"Look out!"

Ahead of us,  lized
the rear trailer ntail,
swinging from arcs.
The squeal of tires on dry pavement rent the stillness, followed by the screech of metal on concrete
as the big truck flipped over onto its side.

The chain reaction of collisions had almost reached
us when I swung the wheel sharply to the right and
aimed for the grassy verge alongside the highway.
For a moment I thought we'd made it. Then the front
wheels hit the wire fence meant to keep deer from
wandering onto the road, and the world exploded
into flying tree limbs and a white cloud and then
nothing.

★

Gladys Jiménez - August, 2008

SANCTUARY HILL
Kathryn R. Wall

WORLDWIDE®

TORONTO • NEW YORK • LONDON
AMSTERDAM • PARIS • SYDNEY • HAMBURG
STOCKHOLM • ATHENS • TOKYO • MILAN
MADRID • WARSAW • BUDAPEST • AUCKLAND

*This book, like all those before and all those
that will come after, is for Norman.
With love. Always.*

SANCTUARY HILL

A Worldwide Mystery/August 2008

First published by St. Martin's Press, LLC.

ISBN-13: 978-0-373-26646-3
ISBN-10:   0-373-26646-4

Printed in U.S.A.

Acknowledgments

In researching the native island aspects of *Sanctuary Hill,* I found one book particularly helpful. *Blue Roots* by Roger Pinckney (second edition, Sandlapper Publishing Company, 2003) gave me wonderful ideas for some of my fictional characters and their peculiar brand of folk medicine. I took many liberties in service to the story, and none of what occurs in *Sanctuary Hill* should be construed as an accurate depiction of any individual, group, or religion. I do, after all, write fiction. That said, however, those wishing to explore this fascinating and obscure facet of Lowcountry culture would do well to consult Mr. Pinckney's account.

Now, it's customary for an author to use this page to thank all those who have helped her along the perilous publishing journey. After six previous books, I'm afraid my expressions of gratitude have become repetitive, though no less genuine. I am truly thankful for the support and understanding of my husband, Norman; my family and friends, especially Jo and Vicky; and my terrific agent, Amy Rennert. I do want to express special appreciation to Ben Sevier. Our editorial relationship was brief but very rewarding, and I wish him well. Jen Crawford and I are just beginning, but I look forward to sharing an equally productive partnership with her.

But now I think it's way past time I thanked you, the reader. You've invested your time and money to travel these Lowcountry roads with Bay and me, we've been privileged to have your company. Whether you found us in an independent bookstore, a big chain, or your local library, we hope you've enjoyed the ride. We certainly have. Y'all come back.

ONE

THE STORM BLEW UP out over the ocean, spawned by a cold front roaring down from the north and fueled by the warm waters of the Gulf Stream. For the better part of three days it battered the South Carolina Lowcountry with a biting wind and relentless rain. Thousands of our annual summer visitors, desperate to salvage at least a few of their precious vacation days, had already packed up and escaped down I-95 to the more hospitable beaches of Florida.

"What's so all-fired interestin' out there?"

I turned at the sound of my father's voice, thick and raspy from the cold that had begun the previous week with a few sniffles, then settled stubbornly in his throat.

"Stop it there before it travels," Dr. Harley Coffin had told me just that morning, "or we'll be battling pneumonia before you know it."

I unwound my legs from my perch on the window seat and crossed the heart pine floor of the study-turned-bedroom to where retired judge Talbot Simpson lay stretched out. Since he'd been crippled by a series of small strokes, his world had come to be circumscribed by this house, his recliner, and his wheelchair. I tucked the heavy afghan more tightly around his shoulders.

"Can I get you something, Daddy? Tea?" I checked my watch. "It's almost time for your next pill."

"A shot of bourbon would do me a damn sight more good," he grumbled.

"Forget it."

"Throw another log on the fire, will you, Bay, darlin'?"

I'd had a couple of the fireplaces in the antebellum mansion going ever since the storm had taken up residence. The dampness of this strange summer cold snap had seeped into everyone's bones. I dragged a hunk of oak from the basket and dropped it onto the glowing embers. When I looked back, my father's eyelids had fluttered closed.

I took up my vigil again on the window seat. I used the sleeve of my old Northwestern sweatshirt to wipe away the mist my warm breath had formed on the glass and stared out over St. Helena Sound. Usually placid, it rolled now in the ceaseless wind. I spotted the white…*something* still bobbing along on the chop that slapped against the pilings of our small dock at the foot of the back lawn. Only the tips of the verdant marsh grass poked out from the gray-green water.

I raised the binoculars and homed in on the object.

Closer now than it had been all day, the box came into sharper focus. A Styrofoam cooler, the kind you can buy for a couple of bucks at every convenience store in Beaufort County, banged against the weathered stilts of the dock. I could see now that it had been bound shut by duct tape, the once shiny strips dulled to a soggy gray. For the first time, I noticed a few frayed strands of rope as well.

Somebody wanted to make certain the lid stayed on, I thought, adjusting the field glasses.

My father snorted. I watched him tug at the afghan with his one usable hand and settle back into restless sleep. I sighed and wished for the hundredth time in the past few days that I was home, stretched out on the sofa in the great room of my Hilton Head beach house, dozing as I listened to the storm rattle the palmettos and beat against the glass of the French doors. The morning's *Beaufort Gazette* had reported that many of the roads on the island were flooded, some impassably so. I would have been marooned but content, with plenty of food in the pantry and my collection of old mysteries to keep me company.

Earlier that morning I'd phoned Erik Whiteside, my friend and partner in Simpson & Tanner, Inquiry Agents, and told him to stay home. We only manned the small office three days a week as it was, and I didn't think anyone would be braving what was fast turning into the second Flood to engage our investigative services.

I looked up at the sound of slippered feet shuffling down the hall. Lavinia Smalls, a quilted robe buttoned up to just beneath her chin, stuck her head around the doorway. Her brown fingers motioned for me to follow before she turned and moved off toward the kitchen. I set the binoculars on the top of the cherry highboy, checked my father's wheezy but even breathing, and tiptoed from the room.

I'd been obeying Lavinia pretty much without question for as long as I could remember. In the sacred halls of Presqu'isle, with its priceless antiques and Baynard-Tattnall family heirlooms, the tall, imposing black woman had been the rock of my childhood, my strong defender against the erratic behavior of my late mother. Now my father's housekeeper and tender companion, she still ruled with a firm hand.

"What are you doing out of bed?" I asked as I followed her into the kitchen.

Within a day of my father's falling ill, Lavinia had succumbed to the same pounding headache and raw throat. I knew she had to be nearly at death's door to send out an SOS for me to trek the thirty miles to St. Helena to help her tend to Daddy.

"I'm doin' lots better," she said over her shoulder, her arthritic hands busy with setting the tea things out on a woven sweetgrass tray. She reached into the cupboard and took down a brown prescription bottle. "Soon as I get this medicine into your father, I'm gonna get myself dressed."

"There's no need," I said, pulling out a chair and seating myself at the weathered oak table. "I can handle it."

Lavinia's smile lit her wrinkled face. "I know that, child. Time you took yourself off home, that's all."

I tried not to take offense. While no one had ever accused me of being particularly nurturing, I thought I'd done a pretty good job of dealing with my father's irascible temper while fetching and carrying for two elderly sick people.

"Now don't go gettin' your back up," she said, reading my

mind as she'd been doing for forty years. "You know I appreciate all you've done these past days." She picked up the whis-
tling kettle from the stove and filled the brown earthenware
teapot. Her smile broadened as she turned back to me. "You
even managed to whip up some passable meals."

"I'm overwhelmed by your praise," I mumbled, and she
laughed.

"Come on now, honey, you know I'm just playin' with you."

I rose and wandered over to peer out the rain-streaked
window over the sink. The cooler still bobbed beneath the dock
pilings, one corner of it resting on a thin strip of marshy ground.

"Will you join us for tea?"

I glanced over my shoulder as Lavinia hefted the tray from
the counter.

"Let me get that."

"No need. You comin'?"

The decision seemed to make itself. "No, thanks. I'm going
outside for a little while."

"What on God's green earth for?" The tight gray curls
bounced as she shook her head. "You want to be the next one
down with this summer cold? I don't have the strength to be
nursin' the both of you, running up and down stairs all day
long."

"Yup, you're definitely feeling better," I replied with a grin.
"Go on, take that in to Daddy. I'll bundle up."

"See that you do." I could hear her mumbling—something
about foolishness—all the way down the hall.

I rummaged in the closet behind the stairs and finally
shrugged into one of my father's old hunting jackets, water-
proof and still smelling faintly of the bluetick hounds, Hootie
and Beulah. The dogs—and my father's ability to trek long
miles with them through the marshes and woods of his beloved
islands—had been dead a long time. On the back verandah I
found a pair of mud-caked rubber boots Lavinia used for gar-
dening and stuffed the legs of my jeans into them. I unfurled a
battered black umbrella and stepped out into the storm.

I moved carefully down the steps between the waterfalls cascading off the hipped roof and squished my way toward the rear of the property. The abandoned osprey nest still hung high in the branches of the dead sycamore, its white trunk looking as if someone had stripped and bleached it. One of its heavy lower limbs had cracked off in the storm, and bits of it lay scattered across the edge of the marsh.

The dank odor of the pluff mud exposed by the ebbing tide mingled with the sweeter smell of wet grass as I waded out into the shallow water. The cooler had been canted onto one side just beyond the reach of my outstretched arm. I knew from the days of my tomboy childhood that I couldn't venture too far out in the soupy mud without the risk of getting stuck there until the tide flowed in again.

Protected somewhat by the overhanging branches of one of the live oaks, I closed the umbrella. Wrapping one arm around the slimy wood of the piling, I reversed my grip and tried to snag the remaining strand of rope with the crook of the handle. It was too thick, and I stepped back to consider my next move.

The muted rumbling of motors and faint whoops of glee brought my head up. Not far out on the Sound, two crazy teenaged boys, stripped to the waist, roared out of the mists on jet skis. The noise receded as the wake kicked up by their passing rocked the Styrofoam box.

"Come on, baby," I coaxed, my arms open and extended. "Come to mama."

The third wave edged it a few inches closer, and I lunged, my cold fingers finding purchase on the rope. I pulled with everything I had, and the sea suddenly gave it up, sending me flying backwards to land ingloriously in the muck. But my arms cradled the treasure against my chest, sticky green seaweed now hopelessly smeared all over my father's jacket.

The banging of the screen door made me turn.

Lavinia stood on the verandah, her arms wrapped in the sleeves of a heavy sweater. "Lydia Baynard Simpson Tanner! What in God's name are you doin'?"

I struggled to my feet. "I got it!" I crowed.

"You get your sorry self inside the house this instant, do you hear me, girl? Now!"

I rescued the umbrella from being carried out to sea and stumbled back onto firmer ground. By the time I marched up the steps, my hair hung in soggy strands against my face, and my feet sloshed in the combination of mud and water that filled the snug-fitting boots. I set the cooler on the floor of the verandah and peeled off my sodden coat. I dumped the contents of the boots over the railing and grinned at Lavinia.

"I've been watching this thing float out there for most of the day. It was driving me crazy."

"And that justifies you traipsing around like some fugitive from the lunatic asylum? I promise you, girl, if you end up hacking and sneezing your brains out, you'll get no sympathy from me."

"Fair enough," I said, hefting the cooler and turning toward the door.

Lavinia held up a hand. "Don't even think about it."

I shrugged and set the Styrofoam box down on the bench she used for potting plants. "Will you at least bring me something sharp to cut this tape?"

Grumbling, Lavinia moved back inside, returning a moment later with a butcher knife. Silently she watched as I ripped through the rope and sawed at the gluey strips of duct tape. When I had everything peeled away, I stepped back.

"You want to do the honors?"

"Don't be ridiculous! I swear you're actin' just like you did when you were twelve. Give you the choice of sitting down in a pretty dress with your mama's friends or traipsing off into the woods with your father, I always knew which one you'd choose." She sighed. "Well, go ahead. Open the thing up. But I'm telling you now, when it turns out to be full of rotten fish guts, you got about two seconds to get it off my porch."

"Yes, ma'am." I pushed back my sleeves like a magician about to reveal his most amazing illusion and lifted the fragile lid.

The contents had been perfectly preserved, maybe by the

cold water at the bottom of the Sound. I had no doubt the rope had once secured a weight of some kind meant to keep the box from floating to the surface. Whoever had assembled this obscene package hadn't counted on the worst storm in twenty years shaking it loose.

I barely registered Lavinia's gasp of horror as I turned back the corner of the yellow blanket and stared into the puckered face of the dead infant.

TWO

THE BEAUFORT COUNTY sheriff's cruiser arrived without lights or sirens. I watched from the verandah as my brother-in-law worked himself out of the front seat and trotted up the steps. He shook the rain from his close-cropped brown hair and shrugged out of the clear plastic raincoat covering his uniform before his eyes rose to meet mine.

"Hell of a day for something like this." His boyish face, so much like my late husband's, reflected a mixture of disgust and sadness.

As usual, I responded to the pain coiled in the center of my chest with a burst of anger. "That's a pretty stupid remark. Is there a *good* time for finding dead babies in beer coolers?"

Sergeant Red Tanner shook his head and wiped his feet on the mat before edging past me and into the house. "I swear, Bay, sometimes your mouth gets way ahead of your brain."

"Is that the best you've got?" I called to his retreating back as I followed him down the long hallway and into the kitchen.

Red's and my relationship had vacillated between easy camaraderie and prickly antagonism over the past few years. His brother's murder, almost coinciding with his own divorce from his high school sweetheart, had left him floundering. The fact that I continued to sidestep his attempts to turn our friendship into something more was a constant, nagging undercurrent that erupted occasionally into sarcasm and harsh words. Nobody's fault, I told myself, just the way things were. The way *I* was.

Lavinia rose from the table as we entered. "I'm so glad you came yourself, Redmond," she said, turning to the stove. "Coffee?"

"Thanks, that'd be great."

I moved around them and positioned myself at the back door. "It's out here."

"We'll wait for the coroner," Red replied, seating himself at the table.

"You don't want to see it?"

"Sit down, Bay." Lavinia patted the back of one of the oak side chairs. "Redmond knows his business."

"Fine." I wrapped my hands around the steaming cup of tea Lavinia set in front of me. If that's how Red wanted to play it, there wasn't much I could do. The hard knot lodged just beneath my heart screamed at me to get the cooler and its grisly contents off our verandah. I'd never had children of my own, although Rob and I had talked seriously about it in the months leading up to his death, and I knew that wizened body, so tiny and perfect, wedged into its tacky coffin, would haunt me....

"Why don't you tell me how you came to find...it."

I looked up to find Red pulling a notebook from the breast pocket of his khaki uniform shirt. I recounted the story while he scribbled.

"Any idea where it might have come from?" he asked when I'd finished.

"No. As I said, I noticed it early this morning. Just a speck on the water, but moving. It didn't get close until the tide had run almost completely in." When he didn't respond, I asked, "Why? You don't think there's any chance of finding where it went into the water, do you?"

My brother-in-law shrugged. "Probably not. And we'll need the forensics people to tell us how long it's been down there. That might give us a clue."

I shivered in the steamy warmth of the old kitchen as another blast of cold wind flung rain against the windows. Though not yet five o'clock on a mid-July afternoon, a wintry gloom had settled over us, and we could only partly blame it on the weather.

The soft whirring of his motorized wheelchair preceded my father's entrance. Lavinia had left him napping, but I should have known his lawyer's radar would have picked up on Red's arrival. I'd inherited my nose for trouble from the Judge.

Lavinia and I exchanged an anxious glance as he maneuvered himself closer to the table. "I would have helped you up if you'd called me," she said, and my father grunted.

"Obviously I managed quite well on my own."

"Be nice," I warned him.

"What brings you out on such a filthy day, Sergeant? Are we having a dinner party, and no one thought to advise me?"

Lavinia answered by hauling pots out of the lower cupboards and banging them onto the stove. "Of course you'll stay, Redmond. I'm doing pork chops. There's plenty."

Not the most hospitable of invitations, and Red and I grinned at each other, our earlier sniping forgotten.

"Thanks, but I don't think you'd better plan on me." Red sobered as he turned to the Judge. "We've got a situation here, Your Honor. Are you aware of what Bay pulled out of the Sound?"

"Of course not. As usual when I'm overrun with women, I'm the last to know the least damn thing that goes on in my own house."

I didn't think it would be a good time to remind him that he'd deeded Presqu'isle over to me just the month before on the occasion of my fortieth birthday. There are some dogs you just don't want to go kicking awake.

I let Red tell the story while I rose and wandered to the back door. I'd replaced the lid on the cooler, and Lavinia had draped a blanket over it as if the poor creature inside had need of warmth and protection. *Too late*. He or she—I hadn't been able to bring myself to look any farther than that pathetic face—had been abandoned in the cruelest way by the very people who should have—

"I want to see it." My father's voice cut across my thoughts.

"No!" Red and I said simultaneously.

"We can't risk further contaminating the…contents," my brother-in-law went on more softly. "We need to wait for the crime scene techs. With all due respect, Your Honor."

The Judge harrumphed and glowered, but he knew Red was right. "Well, what in the hell's takin' them so damn long?"

"I don't know, sir. They got the call the same time I did."

We lapsed into silence then, Lavinia's soft humming the only accompaniment to our individual thoughts. She moved efficiently between refrigerator and sink, sink and stove, her old hands performing the familiar patterns born of the thousands of meals she'd prepared for us over the years. It took me a few moments to realize the tune was an old hymn.

"What's the name of that?" I asked. I rose and crossed to the china cabinet where she kept the everyday dishes.

"Hmm?"

"That song. What's the name of it?" I pulled out plates and carried them to the table.

"'Savior, Like a Shepherd Lead Us,'" she said without turning, and I could hear the pain in her voice. "Go to church more often, and you might know it yourself."

"Yes, ma'am," I replied, swallowing my own tears as I laid the table.

WE BARELY MANAGED to finish pushing food around our plates before the crime scene and coroner's people invaded in force. We civilians took refuge in the Judge's study with after-dinner coffee. Lavinia had left a pot warming on the stove with instructions for Red to make sure everyone helped themselves.

They made very little noise, moving about in the macabre dance they'd performed so many times before. The ancient grandfather clock had just struck eight when my brother-in-law tapped on the door frame and walked into my father's room.

"Just wanted to let you know we're pretty much done in there," he said. I could read the sadness in eyes which reminded me way too much of my dead husband's.

"What's the initial conclusion?" the Judge asked.

Red stepped farther inside and lowered his voice. "Girl, newborn. Maybe only a few hours old when they put her in there. No apparent trauma, so cause of death will have to wait for the autopsy. Could have been a stillbirth, but the coroner doesn't think so."

"Any idea how long she'd been in the water?"

He looked at me and shook his head. "Not right now. We'll send some of the samples up to Columbia, to SLED. They've got the best lab facilities. Could be a while before we get any answers though."

The State Law Enforcement Division had worked closely with my state's attorney husband in his crusade to rid South Carolina of drug traffickers. I never heard their name without an involuntary shudder and a gut-wrenching vision of Rob's small plane disintegrating on takeoff. The deep scars that scored my left shoulder and back were permanent reminders of that hideous rain of flaming metal.

"Child needs a Christian burial." We all turned to Lavinia whose worn fingers worked the edges of a crumpled handkerchief in her lap.

"If no one else steps forward, I'll take care of it," I said. "How long before…"

"Not for a while yet," Red answered, his eyes not meeting mine. "We need to make an effort to find out who she is…*was*. Even if she died of natural causes, it's against the law to just throw her out in the Sound like yesterday's garbage." He coughed away the emotion rising in his throat. "We find the parents, either one, and they're gonna have a lot to answer for."

The heavy silence that followed was broken only by the crackling of logs in the fireplace as each of us pondered what level of fear or desperation—or guilt—could have induced someone to abandon a child in such a gruesome way.

"We can never know another person's heart," Lavinia said into the quiet.

"Whoever did this didn't have one," I countered and looked up to find Red's eyes reflecting my own anger.

"We'll canvass the schools and local hospitals, but we won't know for certain how long the child's been dead until we get the labs back. And we can't assume foul play until the coroner rules."

I shrugged because he was right, but I didn't have to like it. Something in me needed to race out into the storm and begin banging on doors and interrogating suspects.

"Don't stick your nose in this," my brother-in-law said, his voice taking on that official tone that made my hackles rise. "I'm sorry you had to be the one to find it, but that's where your involvement ends. I mean it, Bay."

I didn't dignify that with an answer. Out in the hallway we could hear the scuffling of feet on the worn pine floor as the forensics and coroner's people filed out of the house. I shut my mind against the vision of the tiny body they carried out with them.

"Keep me posted," I said as Red turned to follow them. "As much as you can."

He paused in the doorway, one hand reaching into the breast pocket of his uniform shirt. "I almost forgot." He stepped back into the room, a clear plastic bag dangling from his fingers. "Do you recognize this?" He bypassed me and moved directly to Lavinia. "I thought maybe…"

She took the bag and smoothed it out with her arthritic fingers, turning it toward the lamp on the sideboard. She hesitated, and a strange look crept across her face. "Where did you get this?"

"From around the baby's neck," Red answered, "tucked down under the blanket. It looks homemade. Some of us thought it might be a native island charm."

I rose to stand behind Lavinia's chair and peer over her shoulder. The loop was leather and looked too large to have been made for a baby. The ends had been used to secure a small pouch fashioned of faded blue material with some sort of symbol on it.

"Let me see that," the Judge ordered, but Lavinia ignored him.

"Fetch my spectacles from the table there, will you, Bay?"

I located her glasses, and she slipped them on, bending once again over the strange necklace.

"Do you recognize it?" Red asked.

I heard her quick intake of breath a moment before she dropped the bag into her lap.

"Lavinia? What is it?"

"Lord God Almighty," she whispered, and her shoulders trembled. "Deliver us from evil. Amen."

THREE

THE SUN BROKE through the last remnants of the storm clouds just as I topped the crest of the new bridge over the Broad River. The unexpected glare off the calm waters lit the scene from horizon to horizon, bringing the outlines of all the islands into sharp focus. I fumbled my sunglasses out of my bag.

The wind had died about four that morning. I knew because I'd been awake to witness its shift from a northeast gale to the mild southwest breeze that finally chased the unseasonable weather out to sea. The forecast called for eighty-seven and sunny by midafternoon. The tourists would be back.

I'd given up on sleep after two hours of thrashing around in the old four-poster that dominated my childhood bedroom at Presqu'isle. Though no light showed under Lavinia's door as I crept out into the hallway around one thirty, I felt certain she, too, lay awake. I made my way downstairs, avoiding the creaky boards in the staircase, and brewed myself some tea.

I hadn't wanted to look out toward the Sound, but some perverse energy continually pulled my gaze in that direction.

I sat there in the dark and wondered what kind of person could send a baby to such a pitiful grave, what crushing circumstances or twisted logic could have justified it in someone's mind. I'd sipped tea and pondered on life and death and wished to hell I hadn't quit smoking.

We'd all been dumbfounded by Lavinia's reaction to the small pouch. She'd refused to explain, mumbling about root doctors and the old ways. None of us, including Red, could pry anything else out of her. I hadn't seen her that agitated since the night a year before when my father's life hung in the balance.

The whole episode had been spooky and unsettling. Lavinia Smalls was as staunch a Christian woman as you'd be likely to find on St. Helena Island. Though I knew she'd been brought up to respect the traditions of her mother's people, she'd never once in the forty years she'd been part of my life shown the least inclination toward a belief in all that mumbo jumbo.

Traffic picked up as I merged onto Route 278, and I spent the next half hour wondering what I could do to track down the strange necklace looped around the dead infant's neck. When I finally rolled into Port Royal Plantation, I still didn't have an answer.

None of your business, I chided myself, echoing Red's warning.

I eased the T-Bird into the garage and trotted up the stairs to be greeted by the whine of a vacuum cleaner. I dropped my overnight bag in the entryway and leafed through the stack of mail my part-time housekeeper, Dolores Santiago, had left on the console. I carried the pile with me up the three steps into the kitchen and hit the Play button on the answering machine.

"Bay, it's Erik. I missed you at Presqu'isle, and I guess your cell battery must be dead. Anyway, call me. I think we may have a client."

"That would be a refreshing change," I mumbled to myself.

Business had been slow since we'd wrapped up our last case. I'd been spending my time trying to put together an information packet about the agency, something professional I could present to attorneys on the island in the hopes of scaring us up a few paying customers. Thank God Erik had a part-time job at the office supply superstore on the south end. While I continued to carry the expenses of the office—including his salary—out of my investment account, that couldn't go on forever.

Two more messages were junk, and I erased them. Red's voice boomed out of the last. "You know there's not much point in carrying a cell phone if you never charge the blasted thing. Call me."

"And a cheery good morning to you, too," I muttered, then

paused in the sudden silence as the vacuum died. "Dolores," I hollered, "it's me. I'm back."

My rambling beach house on the edge of the dunes had been the scene of some frightening experiences for both of us, and I didn't want to scare her unnecessarily.

The little Guatemalan woman bustled down the hallway, a wide grin splitting her deep olive face. "Ah, *Señora, bueno!* You are home."

"How's everything been?" I tossed the mail on the little built-in desk and crossed to the refrigerator. I retrieved the pitcher of sweet iced tea that never ran empty and filled a glass. "You want some?"

"Sí, gracias."

I poured another, and we moved by unspoken consent to the small glass-topped table set into the bay of the kitchen window.

"El Juez, he is better?"

I forced a smile. "Yes. Grumpy as ever, which is always a good sign. Lavinia's back up and around, so she kicked me out."

We sipped in silence for a while, the comfort we felt in each other's presence having grown with the years of our friendship. Dolores had come to me on the day I'd been released from the hospital. Recovery from the physical injuries I'd suffered when I'd witnessed the explosion of my husband's plane had taken numerous surgeries and months of intensive rehab. The emotional damage had scarred over but would never completely heal. Dolores had saved me from despair with her gentle care of me. I owed her more than I could ever repay.

Twice I opened my mouth to tell her about my gruesome discovery, to seek comfort by sharing the horror, but I knew that wasn't fair. Her mother's heart would be far more wounded than mine by the callous disregard with which some despicable woman had disposed of her child. Her mind would no doubt conjure up visions of her own sweet babies, even though Angelina had gone off to college and Roberto and Alejandro were about to finish high school. Besides, I had no doubt the papers would be full of the story by the next day's edition. Time enough.

I sighed, and it took me a moment to realize Dolores had asked me a question.

"Sorry?"

"I say the cleaning is done, *Señora*. I think I must do the shopping now. There is a list?"

I shook my head. "No, I don't have any idea what we need. Just use your best judgment." I drained my glass and rose. "I have to make a couple of phone calls."

"I do laundry later," she called after me. "Leave *la bolsa*."

"Okay." I bypassed my suitcase and followed the hallway to the third bedroom that Rob and I had converted to a home office back when he was using computers and logic to attack the money end of the drug trade. Except for updating the equipment, I hadn't changed much of anything. I kicked off my shoes and settled in at the desk.

Red's message seemed the most urgent. The dispatcher at the local satellite office of the Beaufort County Sheriff said that Sergeant Tanner was out on a call, but he'd left word that I should try him on his cell. That violation of protocol made my stomach drop a little, and I worried through the minute or so it took for him to pick up.

"Tanner."

"It's me. Bay."

"Where are you?"

His voice sounded tinny, and I could hear the *whoosh* of traffic outside the window of his patrol car. "Home. I just got your message. What's up?"

"I want you to make Lavinia give me some names, people I can talk to about this root doctor stuff. I tried…" The rest of the sentence trailed off.

"Say again, you're breaking up."

"…out on St. Helena, and the damn tower doesn't cover the whole island. I said, I tried to get her to give me something to get started on with the—"

This time he dropped completely off the air. I waited a few seconds, then hung up just as Dolores stepped into the room.

"I go now for the shopping," she said.

"Okay. I'll be here. Want me to start lunch?"

She beamed. The credit for my transformation from a woman who survived on peanut butter and microwave popcorn to a more than passable cook rested almost entirely on Dolores' shoulders. "*Sí, Señora.* One hour."

I waited a full five minutes for Red to call back, then tried my partner's cell. He answered on the second ring.

"Got your message," I said.

"Hey, you're home." Erik Whiteside's cheerful voice brought an answering smile.

"Just walked in the door about an hour ago."

"How're the Judge and Lavinia?"

"Bickering and sniping."

"So everything's back to normal," my partner said, and I cringed.

"Not exactly."

He made all the appropriate noises of shock and anger as I related the details of the body in the beer cooler. "God, I don't understand how someone could do that," he said when I'd finally stumbled to a halt. "You sure you're okay?"

"I will be as soon as I get the image of that face out of my head."

The silence lasted for a few beats. "Are we going to…get involved? The agency, I mean?"

"Red threatened me with dire consequences if I stuck my nose into the investigation."

"When has that ever stopped you?"

That brought a genuine smile. "Good point. I'm pondering on it. So what's this about a possible client?"

"I picked up messages from the office this morning, and there's one from a guy named Billy Dumars. Wants us to find his wife."

I sighed. "This isn't some kind of divorce thing, is it?" We prided ourselves on refusing to do any errant husband- or wife-chasing, although we might be forced to eat those scruples if things didn't pick up.

"Didn't sound like it. More like he was afraid something

might have happened to her. Anyway, he wants you to call him ASAP." He rattled off three local numbers, which I scribbled onto the desk pad.

"Got it. I guess it won't hurt to hear what he has to say. I'll keep you posted."

"I'm going in to work this afternoon, but I'll leave my cell on." The lightness left his voice. "And about the…that other thing? Let me know if there's anything I can do. I'd really like to find out who did this and kick their asses from here to Charlotte."

"Me, too," I said softly. "Me, too."

The moment I disconnected, the phone rang under my hand.

"If you don't hang up once in a damn while, you can't get any calls." Red's voice came clearly down the line.

"What in the hell's your problem this morning?"

He expelled a long sigh. "Sorry. This thing with the baby has me jacked-up. I keep seeing that face…and then somehow it sort of morphs into Ellie's, and it's making me crazy."

Despite the divorce, Red doted on his two kids, Scotty and Elinor, never missing a visitation unless his job interfered. I should have guessed this case would strike too close to home for him, just as it would for Dolores and all the other parents who would read the grisly details in the *Island Packet*.

Despite the sunlight pouring through the tall window, I shivered. "It's been preying on my mind, too," I said.

"Well, anyway, I called Lavinia this morning, asked if she could give me some people to talk to about that charm thing we found. She wasn't exactly cooperative."

"Doesn't sound like her. She seemed more upset about it than any of us."

"I know. I can't figure why she's stonewalling me."

"And you want me to work on her?"

"Yes. I need someone who'll open up to me. It's the best lead we've got while we're waiting for the forensics to come back. They won't have the results of the autopsy for a few days."

I swallowed hard at the image of that tiny body dwarfed by the expanse of a stainless-steel table in the bowels of the morgue.

"I have a couple of sources of my own, but so far everyone's pleading ignorance," Red added.

"I'll see what I can do."

"Thanks. Call me on the cell if you come up with anything." He paused. "I want these people bad."

"Amen, brother," I whispered and hung up the phone.

FOUR

I LEFT MESSAGES at all three of Billy Dumars' numbers and spent the rest of the morning trying to reach Lavinia, with a notable lack of success. The Judge spent a good part of his day keeping tabs on the goings-on around Beaufort County with his network of old courthouse cronies, so the continuous busy signal wasn't all that unexpected. Besides, the rest of the telephone lines around Beaufort were no doubt burning up with the gruesome news of the newborn's body in the cooler, and my father would be the star of the show since the pathetic bundle had washed up on his property. We had a grapevine—especially for bad news—unequaled in the South.

I cursed and slammed down the handset. Erik had once tried to convince the Judge of the benefits of call waiting, but my stubborn, cantankerous father wasn't having any of it. His motorized wheelchair was about as high-tech as he was prepared to go.

I gave up and marched down the hall into the kitchen.

I had just finished making the sandwiches when I heard Dolores' car in the drive. I intercepted her trying to lug two bulging bags up from the garage.

"How many times do I have to tell you not to do this by yourself?" I relieved her of the one that seemed to be weighing most heavily on her arm. "What idiot packed these things? The big stuff's all in one sack."

Dolores shrugged. I tried not to notice the slight limp as she negotiated the three steps to the kitchen. Though the remnants of her injury only showed up now and again when she was tired or overburdened, I still couldn't stem the wave of guilt that washed over me whenever I happened to witness her discomfort. She would never have been attacked if she hadn't been in my house, and no amount of rationalizing could change that.

After lunch I gave the Judge another try, and Lavinia picked up on the third ring.

"It's me," I said after her brisk greeting.

"Your father's just settled in for his afternoon rest, and I don't want him disturbed. Phone hasn't stopped ringin' since early this morning. He was just starting to feel a little better, too, and now he's hacking again."

"Have you talked to Dr. Coffin? Maybe you should ask him to stop by again."

"I don't think that's necessary. Your father just needs to shut up for a while, give his throat a rest." I could almost see the angry shake of her head. "Told him so, too."

The start of a smile tugged at the corners of my mouth before I remembered the reason for my call. "It's you I wanted to talk to anyway," I said. I squared my shoulders and plunged in. "Red needs your help with that pouch they found on the baby. Why are you being uncooperative?"

The silence lasted a long time. If she hoped I'd give up and go away, she should have known better. We'd been locking horns since I was old enough to talk, and neither of us had a reputation for backing down.

"I'm not being uncooperative. I have nothing to contribute."

"Come on, Lavinia. You recognized that charm or whatever it was. You have a pretty good idea who made it, or if you don't, you know someone who does."

"Don't be ridiculous. If I had any information that might help identify that poor dead child, don't you think I'd tell you?"

"I would have thought so. But it's kind of hard to overlook that remark you made last night about delivering us from evil."

Again the pause lasted a long time. "I...that may have been premature," she said, her tone softening.

I sighed. This woman had brought me up as if I were her own. How could I call her a liar? I tried to recall another time in our long relationship when I had been so completely certain she was evading the truth.

"Look, Lavinia," I said, "I understand. Really. I mean, you have a loyalty to the folks you grew up with. I can respect that. But someone threw that baby away like garbage. I can't believe you'd be a party to protecting the kind of...person who could do that."

"You don't know that the one thing has a bit to do with the other," she said, the bite back in her words.

"True enough. But the first order of business is identifying her, and whoever made that little voodoo thing sure as hell knows who he sold it to."

"There's no need for cursing."

I took a deep breath. "Tell you what. Give me a name, some place to start, and I'll look into it myself. We'll keep Red out of it until we know if there's really a connection or not."

She chewed on that a while. "We'll see," she said a moment before the phone clicked in my ear.

I figured that was the best I could do for the time being. I debated whether or not to call Red but decided against it. The mood he was in, he'd be whipping into Presqu'isle's drive and demanding Lavinia cough up her contacts. I knew from long experience that, left alone, she'd ultimately do the right thing.

I let my gaze wander to the wide window over the desk. Although I generally try to avoid the beach during tourist season, the soft white rollers gliding lazily toward the dune that separated my house from the ocean looked more than inviting. I slipped on one of the suits I'd had specially made to cover the worst of the scar tissue across my left shoulder, tossed on a T-shirt, and slipped my feet into Birkenstocks.

"I'm going for a swim," I called to Dolores, who was loading laundry into the washer. "If someone named Dumars calls, tell him to try again in an hour. Or have him leave a number where I'll be sure to reach him."

"Sí, Señora."

"Thanks."

Outside the French doors, I paused on the deck and went through a series of stretches. The muscles of my damaged shoulder tended to tighten up, especially when I hadn't exercised in a long time. The enforced idleness of the past few stormy days had me itching to get the worst of the kinks worked out. I trotted down the steps, across the wooden bridge that spanned the dune, and out onto the wide expanse of sand.

A few intrepid folks from the Westin Hotel just down the beach lay baking under the relentless July sun while their kids squealed and splashed each other in the shallow surf. I pulled off the shirt, kicked out of my sandals, and plunged into the bath-warm Atlantic.

A HALF HOUR LATER I emerged refreshed and with my muscles tingling satisfactorily. As I shaded my eyes against the glare, I saw a tall man in a crisp khaki uniform standing guard over my discarded clothes.

"Hey, Red!" I called, and he waved. "What are you doing here?" I wiped the salt water out of my eyes with the shirt, then pulled it on.

"Couldn't pass up the chance to see you half-naked," he said with a grin.

I slapped his arm. "As I recall, you've already had that pleasure the day you burst into my bedroom unannounced." I couldn't keep myself from flinching at the memory of his eyes on the puckered, shiny flesh of the skin grafts that disfigured my shoulder and back.

He obviously remembered a different part of my anatomy, because his smile widened.

I worked my sandy feet into my shoes. "So answer my question."

"I just clocked out." He paused and studied a sandpiper scurrying across the hard-packed sand. "I thought maybe you'd want to grab a bite of lunch."

"Sorry," I said. "Already ate."

"I just thought…look, Bay, I'm sorry about…you know." He stumbled to a halt, his eyes still on the bird speed-walking along the beach.

"I was a little snarky myself," I said.

I turned for home, and he fell into step beside me. "Did you have a chance to talk to Lavinia yet?"

I let the necessity of taking the boardwalk single file over the dunes give me a moment to decide whether or not to level with him.

"She's thinking about it," I tossed over my shoulder.

"What the hell is that supposed to mean?"

"Hey! Don't start up something you're only going to have to apologize for later."

I could feel the breath of his sigh against the back of my neck. "Point taken."

"You don't know her like I do," I said. "Trust me, she'll come around. She just needs some time to work it out."

We gained the deck and dropped into matching chaises set back under the overhang of the roof.

"You want a beer?"

"Sounds great."

I swung my legs over the side of the lounger, but before I could rise, Dolores stepped out of the French door. She balanced a laden tray on one hip.

"What's all this?" I asked, rushing to relieve her of the burden.

"*Señor* Red, he no have lunch."

My brother-in-law looked up guiltily as I slid the tray onto the side table. "I may have mentioned it in passing," he said.

I handed him the plate, piled with a thick roast beef sandwich, and an open bottle of beer.

"Tea for you, *Señora*."

I lifted the glass and saluted her. "You're the best, *amiga*."

"Absolutely," Red managed to mumble around a mouthful of fresh sourdough bread. "Are you sure you won't marry me, Dolores?"

She giggled, and I could see the blush spreading across her cheeks. "*Señor* Red, my Hector he no like it if I make the other husband."

"Well, you let me know if you ever change your mind."

"*Sí, Señor,*" Dolores whispered, lowering her eyes a moment before she scuttled back inside.

We sat in silence while Red ate and the sun worked its way

around to deepen the shade. Finally he tossed back the last of
the beer and sighed.

"I could get used to having someone wait on me like that,"
he said.

"I know. Sometimes I feel incredibly guilty, but I console
myself with the fact that she needs the money. Hector's landscaping
business is doing fine, but they've got one kid in college and
two more headed there before long." I hesitated, surprised at the
wave of emotion that jumped into my throat. "Besides, I'd miss
her."

"I know. Well, I hate to eat and run, but..." Red slid his legs
over the side of the chaise. "You let me know if you hear
anything from Lavinia, okay?"

I walked ahead of him through the great room and deliberately refrained from answering. I hate lying, especially to a cop.
"And you'll let me know when you get the results back from
the lab."

His noncommittal grunt could have meant anything from
"absolutely" to "in your dreams."

I watched him turn the cruiser around and head out the
driveway before I yanked the T-shirt over my head and padded
toward the bathroom. Sometimes we were so much alike it was
scary.

FIVE

A LITTLE BEFORE SEVEN that evening, I slipped my key into the lock on the door of our tiny office near Indigo Run about midway down Hilton Head Island. I did my best to ignore the stale smell of a place unused for nearly a week while I turned on all the lights. I'd finally managed to rearrange the furniture to make room for a compact bar refrigerator, and I checked to make certain we had an ample supply of soda and bottled water. I opened a Diet Coke and lowered the temperature on the thermostat before I settled myself in my chair.

The sound of a car just outside sent me scrambling to get the stage set. I arranged a legal pad and a couple of empty file folders on my otherwise pristine desk, then ran a quick hand through my shoulder-length hair and straightened the crease in my beige slacks. I'd gone for the business-casual look, adding a black silk tee and low-heeled sandals. At nearly five-ten, I tower over most women and a lot of men, even in my bare feet, and I've come to realize that visiting the offices of a private investigator is intimidating enough on its own.

I rose as the outer door opened, then slumped back in my seat when I recognized the shaggy head of Ben Wyler, our silent partner in Simpson & Tanner. He'd been conspicuous by his absence over the past few weeks. I hadn't been able to reach Erik, and I thought it might be prudent to have someone else sit in on my meeting with Billy Dumars, so I'd left messages on both Ben's home and cell phones with no real expectation he'd actually turn up.

"No-show?" he asked in that verbal shorthand that marked him out as a Yankee transplant the second he opened his mouth.

"Good evening, Detective Wyler," I drawled, "how lovely to see you again."

He ignored the sarcasm. "Yeah, whatever," he said, checking out the narrow reception area before dropping into the client chair. Although he'd been retired from his brief stint with the local sheriff's office for more than a year, he still scanned any room he entered as if expecting to find armed felons lurking in every corner.

Ben and I had met under strange circumstances, and it had taken us a long time to ease our way around to something resembling a working relationship. As a former New York City homicide detective, he and his experience had allowed us to license the inquiry agency, although he'd insisted he didn't want to take any active part.

I smiled to myself. He'd already proved that was a crock. He'd stuck his nose into the Randolph Wade investigation without the slightest hesitation, and I was pretty sure he'd be at it again if Billy Dumars' case presented the least little bit of a challenge.

Wyler pulled a Fresca from the refrigerator and sipped from the can while his gaze roved around the small room.

"So what have you been up to?" I asked, leaning back in my swivel chair to indicate I was just making conversation. "Haven't seen you around for a couple of weeks."

"Busy," he said. "You know. Stuff. This guy gonna show up or what?"

I glanced at my watch. "It's only ten after. He's coming here directly from showing a piece of property, so he said he might be a little late."

"What's his story?"

When Billy Dumars and I had finally made a connection earlier that afternoon, he'd given me the basics. His wife Tracy had gone missing sometime Tuesday afternoon. Calls to friends and family had proved fruitless. Wednesday morning Dumars had notified the sheriff's office, but they'd refused to file a missing persons report until forty-eight hours had elapsed. Dumars was fuming because the deputy he talked to hadn't been particularly sympathetic, hinting that perhaps Tracy had simply left him.

"That'd be my first call," Ben said.

"Except our potential client swears there was no trouble in their marriage, no financial worries—in short, no logical reason for his wife to have taken off. He thinks maybe she's been abducted."

"Anyone contact him for money?" Ben asked.

"Not so far."

"He got it if they do?"

I nodded. "I did a little checking, as much as I could on the Internet. Billy's been in the real estate business on the island for more than fifteen years. For thirteen of those, he's been one of the top five sales producers. With what property goes for around here, that means he's been pulling in some serious bucks. I'd say he could manage it if—"

The outer door swung open.

Billy Dumars wasn't that tall, but his wide shoulders, straining the seams of the khaki sport coat, gave him presence. A bright red polo shirt, buttoned up tightly against the folds of his neck, stretched across a paunch just beginning to hang a little over his belt. He reminded me almost immediately of Big Cal Elliott, my best friend Bitsy's husband—a one-time athlete gone slightly to fat. His carriage as he strode into the office said this was a man with a little power and a lot of money who didn't have any qualms about throwing either one of them around.

"Mr. Dumars," I said, rising. "Come in. I'm Bay Tanner." His hand was smooth, and he didn't feel the need to prove his masculinity by crushing my fingers. I always appreciate that in a man. "My associate, Ben Wyler."

The two men eyed each other as they shook, a process that never failed to amuse me: that alpha male thing, like two dogs sniffing each other out.

"Pleasure," Billy Dumars said.

"Have a seat."

Dumars took the client chair while Ben wheeled in the one from behind the reception desk. My cozy little office suddenly felt like the inside of a crowded elevator. I uncapped my pen.

"What can we do for you, sir?"

"Like I told you on the phone, I want you to find my wife. Tracy."

"Give me some details. When was the last time you saw her?"

Dumars swallowed, his Adam's apple bobbing above the constriction of his tightly buttoned shirt. It reassured me to see the obvious pain in his eyes.

"Tuesday morning. I left early, had appointments. She was still in bed. She was supposed to play tennis with some of her girlfriends—at the indoor courts because of the weather—then go to lunch. We had plans for dinner that night."

"With whom?" I scribbled on the legal pad, although I'd already heard this part before.

"Clients. Folks in from New Jersey looking to retire down here." A brief smile came and went. "Wife didn't want to look at anything smaller than five, six bedrooms, which would have put them in the two-million-plus range."

"So worth an expensive dinner just to soften them up a little," Ben said in a pleasant voice.

Dumars missed the sarcasm. "Right. But when I came home to change, Trace wasn't there. I called around, but her friends said she left right after lunch."

"Did anything unusual happen that morning?" I asked. "Anything her friends might have noticed?"

The big man shook his head. "Not that they said." He pulled a folded sheet of paper from the inside breast pocket of his coat. "Here's all their names and numbers. Figured you'd need them."

I smoothed it out and slipped it into one of the empty file folders. "Good. That'll save us a lot of time if we decide to take your case. Then what?"

He decided to let that "if" go without comment. "I called her sister up in Atlanta, but Chrissy hadn't heard from her in a couple of days."

"So then what did you do?" Ben asked.

"I drove around a little first. I know some of the places

where she and her friends like to hang out. The bar at the Hilton or the Marriott in Palmetto Dunes. Sometimes the Crowne. Places like that. But no one had seen her."

Billy Dumars had begun to perspire, and he lifted up on one haunch to remove a clean white handkerchief from his back pocket. He swiped it across his brow. "Sorry," he said, "I always sweat when I get nervous."

"Are we making you nervous, Mr. Dumars?" Ben edged forward a little in his chair.

This time Billy got the implication. "I have nothing to hide, Mr.—Wyler, is it? The plain truth is I'm scared. Tracy wouldn't just run off like this. Three days, and not one word. The sheriff says they'll be on the lookout for her car now, but that's about all they can do. Even when I told them about the money, that didn't seem to make any difference."

"What money? You didn't say anything about money on the phone."

"I just found out about it. Tracy took a hundred grand out of our joint account late Tuesday afternoon."

"In cash?"

Dumars nodded.

"And you didn't know anything about this beforehand?"

"No. I wouldn't know about it now if Ken Briggs hadn't mentioned it."

Ben seemed to snap to attention. "Briggs?"

"Yes. He's vice-president of First Coast Bank. We play golf sometimes. He called to see if I was going to be available over the weekend for a round or two."

"And he just happened to mention your wife withdrew a large sum of money from your account?"

I glanced at Wyler. If he'd been a bird dog, he would have been on point. His body had tensed, and his eyes were locked on Billy Dumars.

"Tracy told them she was bringing the money to me for a property we were bidding on at a foreclosure sale. We do that sometimes." He smiled. "Makes the whole process a lot easier when you can just hand over the earnest money in cash."

I tried to hide my dismay. That a man would allow his wife to drive around with a hundred thousand dollars in cash seemed the height of stupidity. But then again, I obviously didn't run in Billy's rarefied circles.

"Briggs just asked if we got the property, and I didn't have any idea what he was talking about. So that's how I found out."

Our client seemed to be running out of steam. His shoulders slumped, and I could imagine what dire scenarios were running through his head because they were probably the same ones careening around in mine. None of them envisioned a good outcome for Tracy Dumars.

I sighed and dropped the pen back onto the desk. No way we could take this case now, not since the introduction of the money. This wasn't just some bored housewife who'd taken off for a fling with the tennis pro. At least it didn't smell that way to me. More like blackmail, or drugs, or some other dangerous enterprise that neither Erik nor I was equipped to handle.

On the other hand, how hard would the authorities look for Tracy? I checked my notes. Billy had said *joint* account, so there was no question of theft. You can't steal your own money even if you do it behind your husband's back.

"How is her car registered?" I asked, startling both Wyler and Dumars, who seemed to be locked in some sort of silent staredown.

"The Mercedes? It's in her name. Why?"

"I'm just thinking out loud." So no stolen vehicle report, either.

Both men turned their concentrated gazes on me. Wyler seemed to be trying to communicate something, but I couldn't figure out the message. I'd just opened my mouth to tell Billy we couldn't help him, when Wyler snapped his fingers in my direction.

"Get Mr. Dumars a contract," he said, his hand outstretched. "And let's record the rest of this. We're gonna need a lot more information before we can get started."

SIX

BEN AND I STOOD nose-to-nose on the gray berber carpet of the reception area.

"Hey, did I ask to get dragged into this?" His voice rose. "You called *me,* remember? I was planning on a nice quiet evening with a couple of beers and a *CSI* rerun. So knock off the righteous indignation routine."

I'd just shut the door behind Billy Dumars, and his five-thousand-dollar retainer check sat neatly on the corner of my desk next to the tape recorder.

"Damn it, Wyler! How many times do we have to have this conversation? I thought we were clear on who makes the decisions around here."

"That only works as long as you don't make stupid ones."

The urge to slap his face was so overwhelming I could feel the tingling all the way from my shoulder to my fingertips. Only my certain conviction that he'd slug me back made me spin and march into my office. I drew a long, calming breath before I flung myself into my chair.

"Then explain to me why you're so hot to take this case. There's nothing we can do that the cops can't, and about a hundred times faster and more efficiently."

"And I know how they think a hell of a lot better than you do." He reached for the folder and extracted an eight-by-ten studio portrait. He slapped it on the desk in front of me. "Look at this. Gorgeous blonde, classy. Can't be much past thirty. He's gotta be at least ten, fifteen years older. I'm sitting in the sheriff's office looking at this, here's what I'm thinking—hot little number with a hundred G's in her pocket and a brand-new

Mercedes convertible, having to sleep next to that guy every night? She's outta here."

"So you're saying that law enforcement will wink and nod, pay a little lip service to keep Billy off their backs, and basically shove the whole thing in a drawer?" I shook my head. "Maybe in New York City, Detective, but not here."

Ben shrugged. "You could be right. But in case you're not, this guy has a right to have somebody looking for his wife."

I picked up Billy's retainer and waved it in Wyler's face. "And your motives are entirely altruistic, is that it?"

He snatched the check out of my hands and tucked it into his pocket. "I think I'd better make sure this gets deposited. Mood you're in, you're liable to rip it up."

The thought had crossed my mind.

Ben tapped an index finger on the file. "You got enough here to get started? Maybe have the kid play around with that new program he was telling us about, the one where he can track down credit cards, although I don't know why a woman with a hundred grand would need to charge anything."

"Any other instructions?" I asked through clenched teeth.

"You know what to do. Interview the girlfriends, family. See if you can get some idea of what kind of mood she'd been in lately. Any gossip going around about her. Was she into younger guys or booze or…you know."

"You mean like whether or not she was in the habit of snorting her lunch?" I asked demurely.

Ben's hoot of laughter filled the small office. "I like you, Bay, honest to God I do. Come on, still friends? Let's go have a drink or something."

"You know I don't drink."

"Doesn't have to be alcohol, although it wouldn't hurt you to loosen up a little."

"No, thanks, it's been a long day."

"Suit yourself. I'll follow you home."

"I don't need an escort, Wyler. It may surprise you to know I managed quite well on my own before you came along."

"Just trying to do the gentlemanly thing. Be careful," he added and turned toward the door.

"Wait! What are you planning on contributing to this investigation now that you've dragged the agency into it?"

His wolfish smile faded. "What I do best. Rattle some chains. Kick some butts." A moment before the door closed behind him, he added, "See if I can't shake something loose."

I DROPPED MY BAG in the foyer and climbed the three steps up to the kitchen. The light on the answering machine flashed briefly.

"Bay." Lavinia's no-nonsense voice bit off the word. "I may have an idea about the root found on that poor dead child. I'm not promising, mind you, so please keep this between us. I'll call tomorrow."

There was no "good-bye."

"Okay," I said to the chill breeze pouring from the air-conditioning vents. I wanted to get Erik up to speed on the new case we'd been bullied into taking, but both his home and cell numbers rolled over to voice mail, and I didn't leave a message. I'd see him at the office first thing in the morning.

I crossed into my bedroom, hung up my clothes, and pulled on a pair of flannel pajama bottoms and an old T-shirt. Barefoot, I returned to the office and settled in front of the computer. An idea had struck, and I checked the clock before picking up the phone.

"Hello?"

The soft voice fit perfectly with Bitsy Elliott's diminutive, size six body, and I could picture her long blond hair curling softly against her cheek. We'd been friends since first grade. As a child, Elizabeth "Bitsy" Quintard had been the epitome of everything my exasperated mother had wished for in a daughter: dainty, feminine, biddable. The tall, gawky tomboy she got stuck with had been the principal trial and disappointment of Emmaline Baynard Simpson's life.

"Bits, it's me. How are you?"

"Bay, honey, where in the devil have you been? I was beginnin' to think you'd dropped off the face of the planet!"

"Busy," I said, only slightly ashamed that I seemed to call most often when I needed a favor. "You know how it is."

"I don't think I've talked to you twice since that fabulous party the Judge threw for you." A faint sigh escaped. "I just know Cal isn't gonna do anything nearly that nice for me next month."

I dragged over my desk calendar and scribbled a reminder on the square for August 24. If I forgot Bitsy's fortieth birthday, I'd never hear the end of it. I made a mental note to swallow my intense dislike for her husband, a former Clemson fullback and king of a dozen Big Cal used car lots all over the state, and make sure he gave her a bang-up party.

"Listen, Bits, I need to ask you something."

"Fire away."

"In all your work with the arts council and the junior league and all that, have you ever run across Tracy Dumars?"

"The name sounds familiar. Do you know who her people are?"

I smiled. "Who are your people" was the Southern aristocrat's code for "give me your maiden name and family lineage, and I'll be able to place you in the proper slot in the social pecking order." My mother would have been so proud.

"I have no idea. Her name came up in conversation."

"In what context?"

I hadn't counted on Bitsy's being so reluctant just to gossip for no other reason than that she could. "Does it matter?"

"No, but—wait a minute. Is her husband the real estate broker?"

"Yes. Billy."

"Cal's had some dealings with him. Commercial property for the car lots, I think. Anyway, I know *of* her. She and her crowd don't belong to any of the important organizations." She didn't quite sniff, but she came close. "They're more into shopping and tennis and having fun than in doin' anything to improve the community."

"I see. Okay, I thought it was worth a shot. Anybody else you can think of who might know her a little better? Someone I can talk to?"

"This is a case, isn't it?" I could almost see Bitsy's deep blue eyes widen in excitement. "Oh, Bay, it is, isn't it? Can I help?"

"No!" I took a deep breath and let it out slowly. "I mean, I'm simply gathering information for someone, okay?"

"But, honey, I've got tons of friends. Surely I know someone who knows someone who—"

"Don't go sticking your nose into this, Bitsy. I mean it. No interrogating your pals at the next DAR tea party or whatever. I'm serious."

In the short silence that followed, I realized I sounded exactly like Red.

"Okay, honey, okay." Her long sigh said a lot about life in the upper echelons of island society. "It's just that things can be a little…boring sometimes. Cal's gone for days at a time, and CJ's heading back to college in a couple of weeks. The other three kids are out more than they're in."

That little-girl-lost tone in her voice always got to me. Bitsy had quit college when she became pregnant with CJ, and she'd been a full-time mother ever since. Another few years, and she'd either have to find something else to occupy her time or go nuts in the deafening silence of her sprawling house in Spanish Wells.

"If there's anything you can do to help, I'll let you know," I said.

"Really? You swear?"

"Don't count on it, but we'll see," I said, hoping the half-promise wouldn't come back to bite me.

"How about if I just make a couple of *teeny* little phone calls—"

"No! Don't do anything. I can't have you compromising my confidentiality agreement with my client." *Damn!* Too late to take it back.

"So it is a case. I knew it." Excitement bubbled in Bitsy's voice. "But don't you worry, honey, my lips are sealed."

"Thanks. I'm counting on that."

We chatted for a few more minutes about the kids and their activities before I hung up with another admonition for her to forget I'd ever asked about Tracy Dumars. I sat back in my chair and fought off the urge for a cigarette. What had I been thinking to involve Bitsy Elliott, even peripherally, in an ongoing investigation? Suddenly I had a whole new sympathy for how Dr. Frankenstein must have felt when he first realized he'd created a monster.

SEVEN

I TURNED THE OFFICE thermostat down to seventy and heard the welcome *whoosh* as the air conditioner kicked on. At nine o'clock in the morning, the outside temperature already hovered in the low eighties, and a heat advisory of 105 had been issued for the afternoon for areas away from the immediate coast.

I heard Erik push open the outer door as I sat behind my desk and slipped off my sandals. In a sleeveless cotton shirt and loose, flowing skirt, I planned on keeping cool no matter what.

"Hey," he called.

"Hey yourself. Grab a legal pad and come on in. We've got a job."

I gave him a brief rundown of the information Billy Dumars had left with me the previous evening along with an expurgated version of Ben's bullying.

"You should have called me to come in."

"You were working at the store," I said as I retrieved my notes and the tape recorder from the center desk drawer. "I tried you later on, but you must have had your cell turned off."

Through his customary deep tan, Erik reddened. I loved that about him. Nearly thirty, and I could still make him blush.

"I had a sort of date."

"Define a 'sort of' date."

"I met someone for drinks after work. I don't consider it a real date unless I actually pick the woman up at her door."

"How charmingly old-fashioned of you," I said with a smile, "Anyone I know?"

He paused just long enough to make me certain he didn't want to talk about it. After his breakup with my spacey half fifth cousin, Mercer Mary Prescott, he'd been pretty tight-lipped about his social life.

"Never mind," I said before he could tell me—in the nicest possible way, of course—to mind my own business.

He studied his hands, his eyes avoiding mine. "I don't like you being here alone with Ben. I don't entirely trust him."

I smiled, even though he couldn't see it. "I don't either. Entirely. But we owe him. And he does have a vested interest in the agency. I can't exactly tell him to stay away."

He lifted his head then, and I was shocked by the anger on his face. "Sure you can. It's your money, and we've got the license. We don't need him anymore."

"What brought all this on?"

Erik squirmed a little in his seat, and again the blush tinted his cheeks. "I know he's probably a good detective, and he has contacts we can use sometimes. But…"

"But what?"

"He only hangs around because he's after you." He stared straight into my eyes, challenging me to deny it.

"I'm aware of his interest," I said, trying hard to suppress the smile quivering at the corners of my lips.

"Sometimes the way he looks at you, it's almost like…like a wolf sizing up a meal."

"An interesting if somewhat unflattering analogy. Look, I'm a big girl. And it may surprise you to know I've had a tad bit of practice fending off unwelcome advances."

That brought a grin to his boyish face. In the scant few years we'd known each other, I'd come to think of Erik Whiteside as the little brother my parents hadn't seen fit to provide me. His friendship and caring had helped to sustain me through some of the most difficult and frightening times of my life.

"I appreciate the thought, but I can handle Ben Wyler."

"If you say so," he said, relaxing back into his chair. "What do you want me to do on the new case?"

I HANDED OVER all the Dumars' credit card numbers Billy had provided us and smiled at Erik's obvious joy. He was never happier than when he had a new gadget or program to tinker with. I pulled the list of Tracy's friends toward me and sat staring at it.

What I really wanted to do was call Lavinia. Her tantalizing message had kept me tossing for a good part of the night. I shared Red's belief that if we found the parents, we'd have the perpetrator of this hideous act, and identifying the maker of the charm would take us a long way down that path. I picked up the receiver and tapped in the first three digits of Presqu'isle's number before hanging up.

Again the image of that tiny, wizened face popped into my head, and I didn't realize I was crying until a single tear plopped onto the desk pad. I swiped at my eyes with the backs of my hands and looked up to find Erik standing in the doorway.

"What's the matter?"

"Nothing. Really. It's just—"

"The…cooler?" he asked, and I nodded.

"I'm waiting to hear from Lavinia. She thinks she might have a line on who made the charm they found."

"I didn't think she believed in that kind of stuff, whatever you call it."

"The charm is called a root. They could be used for anything from making someone fall in love with you to causing chickens not to lay."

"Like voodoo?"

"Sort of. I'm not an expert on it. Most of the famous root doctors operated in the fifties and sixties. Before my time, at any rate."

My father had been a contemporary of the late High Sheriff John L. Mackey. Local legend held that John L. had been fascinated by the work of the local conjure-men of the native people of St. Helena Island. Abandoned at the end of the War of Northern Aggression, these descendants of West African slaves worked their newly acquired acres in almost total isolation from the rest of the country, developing their own language and religion, a mixture of their ancestors' tribal beliefs and the harsh Christianity imposed on them by their former masters and

well-meaning missionaries. While many of the old practition-
ers had died off, it was said there were still isolated pockets of
believers scattered throughout the Lowcountry.

"Strange to think of things like that going on in the twenty-
first century," Erik said. "And anyone who would do that to a
baby should be—well, just let me know if I can do anything to
help."

"Sure. How're you coming with that program?" I slid a
tissue out of the box in my drawer and blew my nose.

"All loaded up. I was wondering if we could use the
company credit card for lunch today. I put the information on
it out into the search engine, so I'll be able to tell if the
program's working."

"Sure, just remind me."

The phone rang. "I'll get it," I said, lifting the handset.
"Simpson and Tanner."

"Bay, it's Lavinia."

At last. "Good morning." I itched to ask her if she'd come
up with anything, but I knew better. "How's Daddy feeling?"

"Some better. If he'd stay off the telephone for five minutes,
maybe his throat would have a chance to heal up."

"That's not likely to happen." I waited, but the silence lengthened. Finally, I said, "So did you find out anything about the
root?"

I could hear the reluctance in her voice. "I may have. There's
a young woman—her mother's the cousin of a friend of mine.
But folks don't like talkin' about these things, not right out in
the daylight, if you know what I mean."

"Okay," I said, wondering why she'd bothered to call if she
didn't have anything for me. "Would it be better if I talked to
this woman myself?"

"No! It's not something we…they'll discuss with outsiders."

"I understand," I said.

"I just wanted you to know I'm doin' my best. I'll talk to
you soon."

She hung up then, but not before I heard her mutter, "Sweet
Jesus, hear our prayer."

I BROUGHT BACK Chinese take-out—paid for on the company platinum card—and we ate it huddled around the screen of Erik's laptop. I'd just come back from tossing our cardboard containers in the Dumpster behind the building when I heard his whoop.

"It works!"

He pointed out the little red flag that had popped up next to our OneTrust card account number. "It beeped, too," he said like a proud father. "Now watch this."

He double-clicked on the flag, and the information scrolled onto the screen: date, time, amount, and the name Imperial Dragon, Hilton Head, South Carolina. Even their phone number was appended.

"That is seriously scary," I said, wondering how many other computer screens across the country were right now registering the fact that we'd had General Tso's chicken and shrimp with lobster sauce for lunch.

As if reading my mind, Erik said, "I told you it isn't entirely legal. I mean, law enforcement has a different one, not quite as fast as this, but individuals aren't supposed to have access. This is actually a beta, sort of like a trial run, for an upgraded version. I have a buddy who works for—"

I held up a hand to cut him off. "Spare me the gory details. I'm happy in my ignorance."

"Okay, but I just wanted you to know. We could be in trouble if anyone found out we're using it in the real world."

"I'll console myself with the thought that we're the good guys," I said. "Nice work."

Back at my desk, I ran through the list of Tracy Dumars' friends, connecting with two of the three with whom she'd had lunch the day of her disappearance. Neither had much to add to what they'd already told Billy, except that Tracy had received a couple of phone calls over their crab salad and chardonnay at L'Étoile Verte. No one thought much of it because all of them had made and answered calls, checking for messages and confirming appointments. I'd never understand the current love affair with being in touch 24/7. Apparently I was the last person on the planet who valued solitude. Neither woman had detected any change in Tracy's behavior after these conversations, but they promised to get back to me if anything occurred to them.

I made a note in the file to have Billy check with his cell provider to request a log of Tracy's phone activity on the day of her disappearance. Even Erik couldn't storm that particular bastion, at least not yet.

I left messages with Tracy's one remaining lunch companion, but the woman I really wanted to talk to was Kitty Longworth. According to Billy, she and his wife had gone to middle school together back in Georgia and had come to the island at the same time. Though Kitty didn't run in Tracy's social circle, they'd stayed close. I picked up the tape recorder and ran it back to that particular part of our conversation the previous evening to verify my memory. Billy Dumars had sounded more than a little disapproving of his wife's oldest friend.

"Kitty's got a gambling problem," I heard him say. "She's supposedly in a program now, but that almost never lasts. When she's on one of her binges, she can disappear for days at a time." His sigh on the tape sounded just as exasperated as I remembered. "You'll be lucky to find her if she's fallen off the wagon. Could be anywhere."

The machine whirred through the silence I'd let hang for a few seconds before asking, "And you don't think they could be together? Tracy and this Kitty?"

"No way," Billy had said with conviction. "Tracy knows how she is better'n anybody."

I recalled how his scowl had deepened at my next question. "But if she was planning something, Tracy might have confided in her?" I thought of my long relationship with Bitsy Elliott. "You're telling me they've been best friends since childhood. It would be a natural thing to do."

"Maybe," he grudgingly conceded, "but I haven't been able to track her down."

I snapped off the tape recorder. I wasn't having any better

luck connecting with Kitty Longworth. But I had her address from the reverse directory function on Google. If all else failed, I'd pay her a visit.

AT FIVE WE CLOSED the office and went our separate ways. Erik had the weekend off from his job at the computer store, so he'd planned a trip up to Charlotte to visit his family. He offered to stick around, but he deserved a little time off, and I told him so. He promised to take the laptop along and keep an eye out for any activity on Tracy's credit cards.

As I slid into the bucket seat of the Thunderbird, I considered what to do about food. No Dolores on Fridays, and the local restaurants would be jammed with visitors until late into the evening. I swung by Publix, grabbed a nice piece of sirloin, and fidgeted at the end of a long line in the express lane.

By seven I had the gas grill on the deck fired up and a sweet potato turning golden in the oven. In faded shorts and Rob's old College of Charleston T-shirt, I perched on a tall, canvas-backed chair. I sipped iced tea and let the quiet of the Lowcountry evening settle around me.

The brilliant blue of the afternoon sky had begun its slow fade as the sun edged toward the mainland. A faint blush of pink seeped into the light that tinged the tops of the oaks and gum trees, and the constant onshore wind dropped to a whisper. Across the dunes I could hear the voices of children reluctant to leave the beach mingling with those of their weary, exasperated parents.

I prefer my beef just sort of warmed up on each side, so it took only a few minutes before I set my dinner out on the wrought-iron table in the screened-in part of the deck. I'd been working my way through my incomplete collection of John D. MacDonald's colorful canon, and I had about thirty pages to go in *The Deep Blue Good-by.* I drowned the sweet potato in butter and cinnamon, spread the book open on the table, and cut into the rare sirloin.

I finished the book and the steak at almost the exact moment the phone rang.

"Hey, it's me."

"Hey, Red," I answered. "What's up?"

"Have you talked to Lavinia?" He caught my hesitation and jumped on it. "If you've got something, I want it, Bay. Now."

I bit back the sharp words and let out a long, slow breath. "I don't have anything to tell you," I said, which was technically true.

"But you talked to her. Is she willing to cooperate with me?"

"You've lived around here as long as I have. Surely you know how things work out on St. Helena. Give it some time."

"Yeah, well tell that to the kid."

Again I forced myself to stay calm. "That's not fair, and you know it. Lavinia will come around."

"Maybe they'd all 'come around' a lot faster if I tossed a few of them in the can."

"You're being ridiculous," I said, all pretense of civility gone. "And I'm warning you, Red. Don't even think about messing with Lavinia. If the Judge doesn't make you pay for it, I sure as hell will."

I had a lot more to say, but I suddenly found myself talking to dead air.

EIGHT

BILLY DUMARS had to be out of town—business, he'd told me, and unavoidable—but he left word with his housekeeper to meet me at his home on Saturday morning. I pulled into the drive of the sprawling Lowcountry house in Ribaut Island a little before nine. Mary Stamper was a pleasant, middle-aged black woman who seemed genuinely distressed about Tracy's disappearance.

We stood next to her compact Chevrolet in the shade of the sweeping centennial oak whose limbs crawled across the wide front lawn, while I tried to elicit something from her more helpful than "Yes, ma'am," and "No, ma'am." When she finally told me to leave the key inside and lock the door on my way out, I hadn't learned a single thing of value other than that the Dumars family had found themselves a very loyal, discreet employee.

Despite its name, Ribaut isn't technically an island, although its location at the northernmost tip of Hilton Head Plantation provides spectacular water views of Skull Creek and Port Royal Sound. Billy's house had to be six or seven thousand square feet with the trademark third-floor dormers and covered wraparound porches. Inside, the air conditioning hummed, and the slate tiles in the entryway felt cool on my bare feet when I slipped off my shoes.

Following Mary's directions, I made my way up the split staircase to the first bedroom on the right. Floor-to-ceiling windows overlooked the water, and French doors gave onto a shady verandah. The décor was elegant and understated, a little too modern for my taste with its abstract paintings and minimalist furniture, but the colors were warm and earthy. The walk-in closet alone could have held my entire bedroom with space left over. Both Tracy's and Billy's clothes were arranged by type and color. Who could possibly know if anything was missing? I doubted if even Tracy herself could have told me. A low door at the far end led to what in the plantation days would have been called a box room. Several sets of luggage sat on raised shelves. Again, I had no way of knowing if any pieces had been removed.

I went through the drawers, careful to leave everything just as I'd found it. I wondered how anyone could possibly need so much underwear. The woman could have opened her own branch of Victoria's Secret.

The bathroom finally yielded up the only thing remotely resembling a clue as to what had transpired the day Tracy Dumars disappeared. On the dressing table built into the long granite countertop, several holes in the array of bottles and jars told of missing items. Basic makeup supplies was my guess—mascara, foundation, lipstick. The kinds of things you'd take along if you were showering after tennis and needed to reapply your face before dressing for lunch. I'd bet there was a gym or tote bag, large enough to hold a change of clothes and shoes, unaccounted for as well.

Back downstairs, I made a quick tour of the main living area. At the rear of the house, a study with book-lined shelves and an ornate desk drew me in, but the only paperwork I found pertained to household expenses and correspondence. With only a little twinge of conscience, I leafed through the bills, then did a cursory search of the drawers, but nothing popped out at me. The only item of interest was a brochure for the Plantation on Amelia Island, Florida, an upscale resort that catered to tennis players. I pulled a notebook out of my bag and scribbled down the address and phone number, although I had no idea what significance, if any, it might have.

Returning to the foyer, I slipped on my sandals and dropped the key on the console table. By the time I stepped back onto the front verandah and pulled the door closed behind me, I

realized I was not one bit closer to finding out what had
happened to Billy Dumars' wife.

SUNDAY I SLEPT IN, so I had to scramble to get in my run before
the temperature hit ninety. I showered and changed in record
time and got on the road just after eleven. Being late for lunch
with the Judge and Lavinia wasn't an option if I wanted the re-
mainder of my day to be one of peace and rest.

Not so long ago, I made my weekly duty trip to Presqu'isle
on Thursday nights to clean the pockets of my father and his
friends in a cutthroat poker game that often lasted well into the
next morning. But death and infirmity had whittled away at the
Judge's cronies, and I had been reduced to settling for a sedate
noon meal taken in the cold formality of the dining room. I
missed enough Sundays to keep it from turning into a ritual,
but I knew Lavinia set a place for me every week.

As I waited at one of the endless string of traffic lights on
Route 278, I dug my cell phone out of my bag and tried Ben
Wyler. After dumping the Dumars case in my lap, he'd seemingly disappeared off the face of the earth. I'd been trying to
reach him for two days, but once again I got no answer. I had
a hard time imagining the gruff, cynical detective fidgeting in
the back pew of one of the island's many churches, but who
could say? Although he'd been in and out of my business—both
private and professional—for the better part of a year, I still
knew very little about his personal life.

Probably just as well, I told myself as the signal flipped to
green.

A half hour later I eased the Thunderbird into Presqu'isle's
semicircular driveway and cut the engine. The allée of oaks
lining the rutted approach road marched right across the wide
front lawn to encircle the house in a green, swaying canopy that
helped repel the blazing Carolina sun. I never stepped onto the
split staircase up to the verandah without a mixture of pride and
anger warring inside my chest. It could have been a magical
place to grow up in if only…

Knock it off, I ordered myself as I pushed open the front door.

"Anybody home?" My words echoed down the long hallway that bisected the old mansion.

"Amusing," my father said, appearing from his room, the wheels of his chair gliding effortlessly across the heart pine floor.

"It wouldn't be if you'd swallow some of your pride and let Lavinia get you out of here once in a while," I replied.

"Try to refrain from offering advice unless you're asked for it, daughter." He worked the controls and executed a sharp turn so that I spoke to his back.

"I will if you will."

I heard his snort of laughter over the soft hissing of the tires and followed him into the dining room where Lavinia had adorned one end of the massive mahogany table with a crystal vase of late roses from my mother's garden. The damask cloth held three place settings of the Royal Doulton. The Judge maneuvered himself in close. I raised an eyebrow, and he smiled. "Vinnie does love these old things."

"Here. Set this down," Lavinia said behind me.

I turned to lift the platter of fried chicken from her hands and place it on one of the hotpads she'd scattered across the tablecloth.

"I'll be right back with the biscuits and the beans," she added. "Come bring in the tea."

"Yes, ma'am," I said, trailing her out. "What's up with all the good china?" I asked as we stepped into the kitchen, but she ignored the question, motioning me farther into the room.

"I spoke with the young woman I told you about," Lavinia said softly, glancing over her shoulder toward the dining room, "and she thinks it's all right to give you a name."

"Of the root doctor?"

"Hush!" she whispered. "This is just between the two of us. You don't share this information with anyone else, you hear me?"

"I hear you, but I don't understand. We're trying to find out who bought the charm so we can track down the parents of that poor baby. Sooner or later it's going to have to come out."

"It doesn't come from you, and it can't be traced back through either one of us to the woman who told me. I gave my word on that, and I expect you to honor it."

"Everything okay in there?" The Judge's voice boomed down the hallway.

"Just be a minute," Lavinia called back, but she gripped my arm, her wrinkled face only inches from mine. "Promise me, Bay."

"Okay, I promise. What's the name?"

"Belle Crowder," she whispered, "and that's the last I'm saying on the subject."

Before I could open my mouth, she hefted the serving dishes and headed back to the dining room without a word. I trailed after her carrying the tray of glasses filled with sweet tea. She seated herself beside the Judge.

"Vinnie, I believe it's your turn to ask the blessing."

I shook my head before bowing it under my father's stern glare. My mother had been a part-time Episcopalian, more for the social connections than for any real religious fervor, and my father had been a practicing agnostic until just recently. I sighed and joined in the amens when Lavinia had finished. My father nodded and smiled at the woman who had shared his house—and his heart, I suspected—for nearly four decades.

We ate in silence for a while after we'd passed around the several serving bowls and piled our gold-rimmed plates with chicken, mashed potatoes, and snap beans from the garden.

"Any news about that poor, unfortunate child?" my father asked, and I shrugged.

"I haven't heard anything."

I glanced across at Lavinia, who stared straight at me with a look I could only interpret as fear. I shook my head to let her know I had no intention of betraying her confidence, not even to the Judge.

"Hell of a thing," he said, either ignoring or missing altogether the silent messages being passed as he wrestled with a chicken leg.

"Redmond called," Lavinia murmured behind her damask napkin as she dabbed at her lips. "Said he might stop by later."

"I told him to leave you alone," I said through clenched teeth.

"What are you two whisperin' about over there?" the Judge demanded, his brow furrowed in displeasure.

"Women talk," Lavinia said. "Nothing for you to be worryin' yourself about, Tally Simpson. You want another biscuit? Bay, pass your father the biscuits."

I forced a smile, and we made small talk for the next few minutes, but underneath I was seething. If Red tried to intimidate Lavinia, I'd have his head on a platter. And not the Royal Doulton.

I rose and began clearing the table while Lavinia carried in our usual Sunday dessert, homemade banana pudding sprinkled with pecans and vanilla cookies. My father's head had begun to nod when the heavy knocker fell against the front door.

I waved Lavinia back down in her seat.

Red, his uniform stuck to his chest in sweaty blotches, looked ready to fold up in the midafternoon heat. "Bay," he said, stepping around me and into the dim coolness of the entryway. "I didn't expect to find you here."

"I'll just bet you didn't. You look like you've been swimming in your clothes," I said, pushing the door closed behind him. "Air conditioning not working in the cruiser?"

Red unhooked his gun belt and laid it carefully on the console table, dragging his sodden shirttail loose. "We had a situation," he said, turning at Lavinia's voice behind him.

"Redmond, how nice to see you. We've just this minute finished lunch. Let me fix you a plate." She turned toward the kitchen. "Won't take but a minute. Everything's still warm."

"I don't want to put you to any trouble," he said, sniffing the air where the aroma of fried chicken still lingered.

"No trouble at all," Lavinia called over her shoulder.

"Thank you, ma'am." Red saw the frown on my face. "What? You wanted me to turn her down?"

"It never crossed my mind. And she's too much of a lady not to have asked. But I'm warning you right now. Eat her food, thank her nicely, and then get the hell out of here. If you

start hounding her about root doctors, you'll wish you hadn't."
I let out a long breath and pasted a smile on my face as Lavinia
stepped out of the kitchen. "You want to wash up first? We'll
be in the dining room."

By the time he joined us, Lavinia had a heaping plate waiting
for him. Red slumped into the chair, his hair plastered to his
head in wet comb tracks, his sweat-stained shirt tucked neatly
back into his uniform trousers.

"You have no idea how much I need this," he said.

"You mentioned a situation," I said.

"Not good table conversation," he replied, ducking his head,
but not before I'd seen the look of anguish flicker in his eyes.

I wondered if it had to do with the dead baby or if this was
some fresh horror. For the first time in a long while, I gave
thought to how emotionally exhausting his job must be.

We kept the talk light until he'd been served a huge bowl of
banana pudding and Lavinia and I had carried the rest of the
dishes to the sink. She shooed me out, and I slid back into my
chair in time to catch the tail end of Red's story.

"Body must have been out there at least three or four days.
Thank God I wasn't first officer on the scene." He glanced in
my direction. "The heat, you know? Even with it zipped into a
coroner's bag—"

"Where was this?" I waited for him to tell me none of my
damned business, but he surprised me.

"You know that dirt road off of 170? The one out to the old
camp? Just up from Grayton's Race."

I nodded. Camp St. Mary's. I vaguely remembered the place
had once been some sort of church retreat for kids. Later they'd
turned it into a home for unwed mothers or something like that.

"There's a few houses out there, some really fancy, but
mostly it's just woods. Don't know how the developers missed
it, although a lot of it's probably still owned by the county. The
land runs right down to the river." He paused to sip from his
glass of sweet tea. "Anyway, some photographer poking around
out there in the marsh came across this Mercedes, nose down
in the mud flats. Looks like someone tried to roll it into the river,

figuring the current would take it out, and misjudged things. The guy caught a whiff of the smell and called us."

"What kind of Mercedes?" I asked, the air suddenly chilly against my bare arms.

"You gonna be able to restrain yourself from butting into it?" My brother-in-law fixed me with a look that was half-amused, half-serious.

A shiver whispered down my back, and the certainty of it settled over me like a cold wind. "It was a convertible. New."

"How the hell would you know that?"

"Just tell me."

He ran a hand through his damp hair. "I swear to God, sometimes you give me the absolute creeps." He flicked his gaze to the Judge, then back to me. "Yes, it was a convertible. Hard to tell much of anything about the body, but it was female. She was stuffed in the trunk. Fully clothed, no sign of sexual assault. Handbag was missing."

"Find anything else? A gym bag, maybe?" I swallowed. "Or a lot of money?"

Red's eyes, hard and accusatory, bored into mine.

"No. And you damned well better tell me just what you know about this, Bay, and I mean now!"

"See here, Redmond," my father began, but I waved him to silence.

I paused, wanting to be wrong, but knowing I wasn't. "Tracy Dumars?"

Red stared at me for a long moment before nodding.

NINE

THE JUDGE AND I HELD a brief consultation in his bedroom, leaving Red to stew by himself over a second helping of dessert. It didn't take long to agree I had little choice but to share everything I knew about the disappearance of Billy Dumars' wife.

I pushed my father's wheelchair ahead of me into the dining room and took the seat across from Red. With as little embellishment as possible, I outlined for him the basic facts as they'd been presented to me by Billy.

"You can check, but he told me he'd talked to someone at your office right after she disappeared. No one was interested until she'd been gone forty-eight hours. Then they told him nothing she took could be considered stolen, even the money. And the car was in her name."

"And how long after that did Dumars hire you?" Red was taking it surprisingly well, with none of the bluster I'd expected.

"He contacted the sheriff Wednesday morning and came to see me Thursday night."

"What have you done about trying to find his wife?"

I couldn't admit to Red that Erik had a new way of monitoring personal credit cards even though he'd never really had a chance to use it. "I talked to two of her friends, the ones she had lunch with that day. I still have a couple more names to check out. Billy had already contacted the sister in Atlanta. He had the housekeeper let me in the house yesterday, and I went through Tracy's things. I couldn't tell—"

"I hope you didn't disturb any evidence." Before I could reply to this ridiculous statement, he added, "If you took anything out of there, I need to know about it."

I bit back my anger. "In case you hadn't noticed, I do have a functioning brain. I left everything exactly as I found it. All I was trying to determine was if she'd packed a bag."

"And did she?"

I shrugged. "She has so many clothes, I couldn't tell. There was makeup missing, but she probably had that with her for after the tennis game."

"Doesn't her husband know?" The Judge's voice startled me.

"He's probably more clueless about it than I am," I said. "Their closet could clothe a Third World country." I waited for Red to finish scribbling notes. "Do they know when she died?"

"That's going to be the question. Like I said, ballpark from the guys on the scene is three to four days. It'll be tough because of…you know, the condition of the body. Temperature inside that trunk must have been over 130 once it quit raining."

"So she was probably murdered the same day she disappeared."

Red looked up from his notebook and scowled at me. "I never said it was a murder."

"No, of course not. You think the woman just crawled into her own trunk and died. What'd she do, bury her purse before she did it? And scatter the money to the wind?"

My brother-in-law ignored the sarcasm. "Anything else you want to tell me before I go call this in? Now's the time if you're holding something back."

I stared him straight in the eye. "Not a thing. You've got it all."

"Good," he said, rising. "Someone will be by to take your formal statement. You want it here or back on Hilton Head?"

I followed him out into the hall and watched as he strapped on the heavy belt that held all the tools of his trade: gun, night-stick, handcuffs. I shivered, remembering the invasion of my home by armed deputies the year before. "Have them come to the office on Monday."

"I'll see what I can do." He looked past me toward the kitchen. "Mrs. Smalls, thank you so much for that great dinner. I really appreciate you letting me just barge in."

I turned as Lavinia paused in the hallway. "You're quite welcome, Redmond. Any time."

"And ma'am?" Red stammered. "What I really stopped by for was to…I mean, about that conversation we had? I just want to—"

"No need. We both said some things we probably shouldn't have."

Her nearly black eyes flicked sideways toward me, but she knew I had no intention of giving her up. Belle Crowder was our secret. And my lead. At least for the time being.

"I appreciate that, ma'am." Red had caught the look and now raised an eyebrow in my direction.

I ignored it. "Any progress on the baby?"

"Nothing so far. Autopsy isn't due until the middle of next week. No reports of missing kids, so we'll have to do it the hard way." He opened the front door, and we stepped out into the blast of heat.

"How did Tracy Dumars die?"

Red stopped and studied my face. "Professional interest or just curiosity?"

"Both," I said, earning myself a brief smile.

"Some reporter from the *Packet* was out there nosing around almost on our tails, so it'll probably make the papers anyway." He sighed. "Shot twice in the back." He ran a hand through his short brown hair. "The scene being basically in the marsh—and with all the rain early in the week—there's not much in the way of physical evidence, but they're out there looking anyway. We'll get ballistics." He sighed. "This used to be an easy place to be a cop in," he said softly. "I don't know what the hell's happening to us."

"The twenty-first century," I said as he trotted down the steps toward his cruiser.

I ARGUED WITH MYSELF all the way back to Hilton Head about exactly where my responsibility to Billy Dumars lay. I knew I had absolutely no right to inform him of his wife's murder. I hadn't needed Red to remind me that notification of next of kin was a job the professionals had a lot more experience with. Besides, they placed a lot of store in how a possible suspect reacted to the news, and they wanted to witness it firsthand.

That Billy was a suspect I had no doubt. I ran our interview over in my head, trying to decide at what point he'd begun to perspire. Maybe he'd been keeping something back. I had a hard time believing the something was that he'd actually shot his wife in the back and stuffed her in the trunk of her own car. I didn't want to think he'd just been using me to throw up a smokescreen, but I'd been fooled by a man before. Badly.

I'd pretty much decided I needed to stay out of it by the time I turned in at the Pineland Station shopping center and parked the T-Bird out front of Starbucks. An iced chai would give me the opportunity to sit a while in the dim, cool coffee shop and convince myself I was doing the right thing, even though a niggling voice in the back of my head kept throwing up arguments.

As I rolled out of the bucket seat, I spotted Ben Wyler's car two rows over, parked in the shade of a crape myrtle, with plenty of empty spaces on either side of his precious restored Jaguar. I scanned the lot, sparsely populated on a steamy, Sunday afternoon, but I didn't see him. I slammed the door and clicked the locks with the remote, turning just in time to watch Wyler stroll out the front door of Starbucks, his arm draped casually across the shoulders of a pretty young woman in a yellow tank top and khaki shorts. They were laughing, and for a moment I marveled once again at how attractive the irritating detective could be when he wasn't scowling.

"Ben," I called, "hey! I've been trying to reach you."

"Bay! What… Is something wrong?"

He dropped his arm from the young woman's shoulders and stuffed his hands in his pockets. Even at the height of his deadly charade the past summer, I'd never seen him look so uncomfortable.

"I just came from the Judge's. Red stopped by with some news." I waited a beat, but he made no move. "Hi," I said, thrusting out a hand to the startled girl, "I'm Bay Tanner. Ben and I sometimes work together."

"I'm Stephanie," she said, returning my grip and smiling. "I've heard a lot about you."

I would have guessed her to be somewhere in her mid-twenties, maybe a little younger. She had long, dark hair brushed back into a clip. Pretty enough in that all-American kind of way, but no beauty. I waited in vain for a last name.

"You want to wait for me in the car? This won't take long."

The girl nodded at Ben and called, "Nice to meet you," over her shoulder as she walked away. Ben's eyes followed her.

"Seems nice," I said, but he ignored the implied question.

"What did Tanner have to say?"

Okay, I said to myself, *we can play it this way if you want.* "Remember Billy Dumars and his missing wife?"

"Of course. What happened, they find her?"

His eyes slipped past me in the direction the girl had disappeared.

"She's dead." That earned me his full attention. "Shot in the back and stuffed in the trunk of her car in the marsh out toward Beaufort."

"Evidence? Suspects?"

"Besides Billy? Not that I heard. Preliminary coroner's guess is that she's been dead for three or four days. Probably not long after she went missing."

"Too bad," he said, then shrugged.

"So we're out of it now."

I'd lost his undivided attention. Again his eyes flicked off toward the parking lot behind me. "Right. Okay. I'll see you later."

Ben Wyler almost trotted across the blacktop, heat waves shimmering in his wake. I saw him unlock the passenger door and take the young woman's arm as she slid into the seat before I spun on my heel and marched into the blessed chill of the coffee shop. I'd be damned if I'd give him the satisfaction of standing there like some jilted lover.

And wherever the hell that analogy had come from, I had no interest in examining it any further.

STARBUCKS HAD A COPY of the Sunday *Beaufort Gazette,* so I lingered a while over my iced tea, skimming through the local news section. My father always read the obituaries first. I guessed at nearly eighty that's where he expected to find mention of his contemporaries. I had no real interest in the goings-on in the upper echelons of county society, although I never ceased to marvel at how many of the daughters of my mother's crowd had stayed around to take over the reins of the historical society, the DAR, and the junior league. In a way, I always thought it was a blessing Emmaline hadn't been forced to make excuses for my total lack of interest in the responsibilities imposed on me by virtue of my ancestry. She never lived long enough to see me learn to shoot and swear and smoke and chase criminals. Maybe there was a benevolent God after all.

Finally I tossed the paper aside and forced myself back out into the heat. I followed 278 to the Port Royal entrance and rolled into my driveway a little past five. As I reached for my bag, something caught my eye on the passenger side floor mat. My heart jumped when I realized what it was.

Gingerly, I retrieved the little packet and held it up between two fingers. The crudely stitched pouch of red cloth bulged with things I was positive I didn't want to know about.

It seemed one of my investigations had just gotten a lot simpler.

Belle Crowder had apparently found *me*.

TEN

I DROPPED THE LITTLE PARCEL on the kitchen counter and stepped back to study it. The number 4 was stitched on one side, a crude representation of an eyeball on the other. I didn't know enough about the root business to judge if these images signified good or evil, but I had a feeling the messenger didn't have my best interests at heart.

A dirty white ribbon had been used to secure the neck of the pouch. I vaguely remembered talk among the people who believed in such things that the number of knots and the manner of their tying had significance. Mine was tied twice, with a space of about half an inch in between.

On my way into the house, I'd fingered the bag in my hand, trying to judge the contents without actually opening it up. It felt like sand or maybe dirt, mixed in with something dry and crackly, possibly leaves of some kind. I breathed a sigh of relief that it didn't seem to contain a bone. Even a backsliding, white Episcopalian like me couldn't grow up in the Lowcountry without knowing the significance of bones to a root doctor.

I dragged my mind back to the twenty-first century and searched the cupboards for where Dolores kept the plastic bags. I snapped one out of the box and dropped the pouch inside, making certain to seal it tightly.

There, I thought, *take that.* Dr. Snake meets Ziploc. We'd see whose magic was more powerful.

I washed my hands twice and dried them on paper towels before pouring myself a glass of tea. I carried it and the strange package into my office and turned on the computer. I plugged

Belle Crowder's name into Google, taking a stab at the spelling. Amazingly, I got a few hits. The most promising was a link to Amazon.com and a book entitled *Lowcountry Magic: The Healing Arts of the Descendants of West African Slaves on the Carolina Coast.* I clicked through and scanned the publisher's description. The author, a professor of anthropology at the University of South Carolina, claimed to have conducted exhaustive studies of the history and culture of this little-known group. The blurbs were all from other professionals in the field attesting to the accuracy and insight the author brought to the subject, one even calling the book "the definitive study of this honorable and often misunderstood facet of African-American culture."

I copied down the book's identifying number and the author's name: Henry P. Crowder, Ph.D.

Coincidence? I wondered before the phone startled me. Red's voice sounded tinny and very far away.

"Can you hear me okay?" he asked.

"Not very well. Why don't we buy some land and put up a few cell towers? We'd make a fortune."

"Not a bad idea. Or it would be if I had any money. Listen, I wanted to give you a heads-up about your statement. Someone will be at your office around ten tomorrow. That okay?"

"Fine. Have you contacted Billy Dumars yet?"

The line crackled. "…been able to locate him. You have any idea where he hangs out when he's not at home or his office?"

"Not really. Every time I talk to him he's either heading to or coming from an appointment. Sounds to me like he works pretty much 24/7."

"Right. I guess you don't sell millions of dollars of real estate every year by spending your time on the golf course."

"I've got his cell number at the office if that would help," I offered.

I couldn't tell if the silence was intentional or if Red's phone had cut out again. "You still there?"

"Yeah. I'm just recovering from the shock of having you be so cooperative. You sure this is the real Bay Tanner?"

"Almost funny. So Billy still doesn't know about his wife," I said, sobering. "You can't let him hear about it on the news."

"Doin' the best we can. And we've already got his cell, but he's not picking that up either."

"Okay. Be careful out there."

"You, too," he said before clicking off.

I shut down the computer and gathered the sheets I'd printed out into a file folder. I put it and the plastic bag containing the red pouch into the right-hand drawer of my desk and went to scrounge up something for dinner. I'd just opened the refrigerator when the phone again interrupted me. This time I let the machine get it.

"Bay, it's Lavinia. If you're there, please pick up. It's important."

She sounded grave. I crossed the room in three strides and grabbed the handset.

"What's wrong?"

"We're fine," she said, reading my mind. A pause. "Have you spoken to anyone about our…conversation in the kitchen?"

My eyes shot to the empty hallway leading back to the bedrooms and my office. To the little red pouch in the plastic bag.

"No, ma'am."

"You're sure?"

"Yes, absolutely. Why? What's the matter?"

Lavinia drew a long breath. "I was just on my way out to Sunday night service when I got a call from my friend Evelyn. I usually pick her up, and she wanted to let me know she wouldn't be going to church because she had to go sit with her cousin's daughter's children. Their mother had to be taken to the emergency room."

I swallowed hard. "And this has something to do with…" I couldn't bring myself to speak the name.

"Yes. It's this young woman who provided me with the information I gave you."

The silence stretched out while my mind whirled with the implications. "What's wrong with her?"

"They're not sure. According to her husband, she complained all day about having a bad headache. He found her a little while ago sittin' on the front porch just staring off into space. He couldn't rouse her, so he called Evelyn for help and drove his wife straight to the hospital."

She paused for breath, and I leapt in before she had a chance to continue.

"Lavinia, if you're thinking this has anything to do with your giving me that name, I'm not buying it." I brushed away the image of the crudely stitched eye on the pouch resting in my desk drawer. "You're implying she's been hexed or something, right? For talking to you?"

"Rooted," Lavinia said without hesitation. "Or maybe mouthed."

"Mouthed?"

"Not as strong as a root, but it can be just as effective."

"Are you telling me you believe all this stuff?"

"Don't be ridiculous. Just because I have a little knowledge doesn't mean…I'm just calling to pass along the information. And to tell you to be careful. That's all."

I could almost hear her jaw snap shut. I knew that sound well. End of discussion.

"Fine," I said. "Will you let me know how she makes out at the hospital?"

"If I hear. I'm going to be late for church. You take care." She hung up without saying good-bye.

I replaced the phone in its charger and stood for a moment staring across the great room and through the French doors to the ocean beyond. The whole thing was getting too bizarre. I strode back down the hallway, retrieved the information I'd printed out, and headed for the car. Barnes & Noble would be open for a few hours yet. If Henry Crowder, Ph.D., was a local, they'd have his books. Somehow I had to track down Belle before anyone else ended up in the hospital. Or dead in a beer cooler. I pushed aside the disturbing images that thought conjured up and roared out of the garage.

AT FOUR THIRTY the next morning I jerked awake, sending the pile of books and papers tumbling from my lap onto the great room carpet. I blinked to focus my eyes in the glare of the one reading lamp blazing in the darkness. My head and neck felt as if someone had clamped them in a giant vise, and my entire left side had gone numb. I stretched and yawned, then bent to retrieve *Lowcountry Magic,* which had landed upright on the floor.

After returning from the bookstore with half a dozen volumes on the subject of local folk medicine and black arts, I'd set up shop in a corner of the sofa with a pot of tea and a legal pad. I'd hopped between books, double-checking facts and references and taking notes, searching for anything that might lead me to Belle Crowder. Although women conjurers were rare, a couple of the other books I'd carted home talked about female healers and midwives who also dabbled in roots.

I'd hit pay dirt about a third of the way through Dr. Crowder's treatise, a brief mention of his aunt Isabelle who claimed to have inherited her powers from her grandfather. So much for coincidence.

I tidied up and piled everything on the coffee table before carrying the dregs of my tea out to the kitchen. I drained two full glasses of cold water before I felt awake enough to stumble back down the hallway and throw myself across the bed.

I dreamed of a floating eyeball, its intense black gaze fixed on me no matter which way I turned.

I CAME TO A LITTLE after eight, still completely dressed. Restored by a steaming shower and fresh clothes, I wolfed down an English muffin, stuffed Crowder's book and my folder of notes into my briefcase, and made it to the office about thirty seconds ahead of Erik.

"Good morning," he called as I inserted the key in the lock and pushed open the door. "How was your weekend?"

"Interesting," I said over my shoulder. "How about yours?"

He laughed. "I'm getting way too old for staying out all night drinking."

I remembered then that he'd gone back home to Charlotte for some reveling with his buddies. "I'm getting way too old, period," I said, dropping the briefcase on my desk and reaching for a Diet Coke from the mini-fridge. I'd need a steady stream of caffeine if I intended to stay upright and reasonably coherent.

Erik sat down at the receptionist's desk and checked messages. "Nothing," he said, a note of disappointment in his voice.

"It gets worse."

I gave him the details of the discovery of Tracy Dumars' body. I hoped Red or someone from the sheriff's office had been able to get hold of Billy. The headlines in the morning's *Island Packet* had been pretty straightforward: LOCAL WOMAN FOUND MURDERED.

The story had been short on facts and long on speculation from "informed sources close to the investigation." The photographer who'd discovered the car and called the cops played a big role in the reporter's re-creation of the scene of the crime, although no name had been given. I guessed he'd also supplied the front-page photo of the rear end of the Mercedes, its deck lid raised to reveal the gaping emptiness where Tracy's body had been stuffed.

Erik's face had gone pale beneath his summer tan. "Do they have any leads?"

I shrugged. "You know Red. I'm amazed he told me as much as he did. Obviously Billy will be at the top of their list of suspects."

He chewed on that for a moment. "So they think he hired us just to throw them off?"

"That would be my best guess. Anyway, we can close out that file. Will you type it up?"

"Sure," he said, rising from the client chair. "Are we giving them what we have?"

"Considering it's pretty much nothing, I don't see the problem. Someone's coming at ten to take my statement."

"Maybe I should get that tracking program off my computer just in case they decide to get thorough."

"Good idea."

I took the Crowder book and my notes out of my briefcase

and set them aside while I listened to Erik tapping at the keys of his laptop. I had just retrieved a bottle of aspirin and shaken a couple out into my hand when Erik's yelp sent a dozen pills rolling across the top of my desk.

"What's the matter?" I called.

A second later he stood in the doorway, his face ashen.

"What?"

"I got an alert. Someone just charged a hundred and fifty dollars' worth of gas. With Tracy Dumars' American Express card."

ELEVEN

WE STOOD STARING at each other for a long time before I could bring myself to speak.

"It happened just now? This morning?"

Erik nodded and glanced at his watch. "Less than an hour ago."

I gathered up the spilled aspirin tablets and slid them back in the bottle. "A hundred and fifty dollars. Even with the outrageous gas prices, that has to be something like an RV."

"Boat," Erik said. "They used the card at a marina."

"Where?"

"Amelia Island. Isn't that near Jacksonville?"

The brochure in Billy's study. I shook my head. "Right. But why now, do you suppose? I mean, does the fact that her death has been made public have anything to do with the timing?"

"I don't know. Why would it?"

"I don't know," I echoed, "but I hate coincidences." I paused. "That program gives you the exact name and location of the merchant, doesn't it?"

"Absolutely," he called over his shoulder. "Hang on."

I leaned back and took a calming breath. *Think this through.* Tracy Dumars' handbag and the money were missing from her Mercedes when her body was discovered. So whoever used the stolen AmEx card was most likely the killer. Or an accomplice.

I now possessed information both ethics and the law required me to share with the cops. And there was no reason I shouldn't. Billy Dumars was my client. He was also being lined up as the chief suspect in his wife's murder. Demonstrating that someone else was using her credit card had to exonerate him, or at least go a long way toward diverting suspicion somewhere else. I owed him that much.

On the other hand...

"Okay, got it." I looked up to find Erik in the doorway, a CD case in his hand. "I've off-loaded all the data as well as the program, so my computer is clean." He tapped his forehead with an index finger. "The information we need about the marina is right here."

"Go stash that in your glove box."

"Why?"

"If they come armed with a search warrant for some reason, I can't believe they'd include vehicles. At least not yours."

He smiled. "You're getting way too devious."

I grinned back. "I'll take that as the compliment I'm sure it was intended to be."

The door closed behind him, and I glanced at my watch. I had very little time to decide. I flipped open the Dumars file and punched in Billy's mobile number.

TEN MINUTES LATER I'd left messages on two of his voice mails and with his office. I supposed I shouldn't have been surprised he wasn't answering, but I'd hoped for at least a brief chance to get his take on the startling information that someone had used Tracy's credit card. Informing the sheriff without running it by Billy first seemed like some sort of betrayal, although I remained convinced it could do nothing but help his cause.

Besides, I'd done very little so far to earn his generous retainer.

Erik slipped back in, and we kicked it around for a while. He agreed with me, but the question was moot if we couldn't find our client. We were still hashing out our options when the outer door opened, and a uniformed deputy followed a short, slender woman into reception. Her close-cropped blond hair hugged her skull, and the white blouse and navy polyester pants gave the impression she didn't much care how she looked. When she pulled the wraparound sunglasses off her face, however, the dark green eyes smoldered with intelligence and more than a little anger.

"Lydia Tanner?" Her voice held a trace of the South, but not Carolina. Maybe north Georgia or Tennessee.

I rose and moved around to the front of my desk. "Yes?"

"I'm Detective Pedrovsky. This is Deputy Graves. We're here to take your statement about Tracy Dumars."

"This is my associate, Erik Whiteside."

While we all took turns shaking hands, I tried to size up the opposition, concluding that the woman would be all business. No chatty little exchanges about the weather or local gossip to break the ice. I took my cue from her.

"Who's taking notes? Or are you taping?" I asked, turning my back and retreating behind the bastion of my desk.

"Tape," Pedrovsky said, reaching into the voluminous, faux leather bag she had slung across her shoulder. She slapped the recorder down on the glass desktop and dropped into the client chair. "Small place."

"Adequate for our needs. At present." If she thought the rapid-fire staccato of her speech would intimidate me, she'd never had a conversation with the Judge. Or Ben Wyler.

She flipped on the tape and ran through her canned declaration of time, place, and subject. The black deputy stood guard just outside my office door. The questions seemed fairly routine. Most of them centered around the timing of my meeting with Billy Dumars, the substance of our conversation, and the efforts we'd made to track down his missing wife. I kept my answers brief, volunteering nothing, especially the information about Tracy's American Express card.

If she'd asked me, I wouldn't have lied, but her barely suppressed anger and dismissive attitude didn't invite confidences.

In less than fifteen minutes she clicked off the recorder. "I think that about covers it. Thanks for your time."

The blunt-fingered hand shot out as she rose, and I returned the pressure, perhaps a little more forcefully than was absolutely necessary. Detective Pedrovsky noticed, and a brief smile softened the hard lines of her face.

"I appreciate your cooperation, Mrs. Tanner. We'll be in touch when your statement's been typed and ready for your signature."

"Happy to be of help. I hope you catch the bastard."

The smile disappeared as if someone had slapped her. "Count on it," she said, turning on the heel of her sensible black flats.

"Thank you, ma'am," Deputy Graves said, before following in her wake.

Erik took Pedrovsky's place in the client chair. "That was surprisingly easy."

I thought about it. "Yes. Maybe too much so. She never asked to see the file, even though I left it sitting right here in plain sight. And she never asked to interrogate you."

"Maybe Red or someone higher up told her to take it easy. You're not without friends, in spite of all that crap last summer."

"You could be right. It might account for her hostility."

"So now what?" Erik crossed one long leg over the other and leaned forward. "What do we do about the credit card hit?"

"We—you—check out that marina. Talk to someone there, see if you can get a description of the person who used it." I thought for a moment. "And a name and description of the boat."

"I'm on it."

"And load that program back up on your laptop. I want to know if you get any more hits on her cards."

He veered away from the desk and headed for the outer door, which almost caught him squarely in the nose as it swung open.

"Hey, sorry, kid," Ben Wyler offered, moving aside to let Erik pass. "How's it going?"

"Ben," Erik muttered as he stepped outside.

Wyler stood for a moment looking after him before he strode in my direction. Shaking his head, he pulled up the chair and slapped a file folder onto my desk. "What's up with him?"

"First off, he hates you calling him 'kid,'" I answered.

"Term of affection. I don't mean anything by it."

"Well, try to refrain. It's a bad habit of yours, not using people's names."

He shrugged and cocked his head to one side. "A little testy this morning, are we? You look like you had a bad night."

I had to laugh. "If you're not careful, you could turn a girl's head."

"I keep trying." He leaned over to take a Fresca out of the mini-fridge. "Did the cops I just passed in the parking lot come from here?"

"Yes." I gave him a quick rundown on the interview.

"Life won't be very pleasant for Dumars for the next few days. They're gonna rip him every which way but loose, see if they can shake out a confession."

"That could be difficult if he didn't do it."

"Nine times out of ten, it's the husband. Statistics are pretty clear on that."

"So ten percent of the time it isn't. And unless Billy Dumars was near Amelia Island a couple of hours ago, he didn't do it."

"And you know this how?"

"Someone used Tracy's AmEx card at a marina there." I looked up as Erik stepped back in with the disk and picked up the phone on the reception desk.

Ben sat up straighter in his chair. "Did you share this with the detective?"

I couldn't miss the accusatory tone of his voice, but I wasn't certain which answer was going to get me off the hook. I hedged. "Not exactly."

"This has a direct bearing on the case, and you know it. Withholding information in an ongoing investigation can get your license yanked."

I noted his choice of pronoun. "I'm not an idiot. And I'm not exactly withholding. I like to think of it more as 'postponing.'"

That raised a smile. "You don't want them to know about the…about Erik's tracking program."

"Precisely. We're working on a description of whoever bought gas with the card. If it wasn't Billy, then—"

The thought struck from out of left field.

"What?" Ben leaned forward over his elbows on the desk.

Red hadn't been able to locate Billy Dumars to inform him of his wife's death. A real estate broker who didn't answer his phone or pick up messages? I hadn't thought much about it, but that was highly unlikely. *Where had he been all day yesterday?* Could news of the discovery of Tracy's body have gotten to him first? Could he already be on the run?

"Erik! What's happening with that ID?" I hollered.

He appeared suddenly in the doorway. "It was a woman, tall, good-looking blonde. Somewhere around thirty, thirty-five was the guy's guess, but he admits he's not real good at that kind of thing. 'Built,' he said. He's sure there was someone else on board. He could hear talking, like on a cell phone, but he never got a look. She took care of filling the tank and handed over the card."

"Male or female? The voice."

"He couldn't tell."

"Did he know where they came from?" I asked. "Or where they're headed?"

Erik shook his head. "He was working on another boat when they docked. The woman said she'd pump the gas herself, so he just waited and collected the money. Said he tried to strike up a conversation, but she wasn't having any of it. He says he didn't ask for any ID, either."

Wyler snorted. "Why would he? Probably so busy checking out her ass he didn't care if the card was stolen or not."

"Can you find out if they've picked Billy up yet?" I asked.

"Negative. I swung by the station on another matter on my way here, and the talk was they hadn't been able to locate him."

Another matter? I wondered if it had anything to do with the mysterious Stephanie. "That doesn't look good."

"His office says he went out Saturday ferrying a group of foreign investors around, some guys looking for private islands to buy. He chartered a yacht to take them out to some of the remoter places up and down the coast. They're due back in this afternoon."

"He told me he was going to be out of town on Saturday, but I didn't get any details," I said.

"So he could be legitimately out of touch," Erik offered.

"Or he could be snuggled down with some tootsie on a boat

in Florida," Wyler countered. "Either way, you need to give this stuff to Pedrovsky. ASAP."

"And how do you suggest we do that? And keep our license."

He studied my face for a moment. "Leave it to me," he said.

I OPENED ANOTHER CAN of soda and slipped off my shoes. Leaning back in the chair, I closed my eyes and thought about a scenario in which Billy Dumars had killed his wife in order to run off with a thirty-something blonde. Why would someone in his position risk the death penalty for another woman? Sure, lust could be blind, but he didn't strike me as a stupid man. A divorce wouldn't have been ruinous. At the rate he made money, even taking a hit in a settlement would still have left him incredibly wealthy by most people's standards. Or they could have a prenup.

Not a stupid man. If he wanted to make it look as if Tracy had just run off, why hadn't he packed up a bunch of her clothes and tossed the suitcases in the river? Or left them in the car to be found with the body. *Wife runs off, gets tangled up with bad people, ends up dead.* Much more believable story. Or maybe that's exactly what he did, and I just hadn't been able to tell when I'd searched her room.

Then why come to us? Because the cops weren't taking him seriously? If he had in fact left his wife dead in the trunk of her car and pushed it into the river, where was the upside for him if her body was found? It didn't wash. None of the circumstances made the slightest bit of sense with Billy as the murderer. Unless he knew about the hundred grand before he said he did? I opened the Dumars file and made a note to contact the guy from the bank. Even though we were technically off the case, I wanted to know.

I slid out the studio portrait Billy had given us Thursday night. Tracy Dumars' clear blue eyes stared back at me from the open folder. Straight blond hair curved around the smooth cheeks of a classically pretty face. I wondered what had compelled her to take a hundred thousand dollars in cash out of the bank, what secret or crisis had led her to death on a dirt road.

I leaned back and let my eyes drift closed, the too few hours of interrupted sleep weighing on my neck. My chin dropped down onto my chest, and I must have dozed, at least for a couple of minutes, before my head snapped up.

"Erik!" I yelled, and he appeared almost instantly in the doorway.

"What's the matter?"

"You said the woman who bought the gas was blond? Good-looking?"

"According to the guy who sold it to her. Why?"

I slid the photo of Tracy Dumars across the desk.

"You think— But why? I mean, then who—"

"See if that marina has a fax," I said, my mind whirling with all the implications. "If not, I want you on the road in fifteen minutes."

TWELVE

IT WAS THE Randolph Remington Wade case, I told myself, which had planted the idea in my mind. Perfectly understandable. I couldn't decide if I was relieved or disappointed when Erik, shaking his head, stepped back into the office.

"The guy at the marina says it wasn't her. Same general type, but the woman on the boat looked younger. Different hair." He paused. "Good thinking, though. It never occurred to me."

"Worth a shot."

The phone startled us both. I beat Erik to thc receiver.

"Simpson and Tanner."

"Bay, Wyler. You may have a problem."

I sat up straighter in the chair. "What kind of problem?"

"I was waiting to talk to Pedrovsky when they came hustling your client through the door."

"Billy? I thought he wasn't due back until this afternoon."

"He must have cut it short."

"What a terrible way to find out about his wife. But why is it a problem for us?"

"Obviously he's the prime suspect. Just like I told you."

I glanced across at Erik.

"Hang on a minute, Ben. I'm going to put you on speaker." I pushed the appropriate buttons. "They've brought Billy Dumars in for questioning," I said by way of bringing Erik up to speed. "Go ahead."

"Go ahead with what? That's pretty much it. They can't possibly have conclusive ballistics already and certainly not DNA. There must be something pretty damning that they'd take the chance on hauling in a guy with Dumars' clout, even if they're not formally charging him. Yet."

"You still haven't said why we have a problem. Are you talking about the credit card thing?"

"Of course that's what I'm talking about," he snapped. "I can't exactly drop a couple of gentle hints in Lisa Pedrovsky's ear now, not with them ready to charge Dumars any second. You're gonna get hit with withholding evidence."

Wyler's choice of pronouns throughout the conversation hadn't been lost on me. *You,* not *we.* One of these days we were going to have a long chat about his jumping around between trying to run the show and pretending he didn't have any stake in the business at all. The man needed to decide if he was in or out.

"So what do we do?"

"I figure Dumars will lawyer up. I think your best shot is to get the information to his attorney as soon as you find out who it is. It's definitely exculpatory, and he may not have to reveal how he came by it. At least not up front."

Although he irritated the hell out of me most of the time, I couldn't fault his logic.

"Okay. Are you going to hang around there for a while?"

"I can. Why?"

"I want to know who the lawyer is as soon as he shows."

"I'll keep you posted."

I clicked off the speaker, and Erik and I sat in silence for a few beats. Finally, he sighed and squared his shoulders.

"This is my fault."

"How do you figure that?"

"I know it's illegal for me to run that program. Sometimes I get so wrapped up in the toys, I forget there could be consequences."

"I gave you permission, so I'm as much to blame as anyone." I chewed a moment on the eraser end of a pencil. "Maybe you'd better take it back off your computer again. Print out everything we have that relates to Tracy Dumars and then make it all go away."

He stood. "Got it. Bay, I'm sorry if any of this gets us into real trouble. I'll be glad to take the fall if—"

"No one's taking any kind of fall. And this isn't a complete disaster. If Billy Dumars was out ferrying a bunch of investors around, he obviously wasn't in Amelia this morning using his dead wife's credit card. We're going to be able to help keep him from getting railroaded on a murder charge. That's a good thing."

"I guess," he said before turning to the outer office.

I let out a long, slow breath and pressed my fingers against the hard knot that had settled in the center of my chest.

JUST AS ERIK AND I were trying to decide on lunch, Ben called back.

"What did you find out?"

"You know a lawyer named Finch?"

"No. I mean, I know some people named Finch, but none of them is an attorney. What's his first name?"

"*Her*. Alexandra. Not much to look at, but I could feel the tension level rise around here the second she walked in the door. I have a feeling she kicks the county solicitor's butt on some sort of regular basis."

"Good for Billy," I said. "Did you get a chance to talk to her?"

"No. She's in there now. I suggest you call her office and leave a message for her to contact you. The sooner she knows about the credit card, the sooner she can start investigating it herself. If she gets independent corroboration, you might just be off the hook."

"*We* might be off the hook."

"Whatever. Listen, I've got some things to take care of. I'll keep the cell turned on. Call if you need me."

Again he didn't give me a chance to reply before he hung up.

"Bastard," I muttered and earned myself a grin from Erik.

I looked up Alexandra Finch's law firm in the Yellow Pages. A pleasant young woman took my name and promised to have her employer get back to me as soon as she returned.

I gathered up my bag and keys and stopped in the outer office. "What do you want for lunch? Or maybe you'd rather take off. Nothing's likely to happen until I hear back from Billy's lawyer."

"How about if I try contacting the other names on that list he gave you? The ones you couldn't reach. And we never checked in with the sister. That way someone'll be here if the Finch woman calls."

"Fine. What do you want to eat?"

"Surprise me."

Outside, the humidity saturated the listless air, and the blazing midday sun had turned the blacktop in the parking lot to the consistency of peanut butter. I used the remote to unlock the doors of the T-Bird, my mind so crowded with the events of the morning that I'd nearly reached the back bumper before it hit me. I stared, unbelieving, at the sight of my little yellow convertible squatting on the ground above four flat tires.

ERIK STOOD NEXT to me in the shimmering heat waves rising off the blacktop, while the cheerful driver the AAA had dispatched cranked the T-Bird up onto a flatbed tow truck.

While we'd waited for them to arrive, we'd done as thorough an inspection of the tires as we could under the circumstances. Neither of us had been able to detect any slash marks or obvious punctures. The caps on the valve stems were all in place. We'd split up the other offices in the complex and done a door-to-door, but no one had seen anyone in the vicinity of my car.

"If the cops had noticed—or Ben—surely someone would have mentioned it," I said as I watched the car bumping up the metal ramp and onto the truck.

"You'd think so." Erik brushed away the sweat from his forehead and wiped his hand on the seat of his khakis. "Doesn't leave much of a window of opportunity. Where you gonna have them take it?"

"The dealership, I guess. I want a specialist to inspect them and tell me exactly what happened."

"They had to be cut," he said. "There isn't any other plausible explanation."

Plausible, I said to myself, my mind shifting of its own accord to the small red pouch with the crude eyeball stitched into the fabric.

"Don't be ridiculous," I muttered out loud, and Erik said, "What?"

"Nothing. Will you drive me? I'm sure I'll have to leave it."

"Of course."

We locked the office, and Erik led the way onto Route 278 and into the noonday traffic. The Ford dealership lay just a few miles off-island, but it took us nearly half an hour.

The service rep eyed me a little suspiciously as I told my tale, but he promised to check the ruined tires over and get back to me. He figured sometime late Tuesday for me to pick it up.

We stopped at Dosido's at Moss Creek for lunch and wheeled back into the parking lot a little before three. Inside, the red light on the phone blinked back at us. I left Erik to retrieve the messages and pulled my cell phone from my bag as I settled behind my desk. Time to get some answers.

Lavinia picked up on the first ring.

"Hey, it's me," I said without preamble. "What have you heard about the girl in the hospital? Is she okay?"

"There's not much to report. Evelyn said they couldn't find a thing wrong with her. She came out of…whatever it was about an hour after her husband got her to the emergency room. Seemed perfectly fine. They wanted to keep her overnight and run some tests, but she wouldn't hear of it. Said she needed to get home to her children."

"So they have no idea what caused her to go into this trance or whatever it was?"

"Not according to Evelyn. The doctor said maybe it was heat exhaustion. She'd been working outside in the garden all Sunday afternoon."

Plausible, I thought again, *but not very damn likely.* Aloud I said, "You still think it has something to do with this root stuff? Some sort of hex?"

I could almost feel her considering her next words carefully. "Bay, I believe in God and Heaven and the saving grace of Jesus Christ, Our Lord and Savior. I *believe*. If you asked me to prove it, I could point to the miracle of birth and the perfection of a rose and the fact that people get healed of terrible illnesses by the power of prayer. But proof? I learned a long time ago not to scoff at things just because I can't prove them."

"So you believe it's possible for a scrap of cloth and some dirt and feathers to put someone into a hypnotic state or cure the gout or—" *Or cause four perfectly good tires to go flat,* I thought. What I said was, "Or make a person fall in love with you? You honestly think that's reasonable?"

Lavinia sighed, and the sound seemed to hold a world of resignation and sadness. "Honey, it's not about reason. It's about *faith*. You either have it or you don't. If you have it, all things become reasonable. And if you don't, there's just no way you're ever gonna understand."

There wasn't one damn thing I could say to that. "Okay. Tell Daddy I'll see him soon."

"I surely will. And Bay?"

"Yes, ma'am?"

"I think it would be best if you didn't get any more involved in the death of that poor child. Nothing you do now will change her situation the least little bit."

I swallowed hard against the memory of that tiny, wrinkled face. "I know that. But if I could bring myself to believe in anything, it would be the Old Testament. An eye for an eye. The people responsible need to pay. And if that conjure-woman can shed any light on things, I need to find her. And the sooner the better."

"I'll be praying for you," Lavinia said and hung up.

THIRTEEN

WHEN I RETURNED Alexandra Finch's call, her secretary put me right through.

"Thanks for getting back to me so quickly, Ms. Finch."

"I called as soon as I got back to the office. Your message intrigued me, especially in light of what transpired at the sheriff's office this morning."

"I understand you're Billy Dumars' attorney."

"Yes. And I understand you've been working on his behalf as well."

"He told you about engaging the agency?"

"Yes. I think we should meet as soon as possible."

"Of course. What would be convenient for you?"

"I'm free right now. I've got Billy back home and resting. Mary, his housekeeper, agreed to come over and keep an eye on him for a few hours."

"How did he take it?" I asked, my stomach contracting at the memory of coming to in the burn unit of the hospital in Savannah after the explosion of Rob's plane. The SLED officer had been kind, but hearing my husband's death confirmed by a stranger had almost broken me right then and there.

"Not the way the cops would have liked. They seemed suspicious because he wasn't wailing and tearing at his hair."

"I think he'd probably already considered the possibility that something bad had happened to Tracy. He didn't want to believe it, but I'd be willing to bet he's played the scenario over in his mind more than once. He's had a few days to get a little used to the idea."

"Exactly what I told them. So, can you meet me at my office?"

"I'm afraid I'm without a car right now. Where are you located?"

"In the Indigo Run business park. In the same building as First Coast Bank."

I laughed. "That's handy. I'm right behind you on Lafayette." I glanced at my watch. "How about I stop over around four?"

"Perfect. You can't miss us. We have the entire second floor."

I hung up and summoned Erik. "Do you have all the printouts on Tracy Dumars?"

"In the folder and ready to go."

"Thanks. I'm meeting with Billy's lawyer in about half an hour. Want to come along? She might have questions about the program."

He thought about it. "Maybe it might be better if I don't. That way you can plead ignorance about how it all works. Just in case we need to cover our…selves."

"Okay." I glanced down at the other message slip on my desk. "Did Red leave a voice mail or just a callback number?"

"Voice mail."

"How did he sound?"

He cocked an eyebrow at me. "Fine. Normal. He said it wasn't anything critical. He just wanted to ask you a couple of questions."

"I think I'll hold off until after I've spoken to Alexandra Finch. Just in case I need to cover my…self."

He laughed. "I did a quick check on her. The lawyer."

"Find anything interesting?"

"She wins a lot more than she loses. I can't find that she's ever defended a capital case, at least not around here, but she's done a lot of things involving battered wives and domestic violence. She almost always defends the woman."

"So this is a departure for her," I said, twirling a pencil around in my fingers. "I wonder why."

"I'm sure you'll find out," Erik said on the way back to his desk.

I'D PURPOSELY LEFT myself an extra half hour so I could make a detour to First Coast Bank on the ground floor of Alexandra

Finch's building. The spacious lobby was nearly deserted on a late Monday afternoon, only two of the eight teller windows open for business.

A trim black woman greeted me as I stepped inside. "Welcome to First Coast. Anything I can help you with today?"

"I'd like to speak to Mr. Briggs, if he's available."

"Let me check. May I have your name, please?"

"Bay Tanner."

She crossed the carpeted floor and knocked on a closed door, then ducked inside. I could see her silhouette through the frosted glass, and a moment later she stepped out and motioned me over.

"Ms. Tanner," she said over her shoulder and moved aside for me to enter.

Ken Briggs rose from his chair behind the desk and extended a hand. He was quite tall, well over six feet, and had a body he obviously spent a lot of time on. Thick black hair was slicked back away from his face, and the rimless John Lennon glasses just saved him from being movie-star handsome.

"Nice to meet you," he said, nodding toward an overstuffed chair. "Have a seat. How can I help you?"

I'd prepared and discarded a couple of scenarios on my walk over from the office, but the truth seemed my best ally. "I'm working for Billy Dumars. He initially hired my firm to locate his missing wife, but I'm sure you've heard about her death."

Briggs shook his head, and I felt certain it was genuine shock and sadness I read on his face. "Terrible thing. I still can't believe it. My wife is devastated. The four of us got to be friends when Billy found us our house out in Colleton River. We all just hit it off, right away. You know how that happens sometimes?"

I nodded and glanced at my watch. I didn't have time for too many fond reminiscences. "Are you aware that Billy's been questioned?"

"No! They can't seriously think— Well, that's just ridiculous."

"I'm inclined to agree with you. So our investigation is now geared to helping prove his innocence. Can you tell me about the day Tracy disappeared? From the sound of it, you may have been one of the last people to see her alive."

My words drained a lot of the color from his tanned face. "I hadn't thought about it that way. You could be right." Briggs cleared his throat. "She called, a little before three that afternoon. Said she needed the money right away for a deal that Billy needed to jump on." He sighed. "I tried to talk her out of cash, but she said that's how Billy wanted it. We'd done this before, although we usually had a little more notice. We had to scramble to get it together."

"So it isn't normal for you to have that much cash lying around?"

"It depends. Fridays we always make certain to be well stocked. Payrolls and all that."

"But you got the money for her?"

"Yes. Mostly hundreds, so it wouldn't be so bulky. One of the bank officers assembled the package and brought it here, to my office."

"How did Tracy seem when she arrived?"

"Fine. Maybe a little distracted, but she was always nervous whenever she carried a lot of cash around for Billy. I tried to convince her once to carry a weapon, but she said guns scared her more than robbers." He shrugged. "She had an empty tennis bag with her. We loaded up the bills, and she left around four."

"She went straight to the car? Didn't stop to talk to anyone?"

"No, not that I recall. I walked her out, made sure everything was okay." He paused, frowning. "Well, we did stop for a second, now that I think about it. My boy was on the way in to see me about something. They exchanged a few words. 'Hey, how are you?' 'Fine.' That sort of thing. But that's it."

"I see." I stood and held out my hand. "Thanks for seeing me without an appointment, Mr. Briggs. I appreciate all your help."

"Not much good, far as I can see," he said, following me out into the lobby. "But if there's anything I can do to help Billy—anything at all—you be sure and let me know."

"I'll do that," I said. "Thanks again."

Outside the heat hit me like a slap. Sunlight filtering through the overhanging branches of the sycamores dappled the sidewalk as I made my way around to the outside staircase.

That had probably been a waste of time, I told myself, but at least now I knew that Tracy Dumars had left the bank alone and under her own power. I guessed that was something.

THE OFFICES OF Alexandra Finch, attorney-at-law, did indeed sprawl across the entire second floor of the three-story office building. I noticed several well-dressed young women bent over desks or computers in the rooms I passed as I followed the receptionist down the hall.

Not a man in sight, I mused, recalling Erik's comments about Ms. Finch's clientele a moment before I was ushered into a corner office furnished in tasteful but modest style. The woman who rose from behind the cluttered desk couldn't have been much taller than five feet five, and she carried about thirty pounds she could have done without. I shook the extended hand while remarking to myself that smiling seemed to be a facial expression she had to work at.

"Ms. Tanner. Thanks so much for taking the time to see me."

"Not a problem." I set the Dumars file on the desk in front of me and took the chair the attorney indicated. "Anything I can do to help Billy."

"It's just ridiculous," she said, echoing Ken Briggs' remark while seating herself in the high-backed swivel chair. "This is a modern law enforcement department operating in the twenty-first century. You'd think the knee-jerk reaction of 'the husband did it' would have been put to rest by now."

I thought this a strange statement from a woman who regularly defended battered wives. "Statistics pretty much support the notion," I said, parroting Ben Wyler's observation.

"You have to have something more than maybes and numbers to justify hauling in a man who's just found out his wife's been murdered." The curling of her upper lip might have been intended as a smile, but it came out more like a sneer. "They'll think twice about doing it again."

"What do they have on him?" I asked. "Other than the fact he's the husband."

"Nothing I could pry out of them," she replied. "None of the forensics is back, except they're fairly certain of the caliber of the gun."

"How?" I asked. "Don't ballistics tests take a while?"

I could see her hesitate about sharing any specific information with me and waited while she made up her mind. "Single shell casing at the scene. One of the crime scene techs dug it out of the mud. Of course, they can't prove it's related, but they'll try." Suddenly she shot forward in the chair, startling me into a flinch. "Look, Ms. Tanner—can I call you Bay? Great," she said at my nod. "Here's the deal. I don't think Billy Dumars killed his wife. We can talk later about why." She paused and tapped a stubby finger on the file I'd brought along. "I'm hoping this will help me prove it. Are you available to continue with the assignment?"

"Of course. Billy's already given me a sizable retainer, and I—"

"No. I want you to work for me. I'll pay your going rate, plus expenses." Her laugh took me by surprise, its clear notes somehow softening the hard planes of her face. "Billy will end up paying for it, of course, but this way we can pool our resources, give him the best defense possible if, in fact, he's arrested. I'm hoping what's in your file will forestall that, but I always like to be prepared. What do you say?"

I'd anticipated such an eventuality, although I hadn't let myself count on it too heavily.

"What's my standing?" I asked.

"In regard to what?"

"I'll be an independent contractor rather than an employee. So does whatever I turn up become part of your work product? I guess what I'm basically asking is are the fruits of my investigation covered by attorney-client privilege?"

Alexandra Finch rested her chin on her steepled index

fingers. "It's a gray area, but my position is that they are, and I'll defend that stance vigorously if the need arises."

"Okay, then. I'm in."

"Great! I'll have Claudia draw up an agreement. I'll need your rates."

I opened my bag and removed the standard contract I'd shoved in there at the last moment. "Everything's here," I said and handed over the papers.

"Not as surprised as you let on," she said. "And just a little devious. I like that. Unfortunately it's an essential survival trait for a businesswoman these days."

She lifted her phone and punched in three digits. In moments a tall brunette in a sharply creased pantsuit appeared in the doorway. "Claudia, you can proceed with this as we discussed earlier. Here's the information you'll need."

The woman crossed the muted carpet to take my contract from her boss's hand.

"Bay Tanner, Claudia Darling. No comma," she added, and the two of them smiled.

It took me a moment to get it. "Nice to meet you," I said.

"You, too, Bay. I look forward to working with you."

"Claudia will sit second chair if it comes to a trial, which I hope you'll be able to help us avoid," Alexandra said, again tapping the cover of the Dumars file folder I'd set on the desk.

I settled it back onto my lap. "Based on what you've just told me about work product, I think I should hold on to this until we have a contract in place."

Alexandra smiled, again that same nearly imperceptible lift of her lips I was coming to recognize as her indication that she was pleased.

"I can have it printed out in a few minutes," Claudia said. "Be right back."

She disappeared down the carpeted hallway, and Alexandra Finch and I studied each other across the desk.

"You're originally from Beaufort," she said, letting me know she'd checked me out. "I understand your father used to be a judge."

"Criminal court," I said, "but he's been retired for a long time now." I waited for a couple of beats. "I'm a little surprised to find you defending a man who may be accused of murdering his wife. Don't you usually work the other side of the street?"

"Usually," was all she said before Claudia reappeared with a sheaf of papers in her hand.

It was a fairly simple document, and Claudia had selected rates at the highest end of our scale of services. I affixed my name to three copies and passed them over to Alexandra who did the same. I took mine and tucked it into my bag.

"So give," the attorney said.

I flipped open the file as her associate pulled up a chair alongside me.

"None of Tracy Dumars' possessions was found at the scene. Her handbag and the money are missing. Robbery seems the logical motive. At eight thirty this morning a woman used Tracy's American Express card to buy gas at a marina on Amelia Island, Florida. Since Billy was out on a charter boat with clients at the time, he can't possibly have been with her. Therefore, he's unlikely to be the murderer."

"Flawless logic," Alexandra Finch said as I slid the file across to her. "Except for one little problem."

"What's that?"

She looked up from the documents. "The cops don't know it yet, but Billy's alibi is about to go right down the toilet."

FOURTEEN

WHEN I RETURNED TO THE OFFICE, Erik and I discussed how Billy's whereabouts for the past couple of days might affect his case.

"If he wasn't with these supposed clients, there's nothing to say he couldn't have been in Amelia this morning with whoever used Tracy's credit card," I said in summing up Alexandra Finch's revelations.

"You're right. It's not more than a three-hour drive," Erik said. "I wonder how long it takes by boat."

"I have no idea. It's something we'll have to find out. Alex said Billy called the sheriff from the real estate office, and his employees claim he'd arrived there only a few minutes before."

Erik looked up from the notes he'd been scribbling. "Did Billy say why he didn't just come back home after they had to cut the trip short?"

Alex had told me one of Billy's prospective clients had proved a poor sailor, and they'd returned to the island Saturday night.

"He claims he decided to take advantage of the fact he didn't have anything scheduled and give himself a day off. He figured if he told his staff he was back, they'd just load him up with appointments and messages to return, so he turned off his cell and sneaked off." I tossed the pen I'd been twirling back onto the desk. "I have to say I find it a little strange he didn't check in with us to see if we had anything to report on Tracy's whereabouts."

"Unless he already knew."

"I don't want to think about that. I can't do this—take his

money and work for his attorney—if I don't believe he's innocent. I know defense lawyers represent people they're pretty sure are guilty, but I— I just don't have it in me."

"Me, either. And if the cops find out about the credit card and the marina guy saying there was someone else on board the boat, Billy could find himself more than just a suspect."

"Alex says the worst evidence is the shell casing they found at the scene. Apparently Billy's bought a couple of guns over the years, including a 9mm Sig Sauer, like the murder weapon." I shook my head. "If the ballistics match, there probably isn't much she can do to keep him from being arrested."

"They have his gun?" Erik asked.

"Not yet. They haven't applied for a search warrant, and Alex advised Billy not to volunteer it. He keeps it at the office in a locked drawer."

"Other people have access?"

I shrugged. "I'd assume an assistant or secretary would probably have duplicate keys."

"If he's innocent, why wouldn't she tell him to hand it over? If it's not a match, he's home free."

"That's what I thought, but Alex says she doesn't believe in doing the cops' work for them. They've tagged the registration already, which is why they brought him in for questioning right away. They've probably requested a rundown on Tracy's credit cards, but it'll take them longer than it did you. And eventually, they'll find out he lied about where he was for the past two days. That'll make them sit up and take notice. Right now they don't really have enough to request a warrant, but they'll keep digging until they do. In the meantime, she hopes we can find enough evidence either that Billy didn't do it or that someone else did. In that case, the gun won't be an issue."

"It sounds unnecessarily complicated to me." Erik shook his head. "If you're innocent, I don't see why you don't just cooperate with the police so they can turn their attention to finding out who really did it."

"I agree. But I guess that's why we're not lawyers. Besides, a man like Billy wouldn't be stupid enough to use his own gun, would he?"

ERIK DROPPED ME at the house a little after seven. Even though Tuesday was his free day, he'd agreed to pick me up first thing in the morning. We'd leave the office officially closed so we could work the phones and be available in case Alex Finch had an assignment for us.

I checked the machine for messages and found that Red had tried to reach me at home. My stomach grumbled as I sorted through a thin stack of mail, then crossed to the refrigerator and contemplated the contents of my freezer. Nothing looked appealing, but in the lower section I found the chicken and biscuits from Sunday dinner. Lavinia never sent me home without leftovers. I popped the container in the microwave, set it on Reheat, and picked up the phone.

I tracked Red down just as a loud *ding* signaled dinner was ready. I tucked the handset between chin and shoulder while we exchanged greetings. I removed the steaming dish and set it on the counter.

"You sound like you're eating," he said when I paused to blow across the first forkful of mashed potatoes before stuffing it into my mouth.

I swallowed, then huffed a little as the hot gravy hit my empty stomach. "I am. Late day at the office. What can I do for you?"

"Well, one of my questions has already been answered. I wanted to see if you'd like to join me for some shrimp and oysters at Bubba's."

"Sorry. Raincheck?"

"Sure."

I gnawed on a drumstick and waited for him to continue.

"So tell me where you stand on the Tracy Dumars case," he said after a long pause.

"What do you mean?"

"Are you still working for Billy?"

"Hang on a minute." I carried my makeshift plate to the glass-topped table and took a moment to gather my thoughts. "Why do you ask?"

"You know, that's one of your more annoying habits. Answering a question with a question."

"It's not a habit. And I have a right to know."

"So do I. Seems to me your job is pretty much finished. I mean, if Billy hired you to find his missing wife, that boat's already sailed."

"Pretty lame metaphor," I said, stalling for time.

"You can joke all you like," he replied, his tone lacking any hint of humor, "but the fact is Billy Dumars is the prime suspect in his wife's brutal murder. You'd be doing yourself a favor—personally and professionally—to get a little distance."

"Thanks for the advice." I heard him snort. "No, Red, seriously. I appreciate your being concerned enough to let me know."

My calm, reasoned response threw him for a moment. "Okay. Good. I don't want you getting into any trouble over this thing, that's all. From what I hear, he's going down hard."

"What makes you say that?" I nibbled at a biscuit, a little rubbery from its spin in the microwave. "Has Billy been arrested?"

This time his grunt held a little more of the old, bantering Red. "You just don't quit, do you?"

"Hey, can't blame a girl for asking. I'll talk to you."

"Bay, wait! I—"

"Gotta run," I said and punched the Off button before I was forced to tell any serious lies.

I TURNED TO the Braves game on the TV in the great room but found myself too restless to get engaged, even though Atlanta was ahead by three runs in the sixth.

I lowered the sound and paused in front of the bookcases flanking the fireplace. I'd finished *The Deep Blue Good-by* and couldn't decide if I wanted to tackle another MacDonald right away. Although I was fully aware the books had been written in a different era—when both casual sex and casual sexism were the norm—I still found myself bristling on nearly every page. While Travis McGee did have something of the chevalier about him, some of his Neanderthal attitudes grated on my nerves.

I wandered out onto the deck without selecting a book, my thoughts drifting to Alexandra Finch and her law firm of women. Maybe there was something to be said for taking that whole male-female thing out of the workplace equation, although Erik and I had no problems. He always treated me with respect, despite his occasional ribbing at my expense, and I truly did think of him as a younger brother.

The sun had begun its slow glide into the treetops on the mainland as I sank down onto a chaise and stretched out.

Wyler was another thing altogether. Most of the time, he treated me as if I had an IQ somewhere equivalent to my shoe size. He expressed his interest often, and in far from subtle ways, but his quips and sly glances left little doubt that it wasn't my mind he lusted after. I should have found it flattering, I supposed, especially considering I'd just slid past forty, and things were beginning to crinkle and sag in a number of places I didn't want to think about.

I gazed across the dune, seeing my mother as she'd been on my last trip to Presqu'isle, just before a heart attack had felled her in the middle of tending her prize roses. She had still been trim, still striking, her pure auburn hair untouched by gray. My mother had been a mean alcoholic, and I'd never understood how the drinking could have failed to leave some outward mark, some slackening or coarsening of her flawless complexion. Lavinia had told me she'd found Emmaline curled on the ground, the pruning shears still in her hand, the wide brim of her straw hat casting a shadow across the peaceful smile on her smooth face. It was probably the way she would have chosen to go, there on the dirt of the land she loved so much better than...

I shook my head. No need to go there. The point was I had some good DNA going for me. Even after the strokes, the

Judge's mind was still razor-sharp. So maybe aging gracefully was already in the hand I'd been dealt. And I'd get by because I truly believed a woman could survive just fine on her own, could find fulfillment in profession, family, friends. I didn't need a man to make me happy. I'd had a wonderful marriage, but that was over. The shock and pain of Rob's murder had finally settled into a dull ache I'd carry with me the rest of my life, but I could deal with it. I could smile at the memories now.

My two subsequent attempts at romance had both ended disastrously. And yet, on still, beautiful nights like this one, I felt a wave of loneliness wash over me, a yearning to reach across the empty space and clasp a warm hand...

I felt my eyelids drooping as I nestled down farther onto the soft cushions. Critical self-examination always wore me out. *I should get up and go to bed,* I told myself, but the occasional call of a mockingbird and the rustlings of the nocturnal creatures in the palmettos beside the deck lulled me into a half-doze. The light, almost constant breeze off the ocean died as nightfall crept across the dunes. I turned on my side and snuggled in....

I AWOKE MUCH LATER, the dew heavy on the cushions of the chaise, my bare arms covered in gooseflesh in the damp night air. I stretched and trudged inside. The ballgame was long over, and I snapped off the television. Wide-awake, I prowled the house, finally pulling on my pajamas and settling once again into the corner of the sofa with Henry Crowder's book.

I flipped idly through the pages, pausing occasionally at a depiction of some of the potions and other concoctions the native island root doctors used to ease the miseries of their customers. I glanced at black-and-white photos of innocuous-looking plants and searched for a description of the kind of charm I'd found in my car. Belle Crowder's name jumped out at me from the caption beneath a fuzzy picture of several people standing in front of a set of tall, wooden gates, and a memory suddenly clicked into place.

Sanctuary Hill was a collection of tumbledown buildings out

in the middle of nowhere about twenty miles northwest of Beaufort. It had been founded back in the seventies by a man who'd been unhappy with the lack of progress in the civil rights movement. I shifted myself more comfortably on the sofa and studied Henry Crowder's analysis. The man had organized a sort of commune for others who shared his beliefs. His goal had been some sort of pure African community based on the old ways and the old religion.

What had triggered my memory was the court case, related to me at some time in the distant past by my father. The leader of Sanctuary had declared the compound to be a separate nation, had even established a sort of passport control at the entrance, guarded by the gates in the photo that had caught my attention. Since they believed they weren't part of the United States, let alone South Carolina or Beaufort County, they didn't think they had to pay property taxes. The county treasurer disagreed, and in the end, the government had prevailed.

"Big surprise," I mumbled out loud.

I turned my attention back to the photo. It was hard to make out faces, but the caption clearly identified Belle Crowder as Sanctuary Hill's resident shaman.

And now I knew where to find her.

FIFTEEN

"SO I DID SOME MORE RESEARCH on the internet," I said to Erik as we climbed down from his SUV.

At barely nine o'clock, the sun scorched the asphalt parking lot and bounced off in shimmering waves of heat. Even with the air conditioning set to high, the room felt stuffy when we stepped inside. I veered away from my office door and took the upholstered visitor's chair in the reception area. Erik hooked up his computer and flicked it on before settling behind his desk.

"And what did you find out?" he asked.

"Sanctuary Hill is for real." I reached down to pull Dr. Henry Crowder's book from my briefcase. "The name comes from some incident in the Revolutionary War, but the residents of the place call it something African I can't pronounce. They're pretty quiet, don't make waves in the community anymore. Send their kids to school, pay their taxes. There used to be a couple of hundred people living there, but it's dwindled down to fewer than fifty, at least according to this." I tapped my finger on the book.

"You know what I don't get?" Erik leaned forward on his elbows.

"The things I don't get about this would fill an encyclopedia. Which one in particular do you mean?"

"Lavinia. According to what you've been telling me, one minute she's acting as if even mentioning this Crowder woman's name could bring down the wrath of God, and the next she's all but offering to track her down for you."

"I know. She's definitely been acting strange."

"So what's our next move?"

"About the baby? Nothing right now. Much as I'd like to turn all this information over to Red, I gave Lavinia my word. I have to figure out some way to get out there and arrange an audience with the elusive Ms. Crowder." I sighed. "But I also don't want to blow this chance to work with Alex Finch. We could get a lot of business out of her if we handle this right."

"What's my assignment?"

"Take the list we made up yesterday, and start checking out Billy's alibi. He told Alex he spent the rest of the weekend— through Monday morning—at a condo owned by one of his clients up on Lake Marion. He claims the guy gave him a key and told him he could stay there anytime he needed to get away. Apparently the man travels a lot and only uses it occasionally."

"Nice work if you can get it," Erik said with a shake of his head. "I wonder what it's like to have so much money you own a place just so you can drop in once or twice a year."

"Billy says he didn't talk to anyone. Did a little fishing off a public dock and ate at chain restaurants, so no one's likely to remember him."

"I'm going to have a tough time tracking any of that down. I'm not even sure where to begin."

I gestured to the folder I'd brought back from the attorney's office. "Alex gave us the name of the condo owner and the address. See if you can find out who the neighbors are. Maybe someone saw him coming or going. If worse comes to worst, one of us will have to drive up there and flash his picture around. Billy's a born salesman. I can't believe he spent nearly thirty-six hours somewhere and didn't strike up a conversation with at least one person who'll remember him."

"Okay."

I sensed Erik's hesitation in that single word. "What? You have a better idea?"

"This will only establish Billy's alibi for the morning Tracy's credit card was used. What about the day she was killed? Isn't that more important?"

"You're right," I said, "but until the coroner establishes a definite time frame, this is all we have to work with."

"I get that."

I suppressed a smile at the stubborn set of his chin. Erik rarely questioned me, and I felt more proud than angry that he had his own take on how we should proceed.

"So tell me what you think we should do."

"See if Wyler can find out the time of death. Or Red. We should concentrate our efforts on that so we're ready if they decide to arrest Billy. If he can prove he wasn't anywhere near Camp St. Mary's, none of the rest of it will matter."

"You're actually suggesting that we ask Ben for help?"

I glanced up as the outer door swung open.

"Hey, somebody taking my name in vain?" Wyler crossed the small space between us. "What kind of help do you need?"

"What are you doing here? It's Tuesday."

"I could ask you the same thing. I called your house, and Dolores told me. Where's your car?"

"In the shop." I left it at that because I didn't want to get into any explanations that involved a hex on my tires.

"So what do you want me to do?"

I turned, and Ben followed me into my office. I dropped the briefcase on my desk and seated myself behind it.

"Grab me a Diet Coke, would you?" I said, and Ben reached to pull one from the fridge. I popped the top of the soda and spent the next few minutes filling him in on my meeting with Alexandra Finch. "So, bottom line," I concluded, "we need to know the time of death. I don't know if Billy can account for his whereabouts every minute since Tuesday afternoon, but I'm betting it'll be tough. It would be for most people. We need something definite to work with."

"And you seriously think anybody down at the sheriff's office is going to tell me a damn thing?"

"What about your pal Pedrovsky? You seemed pretty confident you could steer her away from tagging us with withholding evidence. Can't you sweet-talk her into coughing up the goods?"

For the first time in the year since Ben Wyler had exploded into my life, I saw him blush. I almost laughed out loud.

"Touchy subject, huh? Anything you'd like to share, Detective?"

"You can be a real pain in the ass, you know that? Sure, Lisa would probably give me a heads-up if I asked nice, but the scuttlebutt is that the local guy can't get any closer than a forty-eight-hour window for TOD. Body was too…well, you know. They're shipping everything up to the SLED lab in Columbia for further testing. Probably won't know anything 'til the end of the week."

"What about ballistics? Heard any rumors about the gun?"

Ben shrugged. "No more than the lawyer told you. Sig. Nine-mil casing."

"They know about Billy owning one?" I asked.

"Yeah, they know. But there's about fifty of 'em registered between here and Savannah, not to mention the ones that don't show up on the radar. Not enough cause yet to justify a search warrant."

"So I guess we'll just proceed with trying to establish Billy's alibi for the time someone used Tracy's stolen credit card."

I paused, giving him an opportunity to jump in and suggest an alternative, to bully me into doing things his way. In very un-Ben-like fashion, he simply nodded.

WYLER LEFT a few minutes later. I'd meant to tackle him about his new girlfriend, get some straight answers out of the man, but he'd seemed distracted and eager to be on his way.

"Ben's acting kind of strange, don't you think?" I said to Erik after our silent partner had let himself out into the scorching heat. "He seems as if half his mind is somewhere else. Did you notice?"

Erik shook his head. "I guess I'm not as tuned to the finer points of Detective Wyler's moods as you are. He's pretty much the same arrogant pain in the ass as always, best I can tell."

I laughed. "It doesn't matter one way or the other. Do you have the list of Tracy's girlfriends? I'm going to try to track down this Kitty Longworth. Billy said they'd known each other a long time. Maybe Tracy might have confided in her, although you'd think she would have come forward by now if she had any information."

Before I could settle in to the computer, the second line rang. "I've got it," I called, and picked up.

The Ford garage had my car ready. I gulped a little at the total bill for four new tires, but maybe I could claim it on my insurance. I told them I'd be out later to pick it up. I'd just hung up when I heard the outer door open. I leaned sideways in my chair and watched a young woman pause in front of Erik's desk.

"Is Mrs. Tanner in?" she asked in a small voice, then stopped as she spotted me staring at her from behind my desk. "Oh, hi!" she said.

"Hello." I'd recognized her immediately even though she wore a pretty sundress and backless, high-heeled sandals instead of shorts and a tank top. The nearly black waves of hair curling around her face made her seem even younger than she had a couple of days before, standing outside Starbucks with Ben's arm draped around her shoulders.

"I'm sorry to barge in like this," she said, pausing in the doorway.

"What can I do for you? It's Stephanie, right?" I asked, and she nodded. "Please, have a seat."

"Oh, no, thanks. I can't stay. I just wondered if you'd seen my dad today."

"Your dad?" I said stupidly, a moment before the obvious answer hit me.

"I've been trying to track him down, but he's not answering his cell."

I had to bite back the gurgle of laughter rising in my throat, and Ben Wyler's daughter smiled.

SIXTEEN

"BEN JUST LEFT," I said, all sorts of things beginning to fall into place in the couple of seconds it took Stephanie to step into my office. "I think he was heading for the sheriff's office."

"I just came from there," she said, and the words wiped the pleasant expression from her face. "We probably passed each other on the road."

"Have a seat. Can I offer you a soda or a bottled water? It's already a scorcher out there."

Stephanie Wyler hesitated a moment, then seemed to come to some decision that had little to do with being hot or thirsty. "Sure," she said and set her bag on the floor as she dropped into the client chair.

"Right beside you." I indicated the little fridge. "Help yourself."

She slid out a bottle of water, uncapped it, and sipped. "I don't know how you guys stand this," she said. "At least in New York we know the summer heat waves won't last forever."

"I was born here," I said. "I guess I don't think about it much. I spent a few years up at Northwestern, and I have to say I prefer this to five degrees and a wind chill factor of twenty below."

"You get used to that, too."

The silence became awkward as Ben's daughter studied the label on the water bottle.

"So you're visiting your dad?" I asked. "How long are you staying?"

I'd thought it an appropriate icebreaker, but the look on her face told me it had been a loaded question. "I'm not exactly visiting," she finally said, her eyes roving everywhere except to my face. "This is a nice place. Compact."

I smiled at the clumsy change of subject. "A tactful way to say very small and cramped. The agency's been officially in business for less than a year. We only open the office three days a week right now, although I've recently made a connection that could steer a lot more work our way." I studied her face, waiting to gauge her reaction to my next words. "Your father may have to come out of retirement if we get really busy."

"He'd probably love that," she said with an edge in her voice. "Work was always more important than—" She cut herself off and nearly jumped from the chair. "I really do need to catch up with him. Thanks for the drink." She leaned down to retrieve her bag from the floor. "It was nice to meet you, Mrs. Tanner."

"Bay," I said automatically and again saw a glimmer of her sweet smile.

"Bay," she repeated.

As she turned toward the door, I said, "We'll probably run into each other again, especially if you're going to be around for a while." I waited, but she didn't rise to the bait. I followed her out into the reception area. "Oh, you haven't met the third member of the team. Stephanie Wyler, Erik Whiteside."

I knew Erik had heard everything that had gone on just a few feet away from his desk. He rose and took the girl's offered hand.

"Nice to meet you, Stephanie," he said, appreciation bright in his eyes.

"You, too," Ben's daughter replied.

There was no mistaking the little spark that leaped between the two of them, and neither seemed eager to disengage from the handshake. *Oh boy,* I thought. *This could get interesting.*

"Well," Stephanie said, "nice to see you again, Bay. Maybe…"

She left the thought hanging, and I scooped it up. "Maybe we can all get together one evening," I said.

"That's a great idea," Erik said, and Stephanie colored a little.

"I'll call you." I watched her face for a reaction. "You're staying with your dad, I assume?"

The blush spread to her neck and across her bare shoulders. "For now. Gotta run. Bye."

Erik and I glanced at each other in surprise as she nearly bolted for the door. When it had swung shut behind her, he asked, "Was it something I said?"

I laughed. "I don't think so. And in case you're wondering if she's interested, I can tell you that's a definite yes."

"How can someone that pretty and nice be related to Wyler?"

That brought another snort of laughter. "My thoughts exactly," I said before sobering. "I think she might be in some kind of trouble."

"Really? Why?"

"She's wound pretty tightly. And it would explain a lot, like Ben's being incommunicado a lot of the time over the past few days and telling me he'd been at the sheriff's office on 'other' business. Don't you think she looked scared?"

"I guess. But why wouldn't Ben have asked us for help? And why hasn't he ever mentioned Stephanie before?"

I stepped back into my office and picked up the can of soda off my desk. "He's never been very forthcoming about his personal life. I just assumed he didn't have any family since he never talked about them." I thought about my initial reaction outside Starbucks—that Wyler had found himself a sweet young thing. I shook my head. "Another one of those assumptions I'm learning can come back to bite you in the butt."

"You gonna tackle him about it?" my partner asked. "Even if I don't particularly like the guy, he has to know I'd jump in if his daughter's in some kind of jam."

"I think we have enough mysteries on our plate right now. If he needs us, we'll just have to trust that he'll say so." I sipped from the warm diet soda. "Can you take me out to the Ford dealership? My car's ready."

"Sure."

The telephone rang as I stepped back into my office. For it's being a day we were normally closed, we'd certainly had more than our share of interruptions. "Simpson and Tanner."

"Bay, it's Lavinia."

"Hi." I waited a moment, but she didn't respond. "Is everything okay?"

"Yes, of course." Her sigh told a different story. "I've been thinking," she said.

"About what?"

"Our earlier conversation. About faith. And trust."

Again I waited, letting her set the pace.

"I haven't been entirely forthcoming with you," she said. "I believe I can arrange for you to meet with…her." She hesitated but this time actually brought herself to say the name out loud. "With the Crowder woman. Or at least I can put you in touch with someone who can set it up."

Even though I'd figured out where to locate the elusive conjure-woman, having a personal intermediary might make things a whole lot easier. "If it's not going to get you into any trouble," I said. Thoughts of flat tires and strange hypnotic trances had suddenly made me afraid. Not for myself, but for Lavinia.

"Don't you worry about me, honey," she said. "I've been a coward, and that's not what the good Lord expects of me. That poor baby deserves to rest in peace."

"Are you sure about this?"

"I'm sure." Her next words sounded like a battle cry. "Me and Jesus aren't afraid of a little goofer dust."

"Goofer—" I began, but she was already gone.

"BAY? YOU READY?"

I don't know how long I'd been sitting, staring at the phone when Erik's voice finally penetrated.

"Sure." I tossed the empty soda can in the trash and pulled my sunglasses out of my tote bag, shivering as I stepped out into the heat. Maybe I'd retrieve the Seecamp pistol from the floor safe in my bedroom closet. All this talk about curses and hexes was making me jumpy. Suddenly I felt vulnerable, and that was not a word I ever wanted to apply to myself again.

THE T-BIRD SAT to the side of the Ford dealership on four shiny black tires. They'd also given her a much needed wash job, and the yellow finish gleamed in the noonday sun. Erik dropped me off and left to secure us a table at Dosido's.

I stepped into the service department, and the manager ducked under a lift and picked his way across the concrete floor in my direction.

"Hey, Mrs. Tanner. She's all set to go."

"Thanks. What'd you find out?"

He ran a hand across his balding head. "Damnedest thing I ever saw. I couldn't find one mark on those tires—not a cut, not a puncture, nothing. Valve stems seemed to be good, too."

"So why'd they all go flat?"

"Beats me. Only thing I can think of is that someone loosened the stems, waited until all the air escaped, then screwed them back on. It doesn't make a whole lot of sense, but that's the best I can tell you." A wry smile lifted the corners of his mouth before he said, "You tick somebody off lately?"

I could have given him a list. "So you think it was some sort of prank?"

"Maybe."

"How long would that have taken?" I asked. "For all the air to leak out." I couldn't for the life of me figure out how someone had been able to accomplish it without drawing attention to himself, especially in the busy parking lot with two cops and Ben Wyler almost passing each other on their way in and out of my office.

"Not long at all, really. The weight of the car would have made it pretty quick."

I still didn't buy the time line, but I supposed it didn't matter much at that point. I liked his explanation a whole lot better than the one I'd been trying unsuccessfully to push to the back of my mind.

"I thought you should replace the tires anyway," he said, turning to pull a work order from the rack on the wall beside the counter. He unclipped my keys and handed them to me. "You'd have been due in six months or so, and this way you won't have to worry about something like this happening again."

I hoped to hell he was right.

BACK AT THE OFFICE, Erik and I got down to the work we'd been interrupted from way too many times that morning. I tried unsuccessfully to find another phone listing for Kitty Longworth. The idea that Tracy Dumars' best friend had dropped off the radar was beginning to nag at me. I thought about calling Tracy's sister to get some background on the relationship but decided the poor woman probably had enough to deal with at the moment. I'd save that as a last resort.

A few minutes later Erik stepped into the office.

"I located the names of the other three owners in the building Billy says he stayed in last weekend. I've got phone numbers, but I'm not having much luck reaching anyone. Tax records show those units go for around half a million each. I'm guessing these are people who don't hang around there 24/7. Probably off in Aspen or Palm Beach."

"Or they're working two jobs to cover the mortgage. Let me know if you manage to hook up with any of them. I need to give Alexandra Finch some sort of report in the next day or so."

The phone rang. "I've got it," I said. "Simpson and Tanner, Inquiry Agents."

"Mrs. Tanner? I mean, Bay? This is Stephanie. Stephanie Wyler."

The girl sounded panicky, her words coming in breathless whispers as if she was afraid of being overheard.

"What's wrong, Stephanie? Are you all right?"

"I need to talk to you. I mean, if that's okay. If you have time. I know you're really busy, and—"

"Slow down. Take a breath. What's the problem?"

"I can't…I don't want my dad to know." She swallowed, and that simple action seemed to help her get control of herself. "Can we meet somewhere away from your office? Maybe off the island?"

I glanced at our PI license hanging on the wall and shuddered at the memory of Ben Wyler's cold, dark eyes the day he'd served the search warrant on me. In the year since, I'd witnessed his sardonic smile and wry humor countless times, but I'd also watched that barely controlled anger erupt as if someone had flipped a switch. I understood Stephanie's concern.

"You need to tell me what this is all about," I said firmly. "I'm not sure it's a good idea for either of us to be sneaking around behind Ben's back."

"I'm twenty-two years old. I don't need his permission to talk to somebody."

"And yet you seem hell-bent on making sure he doesn't find out." When she didn't respond, I said, "Are you in some sort of trouble?"

"No. I mean, not exactly. But Dad thinks I'm still ten years old and incapable of running my own life." She hesitated. "Look, maybe this isn't fair. I probably shouldn't get you involved. It's just…"

I hated the undercurrent of desperation I heard in her voice. "Let me get back to you, okay? We'll work something out."

"Are you sure? Like I said, I don't want to cause trouble between you and Dad. But I really need your advice."

"Let me see what I can juggle. Are you free this evening?"

"I can be. I'll have to…yes. Whenever you say. You can always reach me on my cell."

I scribbled the number on a notepad. "I'll call you later this afternoon, and we'll set something up."

"Thank you so much. You don't know how much I appreciate this."

"Talk to you soon," I said and hung up.

I rubbed my hands across my face and stared for a moment at the telephone. I couldn't in good conscience turn the girl away, but I had a hard knot of foreboding in the pit of my stomach. My gut told me that this would lead to nothing but trouble.

"As if that's anything new," I mumbled.

"Are you talking to me?" Erik called from the outer office.

"Nope, just myself. Did you manage to reach anybody at the condos?"

He stepped in and sat down in the client chair. "Two of the people were there." He consulted his notes. "Two women, one single, one married. Neither of them remembers seeing any strangers around last weekend. Both of them admitted they hadn't been out much, though, because of the heat."

"That's not good. The married one, did you talk to her husband?"

Erik shook his head. "He's been out of town on business for the past few days. Left on Thursday and won't be back until tomorrow, so he wouldn't be any help."

"And the third?"

"The condo's in the name of…" Again he checked his legal pad. "A guy named Grant Lincoln. No answer at his place. Couldn't locate a cell for him, but I'm still checking."

"So the bottom line is that Billy has no alibi for yesterday morning."

"Afraid not. There's nothing right now to say he wasn't the voice the marina guy heard inside the boat."

"Except we don't believe that." I studied his face, unsure of what I read there. "Do we?"

"I'm not quite as convinced as I was a day or so ago. It's nothing I can pin down, but I have to admit it's getting harder and harder to buy his story."

"Agreed. Which means we have to get a handle on it, and soon. I'm going up there. To Santee. I'll do whatever it takes to nail down his alibi one way or the other." I thought back to Red's admonition about distancing myself from the murder investigation. "And if it looks like Billy's been screwing with us, at least we'll know."

I didn't mention my conversation with Stephanie Wyler, but that had factored into things as well.

"Okay," Erik said, "I'll type up all the info I have."

"Good. Let's shoot for my being out of here by two thirty."

I picked up the phone and tapped in the numbers I'd written down just a few minutes before.

"Stephanie?" I said when she answered. "Are you free right now?"

"Sure. Where do you want to meet?"

"Do you have access to a car?"

"Yes."

"Are you familiar with Gold's Gym just off the island at Moss Creek?"

"Absolutely. I've worked out there a couple of times."

"Meet me in the parking lot—" I paused as Erik materialized in the doorway waving a printed sheet in his hand. "In about twenty minutes," I finished. "I need to take a drive for a case we're working on, and I thought you could ride along. Not much more private place than inside my car. I'll have you back before dark."

"I'll see you in twenty," she said and hung up.

As I gathered my things together and straightened out my desk, I hoped we'd both still be smiling if her father found out what we were up to.

"In for a penny," I mumbled to myself.

SEVENTEEN

STEPHANIE WYLER SLID into the passenger seat of the Thunderbird and buckled herself in. We exchanged pleasantries about the weather and the tourists until I'd broken out of the aggravating stop-and-go traffic just past Sun City and could give her my almost undivided attention.

"So what did you want to talk to me about?" I asked as the girl lowered the bottle of water she'd carried with her and set it back in the cup holder.

"I almost don't know where to begin," she said with a shake of her head. "I'm sure you're not interested in my whole life story."

"Is it fascinating?" I asked, and she returned my smile.

"Well, I guess to me it is, but the general answer would probably be no."

I slowed at the approach to I-95 and took the ramp north toward Florence. When she didn't continue, I said, "Here's what I know. Your father is a retired New York City homicide detective who got a settlement for being wrongly accused of something and moved to the Lowcountry. He did a brief stint as the death investigator for the sheriff's office. After our little…run-in last year, he retired again. He fronted us for the PI license and has dabbled in a couple of cases. He never told me anything about you, not that he even had a daughter. I had no idea you were here in the area until I saw you with him at Starbucks last Sunday." I grinned and risked a quick glance at the young woman's profile. "I'm embarrassed to tell you what I initially thought your relationship to Ben might have been when he wouldn't introduce us that day."

Stephanie's head swiveled in my direction. "You thought I was his girlfriend?"

I shrugged, the motion hampered by the tug of my shoulder harness. "He didn't use your last name. And you two were hugging, so…"

Her laugh filled the small compartment of the car. "I love it! I can't wait to tell him." The smile faded. "When all this is over."

I waited for her to elaborate, but she studied her hands where they lay folded in her lap and fell silent.

"He never mentioned his family in all the times we've talked," I said. "I assume your parents are divorced?"

"They haven't been together since I was about twelve. I hated him for a long time because I thought his work was the cause of it." A little sigh escaped. "Now that I've been in a couple of…relationships myself I realize it isn't ever just one person's fault."

"Is your mother still in New York?"

"No. She got remarried last year. Carl's a really nice guy. They moved to Arizona to be near his kids."

"Brothers and sisters?" I asked.

"Just Melissa. They live in Westchester. Her husband's on Wall Street." A hint of sadness crept into her voice. "I don't get along with him too well. That's why I moved down here after I got mugged instead of going to live with them."

"Mugged? That must have been scary. Were you badly hurt?" I asked.

"No. He didn't have a weapon, just his fists. Anyway, a beat cop showed up in the middle of it, and the guy ran away. Luckily, he dropped my briefcase, so I didn't lose anything."

"You are lucky."

"Yeah, I guess." Stephanie glanced across the console at me. "Thing was, it made me afraid. I hated feeling like that, looking over my shoulder all the time. Dad was helping me with expenses—editorial assistants at publishing houses don't make much money—and he said he'd cut me off if I didn't get out of the city." She smiled. "Didn't take a whole lot of convincing."

"How long have you been on the island?" I asked, wondering how Ben had managed to keep his daughter a secret. And why.

"A couple of months. I really like it here."

With the cruise control set at seventy-five, we were eating up the miles at a rapid pace. "So what's the problem?"

Stephanie seemed to consider her words carefully. "I moved in with Dad because I really didn't have much choice at first, but then I got hired at the company that publishes the *Hilton Head Monthly*. Plus I'm doing some freelance work for the *Island Packet*. I'm saving my money so I can find my own place, but it's going to take a while. Dad said he'd give me a down payment on a condo, but I don't want to keep relying on him. Anyway, I knew we'd have some problems, but I thought we could work them out. Like adults, you know?"

"Sure," I said.

"He promised he wouldn't butt into my private life, but…well, you know Dad."

"He doesn't approve of your dates?" I asked with a smile. I could just picture Ben grilling Stephanie's poor boyfriends as if they were under suspicion of mass murder.

"That's an understatement. Not that I've had that many. I've gone out with one of the staffers at the magazine a couple of times, but it's more like a friends thing."

"So who has your father all worked up?"

She hesitated over giving up the name, then finally said, "Kenny."

Out of the corner of my eye, I watched her chin come up. In that moment, she looked exactly like Ben.

"Why?" I flipped on my turn signal and blew by a lumbering cement truck, then eased back into the right lane.

"Because he'd hate anybody I went out with. Kenny and I ran into him one night when we were coming out of a…a club. When I got home, Dad went ballistic. You know what he can be like." She dropped into a fair imitation of her father's gruff, staccato delivery. "'He's too old for you. Damn hair's too long. He has tattoos, for God's sake. He's scum.'"

"Did he hate your friend from the magazine on sight?" I asked, suppressing a grin.

The momentary hesitation gave me the answer.

"What's the real reason your father's so dead-set against this guy? I know Ben can be a royal pain, but there has to be more to it than what he looks like." She was quiet so long I reached out and touched her arm. "Stephanie?"

"Dad says he's been in jail."

I suddenly found myself with a lot more sympathy for Ben's position than I'd expected when the conversation began.

"In jail for what?"

"I don't know. It was when he was a kid, and all the records are sealed." I risked a glance at her stricken face. "At least that's what Dad said. I didn't believe him, not at first." She swallowed hard. "But now I think there's a chance he might be right."

THE LITTLE TOWN of Santee sits on the southwestern shore of Lake Marion, right off the interstate. I'd passed through it dozens of times and occasionally gotten off for gas or a quick bite to eat on my way to some other destination. As we exited the freeway and pulled up to the light at the top of the ramp, I could see long lines of traffic snaking past in both directions on the main street.

I'd asked Erik to run off a set of directions from MapQuest, but I knew our first turn was a left. While I waited for the arrow, I glanced over at my young companion. She stared straight ahead. Her hands were clasped so tightly in her lap that her fingers had turned bone-white.

"Stephanie—"

"I said I don't want to talk about it anymore."

"I get that. You've been sitting there like a lump for the past twenty minutes. And getting pissed off at me isn't going to solve the problem."

"You can go," she said a moment before a horn blasted behind me.

I swung the T-Bird through the light and rolled down into

the lakeside village of Santee. Through a gap in the almost steady stream of cars, I spotted the familiar red and yellow signs of McDonald's and darted left into the parking lot.

"You want a tea or something?" I asked, easing open my door.

"Whatever." She climbed out and followed me into the cool interior. "I have to use the bathroom," she said and veered off to the right.

I bought two teas and filled the cups myself from the drink dispenser. I settled into a booth and picked up the directions I'd carried in from the car.

According to the printout, the condominium complex where Billy Dumars claimed he'd spent the previous weekend sat on a spit of land a couple of miles outside the town proper. We couldn't be more than ten or fifteen minutes away. We'd hang out for a while and give Grant Lincoln a chance to get home from work.

I looked up from the map as Stephanie slid into the booth across from me.

"Thanks," she said, peeling a straw and jabbing it through the slit in the plastic lid.

"I still don't understand why you're angry with *me*," I said, my voice as calm and reasoned as I could make it. "When you go looking for advice, it's assumed you want an honest opinion. If you didn't want to know what I really think, you shouldn't have asked me."

Stephanie leaned against the back of the booth and crossed both arms over her chest. The classic defensive pose.

"If your big advice is for me to tell Dad, I could have figured that out myself."

I bit down on my lip before replying. "I didn't say you should tell your father. What I said was, this is not something either one of us should be holding back from the authorities. Even if your suspicions turn out to be groundless, we have to advise the sheriff."

"But that's just it! All I heard was the last little bit of a conversation. It might not mean anything at all."

I rubbed a hand across my forehead where the first rumblings of a headache were beating a soft but insistent tattoo. "If your—" I stumbled over the word *boyfriend*. "If this guy was talking about meeting someone out at Camp St. Mary's in the same area where a murder victim was subsequently found, you don't have any choice. Especially when it happens on the same night the woman disappears. And you knew that even before you asked."

"But Dad's going to jump to the same conclusion you did. All I heard Kenny say was that he'd pick them up and that they needed to be out at the old camp before nine o'clock. It could have been about a lot of things. It doesn't necessarily mean—"

I slapped my hand down, hard, on the Formica tabletop, and Stephanie jumped. I ignored the other heads that swiveled in our direction. "You damn well know that's not true! If you didn't think it might have something to do with Tracy Dumars' murder, you wouldn't have gone to all this trouble to get me to check it out for you." I eased back and dropped both my bunched-up shoulders and my tone. "You have to make up your mind if you're going to start acting like the responsible adult you claim to be or go on sticking your head in the sand like some lovesick ostrich."

I wasn't prepared for the tears that rolled silently down her smooth cheeks. I grabbed a wad of paper napkins from the dispenser across the room and shoved them into her hand before sliding back into the booth.

"I'm sorry, Stephanie, really. I don't mean to be harsh, but this is not something to mess around with. I'm up here to check on Billy Dumars' alibi. There's a good chance he's going to be arrested for his wife's murder. Do you really intend to sit back and let an innocent man go to prison just to prove your father wrong? Could you honestly live with that?"

She dabbed at her eyes and shook her head.

"I didn't think so. Then as soon as we get back we'll go talk to my brother-in-law. Red's a really good guy, and you can trust him. Okay?"

Stephanie snuffled and blew her nose. "It's just that…I've

never met anyone like him, you know? He's gorgeous, and he knows everyone at the clubs, and I can just see the envy on the faces of all the other girls when I walk in with him."

I opened my mouth to say something profound about not getting carried away by superficialities when Geoffrey Anderson's face popped into my head. Not as I'd seen it the last time, just before he…died. But on those hazy summer afternoons when he'd pull into the driveway at Presqu'isle, and my teenaged heart would nearly explode with the wanting of him. When he dropped back into my life a couple of decades later, I'd thought myself infinitely wiser and certainly far less susceptible to his easy charm. Even after I'd begun to suspect that the unattainable object of my adolescent fantasies might not be the man I believed him to be, the physical attraction still had the ability to make me do incredibly stupid things. I knew all about the power of bad boys, and throwing stones at Stephanie would definitely shatter the glass walls of my own house.

I checked my watch. "We really have to get going. You okay?"

"Yeah. Sorry about the crying. I never do that."

"You're entitled," I said, "just this once," and she smiled.

BACK IN THE T-BIRD, we buckled up, and I handed Stephanie the creased directions.

"Where to next? I know it's a left out of here." I swung around to the exit drive, and a kind Southern gentleman slowed to allow me to whip through the steady stream of cars. I waved my appreciation.

"Straight ahead for one-point-seven miles."

I could feel Stephanie's eyes on the side of my face. "What?" I asked, glancing over.

"Dad likes you, you know," she said. "I mean, *really* likes you."

I felt like a thirteen-year-old at a sleepover, sharing secrets about boys with her giggly friends. I forced my attention back to the road. "Of course we like each other. We're colleagues,"

I said in what even I recognized as an evasion. We both knew I understood exactly what she'd meant.

"He talks about you all the time. Bay said this, Bay did that. I think it's kind of cute."

I laughed. "Oh, good. 'Cute' is exactly what I'm shooting for at forty."

"Are you interested in him?" Stephanie's tone sobered. "I mean, like that?"

She deserved an honest answer. "No, I'm not. I think we're too much alike. If we spent more than a couple of hours together, we'd be figuring out ways to kill each other."

"I think you'd be good for him," she said with a sigh. "He's pretty lonely most of the time."

I ignored the twinge her remark stirred up in my chest and checked the odometer. "We're almost at two miles from the restaurant. What's next?"

Stephanie let the matchmaking go and guided me through a series of turns that led us down some winding country roads. Eventually we pulled into the parking lot of several two-story buildings nestled among a stand of pines in a large complex that spread across the shore of Lake Marion. I gathered my bag and climbed out of the car.

"If you want to walk around down by the water or something, I shouldn't be too long," I said. "I just need to see if this guy is home and ask him a couple of questions."

"Don't worry about me," the girl said as she stepped out onto the pavement. "I won't go far."

I mounted the steps of the first building, noticing the manicured landscaping and fresh paint on the stairs. The stucco exterior was a soft cream color, and dark brown trim gleamed in pleasant contrast. The door to number three stood off an open corridor on the corner of the second floor, facing away from the lake. I pressed the bell and waited, glancing across the way to the wood panel with the gold 4 attached. This had supposedly been Billy Dumars' weekend hideaway.

I rang the bell again and leaned in a little closer, hoping to detect some sounds of movement inside the apartment. I tried a couple of sharp knocks, but it was apparent no one was home. Without giving it much thought, I turned, crossed the plank floor, and pushed the button beside number four. I was absolutely astounded when a voice boomed from the tiny speaker I hadn't noticed in the wall to my right.

"Who is it?"

I stepped back and sought frantically for the name of the man who owned this condo, Billy's client who had given him free run of the place. No dice. If I'd ever known it, the name had been swallowed up in some dark pool in my memory.

"I…I'm a friend of Billy Dumars," I stuttered. "From Hilton Head. I wonder if I could talk to you for a moment."

For a long time there was no reply. I stood there in the dying heat of the day, only a light breeze off the lake making it bearable in the confines of the hallway, until I heard the muted *clink* of a chain being slid onto its bolt. I stepped back as the door inched open, and one bloodshot eye peered out at me. Again the chain rattled, and this time the door was flung wide.

"Bay? What in hell are you doing here?" Billy Dumars said as he stepped out into the hallway.

EIGHTEEN

"MORE TO THE POINT, what in the hell are you doing here? Alex said you were resting at home."

Billy eased the door almost closed behind him, and I had to move back to keep us from standing literally nose-to-nose. He ran a hand through his matted hair and blinked at the glare from the shafts of sunlight peeking in at the open end of the corridor. I could have smelled the booze on him from half a mile away.

"Damn newspapers and TV reporters! Even when I disconnected all the phones, they kept bangin' on the doors and ringin' the bell. Especially that Henson broad from the *Packet*. About drove me crazy."

His sudden appearance had been so unexpected I didn't know how to react. "Is the sheriff aware you've skipped town?" I asked, and his chin lifted a few degrees.

"I'm not under arrest. I can go wherever I damn well please."

I supposed he was technically correct, but I didn't think Red and his cohorts would be too happy if they had to initiate a manhunt for him. "Does Alex know you're here?"

His expression gave me all the answer I needed.

"It's not a good idea to run numbers on your lawyer," I said, wondering as I did so if he was even sober enough to understand what I was saying. "And getting plastered won't solve your problems, either."

"What are you, the whiskey police?" He scratched his bare chest, and I realized he had on only a pair of wrinkled boxer shorts, his hairy belly hanging out over the straining elastic waistband.

"Maybe we should talk inside," I said and moved toward the door.

"No!" His shout could have rattled windows. "I mean, I don't think that's a good idea," he added, lowering his voice. "I…the place is a mess."

He worked on a reassuring smile, but his face couldn't quite pull it off.

I waited as he dropped his gaze, his big body weaving slightly. I listened intently and smiled to myself when the muted hum of conversation behind the door suddenly ceased. In the silence, I could hear water running somewhere inside.

"You have company," I said, and Billy jumped, his face a jumble of emotions that ran the gamut from fear to anger.

"How—"

"The TV just went off."

My client gathered himself then, striving for as much dignity as a man could muster standing in a public hallway in his shorts. "Look, Bay, I realize you're just doin' your job. I know Alexandra hired you on, and I appreciate that." His lopsided smile softened the harsh effect of daylight on pasty skin. "I know you haven't been doing this detective stuff too long, but everyone says you've got the knack for it." He took another deep breath. "But I just had to get away, you know? Sitting in the house was making me crazy. I kept expecting Trace to just pop around a corner, ask me if I wanted a drink. Instead, I have to live with knowin' some bastard stuffed her in the trunk of her car so the heat could rot her body into something that's not even…not even…"

A single tear rolled down his stubbled cheek and plopped onto the boards between us. His grief seemed genuine, and God knew he was entitled to it. Or maybe it was the booze. And maybe I had no right to judge how he dealt with his pain. But it was fairly obvious he had someone with him, and that knowledge tempered my natural sympathy for his loss. Getting drunk, okay. But shacking up? Again, technically none of my business, but the concept of mourning your dead wife by hopping into bed with another woman made my skin crawl.

"You need to get yourself cleaned up and back to Hilton Head," I said, stepping toward the stairs. "If the sheriff decides he wants to question you again, it won't look good if he has to send a posse out to bring you in."

Some of the sober Billy peeked out from his ruined eyes. "You're right, Bay. You're absolutely right."

"Good." I glanced across the hall. "Do you know where Grant Lincoln is? I need to see if he can substantiate your whereabouts for Saturday and Sunday nights."

"Why?"

"We need to make sure we can account for your movements every minute of every day between last Tuesday afternoon and yesterday morning."

"Okay. I guess I can see that. But I didn't kill Tracy. I swear."

I let it pass. A couple of days ago I might have been more inclined to accept his statement without question. And yet, Stephanie Wyler's revelation might be just the thing that proved Billy's innocence—to his own hired investigator as well as to the sheriff.

"So do you know Mr. Lincoln?" I asked.

"Across the hall? Good-looking black guy?"

"Grant Lincoln. That's all I know about him. He hasn't been answering his phone."

Billy nodded, and the effort sent him swaying again on his bare feet. "Saw him last night when I came in. Beautiful suit. Must work somewhere pretty high-class." He put out a hand to steady himself against the door frame. "I guess he should be home anytime now."

"He lives alone?"

"Far as I know," Billy said.

Inside, the water stopped running.

"You'd be better off at home," I said, my tone softening at the abject look on his face. "Even with the memories." I slung my bag over my shoulder. "I'll call tomorrow and make certain you made it back okay."

"Sure. Thanks, Bay." He fumbled with the knob, then lumbered back through the doorway.

OUTSIDE, I LEANED AGAINST the fender of the T-Bird, nearly hyperventilating with my desire for a cigarette. Somehow, stress was always my trigger, the nicotine longing surging up to grab my chest in a crushing band of need. I knew it would pass. It always did, but in the meantime—

"Bay? Are you all right?"

Stephanie's voice startled me.

"Yes, fine." I drew in a lungful of the damp, piney air and released it slowly.

"Did you find who you were looking for?"

"Not exactly. Listen, do you mind if we hang around here for a little while?" I checked my watch. "My guy may have had to stop at the store or something on his way home. I'd like to give it another half hour or so if you don't have any place special to be."

Stephanie shook her head. "I'm all yours. Just let me call Dad so he doesn't send out the state troopers."

I knew she hadn't meant it as a joke, and I stepped away toward the lake to give her some privacy. The sun had slid far enough down the sky so that its intense glare was filtered through the branches of the loblolly pines that shaded the condominium complex. A light, swirling wind ruffled the surface of the clear blue water. A few yards offshore a fish jumped, its silvery body catching the orange glow. I turned as Stephanie moved up beside me.

"Dad's not home. I left a message."

"Good. Let's sit out here and wait. The breeze is kind of pleasant."

We settled ourselves onto a wooden park bench just beneath one of the towering pines. For the next few minutes neither of us spoke, although I did check out every car that turned into the driveway. By six I'd just about decided to give it up as a wasted trip when a dark blue sedan eased into one of the numbered parking slots in front of Billy's building.

"This could be him," I said, watching a tall, well-built black man in a tan, summer-weight suit pull a briefcase behind him as he stepped from the car. "I'll be right back."

I crossed the narrow stretch of grass. "Excuse me," I called. "Are you by any chance Grant Lincoln?"

"Yes?"

I extracted my wallet from my bag and flipped it open to the card certifying that the state of South Carolina had licensed me to pry into other people's business. "My name is Bay Tanner. I'm a private investigator from Hilton Head. I wonder if I might ask you a couple of questions."

He studied the license for a moment. He was a handsome man, his black hair cut close to his head, his dark eyes soft and intelligent. "In regard to what?" he asked in a voice that held no trace of the South.

"There's a man staying in unit number four, right across the hall from you. I'd like to verify that he was here last weekend, probably from late Saturday until early Monday morning."

"Why?" The question carried no hint of hostility.

"I'm not at liberty to discuss that," I said. "I just need to know if he was here."

"Is the man a suspect in some crime? Are you looking to establish an alibi?"

I remained silent, and a slow smile creased his face. We stood like that for a long moment, neither of us willing to yield.

"Are you by any chance an attorney?" I finally asked, glancing at the briefcase, and he laughed.

"Guilty as charged."

"Then you can appreciate my confidentiality problem. I'm working with his lawyer. And yes, we're trying to establish his whereabouts last weekend."

"Fair enough," Grant Lincoln said, his tone suddenly all business. "Someone was definitely in the condo. There was a dark-colored car in Arden's parking place when I got back from the lake on Saturday, and it was still there when I left for work on Monday morning. At least I think it was the same one. I'm afraid I didn't pay that much attention. Lots of spillover on the weekends, visitors and such, and I never saw whoever was staying in Arden's place, although I did hear the door open and close a few times."

I glanced at the slot on the other side of Grant's big sedan where a black Infiniti sat baking in the late afternoon sun.

"Is that all?" the lawyer asked. "Don't mean to be rude, but I have some phone calls to make before dinner."

I stuck out my hand, and Grant Lincoln took it. "Thanks for speaking with me. I appreciate your time."

"Not much help," he said, stepping toward the stairway. "Have you spoken to the other people in our building?"

"Yes. No one remembers seeing our client around."

"Well, good luck." He sketched a brief wave over his shoulder as he trotted lightly up the steps.

"Thanks again," I called after him and turned back toward the car.

Stephanie joined me a moment later. "Was that him?"

"Yes," I said, sliding into the seat, "but it didn't do me much good." I cranked the engine and turned up the air conditioning. "You hungry?"

"Always. I saw a Shoney's back up by the interstate. I love their salad bar. If that's all right with you."

"Fine."

As I reached to pull the gearshift into Drive, Billy Dumars stomped down the steps, his wet hair plastered to his head. He wore considerably more clothes than the last time I'd seen him. I slid down in the seat and shut off the car.

"Stay still," I said to Stephanie, who threw me a puzzled look. "Watch the man who just came out. Tell me what he's doing."

Ben Wyler's daughter was a quick study. "He's crossing the parking lot. He just used a remote to unlock a big black car. An Infiniti, I think." I heard the engine a moment before she said, "He's pulling up by the entrance and stopping."

I waited, my neck beginning to cramp from the pressure of the unnatural angle. "What's happening?"

"Nothing. He's just sitting there. Wait! A woman's coming down the steps. Blond, maybe your age. She's carrying a canvas bag, like a tennis bag, or something. She's getting in the passenger side. It looks like he's yelling at her. Okay, she's in."

"Is he looking this way? Does he seem interested in the T-Bird?"

"No," Stephanie reported.

I eased up until my eyes were above the steering wheel just as the car did a U-turn and passed almost directly in front of us. Though the woman's head was turned toward Billy, I caught a brief glimpse of her profile as she flipped her shoulder-length hair away from her face.

"What the hell?" I muttered under my breath as the car sped down the driveway.

The woman could have passed for Tracy Dumars.

NINETEEN

I EASED OUT ONTO the street, for once in my life wishing for a little traffic.

As it was, I had to hang way back, afraid not only that Billy Dumars would spot the tail, but that he'd stop arguing with the blonde long enough to realize he'd seen a yellow T-Bird convertible in the parking lot when he'd visited my office. When he pulled up to a stop sign, I coasted over onto the grass shoulder and waited.

"Bay? What's going on?"

So intent had I been on not getting tagged, I'd almost forgotten I had an unsuspecting passenger.

"I'm sorry, Stephanie. Something's going on here that I can't quite figure out. Bear with me."

"Is that him? The husband of the woman who got killed?"

"Yes," I said. Then a random thought struck me. "You don't know him, do you? Never seen him with your friend Kenny?"

"No. I just recognized him from the paper this morning. There was a picture of him coming out of the police station."

"Sheriff's office," I corrected her automatically.

"Yeah. So what's he doing up here?"

"Damn good question. I'm thinking of tagging along and finding out."

"Okay by me," she said with a casual lift of one shoulder. "Is there something I can do to help?"

The black car moved out, and I pulled back onto the road. My maneuver had allowed a couple of vehicles to get between us, and I felt a little better. I'd skipped Tailing Your Client 101 in the private detectives' handbook, and I basically didn't have a clue what the hell I was doing.

"Bay?"

"Yes. Dig my phone out of my bag and call Erik. His cell number's in my directory."

Stephanie did as I asked without question. Despite our earlier confrontation, I was beginning to like this girl a lot.

Billy and his female companion continued on into town where the traffic had begun to thicken again as folks set out for dinner. Almost directly next door to the McDonald's where Stephanie and I had stopped earlier, they turned into a gas station and up to the pumps. I took the first right-hand driveway that presented itself and eased into the crowded parking lot of a restaurant. I circled the building and sat idling on the near side with the nose of the T-Bird pointed back toward the street. Billy climbed out of his car and inserted a credit card before lifting the nozzle.

"Erik, it's Stephanie Wyler. Hi. Bay wants to talk to you. Hang on." Stephanie held out the phone.

"Thanks. Erik? Listen, where are you?"

"Home. Putting a frozen pizza in the oven. Where are you?"

"Santee. I'm tailing Billy Dumars."

"Billy? What's he doing up there?"

"Drowning his sorrows in a bottle of whiskey." I glanced across at Stephanie who had turned her head in a vain attempt to give me some privacy. "And consoling himself with a very attractive blonde."

"Great. That'll sit well with the sheriff. Wait a minute, you said a blonde? As in the same kind of woman who was using Tracy's credit card at the marina?"

"My thoughts exactly."

Billy slid back into the car. I rolled to the edge of the driveway and waited to see which way they turned.

"What are you going to do?"

I switched the phone into my left hand and watched the Infiniti pull over to the side of the station lot and stop. A moment later Billy and his companion got out, stepped over a low concrete wall, and disappeared inside McDonald's.

"Hold on."

I eased toward the street and waited for a break in the traffic. I cut off a pickup truck and immediately whipped into the next driveway. I drove all the way around and slid into a parking slot.

"Erik?"

"I'm still here. What's going on? And why is Stephanie with you?"

"Long story. Look, just hang in there, okay? I'll call you back."

I flipped the phone closed and slid it into the tray under the dash.

"Are you trying to figure out if that woman is someone you know?"

I glanced at Stephanie, who seemed remarkably calm. "Yes," I said.

"I could go take her picture with my cell. Neither one of them knows me. Would that help?"

"I don't want you involved," I said. "Your father—"

"Can be an old woman. It'll only take a second. I'll pretend I just came in to use the rest room." She pushed open the door before I had a chance to protest. "Be right back."

Stephanie walked purposefully across the parking lot, the phone to her ear and her mouth going as if she were gossiping with a girlfriend. She pulled open the glass door and disappeared inside.

I drummed my fingers on the steering wheel, my eyes glued to the fast-food chain's entrance. The line at the drive-up window crawled along next to me, and I smiled at a toddler who stuck her chubby arm out the window of a dilapidated van and waved. The brief contact with a happy, healthy little girl brought the image of the blue-faced infant who would never get a chance to—

The passenger door jerked open. "Got it!" Stephanie said, holding the tiny screen out so I could see.

She'd caught the woman straight on, an angry scowl wrinkling her forehead. Pretty, but a little rough around the edges. Definitely not Tracy Dumars' face. But still the same type. I wondered what creepy scenario was running around in Billy's head.

"Does that help?" Stephanie asked. "Want me to send it to Erik?"

"Can you do that?"

"Sure. Piece of cake."

I kept my eyes glued to the rearview mirror, glancing down only long enough to retrieve my cell. Erik answered on the first ring.

"What's happening?"

"Stephanie got a shot of the woman with Billy. She's going to send it to you."

"What do you want me to do?"

"Can you print it out? Maybe fax it down to the marina and see if the attendant there can ID her as the woman he sold the gas to?"

"Probably nobody in the office this late. But have Stephanie send it now anyway. I'll do a little snooping. Any idea where to start?"

"None. She could just be a—" I bit back the word *hooker.* "Maybe just a casual date. No way to run it by anyone at Billy's office either. We'll probably have to wait until tomorrow."

"What are you gonna do?"

"Follow Billy and see where that leads us."

I heard the concern in his voice. "With Stephanie in the car? Ben will freak."

"Can't be helped. I'll have her send the photo. Let me know if you come up with anything."

"Will do. Be careful."

I hung up and nodded at Stephanie. "Go ahead and send the picture, if you don't mind." I recited Erik's number while my companion punched buttons on her cell phone.

"All done," she said a moment before I registered the black Infiniti moving past my rear bumper.

I backed around, letting a Mustang convertible from the drive-up line get between us, and slipped out into traffic. Life got a whole lot simpler when Billy took the southbound ramp onto I-95. I set the cruise on seventy-two and settled in a few car lengths back.

Beside me, I heard the rustle of a paper bag. Stephanie handed me a miniature apple pie, still slightly warm. "Thought we might not be able to stop for dinner," she said.

"Thanks." I chewed and swallowed. "Heaven. Listen, I'm sorry you got dragged into all this."

"No problem. And I'm sorry for acting so stupid back there. You were right. I asked for your advice, and I'm going to take it. I want to talk to your brother-in-law when we get back to the island."

"Why don't you take my cell and see if you can get hold of him now? Try the mobile first."

We struck out all the way around, but I left messages for Red to get back to me as soon as possible.

We settled into a comfortable silence then, the steady hum of the pavement making me drowsy as the sun slowly eased its way down behind the trees. I was surprised Stephanie didn't rush to fill the void with music, but she seemed to be enjoying the quiet. I glanced over once and found her eyes had slid closed.

Twilight had edged its way across the sky when Stephanie stirred and stretched. "So is your life always this exciting?" she asked with a hint of mischief in her voice. "Dad used to tell me being a policeman was just a lot of tedious paperwork and a bunch of sitting around waiting for people to show up. I had a feeling he wasn't giving me the whole story."

I smiled across the glow of the dash lights. "Most of the time it's pretty mundane. Lots of phone calls and computer searching and sitting on your butt trying to figure things out."

"So have you done that? Figured this thing out?"

I thought about it for a second. "Not really. We've got a lot more information than we had this morning, but I'm not sure yet what it all means."

Gross understatement, I told myself. Erik and I had both been convinced of Billy's innocence, but his actions were putting a severe strain on that belief. His wife's body had been discovered only a couple of days before, and already he'd jumped into bed with someone else. What did that say about his and Tracy's marriage? Could the leggy blonde he'd shared the Santee condo with be a motive for murder? Maybe it had been just a way to console himself, to ease the pain. But if that was true, why was he taking her back to Hilton Head with him? And where did Stephanie's boyfriend fit into the picture?

I shook my head and found her watching me from the passenger seat. "No," I said, "I don't have it figured out at all."

Night fell as we zoomed past the Ridgeland exit with only one more to go before we turned off toward the island. My eyes had grown fuzzy trying to keep the Infiniti's taillights in view, their red glow blurring into the other traffic as it grew darker. I took a deep breath and twisted my head around on my neck, working out the knots that inevitably settled there on long drives. I'd just about decided I'd sell my soul for a tall glass of sweet tea when blinding headlights suddenly filled the rearview mirror.

The huge tractor-trailer swerved left and roared past me going at least eighty.

"Moron!" I shouted above the din of the huge wheels tearing by at eye level, and beside me I heard Stephanie's sharp intake of breath.

I tapped the brake to disconnect the cruise control and let my speed drop. I wanted to give this idiot plenty of room to maneuver the mammoth double-trailer rig back into the slow lane. Instead he kept blasting down the left-hand side of the freeway. I had just started to breathe again when Stephanie suddenly shouted, "Look out!"

Ahead of us, brake lights flashed on, and I realized the rear trailer on the tandem had begun to fishtail, swinging from side to side in ever-increasing arcs. The squeal of tires on dry pavement rent the stillness, followed by the screech of metal on concrete as the big truck flipped over onto its side.

The chain reaction of collisions had almost reached us when I swung the wheel sharply to the right and aimed for the grassy verge alongside the highway. For a moment I thought we'd made it. Then the front wheels hit the wire fence meant to keep

TWENTY

I FELT AS IF SOMEONE had slammed me in the chest with a sledgehammer. For one long, panicked moment I couldn't get my breath. I punched at the enveloping folds of the collapsing air bag and finally managed to draw in a huge lungful of air. I winced at the dull pain just under my breastbone and the noxious odor—like scorched rubber—that filled the interior of the car.

Beside me I heard a soft moan.

Stephanie!

The passenger-side air bag had deployed as well, and Ben Wyler's daughter reached a trembling hand to her face.

"Are you okay? Stephanie?"

Her eyes finally focused and settled on mine. "I think so."

"Let's get out of here." I fumbled for the shoulder harness release. "Thank God," I breathed when I heard the *click.*

I looked out into overpowering blackness. A thin shaft of light from the one surviving headlight pointed directly up into the canopy of trees. The windshield had crazed but held. The litter of glass across my legs had come from the side window.

"My door's jammed," Stephanie said into the deathly stillness, punctuated now by the faint whine of sirens.

"Will your seat belt release?"

"Yes. But I can't open the door!"

I heard the panic in her voice. "Just calm down," I said, as much to myself as to the frightened young woman beside me.

I suddenly realized the engine was still running. I jerked the key back while I fumbled with the door handle and shoved. The screech of the bent hinges sounded like a woman's scream, but

I managed to force an opening wide enough for us to wriggle through.

"Come on," I said, one hand out to Stephanie. "You'll have to crawl across."

"I can't. I'm stuck."

I looked across the roof of the car back toward Ridgeland where the swirling red and blue lights of a convoy of emergency vehicles pierced the soft night sky. Headlamps lined both sides of the road where others had either pulled off to avoid the pileup or stopped to offer assistance.

"Hang on," I said.

I waded through waist-high weeds around the back of the car, glancing in the other direction where mangled vehicles littered the highway and fire licked at the trees.

"Dear God," I mumbled as I reached the passenger door to find it wedged against one of the fence posts. I put my good shoulder into it. Although it wiggled a little, I knew I didn't have a prayer of moving it enough to free Stephanie's door. I forced my way back to the driver's side and leaned in. "Can you get loose?"

"I don't know."

"Try!" I gulped air and blew it out slowly. "Move around a little and tell me what hurts."

With a quick nod, she lifted herself up on her hands. I saw the wince of pain, but she didn't cry out. "My right ankle, but I can move it. Everything else is just sore."

I leaned in across the seat, bracing myself with one knee. "Okay. I'm going to take you under the arms and pull you toward me. Push off with your other foot if you can. I'll try to be gentle, but it's probably going to hurt like hell." From somewhere I managed to dredge up a smile. "Scream if you want to. Ready?"

I knew moving her probably wasn't the best idea, but I felt as if I had no choice. A light breeze had lifted my hair as I'd stood outside the ruined car, and it wouldn't take much for it to send the fire leaping from tree to tree right into our faces.

The first attempt failed, although she did manage to work her left leg free of the dash. I had just drawn breath to give it another go when a deep voice from somewhere over my shoulder said, "Let me, ma'am."

I eased out of the car to confront a tall black man in a blue work shirt. "She stuck?" he asked, and I nodded. "Well, let's see if we can't get you out of there, missy," he said to Stephanie, his tone calm and soothing.

I looked up as an ambulance slowed and moved past us into the heart of the devastation. The cavalry had arrived.

"If we can move the fence post on the other side, she can get out her own door," I said, surprised to find my voice trembling. Some of the adrenaline rush had started to wear off.

I followed the man around to the passenger side. He put his shoulder to the jammed post. I added my own weight and felt it lifting out of the hard-packed earth. When it toppled a couple of seconds later, I almost went down with it. Our rescuer whipped open the door, which moved freely on undamaged hinges, and lifted Stephanie out as if she weighed no more than a sack of groceries. As he carried her back down the road, away from the worst of the accident scene, I reached in and retrieved our bags and cell phones.

The man kept moving north, past several abandoned cars, finally stopping alongside a fairly new pickup. "Can you stand up for a minute?" he murmured.

"I think so," Stephanie said, and he set her gingerly on the ground.

"I've got you," I said, moving up to drape the girl's arm around my neck and let her weight rest against my hip.

The man opened the door and lifted Stephanie onto the seat. "You get in, too." He motioned for me to follow him around the front. We waited for a hook-and-ladder truck to blow by before he drew back the driver's side door and helped me in. "I'll see if I can find a paramedic. You stay still here, okay?"

I didn't trust my voice, so I simply nodded.

"I'll be right back," he said and disappeared into the chaos.

I drew a long, steadying breath and cleared my throat. "You sure you're okay?" I asked, studying Stephanie's face.

"I think so," she said and burst into tears.

IT TOOK NEARLY five hours for the firefighters, tow trucks, and a phalanx of officers from several different law enforcement agencies to clear the carnage from the southbound lanes of I-95. The fires had been extinguished fairly quickly, and Stephanie and I watched ambulances maneuver their way through the twisted, smoking wreckage to streak off into the night.

Our rescuer had returned after half an hour with a young woman carrying a medical kit. She declared Stephanie's ankle only mildly sprained and told her to see her own doctor in the morning. She checked us over and judged neither of us likely to go into shock, thanks in large measure to the quick actions of the truck owner. Finally, she smoothed some sort of ointment on a burn I didn't even realize I had on my left wrist and taped a square of gauze over the wound.

"Probably from the igniter they use to blow the air bags," she said, before stowing her gear.

Triage was obviously the order of the day. She left some aspirin with codeine and a couple of bottles of water with us and had us sign some forms before heading back into the nightmare to attend to the more seriously injured.

After making sure we were secure in the truck, our black knight disappeared again. I could imagine him wading in to help other victims, his soft voice soothing fears, his strong arms offering security.

And I didn't even know his name.

After downing the pills, Stephanie closed her eyes and leaned her head back against the seat. I flipped open my cell phone and dialed Erik.

"Where are you?" he asked. "I've been trying to reach you for half an hour."

"There's been an accident," I said.

"Are you okay? And Stephanie?"

I calmed him long enough to relate what had happened, assuring him over and over that we were both banged up a little but basically all right.

"I'm coming," he said.

"Wait! There's no way you're going to get to us, either from

Hardeeville or Ridgeland. Besides, we're okay. We're dry and warm and out of harm's way. When they finally get this all cleared, I'm going to ask the man who owns the truck if he'll drop us somewhere off exit eight. Let's say the Huddle House and gas station right there at the interchange. If you really want to help, go there and wait for us."

"I'm on my way."

During the next long hours, we dozed a little, talked a little, and actually managed to laugh about how badly both of us had to go to the bathroom. We agreed men had it easier in a lot of ways, not the least of which was being able to pee just about anywhere. I wondered aloud if Billy Dumars and his companion had made it through the accident.

"I lost track of how far ahead of us they were," Stephanie said, stifling a yawn.

Again the eerie silence settled over us. A few minutes later I renewed my insistence that Stephanie check in with her father.

"He'll go ballistic and come racing out here, throw his weight around, and just generally get in everyone's way," she said with a hint of exasperation.

"Do it anyway. Please."

With a heavy sigh, she punched in the numbers. In the end she decided to lie. She reiterated her story from her earlier call that she'd gone out with friends from work, adding her decision to stay over with one of them. I couldn't bring myself to call her on it.

THINGS BEGAN MOVING a little after two thirty, but it was well past three in the morning before Stanley Johnson, master plumber for one of the large hotels on the island, pulled his pickup truck in front of the strip of businesses alongside Route 278 and eased the gearshift into Park.

"You sure you ladies gonna be all right?" he asked. Fatigue dragged at his round, dark face in the harsh overhead lights of the nearby gas station.

I had spotted Erik's black Expedition parked in front of the diner as we'd rolled off the interstate, and through the window

I could see him hunched over a mug in the booth closest to the front.

"We'll be fine. That's my friend there waiting for us." Suddenly I felt my throat close, and my voice wavered. "Stanley, I don't know how—"

"Hush now, Miz Tanner. You and the girl there just take good care of yourselves and lend a hand to someone else when the time comes. That'll be thanks enough."

He hopped out, and I slid along the seat to join him on the ground. He reached out a calloused hand, but I ignored it and hugged him hard. "Thank you."

"Take care," he said again and climbed back into the truck.

I crossed in front to open the passenger door and help Stephanie maneuver her way out. She limped only a little as we made our way into the diner.

Erik leaped up, enveloping both of us in an embrace so tight it took my breath away.

"Sit down, let me get you some coffee. Or tea. Are you hungry? Hey!" he called, waving frantically at the short, round waitress sitting on a stool in front of the counter.

"Calm down," I said. "The first thing we need is the bathroom."

"Amen, sister," Stephanie replied with a pretty good approximation of her sunny smile. "And I'm first."

"We'll go together," I said, linking my arm with hers in case she still felt a little wobbly.

"Order us two of everything," I called over my shoulder and followed Stephanie into the ladies' room.

When we'd relieved ourselves—a totally appropriate expression, I told myself with a grin—we washed up and did our best to repair the ravages. As I reached into my bag for a comb, my fingers brushed an unexpected scrap of coarse cloth. I could feel the lumpy contents even before I pulled it out into the harsh light of the bathroom's fluorescents.

Beside me at the small vanity, Stephanie said, "What's that?"

"It's a root," I said, turning the red pouch with its crudely stitched eye around in my hand.

"What does it mean?"

I fingered the three knots, tied in red yarn this time, and met her eyes in the cloudy mirror.

"It means Stanley Johnson didn't just happen on us by chance."

"What are you talking about?"

"It's a long story." I drew in a deep breath and raised my chin before dropping the little bag back into my purse. "And I think it's time I met the author."

TWENTY-ONE

I AWOKE JUST PAST NOON. I probably could have slept the clock around, but my friends apparently had other plans.

I remembered Dolores hovering over me a couple of times when I'd roused long enough to roll my aching body into a more comfortable position, and I knew it had been Ben's angry voice I'd heard out in the hallway. Before someone else came charging into my room, I decided I needed to haul myself to the shower and assess the damage.

Under the warm, soothing spray, I inspected the bruises, scrapes, and burns peppering the upper half of my body. Nothing major, I concluded, although the purpling imprint of the harness from my left shoulder to right hip was going to hurt like hell for a long time. I toweled myself off gingerly, applied some ointment to my wrist, and donned a tank top in place of a bra under a loose cotton blouse.

I found Erik and Stephanie seated around the small kitchen table, nearly empty iced tea glasses in front of them. I remembered guiding Ben's daughter to the guest room only seconds before I'd collapsed into the haven of my own bed.

Dolores turned from the stove at my entrance. "Ah, *mi pobre Señora!*"

I waved her away as she moved toward me, arms outstretched. "I'm fine. Really." I raised my hands and wiggled my fingers. "See? Everything's working." I eased out a chair and dropped into it. "How about you?" I asked Stephanie. "How's the ankle?"

"It's okay. A little sore, but I can walk on it."

"Good. Hey, Erik."

My partner nodded at me. "I think you both need to go get checked out," he said, and across the room I heard Dolores mutter, *"Es verdad."*

Stephanie and I shook our heads in unison, then smiled at each other. I looked up as Dolores set a glass of tea in front of me.

"Thanks." I sipped, then turned to the young woman wrapped up in one of my old chenille bathrobes. "Was your father here earlier? I thought I heard his voice."

She laughed. "I think they could probably hear him in Pittsburgh. He's not real happy with either one of us."

"Understandable, although the blame lies squarely on my shoulders. Tell him I said to leave you alone."

"Tell me yourself."

Wyler's voice made me jump, and the sudden movement drew a gasp as my bruised ribs protested. He strode up into the kitchen and seated himself in the remaining chair.

"Where the hell did you come from?" I demanded.

"I've been sitting out on your deck trying to decide whether to murder you for putting my daughter in danger or hug you for thinking fast enough to keep you both from getting killed."

"If those are my only two choices, I think I'll pass," I said.

He tossed the front section of the *Island Packet* onto the table. FIVE DEAD IN MULTI-CAR PILEUP, the headline screamed.

I scanned the article quickly, but no names had been released in time for the early-morning production of the local paper. The consensus seemed to be, however, that the death toll could rise due to the serious injuries of several victims.

"Any news about Billy?" I asked, turning to Erik.

"Dumars made it home okay," Ben interrupted.

"How do you know?"

"I filled Ben in on what you and Stephanie were doing up in Santee," Erik said.

I nodded to let him know I had no objection. Sooner or later Wyler would have found out, with or without the accident.

"Dumars' Infiniti is in the driveway," Ben said. "Can't say whether his companion is with him or not." He rose from the table. "So we need to find out who she is and where she ended up. I'll get on that." He eyed his daughter. "Go get your clothes on, and I'll take you home."

Stephanie's glance darted to Erik, and again I saw that little spark of understanding pass between them. I hoped Ben hadn't noticed.

"Erik's going to take me out to pick up my car at Gold's Gym," she said, not meeting her father's stern gaze. "And we have to help Bay with a rental." Her chin rose a fraction. "You go do whatever you have to do. I'll be home in a little while."

I waited for the explosion, but it never came. "I called the magazine and told them you'd been injured and wouldn't be in for a couple of days," her father said. "Don't make a liar out of me by running all over the damn county in broad daylight."

"No, sir," she said meekly. "I'll be there soon."

"I'll call you," Wyler snapped at me and marched down the three steps. In a moment we heard the front door slam behind him.

NONE OF THE RENTAL CAR companies at the Hilton Head airport had anything remotely resembling my Thunderbird, so I settled for a Chrysler 300, massive and sturdy, with every accessory known to man. I'd already spent more than an hour on the phone with my insurance agent, arranging for the rental and the tow of my poor little yellow convertible to a local body shop for inspection. As I turned onto Beach City road, I wasn't sure what I wanted the verdict to be. The plush leather seats and smooth purr of the big Chrysler already felt familiar, as if such luxury could lure me permanently away from my love affair with sports cars.

I'd also spent some time debating about where my loyalties lay. Red still hadn't returned my calls by the time I left home, but I knew he had to hear Stephanie's account of the overheard phone call as soon as possible. If he didn't respond soon, I'd go over his head to Detective Lisa Pedrovsky.

I could tell my call to Alexandra Finch about the events in Santee and my close brush with the fatal accident on I-95 had shaken the attorney, although I wasn't certain which part had caused her the most distress. She seemed genuinely concerned about my brush with death, but I could also sense her anger at the actions of our mutual client. We made a date to meet the following morning to discuss what effect Billy Dumars' romantic entanglement might have on his chances of being arrested for his wife's murder.

Whether strictly ethical or not, I held off telling her about the possibly exculpatory phone conversation Stephanie had overheard. The authorities should hear it first, then there could be no accusation of manufacturing evidence that might exonerate Billy Dumars. I wasn't sure of the protocol, but it seemed right to me.

As I drove past the library and took a right onto Route 278, it occurred to me that I'd never heard the gorgeous, tattooed Kenny's last name.

THROUGH SHEER LUCK I had gotten on the road just ahead of the afternoon exodus, and I made good time through the construction zone of the 278 widening project. I turned off at 170, chiding myself only a little for ignoring all the things I should be doing in order to chase down something that could only be described as personal business. My hand strayed to my tote sitting next to me on the passenger seat where both little red pouches now rested in plastic bags.

I'd called Lavinia from the rental car office as soon as I'd been certain they had a vehicle for me. It was way past time to get some answers—about Belle Crowder, about these roots that kept appearing on my doorstep, and most importantly about the dead child. Everything else on my plate would just have to wait. The sun wasn't going down until someone on St. Helena Island came clean about this whole grisly scenario, and I found out who was gunning for me. And why.

I FOUND LAVINIA on the back verandah, her feet propped up on a low stool, her head resting against the back of one of the plantation rockers. At first I thought she might have been asleep as

I crept out, easing the kitchen door closed behind me, until I detected the gentle motion of the chair.

"It's me," I said softly.

"I figured," she replied. "Your father's still napping."

I set my bag on the worn boards and sat down next to her. "As I told you on the phone, it's you I really want to talk to."

Her sigh held a world of meaning I could have interpreted in any number of ways. "So you said."

I reached down and lifted the two bags out of my tote. "What do these mean?"

Lavinia took the packages and fingered them without unzipping the sealed plastic. She shook her head and laid them gently on her lap. I followed her gaze across the lawn to the smooth waters of the Sound where a triangle of pelicans glided low over the surface. The lead bird pulled up, and his two companions followed, rising and banking right in preparation for another run. I let the quiet settle around us, certain the answers would come more quickly if I just sat back and waited her out.

"What you've got to understand, honey, is that I don't know a whole lot more than you do. Not about the specifics. You've heard the stories about Dr. Buzzard and the old high sheriff. I know your father's told them to you a dozen times."

"That's true. But you grew up in that world."

The wind off the Sound rustled through the palmettos, their razor-sharp leaves clacking together like Lavinia's knitting needles on a quiet evening. Still the air hung heavily, laden with humidity and a hint of that metallic smell that often presages a storm in the Lowcountry. I inched my chair around and slipped off my sandals so I could prop my bare feet up next to Lavinia's on the worn stool.

"I put all that behind me a long time ago, when I found Jesus. I've had no truck with roots and such for more years than you've been alive." She smiled to take any sting out of her next words. "But the old islanders don't like white folks meddlin' in their business."

I reached over and retrieved the red pouches from Lavinia's lap. "So someone thinks I've been meddling, and this is payback of some kind? You know I didn't go looking to get involved, but I found the baby. No changing that. All I've done since is try to get her some semblance of justice, find out who she is. How exactly did that put me on the wrong side of Sanctuary Hill's resident witch doctor?"

Lavinia's head snapped up. "Don't mock things you don't understand," she said, all trace of conciliation gone from her voice.

"I'm not mocking," I said, "I'm angry. I found the first one of these in my car last Sunday after I got home from dinner with you and the Judge. On Monday, I came out of the office to find all four tires on my car had gone flat."

I waited to see if that got any reaction, but Lavinia continued to rock and stare out at the Sound.

"The man at the car dealership said there wasn't a mark on them." I shrugged at her silence and went on. "Then, last night, I was coming home from…from some business I had to see to up in Santee, and there was an accident—"

"Sweet Jesus alive!" Lavinia's head whipped around and one bony hand shot out to grip my arm where it rested on the rocker. "Not that horrible thing on 95? What happened? Are you all right?"

"I'm fine," I said, patting her hand. "Really. Just a few bumps and bruises." I wriggled my wrist with its small white bandage.

"Thank God," she breathed into the late afternoon stillness.

"The point is," I continued, "a black man appeared from out of nowhere and helped me. And after he dropped me off at the gas station at the interchange, I found the second one of these in my bag. So believe me, I'm not scoffing. I'm just trying to understand what the hell is going on."

"Language," she said automatically before lapsing again into silence.

I waited, watching a bank of dark clouds forming on the horizon. That strange smell in the air hadn't lied. We'd have rain before nightfall, probably one of the driving summer thunderstorms that built up over hours and blew through in a matter of minutes.

Lavinia's feet in their sensible, crepe-soled oxfords hit the floor with a *thump,* and the sudden sound startled me. "I need to set out the tea," she said as if our conversation about roots and death had been just a friendly gossip.

"Okay," I said, but she had already pushed up from her chair and disappeared into the kitchen.

I closed my eyes and shuddered. Lavinia wasn't old, not by modern standards, but she had to be in her sixties, and this kind of erratic behavior scared the hell out of me. I'd heard plenty of stories about people a lot younger displaying the first signs of senility. Or Alzheimer's.

What would I do if she became permanently irrational or incapacitated? Not for the first time I pondered on what my life would be like if my father's care became my sole responsibility. I'd already come to terms with the fact that I didn't have it in me to fetch and carry and tend to him the way she did. I wasn't proud of it, but it was the truth. Could I sit by and watch some stranger become the Judge's lifeline? How would I choose someone? How would I ever know who to trust?

"Get the door, will you, honey?"

I rose and held the screen open. Lavinia carried out the tray and set it on the stool. An iced pitcher of tea, a small dish of sliced lemon, spoons, napkins, and the sugar bowl. And three glasses.

"Who—" I began when the doorbell interrupted.

"You wanted answers," Lavinia said, turning without another word and scurrying back into the house.

I had only a couple of minutes to wonder again about her strange behavior when the door once more eased open, and she ushered a small, dark-haired man ahead of her out onto the porch. He had a neat, pencil-thin mustache connected to a short goatee, and his pleasant face above his starched, white shirt collar glowed the soft, mocha brown of a person of mixed race. I guessed him to be about my own age.

"You must be Mrs. Tanner," he said in a low, cultured tone.

"Bay," Lavinia said, her voice a mixture of fear and resolve, "meet Dr. Henry Crowder."

"Please call me Harry," he said into the heavy silence.

I shook off my stunned surprise and took the offered hand. "My pleasure."

Lavinia pulled up another rocker. She poured out the tea and offered the first glass to her guest.

"Excellent," Harry Crowder murmured after his initial sip. "Just what the doctor ordered. Do you find the heat to be a trial, Mrs. Tanner, or have you become accustomed to it over the years?"

Small talk. Fine. "Call me Bay," I said, my eyes meeting the steady, inquisitive gaze of this utterly confident man. "And yes, I have. Become accustomed to the heat, that is."

"I was so pleased to get Mrs. Smalls' invitation this afternoon. I'm delighted I was able to accept on such short notice." He paused, and a flicker of something not quite so congenial passed across his face. "You have quite a reputation on the island."

That slight lift of the eyebrow and the hint of challenge in his voice couldn't have been plainer, and I had no intention of letting this officious little man intimidate me. I picked up the verbal gauntlet he'd flung down. "As do you, Harry. I found your book very…enlightening."

"I'm flattered. It's not something one generally picks up to while away a summer's afternoon."

"But it is an excellent reference book if one has a desire to understand the finer points of the native culture," I said, my gaze fixed on his strange, golden brown eyes. I wondered what combination of genes had produced such an odd color. On a woman, emphasized with liner and mascara, they would have been irresistibly seductive.

"I've told Dr. Crowder a bit about your recent…troubles." Lavinia spoke hesitantly, almost as if she were afraid of breaking the silence.

"Yes, and you have my profound sympathies, Bay. It must have been quite a shock to make such a gruesome discovery."

"I'm not unacquainted with death," I said. "As I'm sure you're already aware."

"Quite." We stared at each other a moment before he added, "You've chosen an unusual occupation for a woman with your advantages of upbringing and education."

I held his gaze over the rim of my glass as I sipped tea. I shot a quick look at Lavinia before I set the tumbler back on the tray, snatched up the two plastic bags, and tossed them at our visitor. Harry caught them deftly in both hands.

"What say we cut to the chase, Professor? Who's responsible for these roots and what do they mean? Who wants me injured? Or dead?"

I heard Lavinia's sharp intake of breath while I waited for him to fire back at me. I was totally unprepared for his bark of laughter.

"Dead, Mrs. Tanner?" He waved the bags in the air between us. "Oh, no, I don't think so."

I watched, mesmerized, as he unzipped the plastic and drew out the first of the misshapen red pouches. He fondled the cloth, his short, well-manicured fingers probing the shapes and textures of the ingredients inside.

"Oh, no," he said again, "quite the contrary. Whoever prepared these roots very much wants to keep you alive."

TWENTY-TWO

I STARED INTO the dancing golden eyes of the anthropology professor, whose totally unexpected pronouncement had momentarily stunned me into silence.

"Are you sure?"

"Oh, absolutely. Let me show you."

He took the first pouch, the one tied with white ribbon, and his fingers worked at the knots. When he had them both loosened, he opened the little bag to peer inside.

"A few herbs—" He paused to sniff. "Peppermint, I'd guess, salt, and red candle wax," he said, smiling up at me. "Maybe a little goofer dust, but I'd bet it's from a Christian burial."

"Burial?" I leaned back involuntarily as if the bag might reach out and burn me.

"It's grave dirt, gathered at midnight from the area just above where the heart would be," Harry Crowder said matter-of-factly. "If the deceased was a good person, someone who lived an exemplary life, then the dust can only work in good roots, like this one."

"How can you be sure this is good…goofer dust?" I asked, astounded I was actually having this conversation in the first decade of the twenty-first century in broad daylight on my father's verandah.

"There'd be animal bones or crow feathers. Maybe a salamander's feet." He turned the little bag over. "And then there's the eye. That's meant to watch over you, protect you."

He loosened the knots on the other pouch and performed the same ritual of sniffing and poking around inside. When he finally lifted his eyes to mine, the golden highlights seemed to shimmer in the dark shade of the sloped roof.

"You're a fortunate woman, Bay. Someone is taking very good care of you."

"Someone?"

I waited for a response that didn't come.

"Then explain this to me. Two days ago, less than twenty-four hours after I found the first one of these, all four tires on my car went flat. How was that meant to protect me?"

The dapper professor smiled. "Assuming the root had something to do with it."

"Well, the mechanic couldn't find anything wrong with the tires, but I replaced them all anyway."

"Hmmm," was his only reply.

"And then yesterday—last night—I almost got killed in that big pileup out on the interstate. It doesn't seem as if my luck is exactly running high right at the moment."

Crowder steepled his index fingers and rested his chin on them. He sat that way for a long moment. Even Lavinia had turned around to study his face.

"How exactly did the accident happen?" he shot out, making us both jump.

I gave him a brief account, including my rescue by the mysterious Stanley Johnson. The professor's facial muscles relaxed as he listened. A couple of times he nodded.

"It seems to me the roots are working perfectly," he said when I'd concluded my story.

"You're going to have to expound on that," I said, "because it makes absolutely no sense to me."

Dr. Crowder leaned back in the chair, this time lacing his fingers together. "Here's how I see it. Your tires went flat for no apparent reason, causing you to buy new ones. The same day you're involved in what could have been a fatal accident. Tell me, what do you think would have happened if one of your tires had blown out while you were trying to avoid the other vehicles around you?"

I didn't need to think about it. "I probably would have lost control of the car."

"And maybe not been fortunate enough to maneuver yourself

off the road and out of trouble. It seems to me whoever rooted you has probably saved your life. I don't believe you can fault my logic."

"I think Dr. Crowder's right," Lavinia said softly. "It makes sense."

I stared at them for a long time. *Logic* and *sense* were words I found hard to apply to this situation.

"Look," I said, "I don't have enough knowledge to debate you on this. It could all be coincidence. Or you could be a hundred percent right. What I really don't understand is who's doing this? Who's taking this much interest in my health and well-being? And why?"

"That I can't help you with, although I know someone who can." His smile lit the contours of his face but never quite made it to his eyes. "My Aunt Belle would very much like to meet you."

I HAD A LOT MORE questions for Dr. Harry Crowder, but a few moments after his totally unexpected announcement, he pled an urgent appointment. After we'd made arrangements to meet that evening at the little roadside store on Highway 21 near Gardens Corner, Lavinia led him back through the house, returning a moment later to settle once more into the rocker.

"You actually buy this stuff?" I asked, swirling half-melted ice cubes around in my glass of diluted tea.

Lavinia picked up the red pouches and fingered the knots the professor had retied. "You're here, aren't you?" she asked softly. "And safe?"

Again I had no ready answer. The sound of my father's motorized wheelchair forestalled what would probably have been another pointless discussion about faith, the power of suggestion, and grave dirt.

"Who was that pulling out of the driveway just now?" The Judge rolled down the porch from the entrance off his bedroom, coming to rest between our two rockers. "You've had company."

It sounded accusatory, although I was pretty certain he hadn't meant it that way.

"Dr. Crowder. He's an anthropology professor and writes about the local folk magic." I handed the Judge the red cloth bags. "He was explaining about these."

"Where'd they come from?" he asked, weighing the pouches in his one usable hand before turning to Lavinia. "Good or bad?"

"Dr. Crowder says good," she replied. "He's Belle Crowder's nephew and an expert in the field. I take his word."

"Explain," my father said to me, his deep-set gray eyes locked on my own.

"I should start dinner." Lavinia pushed herself up out of the rocker. "You two don't need me for this."

I watched her quick exit through the door into the kitchen before turning back to the Judge. With a sigh, I launched into my story.

I PASSED ON THE collard greens but loaded my plate with barbecue, dirty rice, and biscuits slathered in butter. As usual, there was extra sauce in a gravy boat, and I drowned the pulled pork with it.

"I don't like the idea of you gallivantin' around the county at night with some man you just met," the Judge said, wiping his mouth with the napkin in his good hand.

"Lavinia can vouch for him," I said, and she nodded from across the table. "Besides, why would I have any reason to be afraid of Harry? He only comes up to my shoulder. I think I could take him if push came to shove."

"That's unkind of you, Bay," Lavinia said.

"Sorry. But we're just going to meet his aunt. It'll still be sort of light at seven, if that's what you're worried about."

"What I'm concerned about is your ending up out at . There's not a lot known about that camp these days. I've never actually seen it myself, but I hear it's way back in the woods out toward Yemassee." He slapped his fork hard on the wooden table. "I don't like it."

"I've got my phone if I run into any trouble. Besides, we're not even going to the actual compound. Harry said Belle lives outside the gates. Either way, it's certainly not dangerous. Dr. Crowder is a perfectly respectable college professor who looks to me as if he'd run from the first sign of trouble."

I carried my dishes to the sink and began gathering up the leftovers.

"You have the Seecamp on you?" My father's chin rose as if he expected me to challenge him.

"Yes."

"Good," he said, rolling himself back from the table. "Excellent supper, Vinnie," he tossed over his shoulder as he moved toward the hallway. "Stop in my room before you go, daughter."

"Yes, sir," I called after him. I knew he was off to savor his after-dinner cigar out from under Lavinia's disapproving glare.

We cleaned up the kitchen in silence, both of us lost in our own thoughts. At six thirty I stuck my head around the door of the Judge's study. He sat in his recliner, the cut-crystal ashtray at his elbow, the pungent aroma of good tobacco permeating the room. I set his glass of bourbon and lemon on the side table within easy reach.

"I didn't want to say any of this in front of Vinnie," he said as I perched on the arm of the wing chair by the fireplace, "but I don't entirely trust these people. Why the hell do you feel you have to get yourself mixed up with them?"

I could sense the genuine concern under his gruff words. "You know I don't really believe all this mumbo jumbo about my being protected by some leaves and wax, but everything keeps coming back to Belle Crowder and these roots. Someone hung that charm around a dead child's neck, and I'm more interested in who it was made for than what its purpose was." I sighed and stood. "Red needs to know the baby's identity if he has any chance of finding out who did this to her. This just seems like the best lead."

"And of course, no one at is going to talk to a sheriff's man," he said with a nod. "Understood. You just be damned careful out there, you hear me?"

"Yes, sir," I said, stopping to plant a kiss on the top of his head. "I'll probably go straight back to the island tonight. I've got a meeting first thing in the morning. But I'll call you when I'm on my way. Don't worry."

"Humph," was the only answer I got as I stepped out into the hallway and closed the door behind me.

A little ripple of fear slithered down my neck. *Just a goose walking over your grave.* The childish words didn't sound so silly at the moment.

TWENTY-THREE

HARRY CROWDER DROVE a battered old Volkswagen bus that would have felt right at home parked in the middle of the Haight-Ashbury district of San Francisco in the seventies, although his bumper stickers had more to do with global warming and saving the planet than free love and Vietnam. I pulled the Chrysler in behind him in the narrow parking area in front of the closed store. All the antique farm tools and garden benches had been taken inside for the night. As I stepped out of the car, a semi roared by down Route 17 from Charleston. The wake of it kicked up eddies of dust and gravel that swirled around my bare ankles.

"I'll drive," Harry said.

"Fine." I moved around to the passenger side while the professor reached across and jerked on the door handle.

"Doesn't open from the outside," he said as I climbed into the sagging seat. "I really must apologize, Bay, for the transportation, but the road back to Auntie's isn't very good, and not much more can happen to this old wreck. It's my son Deshawn's latest project," he added with a laugh as the engine sputtered to life. "He loves to tinker with these old things, but he won't end up working with dirt underneath his fingernails. No, ma'am. He's an absolute genius at physics. Deshawn is headed to MIT. Even at eighteen, he's got some ideas about how to stop global warming." He darted a glance in my direction. "My son could change the world."

I let the veiled invitation to political debate slide and put the hyperbole down to understandable paternal pride.

We lumbered out onto the deserted highway and headed

west. After a mile or so of silence, the professor said, "Do you know the story of ?"

"Which one? I know the British routed the Continental Army somewhere around here in a small battle that nobody much remembers anything about."

"I think you underestimate its importance. The British burned Sheldon Church."

"I thought that was Sherman on his march to Columbia after he took Savannah."

"That was the second time. No, had a huge impact on this area." He paused to glance across at me. "Local legend has it that one of the participants in the battle was Francis Marion, the Swamp Fox."

"Interesting. So this compound where your aunt lives took the name of the battle site?"

"Yes. The concept of sanctuary has a special significance in their religious beliefs."

We'd driven west, then north for several miles, turning down ever-narrowing roads, when he finally slowed. He swung the rattletrap van into a small cut in a kudzu-draped hedge. There was a faded sign, but it was almost completely overgrown. I never would have found the place on my own.

My head slammed into the barely padded roof when we hit the first pothole in the dirt track.

"Sorry," Harry said, slowing the van nearly to a crawl.

We entered a long tunnel of overhanging trees and vines, and the soft evening light all but disappeared. I pulled my arm away from the open window as branches slapped against the side of the Volkswagen.

"What happens if a car is coming from the other direction?" I asked.

He turned to grin at me. "Someone has to back up."

The trail—I couldn't bring myself to accord it the status of a road—wound back among the trees for what seemed like forever. Actually, it couldn't have been more than a few minutes before we broke through the dense canopy into a dirt clearing. A huge live oak stood sentinel over a series of rickety wooden

fence posts with sagging chicken wire strung between. There
was a closed gate made of weathered logs held together by
some sort of straps. A faded sign announced something in a
language I assumed to be African of some sort. It looked as if
it had deteriorated a lot since the picture I'd seen in Crowder's
book had been taken. The weak headlamps of the battered old
van swung across wooden houses sitting up on short stilts.
From the foot of a set of open steps, a barefooted child dressed
in shorts and a Spider-Man T-shirt turned to stare at us.

But before I had a chance to take in more than a few details
of the interior of the compound, Harry swung the wheel left,
circling the oak, and heading off into another barely discernible
break in the rampant vegetation. This time the vines and limbs
trailed across the windshield, and the dark tunnel seemed to
crowd in around us from all sides. I forced myself to relax, over-
coming an instinctive desire to reach for the pistol at the bottom
of my bag. The holes in this track made the other dirt road seem
like a freeway. We jounced and bucked down it for a couple of
hundred yards, before the professor eased to his right at a break
in the undergrowth and onto a narrow strip of grass. He turned
off the engine but left the headlights on. In their harsh glare I
saw that the road petered out only a few yards ahead of us into
an impenetrable wall of scrub palmetto and vines.

When he reached for the door handle, I gave my paranoia
free rein, lifted the tote bag onto my lap, and scrabbled for the
grip of the Seecamp. By the time Harry had worked his way
around to help me wrestle open the passenger door, I had the
pistol nestled comfortably in the right-hand pocket of my
slacks.

"Where are we going?" I asked, proud that my voice
quavered only a little. "Why didn't we stop back there at the
gate?"

"I told you, Auntie lives outside the compound." In the
nearly total darkness, his sardonic smile stood out like the
Cheshire cat's. "Please don't be alarmed, Bay. It's just over
here."

I drew a calming breath and stepped out onto the night-damp grass. The silence couldn't have been more absolute if we'd been locked in a tomb. I shook off that unsettling analogy and followed Harry Crowder onto a stone path that seemed to have materialized out of nowhere. Over his head I could just make out a dim glow amid the tangle of vines and twisted limbs.

The light grew as we wound our way through the trees until we finally emerged into another, larger clearing. I couldn't make out many details, but the house seemed to nestle into the woods as if it had always been there. The weathered siding melted into the silvery gray of the trunks that surrounded the little cottage. Some sort of creeper had wound itself around the posts of the narrow porch, and I thought it might be the scent of night-blooming jasmine that floated on the humid air.

When an outside fixture suddenly snapped on, it was as if a dozen flashbulbs had gone off all at once. I stepped back as the door opened, spilling more light out onto the parched grass where we stood. Off in the distance I heard a rumble of thunder.

"Henry?" a female voice said into the glare. "Is that you?"

I could just make out the shape of someone standing in the doorway.

"Yes, Auntie. I've brought her."

"Well get yourselves on in here, then. It'll be pouring in about two minutes."

"I'd better see to the windows on the van," Harry said, turning so quickly he nearly ran me down. "Go ahead, Bay." Again his smile flashed out of the night. "You're expected."

He brushed past me, and I suddenly felt as if I were on a stage, the footlights blinding me and the audience shrouded in the anonymity of the dark theater.

I expelled a long breath and stepped up onto the porch. "Good evening, Ms. Crowder," I said, extending a hand. "I'm Bay Tanner."

The woman ignored the gesture, and even in the glare I could sense her eyes on me. I let my arm drop to my side a moment before she said, "Come in, child."

I hesitated and heard her low chuckle just as the first fat drops of rain plopped onto the dusty steps behind me.

"Don't be afraid," the woman said, her voice now low and seductive. She moved aside, indicating I should pass in front of her.

I squared my shoulders, eased around her, and into a surprisingly familiar world.

WE SAT AROUND an old oak table not unlike the one in the kitchen at Presqu'isle. Harry mopped the water from his face and beard with a hand towel and took the chair on his aunt's left. She'd seated me directly across from her. Belle Crowder had served me tea in a delicate china cup without inquiring about my preference before setting out heavy mugs of coffee for herself and her nephew. Overhead, the storm beat down, the driving rain tapping out a distinctive tattoo against the roof of the cottage.

I wasn't entirely certain what I'd expected, but it hadn't been this time warp back to the early plantation days of the county. Every heavy, oversized piece of furniture crowding the small rooms looked as if it belonged in a museum or in one of the many antebellum houses in Charleston clinging to the long-dead glory of the Old South.

"You're surprised," the strange woman had said, accurately reading my face when I'd first stepped into her house. "I expect you figured I'd be swathed in turbans and bangles, with carved masks and animal skins hanging on the walls."

The accuracy of her barb made me squirm, even while I denied it. Who would have assumed that the shaman of a self-styled, independent African nation would look like a prim schoolteacher? She stood about halfway between her nephew's height and my own, with a body that had probably been naturally thin, now thickened a little around the waist and hips. The tan slacks were pressed into a sharp crease, and the pale pink polo shirt was buttoned up to her neck. The Birkenstock sandals she wore could have been the matching pair to my own.

But the most astounding thing about her was her face, serene and beautiful, beneath a cap of snow-white hair that curled softly over her ears. She had her nephew's café-au-lait skin, but hers had none of the splotches of darker color that spread across his cheeks. The eyes, golden brown and shimmering, looked just as good on a woman as I'd expected they would.

"Really, Henry, I'm surprised at you." Her voice held the barest trace of an accent, South Carolina mixed with something exotic, foreign. "Dragging this poor woman out in a storm and forcing her into that disreputable pile of junk." Her tone sharpened. "Where's Deshawn?"

There seemed to be some silent message being conveyed, and I tried to interpret the look that passed between them. *Hostility* was the word that sprang immediately into my head, although that made no sense.

"My son is where he needs to be," Harry said. He leaned back in the chair and folded his hands in his lap.

The tension seemed to leave Belle's shoulders. "I can't think why you let him tinker with those old wrecks. Boy should be studying, specially if you expect to get him into one of those fancy colleges of yours."

"He does fine, Auntie. You know both the children do well in school."

"They best do," she said with a quick shake of her head. "Not much of a life out there for ignorant people."

Again they exchanged that strange, challenging look.

I sipped at the tea, some exotic blend I couldn't place, but soothing and comforting as the rain pelted the windows outside. I had just decided to bring up the subject of my visit, when Belle spoke first.

"You're troubled about the roots."

"Did you make them?" I asked.

"That's not important," the woman said.

"It is to me. I don't much like the idea of people I don't know leaving things in my car. And my handbag."

She stared into my face as I spoke, as if she needed to concentrate hard on my words, but remained silent.

"Look, Ms. Crowder, I'd prefer it if you could just answer

my questions. I don't mean any disrespect, but I don't buy into all this…into your belief system."

"And yet here you are."

I looked over at Harry. His golden eyes were fastened on my face, and his intense scrutiny was beginning to make me uneasy.

"I'm here for information. Your nephew assured me that those little red pouches are meant to protect me. In fact, he's convinced they already have. But I—"

"You've been in danger?" Belle Crowder leaned forward, her shimmering eyes alight with something I couldn't name.

I told her briefly about the tires and the accident on I-95. She never moved throughout the short recitation.

"Did you send Stanley Johnson to me last night?" I asked.

She eased herself back in the chair, and her gaze finally dropped to the table. "No one sent Stanley to you, not in the sense you mean." She paused, choosing her words. "Can you accept that…*elements* have been put in motion that resulted in your good fortune? It really isn't much different than someone praying for you and having everything turn out all right, is it?"

"I don't much believe in that, either," I said.

"How sad," the woman replied, her eyes full of what looked like genuine regret.

Her pity rankled. I resisted the urge to pat my pocket where the Seecamp pistol nestled next to my thigh. "I prefer to put my trust in things I can see and touch."

"I understand. There aren't many who still believe in the old ways, of whatever religion they've been exposed to. Isn't that right, Henry?"

He jumped, surprised to find his aunt's intense stare fixed on him.

"I don't know what you mean, Auntie. Bay is here partly because she read my book."

Belle Crowder waved his words away with a flick of her hand. "You have a *head* knowledge, Henry. It's your heart that concerns me."

I opened my mouth to head off what could turn into one of

those endless, circular arguments about the merits of one religion over another, but Belle forestalled me.

"Do you have the roots with you?"

My eyes dropped to where my bag rested on the floor. "Yes, ma'am." I leaned over, but she reached a restraining hand across the table.

"Just keep them close. You won't be receiving any more if you keep those by you all the time." She smiled at the look on my face. "What can it hurt, child?"

I had no answer for that.

"Storm's over," she said, rising to retrieve the teapot from the counter and refill my cup. When she'd reseated herself, she placed her right hand, palm up, on the table between us. "Do you mind?"

"Really, Aunt Belle, do you think that's—"

"Be still, Henry." Her face softened as she looked back at me. "Please?"

Reluctantly, I stretched out my left arm. I felt Harry stir next to me, his breath quickening as he leaned in.

Belle Crowder eased my hand closer and gently grasped the tender flesh between my thumb and index finger. It didn't hurt, but I could feel the warmth of her skin where it touched mine. The silence in the little cottage wrapped itself around me, and I felt as if I could drift off to sleep.

"You've had great sorrow," Belle said, her gaze fixed somewhere over my shoulder. "It's eased a bit, with time, but the memories come back. It's good to remember, especially the love. Let that love wrap itself around your pain, like a soft blanket, smothering the sadness. Let go, and find happiness. It's near. You just can't see it yet."

I felt an overpowering urge to yank my hand from her grasp, but the strength of her fingers—or her mesmerizing voice—held me fast.

"There is still danger, child, swirling around you like the winds of the storm. Don't trust your head. It's telling you the way things should be, not the way they are. You'll know the truth. You'll hear it in the voice, and you'll know. Believe in your instincts. Act on them."

I had no idea what she was talking about, but the utter *rightness* of her words settled over me like a warm cloud. It took me a few moments to realize she had released my hand and sat back in her chair. Outside, a final clap of thunder rolled across the night.

"Tell me about the baby," I said, my eyes fixed on hers. "Who made the charm we found around her neck?"

"I take it the authorities are no closer to finding out what happened?" Harry's voice broke the bond between his aunt and me, as surely as if he'd severed it with a knife.

"Not so far, but they're working on it," I said, my eyes still locked on Belle's.

"You can tell them it has nothing to do with…with my aunt or her community. We have no control over the purposes to which their medicinal concoctions are put."

"That's not what the sheriff's interested in." I wanted to slap him into silence, afraid his interruptions had ruined whatever rapport I had begun to establish with Belle. "If we know who made the charm, we can find the parents."

"The hand that fashioned the root is unimportant," she said. "It has great power, meant to protect the spirit of the child in death. You disturbed it. That was the start of your troubles."

Harry Crowder leaped up out of his chair. "We should be going now, Bay. My aunt tires easily." He stepped toward the door, but both of us ignored him.

Across from me, Belle Crowder closed her eyes. "Seek her in the reeds, in the grasses. Like Moses, she was set upon the water."

"Moses?" I said, and her eyes popped open.

"Surely you know the story?" she said, a smile twitching at the corners of her mouth. "A good Episcopalian girl like you surely knows the story of Moses in the bulrushes."

"Of course," I snapped, "but what does that have to do with the dead baby?"

I jumped at the touch of Harry's hand on my shoulder. "Really, Bay. We need to go."

Belle Crowder slumped back in her chair, all the energy

seemingly drained from her body. "Knowledge comes when it's needed," she mumbled.

I wanted to shout my frustration, but I realized it would have little influence on the shaman of Sanctuary Hill. I sipped the last of the lukewarm tea, and Belle pushed herself up from the table.

"Thank you," I said, gathering my bag and standing, although I wasn't sure exactly what I'd gained. "I appreciate your taking the time to see me." She nodded. "May I call on you again if I have more questions?"

Harry stepped around as if to plant a kiss on his aunt's cheek, but she turned away. Again I saw the look of anger flit across his face.

"I think not," the old woman said. "Little would be gained, and I think you have all the information you need now. Keep the roots with you and have no fear. You are protected."

Belle Crowder moved to the door and opened it. The air smelled damp, heavy with the ripe odor of vegetation. Water dripped from a million leaves, and a chorus of tree frogs serenaded us as Harry and I stepped out onto the porch. Before I could turn toward the steps, her thin hand grasped my arm.

"Trust yourself," she whispered and closed the door firmly behind us.

TWENTY-FOUR

I SPENT THE NIGHT TOSSING, images of the strange woman and her enigmatic warnings floating in and out of my mind.

I'd tried to press Harry for answers, but he had lapsed into an almost sullen silence that lasted throughout our short journey back to my car.

"I hope you don't take any of that too seriously," he said when I climbed down out of the van in the deserted parking lot of the country store. "Auntie believes strongly in the power of the root, as do I, but the fortunetelling…well, I just wouldn't put too much store in it."

It seemed an odd remark for a man who'd spent a good bit of his life researching and writing about just such things. Perhaps he and his aunt didn't get along all that well. Perhaps those undercurrents I sensed were simply the normal conflicts any family can experience from time to time.

As I climbed the stairs to Alexandra Finch's office on Thursday morning, Belle's final words floated ahead of me: *"Trust yourself."* At least that was advice I could take to heart, even if my visit hadn't gotten me any closer to solving the mystery of the body in the cooler. In fact, in retrospect, it seemed as if I'd provided more answers than I'd received.

There was no mystery about what had Billy's attorney pacing the beige carpet, her pudgy arms swinging from her sides as if she were on a parade ground. I cast a quick glance at Claudia Darling, her head bent over the legal pad resting on her crossed knees, but she was engrossed in the notes she was scribbling as her employer ranted.

"The stupid son of a bitch! I should have known better than to represent a man!"

"Calm down, Alex," Claudia said without looking up. "You'll give yourself a stroke. It might not be as bad as it looks."

"Of course it's bad! Haven't you been listening to Bay? The moron was having an affair less than two days after his wife's body was discovered. If the sheriff gets his hands on this, Billy's ass is toast!" Alex dropped into the swivel chair behind her desk. "I just wish they'd think with their brains once in a while."

"We don't know for a fact it's an affair," I pointed out. "It could have been just a business transaction."

"Has your operative been able to locate the woman?" Claudia asked.

I had to suppress a smile at what Ben Wyler might say about being described as my *operative.* "I spoke with him last night, and it doesn't appear she's staying at Billy's house, but so far he's struck out everywhere else. He'll continue to flash her picture around the island, but I wouldn't count on that turning up anything. She could be almost anywhere."

"Here's how I see it." Alexandra rested her elbows on the pile of papers spread out over her desk and leaned forward. "Even if Billy and his hooker can alibi each other for Monday morning, that means squat. No one else can definitely put them in Santee when someone used Tracy's credit card. For all we know, they could have been outside Jacksonville on that boat. And if it's not just a casual fling, it provides our client with a hell of a motive."

"You're making assumptions based on facts not yet in evidence," Claudia said, looking up from her notes.

"Guilty. But you know how I like to operate, Claud. Deal with the worst-case scenario up front. I hate surprises, especially from clients."

"So where do we go from here?" I asked.

"What would your game plan be if you were calling the shots?" Alexandra studied me from across the desk.

I took a moment to gather my thoughts. "Okay. It seems to me we need to know a lot more about Billy and Tracy's marriage. Did they have financial problems? Did her taking off with a hundred grand put a serious dent in his cash flow? And why did she take the money in the first place? Drugs? Gambling? Blackmail? Would any of those give Billy motive? We need to find out how long his affair—if that's in fact what it was—has been going on." I took a breath. "And what about Tracy? Was she running around on him? And if so, with whom? Again, motive. The most crucial piece of information we're missing is exactly when Tracy died. Without that, we don't know if Billy has a viable alibi or not."

In the silence that followed, Alexandra Finch stared off into space. The only sound in the quiet office was the scratch of Claudia's pen across the legal pad.

"Well, that's pretty damn depressing," Alex said after a moment. She reached for the phone and pushed a series of buttons. "Leslie, will you bring the Dumars financial file in, please? Thanks."

"I didn't know you do tax law," I said as we waited.

"We don't. But the firm has a couple of attorneys who specialize in estate planning, and they keep copies of the client's annual filings."

The door opened to admit an older woman who set a bulging file on Alex's desk.

"Thanks. Here," Alexandra added, pushing the bulky folder toward me. "You'll be able to make more sense out of these than I will. As for your questions about the marriage, I would have said it was pretty solid, at least up until yesterday. It's Billy's second go-around. Tracy's first. There was some difference in their ages, maybe ten years, but it wasn't a sugar-daddy kind of thing, at least not that I ever saw."

"Do you know if they have a prenup?" I asked.

"No, they don't," Alexandra said. "Actually, I advised Billy to set one up, but he didn't like the idea. Said if Tracy ever wanted out, he'd be glad to see she was well taken care of."

"The man's a saint," I said wryly, and Claudia laughed. "How about the ex-wife? Anything there?"

Alex shook her head. "No. Pretty amicable divorce. Billy gave her a fair settlement. They have a son, probably in his twenties by now. Lives out in California. Something to do with entertainment law. Billy doesn't see much of him. Wife remarried a couple of years after they split. I don't know where she is now." She paused. "You don't think she could be involved, do you?"

"I have no idea. I'm just groping around for a handle here. We're all assuming Billy's innocence, right? That means someone else shot Tracy, either for some personal reason we haven't figured out yet or for the money." I glanced up to find Alex studying my face intently. "Or maybe I'm way off base here. I'm kind of new at this, so you tell me."

"No, it's good to explore alternate theories of the crime. It's just…"

"Are you having second thoughts?" I asked. "About Billy?"

"Maybe," she said. "I would have bet my last nickel he didn't kill his wife. If I'm that bad a judge of character, I need to give this up and go sell perfume at Belk's. But I'm less sure about getting him off than I was before."

That would have been the perfect opening for me to introduce the phone call Stephanie Wyler had overheard, but I still hadn't run it by Red. And without the girl herself to verify the information, it was all just hearsay.

"So what do you want me to do?"

"Give the financial stuff a once-over and see what kind of shape Billy's in." She paused. "You already have a time line of Tracy's movements the day she disappeared, right?"

I nodded. "She played tennis, then lunched with her doubles group. All confirmed, except for one member we haven't been able to reach. She and Billy were supposed to have dinner with clients, but when he got home, she wasn't there. It looks like the last person to see her was the vice-president of the bank who handed over the money."

"What bank?" Claudia asked.

"First Coast. Right downstairs."

"Crazy." Alexandra sat back in her chair. "And nobody thought about how dangerous it was for a lone woman to go running around with that much cash?"

"Apparently she'd done it before," I said and recounted both

Billy's and the bank manager's assertions that the scenario wasn't that unusual.

"Both of them need their damned heads examined. It's like an engraved invitation for trouble."

"You're thinking maybe someone knew about her sometimes having a lot of cash on her?" I thought about that for a moment. "So it could have been just a random thing. The wrong person saw her stuff money in a gym bag, followed her, and killed her for it?"

"But if Billy didn't know about the withdrawal, we're still left with the question of why she took the money in the first place." Claudia's clear voice enunciated the crux of the mystery.

"Right," I said, scribbling on my notepad. "And then there's the location of the body."

"You mean the trunk of her car?"

I nodded. "That and the attempt to dump the car in the river. I can see a scenario where someone forced their way into the Mercedes. But why drive all the way out to Camp St. Mary's? Why not just take the money, maybe knock her out, and split? And something else has been bugging me."

"What's that?" Alexandra asked.

"Why take her handbag? Using stolen credit cards can be a sure-fire way to get tracked down and busted. If you've already got a hundred grand in cash, it would be stupid to take the risk."

"Right. It's the meticulousness of the crime that makes me think it's more than just a random thing." Alexandra leaned back and crossed her legs. "Stuffing the body in the trunk and trying to push the car into the river isn't something a random carjacker would worry about." She cocked her finger and pointed it across the desk at me. "*Bang, bang,* you're dead, take the money and run. It just doesn't feel like a crime of opportunity."

"I agree. It sounds more personal," I said.

"Let's hope the cops aren't thinking along the same lines." Alexandra shook her head. "So far the only one with a personal motive is Billy."

"All this speculation is pretty much pointless until we know

Tracy's time of death," I said. "Any chance you can speed that process along?"

Alexandra laughed. "Yeah, sure. I'm a big hit at the local cop shop. Not to mention the solicitor's office," she said, sobering. "If Billy's charged, they'll have to give me copies of all the reports, but they've been known to drag their feet right up to the edge of the statute. In the meantime, I'm counting on you to worm the information out of your partner. Or your brother-in-law, if it comes to that." She paused again, and her expression softened. "I don't want to bring up any painful memories, but don't you still have connections at SLED?"

The image of the explosion that killed my husband flashed briefly across my vision before I shook my head. "I was never at the top of their hit parade, even when Rob was alive. And I gave them such bloody hell when they didn't arrest anyone for his murder, they completely wrote me off. Besides, most of the people I knew there have probably moved on by now."

"Okay. Just a thought. So scope out the financials, maybe recontact all the people on the list you have of Tracy's friends. And we need to hear the minute SLED arrives at an accurate time of death. Because if Billy wasn't having an audience with the Pope or knocking back a beer with the sheriff himself, I have a feeling they're gonna haul his butt off to jail in a heartbeat."

TWENTY-FIVE

I PUSHED OPEN THE DOOR to the office a little after ten thirty, locked it behind me, and hefted the bulk of Billy Dumars' financial records inside. Erik's chair sat empty as I moved past it and dumped the file onto my desk. I'd insisted he show up for his scheduled shift at the office supply store, despite his repeated attempts to change my mind. I pulled out a soda and settled in to work.

Billy and Tracy Dumars' prior year's tax return seemed pretty straightforward. Their adjusted gross income had been just over 1.3 million dollars. After charitable and other personal deductions, they'd paid tax on just a little more than half of that. I gulped at the amount of the property taxes and mortgage interest on their home on Ribaut Island in Hilton Head Plantation. The real estate business was incorporated and also showed a reasonable profit, though it appeared Billy took most of it out in salary and bonus. Good thing, because his other possible sources of income—interest and dividends—didn't amount to two percent of his gross. I went back over two more years of records but could find nothing that jumped right out at me, except that they seemed to do a lot of trading in the stock market. Not very well, it seemed, as their capital gains appeared pretty paltry for the amount of money they moved around in the course of a year.

"And so what?" I said into the empty office. The fascination with day trading had just been hitting the public about the time I'd given up my accounting and financial consulting practice. While I'd counseled all my clients against the risk of trying to beat the system, I knew several had been seduced into thinking they could outsmart the professionals. I didn't remember one of them who'd been successful at it. At least Billy hadn't lost his shirt, but he hadn't made a killing, either.

I stuffed the returns back in the folder and tucked my scribbled analysis on them into my own file. I'd just flipped open the notes I'd taken that morning in the attorney's office when the rattle of the doorknob froze me in place. Without thinking, I slid open the bottom drawer and wrapped my hand around the pistol. A loud rapping was followed by Ben Wyler's demand for me to "open the damn door."

"I'm coming!" I yelled in reply to his continued ranting a moment before I wrenched open the outside door.

"About time," he said, brushing by me so closely I could almost smell his anger. "I want a key to this damn place."

"Calm down," I said, following his stiff back into my office.

He dropped into the client chair and crossed one long leg over the other. "I shouldn't have to stand outside like some door-to-door salesman begging to get in."

"I'll get you a key, okay?"

Ben pushed the heavy financial file aside. "What's all this?"

"Billy's tax returns. I'm trying to work here."

"Well, I haven't exactly been sitting around with my thumb—" He must have read the aggravation on my face, because he cut himself off. "I have news. You'll want to hear it."

"About what?"

"Two items of interest. I just came from the sheriff's office."

Into his calculated pause, I said, "Tracy Dumars?"

Ben nodded. "SLED hasn't been much more successful than the coroner on pinpointing time of death. What day did she go missing?"

I swiveled around and removed the file from the Active drawer. "A week ago Tuesday," I said.

"The body was found last Sunday. And the state lab says she'd been dead between four and five days when she was found. Best they can do."

"So she must've died the day she left."

Wyler nodded. "Right. Or it could have been that night, but probably not much later."

I leaned back in my chair. "So what does it mean? For Billy?"

"It means he'd better be able to account for his whereabouts for that twenty-four-hour window."

"Tuesday evening the New Jersey clients will alibi him." I checked my notes in the file. "They had dinner at Jaxx. I don't know about after that. We'll have to check with him. What if he just went home and went to bed?"

"If he was alone, that could be a problem. What about earlier in the day?"

"The guy at the bank said he saw Tracy off with the money around four. So she was obviously alive then."

"Briggs actually handed over the money? Personally?"

"Yes. Why? Does it matter?"

Wyler didn't answer for a moment, then shook his head as if to clear it. "No. Never mind. Still leaves a lot of time unaccounted for," he added.

"Not necessarily. I'll call Billy's office, see if I can get a peek at his schedule."

"I don't understand why you're so convinced he didn't do it. Especially after that stunt he pulled yesterday."

I began gathering up the papers spread out on my desk, arranging them into neatly aligned piles. "I don't know how to explain it. Just a gut feeling, I guess, even though I agree his shacking up with someone so soon after Tracy's body was found was incredibly stupid."

"Seems to be a lot of you ladies ready to ride to his defense. I sure as hell don't get what the attraction is."

"Oh, please," I said, restraining myself from flinging something at his head. "Shallow is your gender's department, not mine."

His laugh caught me off guard. "I love rattling your chain. You should see your face."

"I'm glad you find yourself so amusing. You said two items of interest. What's the other one?"

He sobered. "Yeah, right. That baby you found in the beer cooler? They've completed the autopsy."

A band tightened across my chest. "And?"

"And she was smothered. Probably with a pillow or a blanket. Found fibers in her throat."

"They're sure? It wasn't a stillbirth?"

"No way. Born alive, lungs fully inflated, killed maybe a couple of hours later."

"Bastards! The incredible bastards!" I leaped up, and my chair slammed against the filing cabinet with a clang.

"Hey, take it easy! Don't shoot the messenger." He held out a placating hand as if I were a skittish horse. "Calm down. It's not like it was somebody you know or anything."

"Shut up, Ben! Just shut the hell up!"

I raked my fingers through my hair. I needed to hit something. Or someone. I pushed past the startled detective, crossed the carpeted reception area, and yanked open the outside door, banging it against the wall as I stormed out into the dazzling morning. The glare off the windows of the parked cars nearly blinded me. I turned right and stomped past the end office into the small band of uncultivated woods that separated our building from the one behind. I could feel myself hyperventilating as I plunged into the jumble of undergrowth, mindless of the holly that tore at my slacks or the sharp branches that slapped against my bare arms. A few yards in, the wild tangle defeated me, and I stopped. Behind me, I heard Ben calling my name.

I wrapped my arms around the trunk of a young sweet gum, lay my forehead against its scratchy bark, and wept.

"JESUS, YOU SCARED the crap out of me," Wyler said when we'd settled once more into our chairs in the office.

"Sorry," I mumbled, dabbing at the tiny cuts and scratches on my arm with a damp paper towel. "I guess I sort of lost it."

"You think?"

I looked up and found his eyes still clouded with concern. I tried to think of something I could say to explain my bizarre behavior—to myself as well as to Ben.

"I guess I've been hoping it was natural causes. That maybe it was just a kid who panicked when her baby died, and she didn't know where to turn. You could almost forgive her for something like that." I switched the pink-stained towel to my other hand and began working on my right arm. "But to kill a baby. Deliberately."

I swallowed hard against the grief welling up again in my chest. Grief for the dead child. Grief for my own unborn children, Rob's and mine.

"Hey, I'm sorry." Wyler's hand lay gently on my wrist. "Let's talk about something else."

For the first time in our strange and stormy relationship, I saw tenderness in his eyes, and it nearly undid me. I forced back the tears and cleared my throat.

"It's okay. What else did you find out?"

Ben leaned back, his wary gaze focused on my face. "You sure?"

I nodded. "I need to know."

"Kid had some kind of abnormality of her heart valves. Might have been corrected with surgery, but it would have been a long road. With no guarantees."

"And they're sure that isn't what she died from?"

"Absolutely."

"How long had she been in the water?"

"Hard to say. Best guess is less than a week."

"Suspects? Or any leads on identifying her?"

"Nope. Your brother-in-law has organized a canvass of the local high schools. Looking for anyone who missed a lot of time or was pregnant and never came back. Nothing's popped so far. It could be it's not a local, maybe someone who came here just to dispose of…just to do the burial at sea thing." He sighed and ran a hand over his face. "I'm not holding out a lot of hope on this one. Unless someone comes forward, it's going to be a bitch to identify either the little girl or the parents."

But someone will come forward, I said to myself as the serene face of Belle Crowder drifted across my mind's eye. *Whether they want to or not.*

IT TOOK ME ANOTHER fifteen minutes to finish cleaning myself up and convince Ben to go away. His hovering concern had begun to scratch against my nerves, and I needed time alone to think. He said he'd get back on tracking down Billy's girl-friend and made me promise to call him later.

I opened a fresh can of soda and rubbed its icy metal across my forehead. A couple of the scratches on my arm were oozing blood, and I made a mental note to get some first aid stuff for the office in case one of us went totally nuts again and tried to blaze a trail through the woods with our bare hands. The thought made me smile, and I felt most of the tension uncoil from my chest.

I took a long swallow of Diet Coke, flipped to a fresh page in my notebook, and dialed Alexandra Finch's office. She was out, but Claudia Darling took my call.

"Listen," I said, "I've got Tracy Dumars' time of death." I gave her the same information Ben had passed to me, along with the obvious implications for Billy. "We need his appoint-ment book. If we can verify his whereabouts from the time Tracy took the money out of the bank until the next morning, he's home free."

"Good work," Claudia said, "although I'd be willing to bet the sheriff already has his hands on that appointment book. I wonder if he has a PDA or a BlackBerry?"

I had a vague idea of what a personal electronic organizer was, but not much past that. "You want to handle contacting his office or should I?"

"Why don't you take it? We're preparing for trial on another matter, and both of us are going to be tied up the rest of the day." I heard her flip through some papers. "Try his assistant, Sally Longworth."

That stopped me cold. "Any relation to Kitty Longworth?"

"I have no idea. Why?"

"According to Billy, she's Tracy's best friend."

"Interesting. Could just be a coincidence," Claudia said. "It's not that unusual a name."

"Could be," I replied, trying hard to ignore the little flutter in my chest. "Anyway, I'll call the office. Listen, I had a chance to do a quick run-through of Billy's taxes. Everything looks on the up-and-up, although I was surprised at his income. Somehow I expected it to be a lot higher."

"I'll tell Alex you didn't find anything out of line."

"As soon as I have Billy's itinerary for the day Tracy disappeared, I'll get started on interviews."

"Great. And thanks for the update. Alex will be grateful, I know."

I hung up and leaned back in my chair. I had only a moment to ponder on the strangeness of two women named Longworth having a connection to the Dumars when the phone rang.

"Bay! It's Red."

"So you finally picked up your messages. I've been trying to connect with you since Tuesday night."

"Sorry. We've all been doing double duty since the accident."

I considered relating my own involvement in the pileup, then decided against it. I really didn't want to get into all the gory details.

"So what can I do for you?" Red asked.

"I might have a couple of things you can use." The pause lasted only a couple of seconds, but I didn't miss its significance. "Yes, this is the real Bay Tanner, and yes, I'm actually volunteering information."

"About what?"

"First off, the Baby Jane Doe. Ben told me about the autopsy."

"I don't know where in the hell the man gets his information. One of these days I'm going to find his leak and plug it."

I sighed audibly. "I'm really not in the mood, Red. Do you want to hear what I have or not?"

"Hang on a minute." I could hear drawers opening and closing and paper rustling in the background. "Okay, shoot."

I spent the next five minutes giving him everything I could remember about Harry Crowder, his book, and his aunt Belle. For once in my dealings with Red I didn't leave out a thing.

Except Belle's little mind reading routine, or whatever that performance had been.

"But nothing about who might have made that pouch we found on the baby?" Red asked when I'd finished.

"I'm pretty well convinced she made it herself." I thought a moment. "You know, some of the stuff I read the other night said that the root-women were often midwives. You don't suppose she had anything to do with delivering the Jane Doe, do you?"

"I think she'd have to have a license of some kind to deliver babies. I can check that out." He paused. "We might be able to use it as leverage."

"I don't know. If she doesn't take money, it's not like she's practicing medicine, is it? And who out there would ever turn her in?"

"What about forgetting the strong-arm tactics and appealing to her better nature?"

"I tried that. You might have more luck, but I seriously doubt it. First off, it's going to be tough to locate her place without a guide. And secondly, I wouldn't imagine a representative of the government, even a local one, is going to be a big hit out at Sanctuary Hill."

"You've got a point." Again that momentary silence. "Could you find it again?"

"I think so, but I'm not sure. It's so far back in the woods, and the place is seriously creepy."

"Let me check around and see if anyone here can get me in. I'd feel a lot better if you stayed under their radar."

Red's voice held a hint of the old tenderness I remembered from the days right after his brother's murder, days when I would wake in the burn unit of the hospital to find his face hovering over the bed, his eyes studying mine with a mixture of fear and longing.

"It's not that," I said, determined to dispel any notion he had that I was scared. "I'm just up to my ears with the Dumars case right now."

The silence lasted a long time. "I thought you were going to back off on that."

"I don't remember making any promises. And while we're

on the subject," I hurried on, "I may have another lead. I talked to someone who overheard a conversation in which the caller was arranging to meet someone out at the camp. This was Tuesday, the same day Tracy Dumars disappeared. You interested in talking to…this person?"

"Absolutely. Give me a name. Lisa Pedrovsky will want to sit in, too."

"No. Just you, me, and the informant. That's the deal. I gave my word. Tell me where you'll be for the next couple of hours, and I'll get back to you."

"Damn it, Bay, quit jerking me around. If you're so all-fired hot to get Dumars off the hook, give me a name."

"Stay by your mobile. I'll call." I hung up before he had a chance to start yelling.

STEPHANIE WYLER was having second thoughts.

"I'm not sure I want to get involved," she said when I reached her at Ben's house. She'd taken an extra day off work when her ankle had begun to swell. Her doctor had advised her to stay off it for another twenty-four hours.

I forced myself to speak softly. "You're already involved, Stephanie, like it or not. Once you admitted to having information about an ongoing homicide investigation, you gave up the right to change your mind. My brother-in-law is expecting to hear from you in the next hour or so."

I could almost hear her spine stiffening.

"I don't have to talk to him if I don't want to. Maybe I made a mistake. Just because Kenny got into trouble as a kid doesn't mean he had anything to do with that woman's murder." Her voice hardened. "A lot of it wasn't his fault. His father is just such a straight-arrow. His dad could have gotten him out of trouble, but he chose to let them put him in jail. To teach him a lesson."

Where has this sudden about-face come from? I asked myself, and the answer popped unbidden into my head. "Have you talked to him?"

The split-second hesitation gave her away. "No, of course not."

"Don't lie to me, Stephanie. This isn't some game. You told me you wanted to do the right thing. Don't back out on it now."

"I'm not lying! But what if I did talk to Kenny? That's not a crime, is it?"

"Where is he?"

"I'm feeling sick to my stomach. I have to go now."

"Wait!" I yelled. "Please." I could hear her breathing on the open line, so I plunged ahead. "You're right, I can't force you to meet with Red. But at least tell your father about what you heard, okay? It's not safe if Kenny thinks you're the only one who knows. Please, Stephanie. Promise me." When she didn't reply, I added, "If you don't, you won't leave me any choice."

TWENTY-SIX

THERE WAS NO POINT in calling Red back. Stephanie had consistently avoided giving me her boyfriend's last name. I decided I'd give her until the close of business, then get in touch with Wyler. I hated being put in the position of ratting the girl out, but I didn't know what else to do.

The phone rang a moment later, and I hoped it was Ben's daughter telling me she'd come to her senses. No such luck.

"Bay? Hey, honey, it's me."

"Hey, Bitsy. What's up?" It seemed like forever since I'd tried to pick my best friend's brain about Tracy Dumars' place in the social pecking order of Hilton Head Island.

"Well, I think I may have some information for you. And before you start yellin' at me, I didn't go looking for it, I swear. I happened to be having a perfectly innocent conversation with Roselyn Dupres, Roselyn Ravenel she used to be. Remember her?"

"No. Should I?"

"Well, maybe not. I think she went to private school up in Atlanta, but her mama and daddy lived in that big ol' place in The Point that took up an entire block. The one with the big wrought-iron fence around it?"

I rubbed my temples where the start of another headache was thumping. Maybe I needed my eyes checked. "Bits, I'm kind of busy here. What did the conversation have to do with me?"

"I'm tryin' to tell you. Roselyn knows Chrissy Lyons. Well, she was Chrissy Welton back then."

"I have no idea who you're talking about."

"Chrissy Welton! Tracy Welton Dumars' sister. From Smyrna, Georgia?"

I sat up straighter in my chair. "What did she have to say about what happened to her sister?"

"Roselyn said that Chrissy was just devastated. She couldn't believe it. She said she always figured it would be Tracy's friend, Kitty Longworth, who ended up dead like that. Chrissy said the two of them had been tight as ticks for just about forever and that Kitty was always gettin' into trouble."

"How did Kitty's name come up? Exactly?"

"I think Roselyn said Chrissy had been trying to reach this Kitty person and hadn't been able to get hold of her. She was fumin' because she said it was just like Kitty not to be there when someone needed her."

So where was Kitty Longworth? And what did it matter?

I had no idea what it all meant. "Thanks, Bits. That could prove helpful down the road," I said, although I had my doubts.

"Wait! There's more. Did you know that Kitty's sister Sally works for Billy Dumars? She's been his confidential assistant for a couple of years now."

So there was a connection. There's a reason I don't believe in coincidences.

"Anything else?" A long silence followed my question. "Bits?"

"Well, honey, I have heard a couple of catty little remarks about Billy and his assistant, but I wouldn't put much stock in them. Some people just didn't like Tracy and her wild friends, and women like that will say just about anything, whether there's any truth to it or not."

Billy Dumars and Sally Longworth? I thought about the running shower inside the condo at Santee and the trim blonde who stormed down the steps and into Billy's Infiniti. Could it be that mundane? The business executive and the secretary?

"Honey? You still there?"

"Sorry. I appreciate all this, Bitsy, I really do. Thanks."

"Glad to help. If I run across anything else, I'll let you know. We need to do lunch one of these days. I'll call you."

I hung up and immediately punched in the number for Dumars Realty. They picked up on the second ring.

"Hi," I said after the woman had finished her canned spiel, "is this Sally Longworth?"

"No. Uh, Sally's not in. This is Sharona. How may I direct your call?"

"I'm really trying to reach Sally. Will she be back soon?"

The pause lasted a few seconds. "I really couldn't say. She's actually, uh, sort of on vacation."

"So when will she be back?" They weren't tough questions, but Sharona seemed to be having trouble with them.

"Actually, it was kind of sudden. I'm afraid I can't help you. Maybe you should speak to the administrator."

"That's okay. I'll catch up with her another time. Thanks so much."

I cradled the handset against my chest. What—if anything—did all this mean? If Billy had a solid alibi for the night Tracy died, it wouldn't make a damn bit of difference who he was screwing around with, his secretary or someone else. Still it was another one of those nagging little inconsistencies that made the hair on my arms stand up.

I slid the keyboard toward me and pulled up switchboard.com. I had Kitty's last listed address as an apartment complex on the north end of the island near the public school campus. I brought up Sally's information. She lived in what was probably one of the renovated bungalows just off South Forest Beach Drive. *Billy Dumars must pay her well,* I thought, as I signed off the computer. Most of those early beach cottages from the sixties had been torn down and replaced with updated residential units that went for serious money.

My stomach rumbling reminded me that I'd skipped breakfast. I gathered together the files spread out all over my desk and stacked them into a neat pile. I locked up and stopped on the sidewalk, shocked for a moment when I couldn't locate my little yellow T-Bird. Then it all clicked, and I walked quickly across the gooey blacktop to the imposing Chrysler that had become my new ride. I made a mental note to check in with the insurance company as I cranked over the big engine and set the automatic temperature control to sixty-eight.

I hadn't been to the Market Street Café down by Coligny for a long time, and it was close to South Forest Beach. The place was jammed with tourists taking a break from the beach, but they managed to squeeze me in to the single table set out under the sprawling oak tree that shaded the small Greek restaurant. I watched the parade of families and couples as I wolfed down a ham-and-cheese wrap and drained two full glasses of sweet tea. I left money on the table and worked my way through the crowds back to the car.

I slid into the warm leather seat and pulled the note with the addresses out of my pocket. I swung through the Coligny circle, a smaller version of the famous Sea Pines roundabout, past the Holiday Inn and down South Forest Beach Drive. The little side street lay to the right just past the well-shaded entry to First Baptist Church. I made the turn and crept down the narrow pavement, checking house numbers. I swung the Chrysler into a gravel drive behind a lime-green VW Beetle and cut the engine.

I sat for a moment, unsure of just what I intended to accomplish. There was absolutely no evidence that either of the Longworth women had a single thing to do with the murder. Still, I didn't like it that both sisters had a connection to the dead woman and her husband. It could all be perfectly legitimate, and yet—

I'd just about decided to get the hell out of there before I made a fool of myself, when movement caught my eye. I studied the front of the narrow house, not one of those that had been refurbished as I'd assumed, but a neat little cottage of weathered boards that looked as if it had held up well under the assault of the damp, salt-laden breezes off the ocean. The tiny front yard was well kept with a row of camellia bushes hugging the foundation and a bright purple bougainvillea twining around the mailbox post.

When the flicker came again, I realized it was the white drape hanging over the front window. Before I could change my mind, I grabbed my purse from the seat beside me, slid out into the shimmering heat, and marched up the driveway to the front door.

No one answered my first knock. I waited a moment, then rapped again more forcefully. I heard footsteps on tile flooring a moment before the door eased open a fraction.

"Yes?"

In the glare of the afternoon sun, I couldn't make out anything of the person huddled just inside the door.

"Ms. Longworth? Sally Longworth?" She didn't acknowledge the question, so I pressed on. "My name is Bay Tanner. I'm working for Billy Dumars. And for his attorney as well. Billy hired me to find Tracy before…well, before we found out what had happened to her." Again the silence. "I wonder if I might ask you a couple of questions."

"I've already talked to that woman from the sheriff's office."

So Detective Pedrovsky probably had the appointment book. Score one for the professionals.

"I understand, but they're not exactly on Billy's side. It's possible you could have information that could help us clear him."

"I don't want to get involved."

That stopped me for a moment. "I understand you've worked for him for a couple of years as his confidential assistant."

"So what?"

The level of her anger puzzled me. Or was it fear? Hard to tell from just the thin sliver of her face visible between the chain and the door frame. "If I could just come in for a moment? Perhaps—"

"I don't know anything. Just leave me alone."

"But you might be able to help clear him of—"

"Please. Leave me alone."

The slam of the door rattled the windows and nearly knocked me off the steps.

I TURNED AROUND in the church parking lot and pointed the car back toward the street. Even before I had the gearshift shoved into Park, I had the cell phone in my hand.

It took forever for him to answer the page, but eventually I heard him say, "Computers, this is Erik."

"Hey," I said, "it's me. Can you get away from there without totally losing your job?"

The pause lasted only a couple of seconds. "Sure, I guess. I can claim I'm sick. Why? What's the matter?"

"I need you for a stakeout. South Forest Beach. You know where the big Baptist church is?"

"No, but I can find it."

"Good. I'm in the parking lot. In a white Chrysler 300. Hurry up."

"Give me ten minutes."

I eased back against the soft leather seat and let my breath out in a long stream. I fixed my gaze on the traffic moving along the roadway and thought about Sally Longworth.

Her reaction had been bizarre, to say the least. Rather than throwing open her door to someone who was being paid to clear her boss—and maybe lover—of a possible murder charge, she had slammed it in my face.

Why? I asked myself, but of course I had no idea what had sparked her reaction. More fear than anger, I decided after replaying her words again in my head. But fear of what? I hadn't seen enough of her to positively identify her as the woman who'd accompanied Billy back from Santee and who'd narrowly escaped death in the pileup on I-95, but she was certainly blond. And whoever my client had been with, they'd clearly been familiar with each other. You didn't generally argue like that with a stranger, even a hooker. Insufficient data, as Erik was fond of saying.

What I did know for certain from a quick glance into the VW as I'd walked back to my car was that she was on the verge of taking off. The backseat had been crammed with clothes on hangers thrown carelessly across two good-sized suitcases, way too much for a long weekend and way too hurriedly done to be a vacation trip. So where was she going in such a hurry?

I checked my watch for the third time in as many minutes. "Come on, come on," I said into the air-conditioned stillness.

I didn't want to lose her, and there had been no way to lurk around the area on that narrow, quiet street without being spotted. She'd already had a good look at my car—and me—

and there was no place to hide. The Marriott Grande Ocean across the way would have provided good cover, but it was a gated timeshare complex. Security would have been on me in a second even if I'd managed to bluff my way in. The problem was that there were two ways for her to go once she left her neighborhood. The good news was that her bright green Beetle wouldn't be tough to spot.

Erik's black Expedition filled my vision as he turned into the driveway of the church, made a wide circle in the parking lot, and eased in beside me. He left the motor running and moved around the front of the big SUV as I lowered my window.

"What's up?" he asked, leaning in.

"About halfway down the next street to the right. Firethorn. The house is on the left. A VW Beetle, green. I need to know where she's going." I kept my eye on the traffic as we talked.

"So it's a tail?"

"I'm thinking yes. The car's full of clothes thrown in the back. Looks as if she packed in a hurry. I'll hang here until somebody comes along to throw me out, but she could go the other way, toward the back gate of Sea Pines, and swing around to Pope Avenue. I think one of the condo parking lots along Cordillo would be a good spot to watch from."

"Okay. I'll call you as soon as I'm in position. You can explain everything then."

"Go," I said, and he trotted back to the Expedition, jumped in, and headed off.

I glanced at the gas gauge, pleased to see I had better than three quarters of a tank. I could shut the car off for periods of time, and the shade from the magnificent oaks surrounding the church would keep it from turning into an oven. But if Sally Longworth came my way, I had no idea how long I'd have to be on her trail.

As I settled more comfortably into the seat, I also regretted those two glasses of iced tea at lunch.

No more than five minutes later, Erik called to say he'd found a decent vantage point in another church lot and had an unobstructed view of the street.

"I pulled into the first driveway on Firethorn and walked a little way down the street on my way by. The VW's still in the driveway."

"Good. Quick thinking."

"I come up with a decent idea once in a while," he said. "So what's the scoop? Who is this woman we're lying in wait for?"

I told him about Sally Longworth's connection to Billy Dumars and about her strange reaction to my visit. "You remember the list of Tracy's friends Billy gave us when he first came to the office?"

"Yes. There was a Kitty Longworth. The one with the gambling problem."

"Right. Supposedly Tracy's best friend."

"Are they related?"

"Sisters," I said. "Or at least that's what I hear."

"So what do you think's going on?"

"I don't have a clue. But I haven't been able to reach Kitty for almost a week, and now Sally looks like she's ready to skip town. A few too many weird things going on for my taste. I'm willing to spend a little time trying to find some answers. What do—"

"Hold it! Here she comes."

"You sure?"

"Is she a blonde?"

"Yes."

"Then it's her. Hang on."

I eased the shifter into gear and waited for a few cars to pass before turning right out of the church parking lot onto South Forest Beach Drive. The gated back entrance to Sea Pines Plantation appeared ahead in a matter of moments, and I took the right onto Cordillo Parkway.

"I'm behind you," I said into the phone.

"Don't get too close."

I eased off, although there were several cars between me and the high profile of his SUV. We slowed for the light, which turned red as we approached.

"She's got her left turn signal on."

"What's your gas situation?" I asked.

"I'm good. Filled up last night."

"Do you see any sense in both of us tailing her at this point?"

"No. She doesn't know my car, and besides it's only one of hundreds of SUVs around here. No reason she should get suspicious."

"What if she heads for the interstate?"

The signal changed, and I stayed right on the bumper of the Audi ahead of me. I made it through just as the light flipped to yellow.

"I can handle it," Erik said, "but I don't know what you want me to do from there."

"Neither do I. But something's not right about the way she's running." We negotiated the Sea Pines circle and headed out Palmetto Bay Road toward the Cross Island. "Let's just say I've got a feeling." I smiled to myself, remembering a number of times when Ben Wyler had said those very words to me. Maybe I was beginning to get the hang of this detective thing after all. And Belle Crowder had told me to trust my instincts. "Let's just go with it for now."

"Okay," Erik said.

"Listen, stay with her if you can. If you lose her, the world won't end, but I'd really like to know where she's going. If you run low on gas or you have to stop for some other reason, at least we'll know what direction she headed. Even that could tell us something. But don't put yourself in any danger, you hear?"

"Got it," he said, and I heard the excitement in his voice. "I'll check in when I can."

"Be careful."

"Yes, ma'am."

Our bizarre convoy topped the bridge over Broad Creek just where it began to widen into Bishop's Reach. All three of us had transponders affixed to our windshields and rolled smoothly through the Palmetto Pass gate of the toll booths. As I veered off the exit ramp to Marshland Road, Erik's Expedition slowly disappeared into the shimmering heat waves rising from the pavement.

TWENTY-SEVEN

BACK IN THE OFFICE, I sat staring at the PI license on the wall and trying to concoct a scenario in which Sally Longworth's sudden flight made any sense. Or maybe it just didn't, I told myself. Maybe I was trying to force puzzle pieces into slots where they didn't belong. I'd probably sent Erik off on a wild-goose chase and put his job at the computer store in jeopardy on some stupid hunch I was trying to label *instinct*.

But it wasn't my imagination that both the Longworth sisters had a connection to Billy and Tracy Dumars. It had to mean something.

I grabbed my bag and headed back out.

A few minutes later, I turned right onto Gumtree Road, then left into the Marshside complex across from the entrance to the school campus. I checked the address from the note I still had stuffed in my pocket, then wove through the cluster of densely packed buildings, finally pulling up in front of Kitty Longworth's unit. Since the parking slots weren't numbered, I had no idea if either of the two cars parked nearby was hers. I swung into a space marked visitors and cut the engine.

There weren't a lot of people around on a torrid Thursday afternoon in the middle of July. In fact, I didn't see a soul. Kitty's apartment sat in the center of one of the buildings that backed up to a lovely little lagoon. I mounted the steps and pounded on her door. There was a sidelight window, and I leaned over to peer through it, but a thin curtain effectively obscured the interior. I knocked again.

Fat bees droned around the orange hibiscus planted next to the porch, but nothing else broke the somnolent stillness. I backed off and edged around to the rear of the building. Each unit had a small deck attached. A couple sported lounge chairs and plants, but Kitty Longworth's stood empty. A young gator, sunning himself on the opposite bank of the lagoon, kept me in his sights as I made my back around to the drive. I had about decided to give it up when the door on the end unit popped open, and a young woman with a toddler on her hip stuck her head out the door.

"Can I help you?" she said in a soft drawl that held just a hint of challenge.

"Good afternoon. I'm looking for Kitty Longworth. Do you know if she's around?"

"No, ma'am, she sure isn't. I haven't seen her for more than a week."

"Really? Any idea where she went?"

The wary look stayed in her pretty blue eyes as she shifted the little boy to her other hip. "Are you a friend of hers?"

I decided on a version of the truth. "I work for an attorney. We're trying to locate her."

The chin lifted a fraction. "Is she in trouble?"

I didn't want to spook the young mother, but I was starting to melt out in the blazing sunlight. I moved slowly up onto the first step under the shade of the overhanging porch roof.

"No, nothing like that. I just need to ask her a couple of questions."

The baby began to fuss, squirming and flailing his chubby arms. I could see the indecision flickering across the girl's face.

"That's okay. I'll just check with Sally," I said, hoping it sounded offhand enough.

Relief made her shoulders relax, and she shushed the boy in her arms. "You know Sally, then."

"We're acquainted," I said with conviction. It was technically true, if you counted our brief exchange earlier in the afternoon.

"She'll probably know where to find her. I think they're pretty close. At least, I know Sally's helped her out a few times when she got into jams."

I had been about to thank her and move on, but that stopped me. "What kind of jams?"

"You know. Money, mostly." The young woman seemed to regret the statement almost immediately. "Not that she's into anything bad. I mean, Kitty's a really nice person. She keeps an eye on Chipper if I have to run out to the store or something."

"I'm sure she is." I stepped onto the pavement. "Well, thanks for your help."

"Ma'am?" Her voice turned me back toward the porch.

"Yes?"

"I'm sorry I was a little unfriendly back at first. It just made me jumpy, all these people hunting for Kitty."

I could feel that familiar flutter in my chest. "Someone else is looking for her?"

She nodded. "There was a man here yesterday. Looked like he could have been a bill collector or something like that. He was doin' like you done, walking around and looking in Kitty's windows."

"You didn't speak to him?"

"No, ma'am. He knocked, but I didn't answer. Charlie don't like me to open the door to strange men."

I tried to think how this could have anything to do with my investigation and came up blank. But I'm a firm believer that you can never have too much information.

"What did he look like?" I asked.

"Older, maybe in his fifties. Sort of tall. Drove some kind of fancy car. I didn't get a real good look at him." She hesitated. "This doesn't have anything to do with her boyfriend, does it?"

"Why do you ask?"

She shrugged as best she could with twenty pounds of squirming little boy hanging around her neck. "I know it's not a nice thing to say, but I don't like him overmuch. Always makes me uncomfortable. You know the kind of guy who sort of looks you over, like you was a piece of meat?" She glanced around as if Kitty's boyfriend might be lurking nearby. "Just bad news, if you know what I mean. I told Kitty she couldn't bring him over if she was looking after the baby."

I moved back onto the bottom step. "Have you seen him around lately?"

"Can you hang on a minute?"

The young woman turned and disappeared inside. Through the open door I could hear her talking to her son. She reappeared a moment later, empty-handed.

"Sorry about that. He gets so heavy. I stuck him in the playpen for a while with his toys."

"I was asking if you'd seen Kitty's boyfriend around."

"No, ma'am, I sure haven't. Not since Kitty's been gone." She pointed toward an older Ford Taurus, its left front fender dented and the blue paint faded by the relentless Lowcountry sun. "That's her car there. I've been gettin' a little worried, though it's not the first time she's taken off without it." Her smile seemed tentative. "No denying Kitty does love to have a good time."

"Ever hear her talk about maybe gambling a little too much?"

The pleasant face closed up. "She likes those casino boats, the ones where you can play poker? And I know she plays on her computer, too. On the Internet. Never saw any harm in it myself."

I could tell I was losing her. "Just one more question, and then I'll let you get back to your little boy. Do you know the boyfriend's name?"

"It's Kenny. I don't recall I ever heard the rest of it."

Kenny? There couldn't be two of them—could there?

"Can you describe him?" I asked and saw her glance over her shoulder toward the inside of her condo. "I'm sorry, but this is important."

"Tall, black hair. Good-lookin' in a rough kind of way, if you know what I mean." She thought a moment. "Has some tattoos. I don't care for 'em myself, but I guess a lot of guys think they make 'em look tough." Her smile softened her angular face. "I told my Charlie he'd be sleeping by himself if he ever came home with one."

I fished in my bag for a business card and passed it over. "If you think of anything else, or if Kitty comes home, will you give me a call?"

The girl read it but made no comment. "Sure. Glad to." She studied me with worried eyes. "You don't think she's in any real bad trouble, do you?"

I put as much sincerity as I could muster into the lie. "No. I'm sure she's fine."

BACK IN THE CHRYSLER, I pulled around by the pool and parked in the shade, the motor running to keep the air conditioner pumping. Erik answered on the first ring.

"Where are you?" I asked.

"Heading south down I-95, just passing the exit for Richmond Hill. She's in the right lane, staying dead on seventy, so I've had to keep back a ways."

"South. And you're already past Savannah."

"Yeah. What are you thinking?" my partner asked.

"What are *you* thinking?" I countered.

He waited a beat before responding. "Amelia Island?"

"We're on the same page. Listen, I want to run something by you."

I told him about my visit to Kitty Longworth's apartment and shared the information I'd gotten from her neighbor. "You'll probably think I'm crazy, but what if Kitty was the woman using Tracy's credit card? Her sister's a blonde, so it's a fairly safe assumption she could be, too. I should have thought to ask that girl. Age-wise, I'm guessing she'd fit the description we got from the marina guy down in Florida."

"I suppose it's possible. But why? I mean, have you worked out a scenario where that makes sense with everything else?"

"No," I said, "except her sister is apparently heading in that direction. I know it's weak, but let's just ruminate, as the Judge is fond of saying. Kitty's got a boyfriend, someone who gave the nice young mother next door the creeps. And listen to this."

I filled him in on Stephanie Wyler's revelation about overhearing the reference to "the camp" on the same day the coroner's people figured Tracy had been murdered and about her reluctance now to tell her story to the sheriff. Or her father.

"What the hell is she thinking?" Erik asked.

"I have no idea, but I gave her until end of business today to change her mind, or I'm going to Ben myself. And then Red. But wait, it gets even weirder. Kitty's boyfriend's name is Kenny, too. He's tall, good-looking, and tattooed. Almost exactly the same description Stephanie gave me. It has to be the same guy." I paused to let the full effect of my next words sink in. "And the girl said neither Kitty nor the mysterious Kenny has been around since the day Tracy disappeared."

"Didn't Billy say she was into gambling? Makes more sense to me that she's taken off for Vegas or Atlantic City."

"The neighbor says she prefers online poker and casino cruises. And there's the man who came looking for her yesterday."

"I still don't get what all this has to do with the murder."

"Try this on for size. If Kitty was in serious trouble, like with loan sharks or some big-time gamblers she owed money to, she could have seen Tracy as a quick source of cash to bail herself out. And they've been friends since grade school. Don't you think Tracy would have come to her rescue?" I twisted around in the seat and slipped off my shoes. The more I talked this through, the better I liked it. "It would explain the money. And her not telling her husband what she was up to. I can't think Billy would be thrilled to see his hard-earned cash flushed down the toilet like that."

"You seriously think Kitty would murder her best friend for money?" Erik asked.

"Why not?"

The silence lengthened. "I don't know. I guess I just can't see women running around knocking each other off."

"Ah! Sexism rears its ugly head."

"I'm serious, Bay. Tracy was shot in the back. That's cold. I can see a woman maybe flying into a rage and killing somebody, but to execute your best friend like a rabid dog? I'm sorry, sexist or not, I've got a real problem with that."

"Okay. How about the boyfriend? What's to say he didn't do the actual killing?"

"While Kitty just stood there and watched? And you don't even know for sure he was there."

"You're awfully protective of a woman you've never actually met."

"And you're awfully quick to label her a murderer," he snapped back.

"Look, this is probably useless. But one thing that's not open for debate is that Sally is on her way south. Toward Florida. Maybe she really is off on vacation, but I'm not buying it. At least not yet. It's imperative now that you stay on her tail."

"Not a problem. By the way, we're coming up on Midway now."

"Keep me in the loop," I said. "And be careful."

I clicked off and a moment later punched in Ben's mobile number. It had suddenly occurred to me that he already knew the last name of Stephanie's boyfriend. He'd told her Kenny had been in jail, so he had to have a full name to run through the sheriff's database. I waited for what seemed like forever, but he wasn't picking up. I had a bad feeling that everything was coming together, and I was running a step behind.

Time to go to Plan B.

TWENTY-EIGHT

HE SAT AT THE MOOSE TABLE directly underneath Waldo's imposing rack of antlers. In the winter, we always tried to get close to the fireplace at Jump & Phil's, but I had already worked up a sweat in the short walk from the parking lot. I tossed my bag into an empty chair and pulled out the one across from my brother-in-law.

"I ordered you a sweet tea," he said, sliding the glass across to me.

"Thanks."

I laid my sunglasses on the table and sipped greedily.

"You gonna eat?" he asked.

"I don't think so. But you go ahead if you want."

Red signaled the waitress and ordered a burger and fries with cheese. "This is gonna be lunch and dinner, I'm afraid," he said as if he owed me an explanation. "I've been taking a report in Sea Pines from some guy who had his car stolen right out of his driveway. A brand-new Porsche Boxster. Middle of the day, can you believe it?"

"If it was red, you might want to check my garage."

He smiled, looking expectantly at me across the table. "So what's this all about? You ready to come clean with a name on this mysterious informant of yours?"

I glanced down at my watch. "Not just yet. But I do want to talk about Tracy Dumars."

His face tightened. "You know I can't discuss an ongoing investigation."

"I don't want you to talk," I said. "I want you to listen." I paused as a thought struck me. "Actually, I do need to ask one question. You can just nod, if you're worried about violating protocol."

"We'll see. What's the question?"

"Have you checked out Tracy's credit cards to see if there's been any activity since she disappeared?"

The waitress picked that moment to slide the burger and a huge plate of French fries dripping with cheese onto the table between us. "You need a refill?" she asked, and I shook my head.

After she'd moved off, Red stared straight at me, ignoring the food. I waited as he studied my face, although I had no idea what he was looking for. A long moment later, he nodded. "Yeah, we checked it out."

"Okay," I said, "so let's play hypothetical here."

"Sounds like one of the Judge's games." Red buried the fries in salt and worked one loose from the tangle of cheese.

"You eat, I'll talk. Let's assume that Billy didn't kill his wife." I held up a hand as he swallowed and seemed about to protest. "Hang on. Go with me here. So what motive could someone else have for killing her?"

"A hundred grand in cash springs immediately to mind."

"Exactly. So let's look at why she took the money out of the bank in the first place. Even if she and Billy were having problems and she was running away from home, why take the money in cash? She's got legal access to their accounts. She could have taken it all in a cashier's check, cleaned him out entirely if she were trying to start a new life. As the sheriff told Billy the first time he reported her missing, it's not stealing if you take your own money."

"Go on."

I couldn't tell from his expression if he was buying any of it or not. "Okay. So I understand someone used one of Tracy's credit cards down near Jacksonville. A woman."

He paused, a dripping fry halfway to his mouth. "How— No, wait. Don't tell me. Wyler."

For once I could deny his accusation with complete honesty. "No. Ben had nothing to do with it. And it doesn't matter, anyway. Let's just say I know it's true." I drew a deep breath and leaned in toward him. "Think about this as a scenario. Kitty Longworth is—*was*—Tracy's best friend. She's also a gambler. What if Kitty got in so deep they were thinking about rearranging her face or something, and she went to Tracy to bail her out? Kitty's got a boyfriend I hear isn't a stranger to trouble, either. Tracy agrees to give Kitty the money, there's some kind of argument during the exchange, maybe with the boyfriend, and Tracy ends up dead. Kitty's an accessory now, so she runs with the boyfriend, taking the money and Tracy's purse with her. Granted, they've got the hundred grand, but it's the kind of thing a woman would do. Or maybe they're hoping to make it look like a random robbery or delay identification of the body if it's found. They make their way down toward Jacksonville where they're holing up. Probably on a boat. Not being the brightest bulbs in the chandelier, they use one of the credit cards to buy gas."

I sat back and crossed my arms over my chest. I'd been concise, logical, and unemotional. Hell, I'd almost convinced myself it was the way the murder had gone down.

Red wiped his fingers on his napkin and sipped from his glass of Coke. "Interesting."

"There's more. Kitty's sister, Sally, is Billy Dumars' secretary." I glanced again at my watch. "About three hours ago, Sally took off from her house with her car jammed with clothes. Right now she's heading south on I-95. I think she's meeting up with Kitty, maybe somewhere around Amelia Island."

When he didn't respond, I succumbed to temptation and extricated a cheese fry from the dwindling pile on the plate between us. His face gave nothing away.

"It has possibilities," my brother-in-law finally said.

"So what happens now?"

"What do you mean?"

I swallowed my frustration. "If they're in Florida, do you have to work with the local police down there? Can you ask the Highway Patrol to tail Sally? Erik hasn't checked in for—"

"Erik? What does he have to do with this?"

"He's following Sally Longworth. Didn't I say that?"

Red shoved the rest of the uneaten fries away from him. "No, you damn well didn't say that. Get him on the phone. Now!"

I gave a thought to fighting him on it, but what was the point? I'd come to him because I felt as if Erik and I were getting in over our heads. If I was even marginally close to the truth of what had happened, Erik could be driving blindly into a confrontation with a murderer. Or two. We needed help, and I'd finally come to the realization that asking for it was the smartest thing to do. Since I still couldn't reach Ben, I felt as if I had no choice, but I didn't have to like it. I fed Erik's number into the cell phone and leaned back in the chair. Red's gaze stayed locked on my face.

"Hey, it's me. What's happening?"

"We're still heading south. Just crossed into Florida."

"I'm sitting here with Red." My brother-in-law gestured for the phone. "Hang on, he wants to talk to you."

"Erik, it's Red.... Yeah, we've been discussing the Dumars case." He looked up and smiled across at me. "Yeah, kind of surprised me, too." His face sobered. "I know, but you have no idea what you could run into if what Bay's been telling me isn't completely out in left field. You could be riding into real trouble.... No! That's exactly what I *don't* want you to do.... What? Erik!"

He shook the phone. "Damn it! He hung up on me."

I reached across and took my cell out of his hand. I hit redial and waited, but the message said the number was not in service.

"He turned it off," I said. "What happened?"

"He said this Sally was getting off the interstate. Route A1A. He said he needed to concentrate on not losing her."

I thought for a moment. "A1A. Isn't that the road you take to Amelia Island?"

"How the hell should I know? You're the one with enough money to hang out in swanky resorts, not me."

I gave him a moment to get himself together. "That wasn't entirely fair."

He ran his hand through his close-cropped hair, one of those gestures that reminded me so much of his brother. A sigh loosened the lines of tension on his face. "I know. Sorry."

"I saw a brochure from a resort on Amelia Island in Billy's study when I checked out their house. And that's where the credit card was used."

Red shook his head. "I get it. But the dead body is definitely Tracy Dumars. Preliminary DNA confirmed it. So this isn't another one of your doppelganger situations like the Wade thing."

"I know that. I'm just saying that Kitty may have gone along with Tracy on some of her tennis trips. She could feel comfortable in the area. Besides, it's not that far from Jacksonville, and I'm guessing there's plenty of marinas around there where they could dock a boat."

The waitress seemed to sense we were in the middle of something she'd be better off not interrupting. Silently she slid the plates off the table and replaced them with the check. As Red reached for his wallet, my phone chirped.

"Erik." I flipped it open, and Red leaned in.

"Hey," I said into the phone. "What happened back there?"

"I didn't want to get into a big hassle with Red," my partner said. "We're definitely on the way to Amelia Island. At least according to all the signs I keep seeing."

"Amelia," I said aloud for Red's benefit. "What are you going to do when she finally stops?"

"Make note of the address, hang around a little to see if she looks like she's staying put for a while, and then find some place to take a leak."

My laugh startled Red, and he glowered back at me.

"Okay," I said, "but on no condition are you to approach her. Once she lands somewhere it's a stakeout. Are we clear on that?"

"Crystal," he said. "I'll let you know the minute she comes to roost."

"The minute," I said and hung up.

"Well?" Red's expression had hardened again.

"He'll call as soon as he has an address. No heroics. He'll just hang around and wait for instructions."

My brother-in-law pushed back his chair. "I need to check in with the office. You stay here. And let me know the second you hear from him."

I flinched a little at the officious tone of his voice as he strode out the door toward his cruiser. Taking orders has never been one of my strong suits. But I'd come to Red for advice, and it would be stupid of me not to take what he offered. By the time I'd gotten a refill on my tea, he was back.

"I've got things in motion. The sheriff will contact the local PD down there if and when we have something solid to go on. Right now we have absolutely no proof that either one of these Longworth sisters or the boyfriend is involved in Tracy Dumars' death. It's all just speculation." He sighed. "In fact, everyone seems convinced they'll eventually be able to nail the husband. But the sheriff is at least willing to listen to other scenarios."

"What kind of proof does he need? Is it something Erik—"

"No! All we need from him is the address. If he spots the other two in the area, that could help bolster our theory, but—"

"*Our* theory? You mean you're signing on?"

"Not entirely. I'm just willing to entertain the possibility. There's a couple of things you don't know, and you didn't hear them from me, got it?"

I leaned closer. "Got it. Like what?"

"We executed a search warrant for Dumars' home and office. No signs of any struggle at either place. We did a preliminary on the gun he keeps in his desk at the real estate place. No match."

"Does he have an alibi for the night of the murder?"

"Lisa's working on that. According to his schedule, he had appointments all afternoon, and he was wining and dining some clients on Tuesday evening. Everyone's confirmed his story so far. He says he stopped off for a drink after he left the New Jersey couple. We've verified he was in the bar at Conroy's at the Marriott until sometime around eleven, but it gets a little murky after that. Doesn't exactly sound like the actions of a frantic husband, does it?"

"The fact that he was out boozing when he didn't have a clue where his wife was makes him a jerk, not a murderer."

Red slurped diluted Coke and stared straight into my eyes. "Hearing from your mystery informant would go a long way toward helping his cause."

"I'm working on it. So Billy's pretty well clear then until, say midnight. Doesn't that put him out of the running?" When he didn't immediately reply, I said, "Doesn't it?"

"Theoretically. But without an exact time of death, there's some gray area."

I leaned in closer. "Come on, Red. No struggle, no ballistics match, no real motive, and probably an alibi. What the hell else can the poor guy do to convince you?"

"That's not entirely accurate. There is a possible motive."

"Like what?"

"Money," he said. "Things haven't been going that well for him. After the big boom a couple of years ago, with everyone flipping and driving up the property values, the market has sort of leveled off. The number of folks looking for million-dollar-plus homes has hit a plateau. Or at least that's what our contacts in the real estate business tell us."

"So you think he'd kill his wife to get back the hundred grand she withdrew? Would it have made that much difference to him?" I remembered his last year's tax return, the 1.3 million adjusted gross income. And then his Schedule D numbers popped into my head. Maybe his stock speculation games had gone south in the past few months. Maybe…

"Even for someone in his league, that's a pretty good hit." Red's voice drew me back. "And there's something else you've forgotten about."

"What?"

"Even if Dumars didn't do the actual shooting himself, there's nothing to say he didn't hire it done."

I didn't have an answer for that. Maybe Tracy had decided she wanted out, and the lack of a prenuptial agreement had come back to bite Billy. A hit man would certainly have cost less than what his wife could have taken him for in a settlement.

Especially if she'd caught her husband screwing around. Divorce lawyers loved a cheating spouse when it came to wringing money out of the other partner.

But that still didn't explain the hundred grand in the gym bag.

"So that's why we're not ready to write off the husband, even though there's squat in the way of physical evidence." He leaned back in his chair, and his cool eyes studied me. "I'm sorry if that messes up your theory, and I have to admit it's not entirely out of the running yet. But my gut tells me Dumars is the one. I just think we'll play hell proving it."

I drummed my fingers on the table and stared out across the parking lot.

"What are you thinking?" Red's voice from across the table startled me.

"I'm reassessing," I said, and he smiled a moment before my cell phone chimed its notes.

"Erik," I said, checking the display. "Where are you?"

"I'm not sure," he replied. "It's some sort of marina about twenty miles south of Amelia. I didn't see any city limit sign. The VW turned in at this restaurant on the water, right near the docks. I followed her inside, and she's in the ladies' room. Hang on."

Red slapped his hand on the table, and I jumped. "What's going on?"

"Erik followed Sally to some marina south of Amelia. She's in the rest room."

"Give me the phone."

I held up a finger as Erik spoke again. "She's back. Speaking to the hostess. She's taking her out to a table on the deck. She's making a call on her cell now. Let me see if I can get close enough to hear what she's saying. I'll call you back."

"No, Erik! Don't—" I looked across at Red. "He hung up."

"Damn it, Bay!" Red's face had gone purple with anger as I clicked off the phone. "Get him back on the line. Now!"

"They're at a restaurant, and it looks like Sally's waiting for someone. She's making a call. He's just going to hang around and observe."

"I can have his ass hauled in for obstruction, you know that?" He pushed back his chair with such force the solitary drinker at the bar turned a bloodshot eye toward him.

"Really? In Florida?" I kept my voice level. "I don't think so."

"*You're* not in Florida," he said through clenched teeth. "I suggest you keep that in mind."

Our eyes stayed locked for a long time before he spun on his heel and marched out into the steaming July afternoon, his anger trailing behind him like smoke in the wind.

TWENTY-NINE

I SAT FOR A LONG TIME, the enigma of Billy and Tracy Dumars and the Longworth sisters running around in my head, before I finally stood and slung my bag over my shoulder. A part of me wanted to jump in the Chrysler and head south, but that seemed premature. In the end, I decided to go back to the office and wait. I seemed to be doing a lot of that lately.

I had just stepped out the door of Jump & Phil's when my cell phone chimed. *Excellent,* I thought when I saw the number.

"Ben, thanks for calling back." I sat down in one of the plastic chairs in the outdoor seating area next to the restaurant.

"Well, make it snappy. I've got things to do."

I took a few seconds to organize my thoughts. "A couple of things. Have you had any luck tracking down the woman Billy brought back with him from Santee?"

"Not exactly. A couple of the hookers we crossed paths with last spring said they'd seen her around, but the only name I've got so far is Jasmine. Probably not her real one. Pretty high-class, expensive broad, and rumor has it she and Dumars aren't exactly strangers. I'll keep on it." He paused for breath. "What else?"

So much for my boss-secretary scenario. Maybe. I bit my tongue and ordered myself not to snap back. "This is a little sticky, Ben. I'd really like to talk to you about it in person. Any chance you could meet me at the office?"

The decision not to get into the subject of Stephanie's boy-friend over the phone seemed prudent.

"I'm in the middle of something here. Can it wait?"

"I really don't think so. It's sort of about your daughter."

"What about her?"

"Can you just meet me? I promise it won't take long. Please."

"Where are you?" he snapped.

"On the south end. It won't take me—"

"Ten minutes," he said and hung up.

THE JAGUAR SAT OFF to the side of the parking lot in the shade when I pulled in precisely eight minutes later. Ben climbed out of the low bucket seat and stalked in my direction as I put the key in the lock.

"Thanks," I said when he held the door open and allowed me to precede him inside.

"I don't like people sticking their noses in my private life," he said, following me into the office. "Even you. My girls are off-limits."

"Understood." The mood he was in, I decided to skip the preliminaries. I checked my watch. Exactly five-ten. Stephanie's deadline had run out, so I was not technically breaking my word. "Has she talked to you about the conversation she overheard Tuesday night?"

"Steph? No. What conversation? And how do you know something about my daughter that I don't?"

"She told me while we were riding around up in Santee."

"Speaking of which, I never did get a satisfactory explanation of what she was doing with you in the first place."

I told him the story of her asking for my advice about her boyfriend problem. The moment I mentioned Kenny's name, Ben shot straight up out of his chair.

"That son of a bitch! I should've hauled his ass off to jail the minute I caught him sniffing around my daughter! What's he done?"

"I don't know that he's done anything. But Tuesday night she heard him tell someone he'd pick them up so they could be out at 'the camp' before nine. That's the night Tracy Dumars disappeared and was probably murdered. Her body was found in the marsh near Camp St. Mary's. Stephanie made the connection herself after she read about it in the papers, but she was scared to tell you. Still is, apparently."

He turned without a word and strode across the carpet.

"Ben! Wait! Don't go running off half-cocked. There could be a perfectly reasonable explanation—"

The slam of the door cut me off. I sat back in the chair and ran a hand through the tangle of my hair. If there was a more aggravating man on the planet, I'd yet to meet him. And I still didn't know the elusive Kenny's last name.

I WAITED UNTIL almost seven thirty, but no one called. I'd thought about giving Stephanie a heads-up so she'd be prepared for her rampaging father, but I decided just to stay out of it. I'd call Red later and give him the information. I'd done all the damage I could for one day, I thought as I dragged myself out the door. I'd started on a hunger headache, amplified by my worry about Erik and Ben's daughter, so I used the drive-through at McDonald's to grab a burger. I'd managed to wolf down all but a few French fries by the time I turned into my driveway. I'd just pushed open the heavy door of the Chrysler when the sound of a vehicle pulling in behind me made me turn.

The black Camaro, its side windows tinted a deep, impenetrable gray, eased up next to me, and Red stepped out into the rosy twilight. I wondered why he didn't shut off the engine.

"Hey," he said, leaning on the roof of the car, and I noticed he wore civvies.

"Hey yourself. Where'd you get the wheels?" I reached back in to retrieve the empty food bag.

"Fruits of our labors," he said, striving for a lightness that didn't quite make it into his voice. "Confiscated it from a local drug dealer who won't be needing it anymore. We use it sometimes for stakeouts or speed traps."

"Nice." We stood facing each other across the roof of the sports car, the only noise the muted wash of the waves against the beach on the other side of the dunes and the low rumbling of the big engine. Even the birds had gone silent.

"I…we need a favor," he said, glancing down.

"Really? Why don't you just arrest me for obstruction of justice? Then you can make me do whatever you want."

At least he had the decency to blush a little. I thought he mumbled, "Sorry," but I couldn't be sure. So many of Red's and my conversations went like this. We sniped and dug at each other, anger boiling over, but eventually we worked our way back. Neither of us was terribly good at apologies.

I decided to let him off the hook. "Come on in, and we'll talk."

"It's kind of pressing," he said, his gaze again darting toward the vehicle.

"Someone with you?" I asked, and he nodded.

"Malik. Deputy Graves." The passenger side window came down, and the pleasant black face of the man who had accompanied Detective Lisa Pedrovsky to my office smiled up at me.

"Evenin', ma'am," he said.

"Good evening, Deputy." I slammed my door shut and stared at Red. "What's going on?"

"It's like this," the earnest young man said. "I got a cousin who knows Miz Crowder out to the Sanctuary, and she cleared it for us to go out there and talk to her. About that poor little girl you found in the cooler."

"That's good. So what do you need me for?"

"She asked for you," Red answered, his eyes locked on mine. "Specifically. Said she wouldn't see us unless we brought you along."

"That doesn't make any sense. When I was out there with her nephew, I asked if I could come back, and she said it wasn't necessary, that I had all the information I needed."

Malik Graves shrugged. "I don't know what to tell you, ma'am. My cousin says that old woman has flat-out got a head full of snakes. But if she has any solid information about that little baby, I sure do want to hear it." He paused a moment, then lifted his chin a fraction. "Don't you?"

The unspoken challenge raised my hackles, but I replied civilly. "Of course. If you think I can help. Let me just check my answering machine and freshen up a bit." I flipped open my phone and stared for about the hundredth time at the empty screen. "You're welcome to come in if you like."

"No thanks," Red replied. "We'll wait out here."

"Suit yourself."

The only message was from my father, a halfhearted attempt to guilt me into coming to dinner on Friday night. He whined a little about not being kept in the loop on any of the agency's cases, but he didn't put a lot of effort into it. I made a quick stop in the bathroom and lifted a sweater off a hanger in my walk-in closet. I patted my handbag where the Seecamp pistol rested, slung it over my shoulder, and reset the alarm before I walked back out to the driveway.

RED HANDED ME a sheaf of papers, and I spread them out on my lap as we roared out 278 toward Beaufort. Malik Graves had insisted on climbing into the back.

"I've already heard about the autopsy," I said, sliding that file back into its jacket. I knew there were photos inside that I definitely didn't want to see, even in the fading light of the evening.

"Take a look at the interviews," Red instructed, and I extracted a slim folder.

"Interviews of whom?"

"Mostly at the school. Yours is in there, too."

"You obviously didn't find any recently unaccounted-for pregnant teenagers," I said, and he grunted.

"Two, but there doesn't seem to be anything sinister about them. One's African-American."

He didn't have to expound on that. The tiny girl in the cooler had been light-skinned, the soft fuzz on her scalp medium brown. I banished the image by force of will. Anyway, she was an unlikely by-product of a black couple. An interracial relationship, maybe. *Stretching it,* I thought. Still, it happened, this sudden appearance of a baby with recessive genes that harkened back to the dark days of our history when white masters roamed the slave row uncontested.

"And the other?" I asked.

"Girl went up North to stay with her mother until the baby was born. Pennsylvania. It's in the file. She'd been living down here with her father. Some sort of custody battle. Ugly, from what I gathered from the mother."

"You talked to her?"

Red didn't answer for a moment, taking the off-ramp onto 170 and easing into the sparse traffic. "Yeah. Well, no, actually, not the girl. Talked to the mother for way longer than I wanted to. She told me her daughter had delivered a seven-pound boy just a couple of days before I called. Everyone doing fine."

"You believed her?"

Red turned to stare at me in the glow of the dash lights. "Why wouldn't I?"

"Because if your daughter had killed her child, then come running home to mama, wouldn't you cover for her?" The quiet in the car stretched out as I leafed through the interview transcripts. "What's the name?"

It took him a while to answer, and I wondered if he was busy reassessing his easy acceptance of the woman's story.

"Wilma something. It's in the file."

I located the folder and held the sheet up to the map light I'd snapped on a few miles back. Night was rapidly descending, and I hoped we'd make it to before full dark. Malik claimed to know his way onto the potholed road leading to the compound, but I'd feel a lot better—

"Jesus, Mary, and Joseph!"

"What?" Red demanded, his voice taut. "What's the matter?"

I'd been scanning the interview with half my brain engaged, the other half worrying about getting lost in the impenetrable jungle surrounding the Crowder place, when the name seemed to leap off the page. My heart constricted, and I felt a wave of dizziness wash over me. *She was right!*

"Bay! What's going on? Talk to me!"

I heard him as if from a long distance, my mind tangled in the glow of the lamps in Belle Crowder's kitchen, her soft voice telling me to use my instincts, to trust them. Speaking what I'd thought was nonsense, something about Moses. Assuring me that I'd understand when it was time.

"She said the baby was set upon the water, like Moses."

"Who said? What the hell are you talking about?"

It took me a moment to realize that Red had pulled the Camaro off the road and into the old entrance to Grayton's Race. The bare patch of ground where the Welcome Center had once stood gleamed brightly in the glow of a three-quarter moon. After the fire, nothing had ever grown back in that spot. My mind shifted to Geoffrey Anderson's face, his hands clawing at the window, and a shudder ran through my entire body. I felt Red's fingers dig into my shoulders.

"Bay! For God's sake, what's wrong with you? Are you having some kind of fit? Come on! Talk to me."

I shook my head and pushed all the hideous memories back in their hole. I turned toward the anxious face of my brother-in-law.

"I'm sorry. It's just…let me think a minute." I drew in a long breath and exhaled slowly. "Okay. When I went to see Belle, she didn't want to talk about the root. But when I asked about the child, she told me to look for the answer in the grasses. To remember about Moses in the bulrushes."

"I don't understand." Red's breath was warm against my cheek. "What does it mean?"

I held the first page of his interview with the woman from Pennsylvania out to him and pointed at the name of the pregnant teenager who'd supposedly just delivered her child. "She said the knowledge would come to me when I needed it. Moses in the bulrushes. Grasses."

In the dim glow from the instrument panel, I saw the light dawn in Red's eyes.

"Marsh. Elizabeth Marsh. Son of a bitch," he said, and I nodded.

THIRTY

"WHAT DO WE DO NOW?" Malik's soft question hung in the chill air of the Camaro's dim interior.

Red leaned forward, his arms resting on the steering wheel, his gaze fixed on something far away. "I can't believe I let that woman scam me. She sounded"—he lifted his right shoulder a fraction—"perfectly normal, like a proud new grandmother."

"Protecting her child," I said, the buzzing in my ears and the surreal feeling of being outside my body having subsided. Sitting right next to the spot where I'd witnessed someone burn to death, however, was giving me the serious creeps. "Can we get going?"

Red glanced around and suddenly realized where we were. "Oh, God, Bay. Sorry. I didn't think." He checked for traffic and swung the Camaro back onto the roadway. "I need to call in, get some paperwork rolling. We'll check records, see if this girl really did deliver a baby. May take some time, though. Scranton isn't a little town. Could be several hospitals. Or it could have been a home birth."

I opened my mouth to say Erik could do it in a flash, then realized he still hadn't checked in. I'd almost forgotten about the whole Dumars-Longworth scenario.

"Listen, Red, there's something else." I glanced back over my shoulder and encountered Malik Graves' intelligent dark eyes.

"What?"

"That matter we were discussing at lunch?" I hoped he wouldn't make me spell it out.

"Yeah, the Florida thing. What about it?"

I chose my words carefully. "My friend hasn't called in several hours, and I can't reach him. I'm getting a little worried."

I couldn't read his face, but I heard the mixture of anger and concern in his voice. "I tried to tell you it wasn't a game for…for your friend." He, too, glanced back toward the deputy. "How serious do you think it is?"

"I don't know. He could just be keeping a low profile. Or maybe he can't get cell service. Like on St. Helena sometimes."

"That's probably it. Try him now."

I pushed redial on my cell phone and again came up empty.

"Let's get this other thing squared away, and I'll check it out for you. I'm sure it's nothing to be concerned about."

I desperately wanted to believe him.

My brother-in-law lifted the radio mike and set the investigation into Elizabeth Marsh in motion as we sped along into the deepening twilight.

The kernel of anxiety lodged in my chest continued to grow as we rolled past Beaufort. For a long time, no one spoke. Red stared straight ahead, and Malik seemed content in the silence. I wondered if everyone's brain was swirling with the same dark scenarios as my own.

"Why are we still going to see Belle?" I asked when he took the turn that would head us out toward Yemassee.

"Because we can, for one thing," he said, casting a quick look over his shoulder. "I don't expect I'm going to get another invitation any time soon. And because this Elizabeth Marsh business could turn out to be a wild-goose chase."

"But—"

"I know, it seems like too much of a coincidence, but it's not proof. While the office is checking on birth records, we might as well cover all the bases."

I settled back into the bucket seat, unable to mount any valid argument, but with a feeling of dread swirling around in my gut. Belle Crowder had made me uncomfortable the last time I'd ventured into her domain, and the undercurrents swirling between her and her nephew Henry had not been my imagination. Not to mention the fortunetelling thing, which had been downright creepy, despite the homey atmosphere of her snug cottage in the woods. I promised myself I'd keep my hands in my pockets this time.

Twenty minutes of back road later, Malik Graves said, "There it is."

Red slowed the sports car to a crawl. He eased onto the dirt track and almost immediately the Camaro bottomed out as the right front tire sank into the first pothole.

"I guess I should have warned you about the road," I said, throwing up my hands to keep my head from banging into the roof.

"You think?" Red slowed until we were barely moving, but still the undercarriage slammed into the hard-packed dirt. "I don't have any room to maneuver around these damn ruts. Should have brought an SUV. Or a tank."

"Sorry, sir," Malik offered. "I didn't know it had gotten this bad."

Red brought the car to a complete stop. "I think we should back up and park off the side of the paved road." He looked at me. "How far is it?"

"You're asking me? You know I'm no good at that kind of thing."

"I don't need a precise measurement," he said, the anger bubbling again just below the surface of his words. "Can we walk in?"

I tried to remember how long it had taken Dr. Crowder and me to bump and sway down this pathetic excuse for a road in his son's battered old van. "I guess. I mean, it's not miles or anything like that."

"Probably walk faster than we can drive in this baby anyway," Malik said.

"Okay. Fine."

Slowly, Red backed down the track, jarring all of us until he whipped back onto the wider road, then parked next to a screen of wild holly trailing choking tendrils of kudzu that lined the verge. We all climbed out of the car.

"Hold up a minute, Bay." He popped open the tiny trunk, and he and Malik retrieved flashlights and their heavy gun belts.

"You think we're gonna need all this?" the deputy asked, his black face glowing in the dim light.

"Probably not, but I don't like the idea of us walking naked into the woods. Holsters and weapons only."

"Yes, sir."

I waited while they unclipped the other cop paraphernalia and strapped on their pistols. Red slammed the trunk lid and clicked on one of the powerful flashlights.

"You take the point," he said to the deputy. "Bay, you're in the middle."

"You make this sound like we're on patrol in enemy territory," I said, hoping for an answering smile and not getting one.

"Let's go," he said, and Malik moved out.

The beams of both flashlights pushed the darkness aside, at least for a few yards ahead of us. The dense vegetation that crowded the road quivered in a light breeze, making the winding track feel like a wavering tunnel. The woods lay eerily quiet, no rustle of foraging night creatures disturbing the heavy silence. We walked single file along the right side of the one-lane path, avoiding the possibility of falling into any of the scattered potholes. A few no-see-ums buzzed occasionally, but even the insects seemed to have turned in for the night.

After a few minutes, I dropped back to edge closer to Red. "What do you think about Erik?" I asked.

"I think you're both idiots for tailing someone across state lines," he said, his voice low and terse. "And for thinking you can do this job better than we can."

"That's not fair! You wouldn't have done a damn thing if I'd asked you to follow Sally Longworth. Your knee-jerk reaction has been to try and nail Billy for his wife's murder right from day one. No one's been the least bit interested in looking at other suspects, and you damn well know it!"

"Problem, sir?" Malik had stopped and turned toward us.

"No, deputy, no problem. Let's keep moving."

"I don't care about all that right now," I said as we spread out again along the side of the road. "I'm worried. It's not like him to leave me hanging like this."

"Erik's not stupid. He may be a little gung-ho sometimes, but he's not going to put himself in harm's way. My guess is it's a cell tower thing." He reached out and patted me gently on the shoulder. "Don't worry so much. He's a big boy."

I held his words in my head, repeating them over and over like a mantra, as we followed the twists and turns of the track. I thought I could see the soft glow of lights from the compound through the heavy screen of trees just a second before the roar of an engine shattered the silence.

Malik Graves had disappeared around a sharp bend, and his shout froze us for a moment. Red's hand gripped my arm. We heard a cry followed by a dull *thump,* and a beam of light cartwheeled against the black canopy overhead. Then the night was filled with the blinding glare of headlights, and the roar of the engine reverberated in my chest. I felt myself being jerked off my feet and flung toward the bushes. Thorns and branches ripped at my clothes. Something big and solid barreled toward us in a haze of dust. I had only a fleeting glimpse as it brushed by with only inches to spare before it careened away down the track.

"YOU OKAY?"

Red's voice came from right next to my ear. I tried to turn my head and realized he lay on top of me, my face pressed into something sharp and stingy.

"Let me up." I felt him shift his weight, and I drew a long, shuddering breath. The air, heavy and damp and redolent with the loamy scent of decayed vegetation, tasted wonderful in the back of my throat. Then memory came flooding back, and I scrambled to my feet. "Malik," I said, fear an almost palpable presence as Red and I held each other's eyes.

He whirled and forced his way through the undergrowth back onto the track. I stumbled out behind him, and we sprinted around the bend ahead. The deputy lay on his back, one arm flung out as if in supplication, his left leg twisted at an unnatural angle. In the glow of Red's flashlight as he knelt over his fallen officer, I could see the white gleam of bone sticking out from his trouser leg. Bright red arterial blood soaked the material from just above the knee. I forced down the bile rising in my throat.

"Is he—"

"Breathing," Red answered, "but not very well."

I dropped down beside him. "What can I do?"

"Hold the light," he said, thrusting it into my free hand. He unhooked Malik's belt, slid the holster onto the ground, and tightened the leather strap around his deputy's thigh. Almost instantly, the rhythmic spurts of blood subsided.

Red sat back on his heels and expelled a shaky sigh. "You got your cell?"

"Help is on the way."

The soft voice materialized out of the darkness lurking just outside the glow of the light. I gasped, and Red rolled, coming up on his knees, his hands gripping both his pistol and Malik's flashlight.

Belle Crowder stood perfectly still, her arms at her sides, and made no attempt to shield her eyes from the glare.

"Red!" I yelled, finding my voice at last. "It's Belle."

The woman moved closer as my brother-in-law lowered his gun. She knelt and placed her hand on the deputy's chest. She closed her eyes and murmured something under her breath, then rose and moved toward the woods.

"Hold it!" Red swiveled the light to keep her in its glow, and his gun hand came up again.

"Shine that over this way, if you please," she said, her calm voice seeming to float in the still night air. "Against this tree."

He hesitated, then did as she asked, the beam illuminating a thick growth of moss clinging to the bark of a twisted trunk.

"Good," the woman said. In one smooth movement, she slipped a folding knife from the pocket of her dark slacks, flicked it open, and sliced off a large piece. Red and I watched in amazement as she opened Malik's shirt and laid the fuzzy green mat against his chest.

"What the hell—" Red began, but the woman silenced him with an upraised hand.

"It will help his breathing. Until the others arrive."

She checked his leg, nodded approval at Red's improvised tourniquet, and stood to face us. Before she could speak, we all raised our heads at the faint sound of sirens in the distance.

"I'll be getting back," she said.

"Wait!" Red ordered, and she turned.

"Mrs. Crowder. Belle. Do you know what happened here?" I asked.

Malik stirred, his moans soft, like a child in the middle of a bad dream.

I stepped closer. "Do you have any idea who that was?" I looked back up the track to where it disappeared into the trees around the bend.

The shake of her head was barely discernible in the heavy darkness, although the glow from Red's flash outlined the edges of her face in an eerie glow.

"Are you sure?" His angry voice sounded like a gunshot in the deep stillness.

Belle Crowder edged farther out of the circle of the flashlight's beam, and again her disembodied voice seemed to ride on the evening breeze.

"I have no idea," she said, her dark eyes darting away from mine, and I knew for a certainty she was lying.

THIRTY-ONE

THERE WAS NO WAY for an ambulance to maneuver its way down the narrow path. Red left me sitting beside Malik Graves, his clammy hand limp in mine, while he sprinted back toward the entrance to intercept the paramedics and lead them to us.

Belle Crowder had melted back into the woods as silently as she'd come.

In the oppressive stillness, with the coppery smell of blood filling my throat with every breath, I squeezed the deputy's fingers and hummed softly. It took a moment for me to realize it was the same hymn Lavinia had sought refuge in back at Presqu'isle the night we found the dead baby. What had she called it? "Savior, Like a Shepherd Lead Us," that was it. I understood now why the simple tune had brought her comfort. I hoped somehow it was reaching through to Malik's consciousness, soothing and reassuring him. There wasn't much else I could do.

Belle's denial still floated on the night air, mingling with the whispers of the wind in the tops of the pines. She knew who had been driving, but we'd play hell getting her to admit it. I continued to hum softly, eyes closed, stroking Malik's hand while I tried to reconstruct that brief glimpse I'd had as the massive vehicle sped past. SUV? Or maybe a pickup truck. Definitely not a regular car. The top had sat too high off the ground. Or maybe my fear had magnified its size. Memory could be a tricky thing. I had the impression of brown, but that could have been just the contrast with the glaring headlamps. Definitely dark, though. I felt certain of that. And a touch of white somewhere, but I couldn't bring it into focus. License plate? Bumper sticker?

Malik stirred, and I laid a hand on his forehead. He didn't seem feverish, in fact just the opposite: his skin had a cold, clammy feel that made me shudder. I looked back down the track, straining for some sound or telltale flicker of light that would announce the arrival of the medics. At least his breathing seemed to have evened out, whether as a result of his own tough constitution or Belle's application of the velvety moss I couldn't have said.

A long time later, I thought I heard a muffled shout and turned my head toward the sound. Lights bobbed crazily in the distance, and suddenly the labored grunts of men carrying heavy gear and running all-out filled the night air. Red was in the lead as they sprinted around the bend and thudded to a halt. So many flashlight beams played over the narrow roadway, I had to throw up an arm to protect my eyes from the glare. I felt hands disentangling Malik's fingers from my own, then Red lifted me to my feet.

"Over here. We'll just be in the way." He led me to a flat spot on the opposite side of the road, and both of us sank to the ground.

Without conscious thought, I leaned into him, and a strong arm encircled my shoulders.

"You okay?"

I nodded. "Yeah. I guess."

"My fault," he said, and I could feel the tremor work its way from deep inside him and shiver down the arm that held me.

"Bullshit," I said.

"I was in charge. I should have had the point."

"Okay, sure. It would be a lot better if that was you splattered all over the road." I felt tears rising, and I swallowed hard. "He's young, and these guys are the best. He'll be fine."

A stretcher had been laid out on the ground, which was illuminated by a wide circle of lanterns the team had carried in. Someone had inserted an IV needle into Malik's arm while another held the bottle of clear liquid high above him. Two EMTs worked on the leg while another monitored vitals. Belle's square of moss had been tossed aside into the dirt.

"Ready to transport."

Red dropped his arm and leaped to his feet at the paramedic's words. In one smooth and practiced motion they eased the young deputy's body onto the stretcher. My brother-in-law hovered, obviously torn between a desire to accompany his bloodied comrade and the need for information on his assailant.

"We'll take good care of him," one of the medics said. "Go find the bastard that did this."

Red stepped back as they moved out, the team walking as quickly as they dared down the dangerous road, the stretcher held perfectly level as they disappeared around the bend.

I hadn't realized a half dozen officers, some in civvies, had been hovering just out of reach of the lanterns' glow until I heard the stern voice of the sheriff himself. "What the hell's going on here, Tanner?"

"Sir." Red moved toward the circle of men, and his words faded.

I waited a moment, forgotten by the cluster of policemen, before picking up Red's fallen flashlight and moving up the road toward the compound.

I ANGLED LEFT at the huge oak, eventually found the stepping stones, and followed their path to Belle Crowder's front porch. As I placed a foot on the bottom step, the door opened.

"Come in, Bay. The kettle's just boiling."

Without waiting for a reply, she turned and disappeared into the soft glow of the interior. I shrugged and followed, easing the door not quite closed behind me.

Belle arranged the silver tea ball in the pot, then poured steaming water over it. Immediately the room filled with a rich aroma: sharp and earthy, but calming at the same time. She smiled and indicated I should take the same chair I'd occupied just—what? Was it possible our previous meeting had been only twenty-four hours before? This day felt as if it had lasted for years.

She seated herself and slid a blue earthenware plate across

the polished table. "Molasses. The recipe's been in my family since the plantation days."

I eyed the dark brown cookies liberally sprinkled with sugar.

Across from me, Belle laughed, a clear, delightful ripple that seemed inappropriate somehow in light of the scene I'd just left. "They aren't laced with anything, my dear. Perfectly harmless. You need something sweet to take that shocky look out of your eyes." She reached across and brought one of the cookies to her mouth. "I'll go first."

"They need to know who was driving the truck."

"The young man will survive. Please put your mind at rest about that. I'm afraid he'll be a long time healing, but his outlook is good."

A nice sidestepping of my implied question. "And you know this how?"

"You have neither the temperament nor the wisdom to understand these things, Bay. Just this once take something on faith."

The challenge should have made me angry, but I found myself nodding.

"Eat," she said, her eyes holding mine for a long moment.

I picked up a cookie and took a tentative bite.

"Come in, Sergeant."

Behind me I felt a rush of warm breeze as the door swung open. Red moved soundlessly across the faded carpet and stopped just short of the table, his right hand resting on the butt of the gun strapped to his side.

"Ma'am," he said. "I need to ask you a few questions."

Belle turned to the stove and poured coffee into a sturdy mug that matched the plate. With the slightest tilt of her head she indicated Red's assigned place. It had been Harry's the night before. Once he'd seated himself, she resumed her chair and slid the cookies in his direction. She offered neither milk nor sugar, and I wondered how she knew Red took his coffee black. I wondered a lot of things about Belle Crowder.

"You know who was driving," he said without preamble.

Belle reached for the teapot and filled mugs for the two of

us. The steam rose, easing some of the tension in my chest. I blew across the surface and sipped cautiously. Without conscious thought, I finished the first cookie and reached for another.

"I never saw the…vehicle, Sergeant, I merely heard it. I came out to investigate and found you and your unfortunate friend." A brief glance in my direction. "And Bay."

I thought about how far it was from her snug cottage to the cluster of houses inside the fences of and from there to the sharp bend in the road where Malik Graves had been struck. Was that possible? Even on a still night like this one, it didn't seem feasible. And why hadn't it roused anyone inside the compound? Before I could raise the question, Red turned to me.

"What's at the end of this path?"

I remembered the headlights of Harry Crowder's van reflecting back off the impenetrable wall of vegetation. "Nothing. It ends just on the other side of this house."

He whipped his head back in Belle's direction. "So the vehicle had to come from here. No way it got up to that kind of speed if it was exiting the compound, not on that road." He paused. "And why would you have gone to investigate? What made you think something was wrong?"

The woman sat completely composed under Red's unwavering stare. "I sensed it."

Red kept his voice level, but the sarcasm was unmistakable. "You sensed it?"

Across the table I saw Belle stiffen. "You were a soldier." She didn't make it a question.

"Marines."

"And you've been a police office for a number of years. Tell me, Sergeant, have you never come upon a scene where everything looks perfectly normal, no signs of trouble or danger, and yet you felt in your gut that something wasn't right? Haven't the hairs on your arms tingled and the breath caught in your throat? Didn't your hand rest more firmly on your weapon?"

Red squared his shoulders at the challenge in her voice before saying, "Of course, but—"

"Then you understand."

"No, ma'am, I don't understand at all. I have a deputy who may lose a leg and a murdered child with one of your charms around its neck. When you agreed to meet with us, you wanted Bay here to come along. I assumed that meant you were ready to tell her the truth. I'm still waiting to hear it."

I sat mesmerized in the soft glow of the lamps while Red and the conjure-woman held each other's gaze across the worn oak table. Belle was the first to look away.

"Trouble, like everything else, will come if it will come," she said and reached for the teapot. "I missed a sign somewhere, and that poor young man has had to pay the price for it. I hope he can forgive me." She looked again at Red. "And you as well, Sergeant."

Again the two of them locked eyes. The double meaning of her words hadn't escaped either of us. This time, Red was the first to blink.

"So you have nothing that can help me."

Suddenly Belle turned her penetrating gaze in my direction, and I could feel heat rising up my throat.

"You're worried about your friends," she said, and I gasped.

"What do you mean? What friends?"

She didn't respond, but her deep, searching eyes never wavered from my face. Her slender brown fingers reached for my hand, and I knew what was coming. I jerked away, startling us both.

I pushed back my chair and jumped to my feet. "We have to go."

"Bay—" Red began, but Belle cut him off.

"She has reason for concern."

I reached automatically for my bag before realizing it still lay out in the woods somewhere, in the tangle of undergrowth where Red had flung me.

"Give me your cell," I said without preamble, thrusting out my hand in his direction.

"They don't work out here," Belle said, her eyes still locked on my face.

I spun on my heel and headed for the door.

"Bay, sit down!" Red snapped. "You can't go anywhere without me."

The profanity died on my lips. He was right. I slumped against the wall and waited.

"Just hold on a minute." He turned back to Belle. "Ma'am, it goes against my upbringing to call anyone a liar, especially a lady, but we both know you're not telling me the whole truth. You know who the parents of that poor little girl are. For some reason, they came to you for help, for that root we found around her neck, and you could name them if you chose. They killed their child, Ms. Crowder. Not a few hours out of the womb, and they put a blanket over her face and held it there until her tiny lungs stopped drawing breath."

In the warm cocoon of the cottage, the hideous image erupted inside my head. "Stop it, Red!"

Both of them ignored me.

"And you know who was driving that vehicle, too. I'm as sure of that as I am of anything. You're protecting murderers, Ms. Crowder. How does that square with your religion?"

Belle had sat perfectly composed under the onslaught of Red's words, but his last question brought her head snapping up. "You can't begin to understand my beliefs, Sergeant."

"Try me."

"It would be a waste of time. Like Bay's, your policeman's mind can only grasp the tangible and the mundane."

I watched Red struggle to control his anger. "Give me the names, Ms. Crowder."

"You already know them." Her gaze slid to me. "All of them."

Red slammed out of his chair, knocking it against the kitchen cabinets with a crash. "Quit playing games with me, lady! I have a murdered baby on my hands. And an officer down. I don't want to hear any more of your goddamned mumbo jumbo!"

I took a step back toward the table, but Belle Crowder had no need of my protection.

She held up a placating hand and spoke softly. "I have no intent to deceive you, Sergeant. Unlike so many of my black brothers and sisters, I've never been questioned by the police before. Forgive me if I've handled it badly."

Red let the barbed remark pass, but I could tell his anger had reached critical mass. "Unless I get some answers, the next time you talk to us won't be in quite such pleasant surroundings."

Belle ignored the implied threat, and her gaze drifted again in my direction. "Do you remember our conversation last night?"

I nodded.

"We spoke of knowledge. You have it now." A long sigh escaped, and she leaned back into the chair. "Use it as you will. I can do no more." She wrapped her hands around the heavy mug and brought it to her lips. "Trouble will come if it will come," she murmured.

Red looked from one to the other of us. When he spoke, it was through teeth clenched so tightly I thought his jaw might shatter under the pressure. "The names, Ms. Crowder. Now."

I studied the two of them, locked in their battle of wills. Their mutual animosity, almost palpable in the charged atmosphere of the cottage, stretched back through the generations, fueled by old fears, old hatreds, old wounds. It hovered in the air like a dark, swirling cloud.

I leaned against the wall and let the crackling silence wash over me, images flickering in front of my glazed eyes like the jerky motion of an old black-and-white movie: the wrinkled face of the dead child; Harry Crowder's golden brown eyes; Malik's cry; and the brown van hurtling toward me out of the darkness....

I shook myself. "The brown van," I murmured, and suddenly it all clicked into place.

Red's eyes caught mine, his anger at Belle still smoldering there. "What did you say?"

"Never mind," I said. "Let's go."

"What—"

"I'll explain later. We have to go. Now."

The urgency in my voice reached him, and he rose from the table. "I'll be back," he said and marched toward me across the faded Turkey carpet.

"Good-bye, Belle," I whispered, but she didn't respond.

Across the room, I saw her head slump against her chest, and a single tear slid down her golden cheek.

THIRTY-TWO

My CANVAS TOTE BAG lay crumpled in a tangle of hawthorn and blackberry bushes.

"Thanks," I said as my brother-in-law crawled back onto the dirt track and handed it to me. I slipped the strap over my shoulder and fell into step just behind him. After a few moments, I asked, "What are you going to do now?"

Red punched the redial button on the cell phone he cradled in his hand while I kept the flashlight trained on the rutted road ahead of us. "Damn useless piece of crap!"

"It'll work as soon as we get out of these woods," I said. "Just another few minutes." I spoke calmly, as if I were trying to reason with a snarling dog. "Or you can radio from the car." He lengthened his stride, and I trotted a little to keep up with him. "Don't worry, you'll get him," I said softly.

He whirled around so fast I almost ran him down. "And what do you think I'm going to use for evidence? That crazy old woman's ramblings or your half-assed deductions? Jesus, Bay, get serious." He spun again and moved off.

I knew he wasn't angry at *me,* but his words stung.

"There has to be damage to Deshawn Crowder's van." I shuddered in the warm night air, remembering the sickening thud as he'd struck Malik. "And blood."

"You can't possibly swear it was the kid's van, and we won't get a warrant without a sworn statement. I sure as hell didn't see anything except a blur that almost took us out along with Graves. There's no way you can say you did."

"I can, Red, and I *will* swear to it." In my mind's eye, back at the cottage, the white rectangle on the front bumper had

popped into focus, clinching it for me: IT'S OUR PLANET—
KEEP IT GREEN. I remembered smiling to myself at the naïveté
of the sentiment the night before in the small parking lot of the
store at Gardens Corner when Harry Crowder picked me up.

Red ignored me, his stiff back clearly visible in the flashlight beam playing out in front of me.

"And the lab has the baby's DNA," I said when he didn't
respond. "All you need to do is get a match."

"And I'm going to get a judge to compel a sample from the
kid based on what? You seriously think his parents will consent
just because you've strung together a bunch of assumptions
based on that old witch's double-talk and a two-second look at
a speeding vehicle?"

"First of all, you don't need his parents' consent if Deshawn
is eighteen. He's leaving for MIT in the fall, or so his father told
me. And everything Belle said made perfect sense to me. She
pointed us at the girl. She said we already knew the names. And
we do. I guarantee you won't find any birth record for Elizabeth
Marsh's baby up in Scranton. She and Deshawn are the parents
of that dead child. I don't know which one of them actually did
it, but one or both of them smothered their own daughter. I know
it."

The encroaching vegetation thinned, the air around us light-
ening as we neared the end of the rutted track.

Suddenly Red whirled, and I skidded to a stop. "That's just
it. You don't *know* a goddamned thing. You're putting two and
two together and getting five."

He turned again and marched toward the paved road.

"Harry Crowder laid it all out for me last night." I puffed
along trying to keep up. "He said Deshawn is brilliant, a kid
with an unlimited future. No way he's ever going to save the
world if he's tied down to a teenaged girl and an illegitimate
baby."

I saw Red glance behind and heard him mutter something I
thought was, "God save me from amateurs."

"Go to hell," I shouted.

The thin light of a waning moon filtered through the trees

and dappled the path in front of us, and Red broke into a trot. I scrambled to keep him in sight, the adrenaline buzz that had fueled me for the last hour beginning to fade. I slowed as he broke through into the clear and wrenched open the door of the Camaro.

I stepped out into the clean night air, and it seemed as if a tremendous burden had been lifted from my shoulders. I turned back toward the long dark tunnel and wondered how the people of could bear to live daily under the oppressive weight of the encroaching forest.

I jumped when Red suddenly materialized in front of me.

"Let's go."

A lot of the anger had drained out of him. He looked as weary as I felt. I let him take the flashlight and guide me around to the passenger side of the car. He slid in the other side and lifted the mike from his radio.

"Tanner," he said when a faint voice crackled back. "You're weak. Call me on my cell."

He shoved the key in the ignition and turned over the engine. A moment later we were hurtling down the dark, deserted road. His phone rang almost immediately.

"Yeah, that's better. How's Malik? Good. Keep me updated if anything changes. I'm on my way in. About twenty minutes out. Any word on the Marsh girl?" He glanced at me, his face unreadable in the wash of the dash lights. "Yeah. Okay. Thanks."

"What?" I asked after he'd disconnected. "What'd they say?"

"They checked every hospital in Scranton. No birth records for Elizabeth Marsh."

I sat silent, my eyes straight ahead.

"Doesn't prove anything."

"I know." I chose my next words carefully. "Look, Red, I understand you don't approve of Belle Crowder, or put any credence in her beliefs. But she's done everything she could to point me in the right direction short of flat-out giving us her great-nephew's name."

"That's exactly what she should have done. Just spit out the name."

I ran a hand through my sweat-damp hair. "You know that doesn't make any sense. It's the same thing I was talking about when we first IDed the Marsh girl. Belle is protecting her own. Like Elizabeth's mother. And Deshawn's father. It may not be right, but it's understandable." I gave the words time to settle before adding, "Wouldn't you do the same for Scotty or Elinor?"

Red didn't react, and I lay my head back against the seat. I felt completely drained, as if every drop of emotion had been wrung from me. I closed my eyes and watched the image of Belle Crowder drift across the blackness, that solitary tear sliding down her cheek. And from somewhere far away I heard her voice, whispering inside my head: *"You're worried about your friends."*

I jerked my phone out of my bag and breathed a sigh of relief when I saw the tiny row of bars marching across the illuminated face. I had one missed call, but it wasn't from my partner.

"Bay, I'm sorry, but I can't worry about that now. I need to get back to the station."

I punched in Erik's number and ignored him. The quiet stretched out as I waited. Nothing. "I don't understand! Where the hell is he?"

My mind slipped away south, to a now darkened marina and a hundred thousand dollars in cash. To a dead woman stuffed in the trunk of her car. And the second part of Belle's warning: *"She has reason for concern."*

"I'm going down there," I said, more to myself than to Red.

"Like hell you are."

I turned to study his familiar face in the faint glow of the dash lights. The angry scowl was back.

"I wasn't asking permission."

"I don't give a damn. You're not going to tear off like some avenging angel into a situation you know nothing about. And certainly not in the middle of the goddamn night."

"And you're going to stop me how?"

He whipped the wheel sharply right at the next intersection, and the tires of the Camaro squealed in protest.

"With reason, I hope," he said. The smile took a lot of effort. "Or I could always lock you up for a few hours."

"You could try."

Red remained silent, slowing as we approached the city limits and traffic thickened.

"Drop me off in town, and I'll get a cab back to the island." When he didn't respond, I added, "Unless you're serious about the jail thing."

"Of course I'm not serious, Bay. God! Don't I have enough on my mind right now? Do I have to add you to the list of things I'm worrying about?"

The simple question made me squirm in the bucket seat. Of course he had more than enough on his plate. He couldn't quite bring himself to believe in Deshawn Crowder's involvement in the death of the child; and, even if he did, he couldn't see a way to bring him to justice. And he had a wounded deputy whose injuries he felt responsible for. I drew in a deep breath and spoke softly.

"I'm sorry. I know you don't need any more grief tonight. Just let me out, and you can get on with it. I'll go home, keep trying to reach Erik on the cell. If I get through—"

"And if you don't? Are you prepared to promise me you won't go tearing off to Florida?"

He'd already known the answer before he asked the question.

"I'll call you first," I said, hoping the promise would satisfy him.

"Try him again now," he said as we turned onto Ribaut Road.

In a few moments we'd be at the jail complex and the main office of the sheriff's department. I hit the redial and waited, but again came up empty. I looked up as we rolled to a stop. Red's voice sounded more than tired.

"Just let me get some things squared away. You can use the rest room, maybe grab a Coke or something. You'll have to

make a witness statement about what happened out there to
Malik. Then—"

"I can call a cab."

"Just shut up for a second, okay?"

"Sorry. Then…what?"

"Then I'll drive you to Florida."

THIRTY-THREE

As IT TURNED OUT, it was almost midnight by the time we finally got on the road. After I gave my statement, I managed to nap a little on one of the hard chairs in the waiting area, but it left me with a stiff shoulder and very little in the way of rest. I yawned widely as we made our way out into the warm, cloudless night.

"What's happening?" I asked.

"Nothing, at least not until morning."

"But Deshawn could dispose of the van by then! You can't—"

"Bay. Please." Red opened the passenger door. "There's an alert out on the vehicle, and Lisa Pedrovsky came in to get started on putting together a case."

"Is someone checking their house?"

"Already done. No one home."

"At midnight? You think Deshawn skipped?"

"I have no idea." He sighed as I slid into the bucket seat of the unmarked Camaro. "At any rate, it's all in the hands of the detectives now. We'll get him because he'll screw up. The amateurs always do," he added and slammed the door closed.

There was that word again: *amateurs*. I didn't let myself examine the implications of it too closely.

Red climbed into the driver's seat and fired up the powerful engine.

"Aren't we going to switch cars?" I asked as he backed around and eased out into the empty street.

"No. I don't want to waste the time."

"They're letting you take this out of state?"

"Unofficially," he said without looking at me. "I'm off duty, remember?"

"What does that mean?"

"The sheriff knows where I'm going and why. I'd never try to run a number on him. But it's sort of like those old *Mission: Impossible* reruns on TV. You ever watch those?"

"Sure. They used to get the tapes that self-destructed."

Red smiled. "And after the voice gave them their assignment, it said something like, 'As always, if you or any of your IM team are killed or captured, the Secretary will disavow any knowledge of your actions.'"

"Pretty good," I said, answering his smile across the narrow console. "So the sheriff will 'disavow' us if we run into any trouble?"

"Not really. He just made it clear this was unofficial. But he'll be there if we need him." He paused. "Try Erik again."

"Nothing," I said a moment later. The sigh came out louder than I'd intended.

Red's fingers brushed across mine. "We're probably going to find him asleep in his car," he said, "and this will turn out to be a wild-goose chase. You always manage to look on the dark side of things."

I thought about that as we hurtled through the night down nearly empty highways. Red had turned off the scanner so that the quiet wrapped itself around us in the dim interior. I remembered how much I'd always loved this feeling whenever I'd been able to hound the Judge into taking me along on one of his fishing or hunting expeditions. Getting up long before dawn and tiptoeing out of the house like thieves, easing down the rutted avenue of oaks, completely isolated in the warm cocoon of the big Lincoln as the headlights picked out the startled eyes of a raccoon or possum interrupted in its nocturnal foraging. Away from Presqu'isle—and my mother—I'd been an explorer embarking on a wonderful journey, the possibility of adventure always just around the next bend in the road. Tucked into the curve of my father's arm, I'd felt excited but safe.

Rob, too, had made me feel like that. Even when we'd been

up to our necks in tracking the finances of drug dealers and mob bosses, I'd always known he'd be right beside me. All I had to do was reach out, and he'd be there, his smile the beacon I could always follow home. His murder had nearly killed me, both physically and emotionally. It had been a long road back to life, a life I'd carved out for myself with determination and intention. I had taught myself to be happy again. And yet…I felt the constant need to peer back over my shoulder, certain somehow that whatever peace I'd managed to wrap around myself couldn't last.

"A lot of bad things have happened," I whispered, embarrassed to hear my voice quiver.

"I know." Red's hand found mine again, and this time he didn't let go. "But you survived."

He glanced away from the road, and for a moment our eyes met. I turned away from the raw emotion on his face and tried to slide my hand free, but he held it fast.

"Relax," he said. "I'm not gonna bite." His soft laughter broke some of the tension. "Not unless you want me to."

We rode like that, our linked hands resting loosely on the console, as the white lines of the highway ticked by in mesmerizing rhythm, and the miles disappeared beneath the humming wheels of the Camaro.

"He's a hard act to follow."

I didn't need to ask what he meant. "Your brother loved you a lot. And he was so proud when you joined the Marines. He thought you were so much braver than he was. He said he just wasn't cut out for shooting at people. He admired you for being able to do what a soldier has to do."

"But he's the one who died. Violently."

His hand tightened around mine, and I squeezed back. "He never expected that. Neither one of us did. Even though we knew what he was doing was dangerous, and he had those two bodyguards the attorney general's office insisted on, we just never…" I could feel my voice breaking, and I clamped my lips shut.

"I know. At least the bastards who did it have finally been made to pay. At least we have that."

I nodded and swallowed down the tears, and we rode without speaking for a long time, rolling along the Georgia coast, its rivers and marshes glinting in the moonlight, its Golden Isles slumbering under the blanket of humid night air. I tried Erik's cell number three more times with no result.

I felt myself dropping off, my neck stretched across the hard leather of the seat back, when Red spoke.

"We're almost to Florida."

I roused myself and yawned. "You know where we're going?"

"I programmed it into the GPS. And it looks like there's only one road off Amelia Island heading south, so we should be able to locate the marina with no trouble."

I sat up straighter and peered at the digital clock on the dash. Ten minutes to three. We'd be riding into trouble completely in the dark.

"You know," Red began, and I glanced at his profile. "When I said Rob was a tough act to follow, I didn't just mean professionally."

As gently as possible, I disengaged my hand from his grip and wiped my sweaty palm on my pants leg. "I know."

"Before we get all wrapped up in whatever…whatever it is we're heading into, I want to say—"

"I know," I said again and felt myself moving away from him, huddling against the passenger door, as if I could escape his words.

"No. You don't know, because you've never sat still long enough to let me say it. And unless you plan on jumping out of a car going eighty miles an hour, you're going to hear it."

I closed my eyes and resisted the urge to cover my ears with my hands. As a child, I'd tried to block out the yelling from my parents' room, my mother's drunken tirades, the Judge's calm, reasoned responses nearly drowned out by her shrieks and profanities. Burrowing under the covers and wrapping a pillow around my head hadn't worked then, either.

"You know how I feel about you, how I've felt almost from the first time Rob brought you home to dinner. Do you remember that day? I could tell you every word you said, every look, every gesture—"

"Don't do this, Red. Please."

"I'm sorry, but it's way past time." He ran a hand through his hair and slapped it onto the steering wheel. "Of course you didn't have eyes for anyone but him, and Mom said afterward she'd be surprised if you weren't married within a month. Took you a little longer, but not much."

I felt him glance at me, but I kept my eyes straight ahead.

"And no one knew how pointless it was more than I did. I told myself I was being an idiot, acting like some lovesick schoolboy. I made myself forget about it, forget about you. But it ate at our marriage, Sarah's and mine. Fifteen years. And eventually…" His voice trailed off.

"Don't put that on me, Red. Don't you dare try to put that on me."

"I'm not, Bay. I never said it was your fault. It just…happened. Don't you think I would've changed things if I could? You don't think I miss my kids every damn day?"

He fell silent again, waiting for me to respond. A voice inside my head screamed, *Shut up, shut up, shut up,* but no words came.

Finally he said, "I waited a year after Rob…died. And how many more since then? I love you, Bay, but I can't go on with this charade of a friendship. And watching you throw yourself into danger, almost as if you're hoping to get hurt? Or killed? I can't deal with it anymore. It's tearing me apart."

A hard knot had settled into my stomach, and my hands had gone icy. I rubbed them together, unable to generate any warmth. "What are you saying, Red?"

"I'm saying you need to decide. I won't—"

I jumped as the notes of my cell phone reverberated through the car. Red and I locked gazes a moment before I stabbed at the button. The number was the same as on the earlier message I hadn't retrieved.

"Bay! Thank God!"

"Who—"

"I can't find Dad. Have you seen him?"

I glanced at Red who raised an eyebrow and mouthed, "Erik?" I shook my head, trying to figure out who would have the nerve to call my cell phone in the middle of the night. Then it hit me.

"Stephanie?"

"Yes. I'm sorry, I know it's late, but…Dad's gone."

"What do you mean 'gone'?"

"He left hours ago, and he never came back. I've tried every place I can think of. It's not like him. I mean, he's never done anything like this before. I'm really worried." The catch in her voice made me sit up straighter.

"Calm down. Start at the beginning."

Out of nowhere I heard Belle Crowder whisper inside my head: *"You're worried about your friends."* Friends. Plural.

"He came home from your office around dinnertime, and we got into this huge fight."

After I told him about her boyfriend's connection to Camp St. Mary's, I thought.

"I'm sorry, but you didn't give me any choice, Stephanie. You should have told him or Red the minute you realized the significance of that phone call."

My brother-in-law turned his head toward me at the mention of his name, one eyebrow raised in mute question, but I waved him off.

"I know. I'm sorry," Stephanie said. "It's just…I mean, I still don't believe… The thing is, I told him all about it, and he went ballistic. He said for all I knew Kenny could be involved in the murder, and I could get arrested for obstruction of justice."

"That's not going to happen," I said, glancing again at Red. "They use that threat all the time, but they rarely follow through. Besides, your father's not a cop anymore."

"He wanted me to go down to the sheriff's office right then and make a statement, but I was really upset." Again I heard the catch in her voice. "I said some really hateful things, Bay. I didn't mean them, he knows that, but I was so angry."

"He'll get over it. But I don't understand what the problem is. You said Ben's gone? Gone where?"

"I don't know! He slammed out of the house after the fight. I tried waiting up for him, but I had a couple of glasses of wine, and I fell asleep. I woke up just a little while ago, and he wasn't here. His car's still gone, too."

"Maybe he's just having a drink somewhere," I said, although I had a difficult time believing Ben would still be out at this hour. Besides, most bars closed at two.

"But why would he have his cell phone turned off? I've left about a zillion voice mails, but he hasn't called back. I tried to get you earlier, but that wouldn't go through either."

No service at the Sanctuary Hill compound, I thought.

I tried to focus my sleep-deprived brain on what had Wyler's daughter so worked up, but I just couldn't wrap my head around it.

"Tell me exactly what you told Ben. Everything."

Stephanie gulped and seemed to pull herself together. "I told him about the end of the call I overheard, about Kenny saying he'd meet someone out at the camp on Tuesday night. That's when Dad said I could be arrested. He asked me when was the last time I talked to him, to Kenny, and at first…at first I didn't tell the truth, because he was so angry! But then he kept screaming about how I could be an accessory to murder." Her voice quavered. "You were right. I did talk to Kenny. Yesterday."

I didn't take any pleasure in being right, but I'd felt certain something had happened to change her mind so drastically in only the day and a half since she'd seemed more than willing to cooperate with the investigation.

"What did he say? Stephanie?" I prodded when she didn't answer.

"He said he had to be gone for a few days and that I shouldn't worry." She paused, and I could picture her square chin rising in defiance. "He said he loved me and that he'd see me soon."

"Do you know where he was calling from?"

"No. But it wasn't his regular cell number. And then tonight, after Dad slammed out of the house, I was going to call him back and make sure he was all right, and—"

"Tell me you didn't do that."

"Why? You and Dad are wrong about Kenny. You are! It was just a stupid coincidence. He didn't have anything to do with that woman's murder."

I tried to remember what it was like being twenty-two and blinded by love.

"Did you get hold of him?"

"That's just it. The caller ID had been erased from my cell phone. Dad must have done it, before he left."

And made a copy for himself, I thought. With the number from Stephanie's phone, Ben could track him down. Always assuming he could get someone at the sheriff's office to lend him a hand. Someone like Detective Lisa Pedrovsky perhaps?

"Look, Stephanie, I really don't think you need to worry. Your dad can take care of himself."

"Can you come over? Maybe we could go looking for him."

I glanced up as we slowed, and a few seconds later Red guided the Camaro onto the exit ramp for A1A.

"I can't. I'm in Florida, on my way to find Erik. I'm at least three hours away."

"What's Erik doing in Florida? I tried to call him, too. Is he okay?"

I groped for a lie she might swallow. "He's fine. He had car trouble, and we're going to pick him up. Listen, I'm sure your dad's all right. Just keep holding on to that thought and try to get some sleep. Who knows, you might wake up and find him passed out on the sofa."

"I'll try."

"And have him call me when he does show up, okay?"

"I will. Thanks, Bay. I'm sorry I bothered you so late."

"No problem." Beside me, Red shifted in his seat, and I realized I had one more question. "Hang on a second. What's your boyfriend's last name?" Since I intended to dump this all in Red's lap, I knew he'd need the information. "Come on, what's the big secret? Your dad knows it."

I waited through what seemed like a long silence before I heard her sigh of resignation.

"I suppose it doesn't matter. It's Briggs. Kenny Briggs."

THIRTY-FOUR

"WHAT THE HELL'S going on?" Red asked.

As we sped toward Amelia Island, I gripped my head in both hands and tried to massage away the pain pounding in my temples. The weariness lay so heavily on my shoulders I felt as if I could slide down onto the floor and sleep for a week. Instead I lowered the window and breathed deeply of the salt-laden air rushing by.

"I don't know yet," I said. I couldn't begin to corral all the chaotic thoughts racing around in my brain. "Basically, Stephanie can't find Ben."

"Who's Stephanie?"

I pulled my head back in and stared at my brother-in-law. Of course he didn't know who Stephanie was. In our brief conversation I'd referred to her only as my "informant."

"She's Ben's daughter."

"Wyler has a kid? Did you know that? I mean, before?"

"No. Not until a couple of days ago."

"So what's the problem?"

"They had a fight, and he took off. He's not answering his phone, and he hasn't come home yet. She's worried."

"I guess I might be, too, at almost four o'clock in the morning, but he's a grown man. There are some things fathers don't necessarily want to share with their daughters."

I heard the smile in his voice, but I couldn't respond. I slumped down in the seat and let my eyes drift closed.

"You said something about her talking to me."

I ignored him. *Briggs!* It had to mean something. Ken Briggs. Vice-president of First Coast Bank. The man who'd

handed over a hundred thousand dollars in cash to Tracy
Dumars. And Kenny had been there. Briggs had told me his son
had dropped by while he was escorting Tracy to her car. Had
Kenny followed her? Or was it something to do with Kitty
Longworth? There was a connection, there had to be, but...I
felt myself falling. For a moment I fought it, struggling to hold
on to the thought, before I surrendered to exhaustion and slid
into sleep....

"BAY. WAKE UP."

"Leave me alone," I mumbled and jerked away from his
hand on my arm.

"Come on. I think we're here."

The lights of the small marina materialized out of the gray
mist hanging over the water. Red drifted left into the gravel
parking lot of the restaurant next door.

"There's the Expedition."

I shook myself awake as he pulled up alongside Erik's SUV. I
stretched and glanced around. The scene was eerie, with thin
tendrils of fog drifting across the three boats tied up at the narrow
dock.

"Stay here."

Before I could reply, Red slipped from the Camaro and
eased the door closed. I watched him circle the SUV, peering
in the windows. In less than a minute, he was back.

"Nothing," he said, and my stomach lurched.

"Where is he?"

"I don't know. Stay here," he said again. "I'm going to take
a look around."

"No way."

Red opened his mouth to protest, but I had already hauled
myself out of the bucket seat, my legs a little wobbly from
almost four hours of being cramped under the low dashboard.
He motioned with his head, and I followed him up the steps
onto the porch that wrapped itself around the restaurant. We
cupped our hands around our eyes to stare into the windows but
encountered only darkness. On the back deck, the chairs in the

outdoor eating area had been stacked on top of the tables. We tiptoed down a ramp and back to the car.

"Let's check out the boats," I whispered.

"Hold on a minute." Red leaned inside the Camaro and came out with a holster. He pulled out his service weapon and checked the clip. While he worked it into the back of the waistband of his shorts, I eased open my door and retrieved the Seecamp.

Red moved around the rear of the car. "Ready?"

I nodded, and we moved off along the dock, not exactly creeping, but certainly not announcing our presence. In the eerie stillness, broken only by the soft slap of water against the pilings, I patted the pistol where it nestled in my pocket.

"There," Red said softly, pointing just ahead to where a thin light showed from the cabin of the middle boat in the row. The others were completely dark. The big craft rocked gently on its mooring ropes, its fenders squeaking lightly against the dock.

Red motioned for me to stay back, but I followed as he edged closer. A few more feet and I was able to make out the shiny gold lettering across the stern: PRIME RATE. Below that were the words HILTON HEAD.

I tugged at Red's sleeve and leaned close to his ear. "This is it."

I could see his eyebrows raised in question. I jerked my head toward the parking lot, and he followed me back to the Camaro.

"What's going on?" he demanded. "How do you know?"

"We don't have time for the whole story, but the man who was talking on the phone about meeting someone out at the camp was Kenny Briggs. He's been in jail, and he's got a connection to Kitty Longworth. Plus his father's a banker, the one who gave the money to Tracy Dumars. *Prime Rate*. Banker? Don't tell me that's a coincidence."

"But—"

"We don't have time for any more talking. What if Erik's on that boat? What if they've done something to him? Come on," I said, whirling toward the dock.

Red grabbed my arm and jerked me back.

"Are you nuts? We have no legal reason to board that boat. No warrant, no probable cause. Besides, I don't have any jurisdiction down here, and there's nothing that suggests anyone's in imminent danger. We could be arrested for breaking and entering, same as if we barged into somebody's house in the middle of the night."

"I don't give a damn about probable cause or any of that crap." I could hear my voice rising.

"Wait! What if you're right? What if someone on that boat is involved in the Dumars killing? She was shot, remember? There's a gun around somewhere."

"You can sit here figuring out all the angles 'til hell freezes over. I'm going in there and get Erik."

I yanked the pistol from the pocket of my slacks, but Red tightened his grip.

"You're not going anywhere until we talk this out. And put that damn gun away before you hurt yourself."

I jerked out of his grasp. "I swear to God, Red, I'll shoot you myself if you try to stop me."

"Just listen a second, will you? I'm not saying we're not going to check it out. I'm just suggesting that we don't go walking into a situation we're not prepared for. Think about it. He could be—"

A car rolled by on the road, its headlights stabbing into the darkness, and we both turned to follow its progress. As it swung by, I saw a flash in the belt of trees that separated the restaurant from the small strip of beach down the way.

"Look!" Before Red could respond, I was running. I heard his feet on the gravel as I skidded to a stop.

The green VW had been pulled up into a thick stand of bushes. We pushed aside branches and forced our way in. The windows were down, and the stack of clothes was still strewn across the backseat.

I looked at Red. "Sally Longworth's car. Still think this is all some figment of my imagination?"

"Quiet," he whispered, and I felt his hand on my arm. "Someone's getting off the boat." He pointed. "Look."

I forced my eyes to focus in the misty dawn. A figure had slipped over the rail and stood frozen on the weathered boards of the dock. A glint of light from the single overhead lamp reflected off long blond hair as the head moved cautiously from side to side before turning in our direction. Instinctively, we both crouched. The woman tiptoed toward us, glancing back with every other step. A few yards from us, she stopped to heft a gym bag onto her shoulder, then gathered herself and ran directly at us. A moment later she crashed into the thicket.

In one swift movement, Red had a hand clamped over her mouth. She struggled in his arms, but he managed to wrestle her to a standstill. I could see his mouth moving, whispering to her, but I couldn't hear the words. In a moment, I saw her go limp. He motioned for me to join them, and he dragged her with us to the edge of the parking lot under a stand of scraggly pine trees. The bag dropped with a soft *thump* onto the gravel.

"I'm a cop," my brother-in-law said, "from Beaufort. We're here to help. If I take my hand away, will you be quiet?"

The blonde nodded, and Red released her.

"Are you Sally or Kitty?" I asked, the darkness under the trees too deep for me to make out her face. Not that it would have helped. I'd never seen either of the sisters up close.

She swallowed hard. "Kitty."

"Take it easy." Red spoke slowly. "Who's on the boat?"

A shudder passed through her slender body before she said, "Kenny."

"Kenny Briggs?" I asked.

"Yes." The tremors shook her once again, and I held out a hand to steady her. "We have to get out of here," she said, panic making her voice rise in the stillness.

"Calm down." I gripped her arm more tightly. "Is there someone on board besides Briggs and your sister? Another man?"

She ignored me. "You don't understand! He's going to kill me! Just like he did Tracy!"

Red moved closer. "This Briggs guy killed Tracy Dumars? How do you know that? Were you there?"

"It was awful! He shot Tracy, just like that. In the back. For no reason! She gave us the money. I told him to let her go!"

Kitty Longworth's voice was sliding into hysteria, and again Red clamped his hand over her mouth.

"Keep it down!" he whispered.

She drew a long breath and nodded, and Red released her.

"You have to help Sally."

"You just ran off and left her? With a murderer?" I wanted to shake the woman.

"You don't understand!" The sob caught in her throat. "Kenny's gone crazy! I was going for help. We have to get help!"

I heard her foot move, as if she was probing for something. I reached down and swooped up the bag she'd dropped when Red first grabbed her. I had a moment to register surprise at how heavy it was before Kitty whirled on me.

"No! Give that to me!"

Red jerked her back, and Kitty swung at him. He yanked both her arms behind her back. "Stay still and shut up. Go ahead, Bay," he said softly, "open it."

I stepped back out of reach and knelt on the bed of crackling pine needles. It took me a moment to find the zipper in the dark.

The stacks of bills still had First Coast's paper sleeves wrapped around them.

"You can't—I need that money! If I don't give it to them, they're going to kill me!" the woman cried through her curtain of shimmering hair. Suddenly her bravado subsided into whimpers. "You have to let me take it to them."

Red tightened his grip on her wrists. "You're not going anywhere." To me he said, "Put that in the trunk and bring me the cuffs."

I hefted the bag and carried it toward the car. I kept my eye on the *Prime Rate* rocking gently on the light swells from the incoming tide as I deposited the money and found Red's handcuffs. Back at the edge of the parking lot, Kitty slumped against Red, all the fight drained out of her.

"I'm sorry, but this is for your own protection." He snapped the cuffs on her, then turned her around to face him. "Now I need some answers. Is there anyone else on that boat besides Briggs and your sister?"

"There's plenty for everyone, you know. Almost a hundred grand. I only need fifty to pay off my debt." Her wide eyes lifted to Red's. "I don't mind sharing. Just tell me how much you need, you and your friend here. How about five? That's not a bad payday for just taking these handcuffs off me. I swear I'll disappear, and no one will ever know."

"I'm going to ask you one more time." Red's voice held all the authority of a longtime cop. "And quit stalling. Tell me who else is on that boat."

"No one," she said, and I could see the lie in the way her eyes slid away. "I'll give you ten thousand, but I have to have some for myself. I need to disappear. You can understand that, can't you?"

Her face had taken on an almost seductive softness, and her voice had dropped to a whisper. "I know you want to help me. I can tell you aren't like Kenny." Instead of pulling away, she moved right up against Red's chest. "Please help me. I'll make it—"

"Shut up," Red said, stepping away. "The only thing I want from you is the truth, but I don't think you'd recognize it if it walked up and kicked you in the ass, lady."

Kitty Longworth clamped her mouth shut and stared defiantly at Red as he led her to the car and helped her into the backseat. He pulled the keys from his pocket and clicked the locks. As we stepped away, I heard her yell, "He'll kill you!"

"She secure in there?" I asked.

"Absolutely. The doors won't open from the inside unless I release them." He paused. "You buying any of that story?"

"Who knows? We'll sort it out later. Let's go get Erik." Once more I turned toward the boats, and once again Red held me back.

"I'm going to call for backup."

I stared at his face, growing more distinct as the sky light-ened with approaching dawn. "You're kidding, right? You want to sit here until your boys show up? Kitty was lying. You know Erik's on that boat. We have to move."

"Bay, wait! You can't—"

I wrenched his hand away. "*You* can't. But I'm not a cop."

I jerked out of his reach and dashed toward the dock.

I was surprised when he didn't start after me. I skidded on the slick boards as I tried to check my momentum. A few yards from the *Prime Rate,* I dropped into a crouch, crab-walking my way toward the stern. I had just eased the Seecamp out of my pocket when I sensed movement on my right. Before I could turn, something snaked out and clamped itself around my wrist and a hand covered my mouth. In a matter of seconds, I found myself sprawled on my back in the thick row of underbrush that separated the marina from the road, looking up into the small, but lethal muzzle of my own pistol.

THIRTY-FIVE

"BAY!"

I'd closed my eyes in anticipation of the *pop* of the Seecamp, but the sharp whisper of my name snapped them open. The gun lowered, and suddenly Ben Wyler was leaning over me.

"God! I had no idea it was you sneaking around out there. What in hell are you doing?"

I stared at the white blur of his face against the backdrop of the thick vegetation. When he held out a hand, I took it and let him haul me to my feet.

"I could ask you the same thing," I said, my voice cracking despite my best efforts. I dusted the pine needles off my pants. "You're pretty quick for an old guy."

A soft rustle announced Red's arrival, and I stepped in front of my partner.

"It's Ben," I said, holding out a hand against the pistol my brother-in-law had pointed straight out in front of him.

Red dropped his arm to his side and worked his way in beside us.

"What in bloody hell are you doing here, Wyler?"

"Sorry, Sergeant, didn't know it was you. Didn't recognize the car when you pulled in, and it was too dark to make out faces." Ben spoke in his usual rapid-fire cadence in the thick whisper we'd all adopted without conscious thought. "I just saw one of them go over the side."

"Kitty Longworth," I said.

"I wanted to follow her, but I figured I'd better stay here and keep an eye on the other three."

I jumped on his last word. "Three? Is it Erik?"

"I think so," Ben said. "I didn't actually see him onboard, but there's definitely another man. Voices. They been arguing off and on since I got here a few minutes ago." He leaned toward Red. "The other one get away?"

My brother-in-law shook his head. "Cuffed in the backseat of the unmarked. She was trying to make a run with the money."

"Figured that was what she had in the gym bag."

"We need to quit talking and go get Erik." I held out my hand, and Ben reluctantly returned the Seecamp, butt first.

"That little peashooter wouldn't stop a gnat. Besides, you're not going anywhere near that boat. What's the plan, Sergeant?"

"Backup's on the way. We just have to sit tight."

I gasped at the muffled report of a gunshot, and Ben pushed me to the ground.

"What the hell?" Red said, crouching beside me. "Did that come from the boat?"

A moment later, Sally Longworth stumbled out of the *Prime Rate*'s cabin, pale hair tumbled over her shoulders as she wove her way to the rail. She moved like a drunk, her hands clutched to her chest.

"What's she doing?" I whispered, and Red held up a hand to silence me.

"Stay here," he said, pulling the gun from behind his back and bringing it up in one fluid motion. "You, too, Wyler."

Before he could move, the woman suddenly dropped, crumpling onto the deck.

Red thrashed through the underbrush and raced down the dock, vaulting the boat rail in one swift movement. We heard the *thud* as he landed, saw the impact rock the trim craft on its mooring lines. The sound galvanized both of us at the same moment, and I sprinted after Ben as he ran toward the boat.

"Stay back," Red called softly as we approached. He turned away, gripping his pistol with both hands.

"Wait!" I cried in a hoarse whisper, but he ignored me and moved purposefully toward the cabin, Ben right behind.

"Get out of here! Now!" Wyler growled over his shoulder.

The two men gestured at each other, Red indicating he'd take the inside. Ben nodded and crept toward the bow. In a moment they'd both disappeared from view.

THE WOMAN LAY IN a heap, blood seeping onto the boards from a raw, jagged wound just below her right shoulder. The left side of her face looked as if someone had hit her with a baseball bat, the skin broken and purpling. I pulled off my shirt and pressed it against the pulsing hole in Sally Longworth's chest. I knelt beside her, my hands trembling as I tried desperately to stanch the flow. I'd seen more blood in the past few hours than I ever wanted to encounter the rest of my life. In the growing pink of the encroaching dawn, I stared straight ahead at the cabin door, straining for any sound. When it came, the reverberation of the gunshot seemed to fill my head.

Instinctively, I covered Sally's body with my own.

The shouts erupted from all directions. I thought I heard Red yell, "Police! Drop your weapon!" and Wyler shouting, "Put it down! Put it down!"

Another report shattered the night, and suddenly there was Erik, stumbling up out of the cabin right in front of me, rivulets of blood running down the left side of his face.

"Down! Down! Down!" Ben screamed, and suddenly he appeared out of the darkness.

He threw himself at Erik, and they crashed to the deck. I heard the crack as a bullet ricocheted off the metal railing a split second before the final shot ended in a high-pitched scream and the splash of something big hitting the water.

I opened my eyes to a red haze.

It took me a moment to realize my face was covered with splattered blood.

Then Red was beside me, calling my name. His voice seemed to come from very far away.

"Bay! Oh, God, oh, God!"

I felt his hands on my cheeks, my neck.

"Where are you hit?"

I pushed him away. "I'm okay, I'm okay."

His body seemed to deflate as the tension and fear drained

out of him. Roughly, he helped me to my feet and pulled me into his arms. "Thank you, thank you," he murmured over and over before I forced myself free of his embrace. I stumbled over something, and Red grabbed my shoulders.

Ben and Erik lay sprawled on the deck, their legs entwined, blood everywhere. I heard a low moan, and Red and I immediately knelt beside the tangled bodies.

"Erik! No!" I screamed as Red lifted Ben and rolled him onto his back.

In the soft light of the pink dawn sky, I saw the gaping hole in Wyler's left side.

"Bay?" Erik lifted his head and struggled to sit up.

Red reached out a restraining hand. "Lie still. You've got a head wound."

Erik reached his fingers tentatively to his temple. "It's just a graze, I think. There's a furrow there, but that's all. I shoved him and threw off his aim."

"Thank you, God," I whispered and helped him to his feet. I wrapped my arms around my partner and held him against me, the slow, steady beat of his heart the most wonderful sound I'd ever heard.

"Wyler's bad." Red's voice cut through the sound of sirens screaming in the distance.

"What about Kenny? Did you get him?" Erik asked. He'd wiped the worst of the blood from his face with his shirttail, and his wound oozed only a little.

"In the water," Red replied, the steel of the cop back in his voice. "But he's not going anywhere. I took him dead in the heart."

The squeal of brakes and flying gravel reached us, and the pulse of flashing blue lights reflected off the windows of the restaurant.

"Make sure they got ambulances on the way." He pulled off his shirt and stuffed it into Ben's side. "Go!" he yelled at me a second before I scrambled over the rail and raced toward the parking lot.

THIRTY-SIX

I HATE HOSPITALS. No matter what kind of disinfectants or cleaners they use, there's always that same, faint stink of sickness and death floating just beneath the surface.

Erik and I hunched in molded plastic chairs and watched morning creep across the sky through the double glass entry doors of the emergency room. The stark white of the bandage contrasted sharply with the pink of his scalp where they'd shaved part of his head before stitching him up. Somewhere behind us, Red huddled with the local sheriff around Sally Longworth's bed. Kitty had been whisked away in a cruiser. According to Red, she was still trying to explain away her part in what had gone down on that blood-splattered boat in the dark hours before dawn. And in a deadly marsh near Camp St. Mary's.

Ben had been in surgery for hours.

"You want anything?" Erik's voiced echoed slightly in the deserted room.

"About three days of uninterrupted sleep," I said, and he smiled.

"I'll bring you a Coke." He rose and fumbled in his pocket for change before approaching the row of vending machines.

We ate peanut butter crackers and sipped sodas while a single black woman in a pink flowered smock hummed to herself behind the sliding glass of the information window.

"I'm going to check in with Stephanie again," I said, tossing my empty can into a plastic wastebasket on my way to the double doors.

Outside, the air hung heavy with humidity, the temperature

already on its climb toward triple digits. I sat down on the low brick wall that bordered the entrance. As I scrabbled for the phone in my purse, my fingers brushed one of the red pouches nestled in the bottom. I should have given one to Ben. Maybe Belle Crowder could…I shook off that ridiculous thought and hit the Redial button.

I'd called Stephanie from the Camaro as we followed the sheriff's car to the county hospital a few miles from the marina. I'd lied about the severity of Ben's injury, downplaying it to the distraught young woman. She had a three-hour drive ahead of her, and she needed to concentrate on arriving in one piece. We'd spoken periodically, and she seemed to be holding up. For now.

Stephanie sounded beyond tired. "Bay. Hi."

"Hey, kiddo. How're you doing?"

"Hanging in," she said. "How's Dad? What are they telling you?"

"Not much. You know how hospitals are. Since we're not relatives, they haven't been very forthcoming. Where are you?"

"Just getting off the interstate. I'm maybe a half hour away."

"You have the directions?"

"I'll find it. Why won't they let you see him?"

I didn't know how much longer I could keep up this charade. I knew in my heart the surgery was taking way too long. "They probably will soon. Besides, you'll be here shortly."

"Call me if you hear anything."

"I will. You just drive safely. I'll see you in a few minutes."

I sat staring at nothing for a long time after I disconnected. Ben would pull through. He was too tough, too ornery not to. The thought made my lips twitch a little, but the half-formed smile vanished as the emergency room doors *whooshed* open, and Erik trailed Red outside.

"Where's Stephanie?" my partner asked.

"Almost here."

My brother-in-law slumped down beside me. We'd all had to borrow shirts from the EMTs, and the material on Red's strained across his chest. He reached for my hand, and I let him take it. "You doing okay?"

I squeezed his fingers. "I'll do. What's happening in there?"

"We're not going to get anything more out of Sally for a while. They thought they had her stabilized, and we were able to talk to her a little. But then she started having trouble breathing, and they threw us out. Her lung collapsed. They're going back in. Doctor told the sheriff he's pretty sure she'll pull through, but she's going to be out of it for the next day or so."

"What about Ben?"

"Still in surgery."

I slumped over, my elbows on my knees, and worked my head around on my neck, trying to ease some of the kinks. I didn't know how I could possibly face Stephanie Wyler if something happened to her father. What would I say? I drew in a long shuddering breath.

Red let go of my hand and began to work the knotted muscles in my shoulders. I had to restrain myself from groaning with pleasure.

"You give your statement yet?" he asked Erik, and my partner nodded.

"I've heard bits and pieces, but not the whole story. Mind going over it again?"

"No, I guess not." Erik picked at the adhesive tape holding the gauze pad on his scalp and turned toward me. "Remember I called you from the restaurant when Sally landed here? And she was talking to someone on the phone?"

I nodded.

"Must have been to her sister, because a couple of minutes later I saw this blond woman come walking up the dock. I figured it must be Kitty because the two of them looked alike. The tattooed guy was with her, had hold of her arm like he was afraid she'd bolt. They all sat down outside and ordered dinner. I got a table close by, tried to eavesdrop, but I couldn't hear much of anything. They sat there until almost dark." He sighed. "I didn't know what to think. It seemed like a friendly enough discussion, but I realize now he must have had the gun in his pocket all along. There's no way they would have gone back to the boat with him otherwise."

Red continued to knead my shoulders, easing off on the left side where he knew the tender scar tissue crisscrossed my back. I let my mind wander to Ben and the gaping hole in his side. I'd already heard Erik's story of how he'd followed them back to the boat then set up to keep watch in the same belt of trees where Ben had surprised me a few hours later, how Briggs had sneaked back out sometime after midnight and moved Sally's car into the bushes.

"I didn't like the look of that," I heard Erik say, "so I thought that would be a good time to see if the women were all right. I also didn't like that he'd left them there alone. I thought maybe he might have done something to them."

Red nodded.

Erik had sneaked on board, finally locating the cabin, and had been about to call out when something had smashed into his head.

"Next thing I knew, I woke up inside with the guy's gun pointing at me."

I'd already expressed my opinion about the stupidity of his trying to rescue the Longworth sisters on his own. Especially unarmed. I suppressed a shudder at how differently things might have turned out if I hadn't insisted on racing to Florida in the middle of the night…if Ben hadn't been able to trace Kenny's call to Stephanie….

"They were all arguing," Erik continued. "About the money and who was entitled to what. Sally kept saying he could keep it all, just let them go, but Kitty wasn't having any part of that. I kept sort of drifting in and out, because of getting hit on the head, so I didn't catch a lot of it. Then all of a sudden I came to, and Kitty was gone. Sally was like a crazy woman, hanging on to his legs so he couldn't go after Kitty. I tried to help, but I was pretty useless."

"Don't beat yourself up about that," Red interrupted. "Getting smacked in the head with a gun butt can definitely slow you down."

"Somehow I managed to get in his way enough that Sally had a chance to run, too. But then she got to the top of the steps, and he knocked me down and…he just shot her. I finally punched him in the side of the head and took off after her, but he nicked me, too." He let out a long, trembling breath. "And then you guys showed up."

I pushed away the awful possibilities of what could have gone wrong. We sat in silence for a long time before Red's voice cut through the still morning air. "We got a little bit out of Sally before they took her back into the operating room. Her story pretty much jibes with Erik's about what happened on the boat. As for the rest of it, all she knows is what Kitty told her, which could be a complete crock. But it sounds like it went down pretty close to the way you figured it, Bay. Kitty told Tracy she had gambling debts she couldn't pay, and the guy was threatening to kill her. She finally convinced her old friend to bail her out."

"And how much of that is true?"

"Who knows at this point? She took Kenny along for protection in case the guys who were after her showed up. So she says."

"So what went wrong?" Erik asked. "How did Tracy end up dead?"

"Briggs couldn't resist getting in on the action. When she saw him, Tracy freaked. She knew as well as anyone the kid was trouble. She tried to take back the money, and Briggs shot her. He made Kitty help him push the Mercedes into the river. He figured it would sink and never be found."

"He killed Tracy just like that?" Erik asked. "For no real reason?"

"In the world according to Kitty Longworth. Via her sister. Keep in mind this is thirdhand information. Kitty claimed Briggs told her she was now an accessory to murder, and they needed to hole up for a few days. Briggs Senior keeps his boat on Skull Creek, so they came back to the island and hid out there."

"Why on earth didn't they try to put some distance behind them?" I asked.

"I have no idea," Red replied, "but when the body turned up

on Sunday, they made a run for it. They gassed up on Amelia Monday morning, and Kitty used the credit card. She told Sally she was hoping someone would notice, but I'm not so sure."

I spoke to Erik. "Remember the man at the Amelia Island marina? He didn't say anything about Kitty's being nervous or looking scared when she handed over Tracy Dumars' stolen credit card. And Kenny was apparently on the phone inside the cabin. She could have run or passed a message or done a lot of things if she was really trying to get away."

"You're right," my partner said. "I'm not totally buying that." He turned back to Red. "So how did they end up here? We're only about twenty miles from that other marina. Why didn't they head out to the Bahamas or somewhere they couldn't be found?"

"Something went wrong with the engine," Red told him. "They pulled in here to get it fixed and had to wait for parts. That's when Kenny decided maybe they wouldn't pay off the gambling debt after all, just keep the whole hundred grand for themselves."

"And Kitty began to wonder if he'd eventually decide he didn't need to split it with anyone?"

Red smiled at me. "Exactly. She called Sally to come bail her out, but Kenny caught her with the phone. He let the sister come ahead, figuring he'd clean up all the loose ends at one time. Sally says she thinks he intended to take the boat out and drop them both over the side."

"This guy was a real piece of work, wasn't he?" I asked no one in particular.

I thought of Ken Briggs, the handsome, easygoing banker in the rimless glasses, and I wondered what he and his poor wife had done to create such a monster. Or maybe that wasn't fair. Maybe they'd done everything exactly right, and their son had turned out to be a murderer all on his own.

Red patted my hand. "Remember how quick Kitty was to name Briggs as the shooter? Since Tracy gave her the money of her own free will, Kitty wouldn't have been culpable for a damn thing except bad judgment. Now, with Briggs dead, she just might make a jury buy her little kidnap story." Red shook his head in amazement.

"Especially if Sally backs her up," I said. "She could actually walk."

The doors slid open, and the two officers who had accompanied us to the hospital stepped out into the sunlight.

Red stood. "Captain? Any word on the woman?"

The older man shook his head. "They're still working on her. You hear anything about your friend?" he said to me.

"No. They won't talk to me. His daughter's on her way."

"Guy's a former cop, I hear," he said.

"Yes. And one of my partners." I glanced at Erik and the white gauze taped to his head. Simpson & Tanner had taken a lot of blows and survived. Ben would, too, I told myself.

"Shame. Hope it turns out okay." He turned to Red. "We're gonna have to keep your weapon, Sergeant. Looks like a perfectly justifiable shoot, especially after hearing that woman's story, but you know the procedure."

"I understand." Red ran a hand through his hair. "You gonna want us to stick around for a while?"

"Sheriff says y'all can head back up north whenever you're ready. Professional courtesy. He figures you'll be willin' to come back down when we need you."

A cruiser rolled up in a swirl of dead pine needles and dust, and the captain turned to pull open the passenger door.

"You folks drive careful now, hear?" He held out his hand, and Red stepped over to grasp it. "Thanks for your help, Tanner. You tell your boss mine sends his regards."

"I'll do that, sir. Thanks."

The three of us stood watching the patrol car roll out of the lot. I'd just taken a couple of steps toward the emergency room doors when a squeal of brakes made me turn. A small Honda bucked to a halt, and the driver's door flew open.

"Bay!" Stephanie Wyler shrieked, and a moment later she collapsed into my arms.

THIRTY-SEVEN

At a little after eleven I walked into the surgical waiting room to find it empty. I gripped the handle of my bag, the bottom dropping out of my stomach.

"It doesn't mean anything," I said aloud. I walked toward the nurse's station, but no one seemed to be around.

I'd taken a break from the tiny area with its two straight-backed chairs, lumpy sofa, and months-old magazines. Erik and I had been alternating, each of us taking a turn sitting with Stephanie while she paced back and forth on the worn carpet. An hour before, they'd brought Ben down from surgery, and she'd been able to spend a few minutes with him. That's how it would go, the nurse told us, just a brief moment every hour or so until he stabilized.

The rural hospital had a surprisingly good trauma staff, or so their brochure claimed. I'd been reduced to reading it thoroughly to help pass the time. Stephanie didn't want to talk, and I was inclined to hold on to the silence as well. There'd been way too much noise and excitement in my life over the past twenty-four hours. Once in a while I let my hand slip into my bag and finger the red pouches Belle Crowder had devised to keep me safe. I willed their power over to Ben and wished, like Lavinia, I believed in prayer. Instead, I recited the Twenty-third Psalm over and over in my head. And hoped.

I'd been fighting sleep, stepping outside whenever Erik took over, attempting to clear my mind with doses of fresh air. I had actually nodded off when he'd come down to tell me Stephanie had gone in for one of her hourly visits. I'd dragged myself into the narrow elevator and pinched myself alert on the short ride to the third floor.

I sat down then and waited for her to come back, but the minutes ticked away. I turned as the elevator doors slid open, and Red stepped out.

"How's it going?" he asked, and I shrugged.

"I think Stephanie's in with him now. She's been gone longer than usual, so maybe that's a good sign. I don't know."

"Let me see what I can find out."

I walked behind him to the water fountain and splashed cold water over my face. I watched my brother-in-law lean his elbows on the counter and speak quietly with a woman in baggy surgical scrubs who'd just stepped out of Ben's room. At one point he pulled his wallet from his hip pocket, presumably to flash his ID. He glanced once at me, then turned his back. I stood frozen in place, my hands gripping the fountain like a lifeline. I saw Red nod, and I read it on his face the moment he turned around. I felt my knees buckling.

And then he was there, his arm around my shoulders, his body taking my full weight as I sagged against him. "Sit down." He eased me onto the hard chair, and suddenly I found my head hanging down between my knees. "Breathe. I'm not going to let you pass out. Come on, now. In and out. That's it."

I felt my brain stop swirling, and I fought against his hand on the back of my neck. I dragged in air through my mouth.

"When?" I asked, and Red eased back, his arm still bracing my shoulders.

"About fifteen minutes ago. The nurse said even though he came through the surgery, they didn't give him more than a fifty-fifty chance. Too much damage. The bullet severed an artery near his heart. Still, there was some hope. But they apparently missed a clot. She said it broke loose. Nothing they could do." When I didn't speak, he said, "I'm so sorry, Bay. It was quick, though, if that's any consolation. He never regained consciousness."

Ben Wyler had been a major irritant in my life for more than a year. He was caustic, argumentative, and sometimes downright scary. More often than not we'd be sniping at each other inside of ten minutes in each other's presence. Nonetheless, silent or not, he'd been my partner. The shock of his death would linger for a long time.

Red stroked my hair, and we sat in silence. I had no words— or tears. I felt sure they'd come later.

"Where's Stephanie?" I asked, suddenly coming out of my daze long enough to realize there was someone who would mourn Ben's passing far more deeply than I.

At the same moment, she appeared in the doorway of the waiting room, her face pinched and blotchy, her eyes nearly swollen shut. I started to rise when, with a cry of anguish that nearly broke my heart, Stephanie Wyler once again flung herself into my arms.

ULTIMATELY, STEPHANIE PROVED to be every bit as tough as her father had been. Her sister Melissa arrived by taxi from the Jacksonville airport a few minutes later. Stephanie had called both her sister and her mother before tearing south to be with Ben.

Melissa burst into the waiting room, and the two girls stood locked in a tearful embrace after Stephanie delivered the terrible news. Their mother, insistent on supporting her girls, would be arriving from Arizona in a few hours. Red and I offered our services in any capacity they might need but were gently rebuffed. They would wait for Ben's ex-wife, and the three of them would make arrangements to have his body transported back to Hilton Head.

Red and I walked out the hospital doors into brilliant sunshine, and he slipped an arm around my shoulders. Erik was nowhere in sight.

"Sit down and catch your breath. I'm going to get us something to drink."

"No!" I grabbed his hand. "We have to find Erik. I don't want him to hear it from somebody else."

"Don't worry. I'll take care of it."

His tender smile seemed to bathe me in a warm glow. For

the first time since my husband's murder, I looked into Red's eyes and didn't see his brother staring back.

The realization frightened me, and I jerked away just as Erik came through the door.

"What's going on? How's Ben?"

Red started to speak, but I cut him off. Painful as it was, this was my job. I had to swallow hard before I could force out the words. "He…he didn't make it."

I waited for his response, which was a long time in coming. "Stephanie?"

"She's doing okay. Her sister just got here, and her mother's on the way. She'll have plenty of support."

"I…I don't know quite what to say." He dropped down onto the low wall next to me. "You know I didn't like him. I mean, because of the way he always treated us, like we were idiots or something. But…"

"I know. He drove me crazy, too, sometimes. But he was a good cop. A good detective."

"He saved my life back there, didn't he? If he hadn't pushed me down—"

"He might have," Red said and put a hand on Erik's shoulder. "There were a lot of bullets flying. You can't blame yourself in any way for this."

"But if I hadn't gone playing hero and gotten myself—"

"Stop it," I said. "Don't ever think that. Ben was there because he wanted to be. He was trying to protect Stephanie first of all. But he would have done it for any of us. He saved the Judge and me, too, last summer. He may have been a major pain in the butt sometimes, but he had a good heart. He loved his daughters, and he almost always tried to do the right thing."

"A man could have a worse epitaph," Red murmured, and I found myself giving up the fight against the tears.

ERIK INSISTED he wanted to drive home alone, so I climbed into the Camaro with Red, and we headed north. We lost him somewhere around Brunswick, and I hoped he'd be all right.

"Don't worry," my brother-in-law said when I voiced my concern. "He has a right to his privacy. It's going to take some time for him to get over feeling guilty." He smiled at me. "We'll help him."

I settled into the seat and tried to close my eyes, but the horrific scene on the boat kept playing over and over in my head. I must have dozed a little, because when I came to we were exiting 95. I glanced at Red when he picked up his cell phone.

"Almost there. I want to check in with Lisa," he said, "see how things are going with the Crowder thing."

I swallowed down my own guilt. I hadn't thought about the dead child and her murderous parents in hours.

I listened to his noncommittal grunts until he clicked off and redialed. "What?" I asked.

"I want to see how Malik's doing, then I'll fill you in."

The deputy was in stable condition Red reported a few minutes later. They'd repaired his shattered leg and were hopeful he'd regain full function. He'd have a lot of rehab to get through first, though, and the consensus was that his career in the sheriff's department was over.

"Will he get any kind of compensation?" I asked.

"We were out of uniform," Red replied, "and we were working the case unofficially. I don't think anybody'll try to fight it, but I'll make sure he gets his disability if I have to petition the state legislature myself."

"I'll be right there with you," I said and earned myself a tender smile. "What about the other?"

"Nothing's popped on Deshawn Crowder. Can't find him or his van. The father's missing, too."

I tried to recall what Harry had said about his family, clawing through the thick fog that clouded my brain. "I think there was a daughter, too. Or at least another sibling. What about the wife?"

"Lisa can't find any of them. It's as if the whole bunch just disappeared off the face of the earth."

"What about Elizabeth Marsh? Is she in Scranton with her mother?"

He shook his head. "No sign of the girl, at least not yet. The mother claims she's out of town visiting relatives with the new baby."

"So she's still sticking to that story." I thought a moment. "Did they check out the compound at Sanctuary?"

"For what?"

"For all these missing people. Every one of them has some connection to the place."

"We can't do that. Private property, and we've got no probable cause."

"So you're saying no one believes I saw Deshawn's van run down Deputy Graves? Do they think I hallucinated it?"

The tenderness I'd seen in his eyes just moments before faded as if I'd only imagined it. "Your statement is being given due consideration. But without something tangible—"

"Just forget it. I don't need to hear the excuses," I snapped and turned my back on him.

A few minutes later we swung into Port Royal Plantation. Red flashed his badge at the guard gate and glided through. He pulled into my driveway with a squeal of the tires.

"I need to get back to the station," he said, his voice tight with anger. "Get some sleep."

I climbed out of the Camaro, then leaned back in. "Find the damn baby-killers," I flung at him before slamming the door shut with all the force I could muster.

He peeled out and roared off down the road, leaving me to stare after him, ashamed and hurt and incredibly sad. For Stephanie and her sister. For Ben and Baby Jane Doe. And for myself...

I STRETCHED AND ROLLED onto my side, one eye forced open to study the digital clock on my bedside table. In the dim light and my own sleep-drugged brain, I couldn't decide if it was eight thirty Friday night or Saturday morning. I tossed off the duvet and stumbled to the bathroom. Regardless of what day it was, I desperately needed a shower.

The hot spray partially restored my ability to string words together into some semblance of coherent thought. Wrapped in my old terry cloth robe, I shook out my damp hair and threw back the bedroom drapes to find evening descending over the sea oats barely visible across the top of the dunes. Only the white, foaming edges of the waves could be seen as they curled gently onto the sand.

I sighed and laid my forehead against the cool glass of the window.

I'd collapsed onto the bed a few hours before, so numb I'd expected to drop instantly into healing sleep. Instead, my mind had refused to slow down, hopping madly from one image to another: the ragged hole in Sally Longworth's chest; the gruesome corpse of Kenny Briggs when they'd fished it out of the water; the pain on Stephanie Wyler's face as she burst into the waiting room. I thought about all the times her father and I had crossed swords, the wounding words, then his sardonic smile making it all seem like some inside joke.

I tossed and thrashed in the wide bed I'd once shared with Rob—and Alain Darnay—and tried to picture a world without Ben Wyler's caustic wit and wry humor in it. He'd had a thing for me, and he never made any secret of it. And he had been quicker to criticize than compliment. But I always felt that underneath he had a grudging respect for my tenacity and my integrity, much as he ridiculed them.

I would miss him.

The real tears came then, along with great, gulping sobs that shook the bed and made me feel as if I might choke on the pain. And sometime in the middle of the storm of emotion and regret, I had finally slept....

In the kitchen I glanced at the answering machine frantically blinking. As I had earlier, I ignored it. I set the kettle on the stove, then walked down into the great room and slid open the French doors. The humid night air rushed in as if I'd created a vacuum, but I could hear the soft *shushing* of the ocean. That sibilant sound had always been a source of comfort to me.

Of its own accord my mind wandered back to the hell of the past two days, to Red's emotional speech in the dark of the car as we raced south…to all the horrors the last forty-eight hours had spawned. So much pain and misery. And my reaction— learned at my mother's knee—was to lash out, to use sharp words and sarcasm to cover my inability to deal with all those other, trickier emotions, like hurt and loss. And love.

And poor Red so often stood directly in the path of my anger.

The whistle of the teakettle sounded like a siren in the heavy stillness of my empty house.

"Sometimes you can be such a complete jerk," I told myself as I went automatically about the task of making tea. I carried my cup, a spoon, and a jar of peanut butter to the table in the breakfast alcove where I sat gazing out the window into the dark. The ringing barely registered until the machine picked up, and the Judge's outraged baritone thundered into the kitchen.

"Lydia Baynard Simpson Tanner! This is your father. Pick up the goddamned phone this instant, do you hear me, girl? You have ten seconds before I hang up and send the entire—"

I crossed the room in three strides and snatched up the receiver. "What?"

"I knew you were there! Why the hell aren't you answering your phone? Do you have any idea how worried Vinnie and I have been about you? I've left a dozen messages—"

I tried to muster my usual tolerance for my father's bad temper and failed. "Hey! I don't need this crap from you right now, okay? Up until a little while ago, I'd had about fifteen minutes' sleep in thirty-six hours. I've watched a deputy get run over by a truck, plugged a bullet wound with my shirt, and Ben's dead! For once in your life, think about somebody's feelings besides your own!"

My hand quivered with the overpowering desire to slam the phone against the wall, to pound it into tiny pieces of wire and plastic. Instead I braced my hands on the desktop, drew a long, shuddering breath, and brought the receiver back to my ear.

"We...I...I just needed to know you were safe." The long pause echoed with our sad history, all the words that should have been said and weren't. And those that should never have been spoken at all. "I'm sorry, sweetheart," my father whispered. "I'm sorry about Ben."

I let myself down onto the wooden chair next to the desk. "I know, Daddy. I shouldn't have—"

"It's okay, sweetheart. It's been a long couple of days for all of us. You get some sleep, and we'll talk tomorrow."

I knew he couldn't see me nod, but it was all I could manage. As I reached to lay the receiver back into its cradle, I heard him say, "I love you, princess."

I SHUFFLED BACK to the table, poured fresh tea over the dregs in the bottom of my cup, and tried to decide what to do next. A million questions rattled around in my fuzzy brain, about the Longworth sisters, Deshawn Crowder and Elizabeth Marsh. And Ben...

I wondered what would happen to the agency now that he was gone. Would our license still be valid? We'd just begun to make a reputation for ourselves. Over time, it might actually turn into a viable, moneymaking enterprise, especially if I could foster the connection with Alexandra Finch. I screwed the lid on the peanut butter jar and asked myself if I still had the stomach for it. It had seemed such a lark in the beginning, the thrill of the hunt, the rearranging of the puzzle pieces until they fell into place. I'd thought of it more as an intellectual exercise, even though the past year had proved how dangerous it could be as well. And how would Erik feel about it? He'd almost died out there. Maybe, like me, he'd grown weary...and afraid.

I lifted my head at the sound of the phone. "Please, God, no more tonight," I murmured as I sat, unmoving. Whoever it was hung up without leaving a message.

I carried my cup to the sink, rinsed it, and put it and the spoon in the dishwasher. With a sigh, I sat down at the desk, plucked a pen and pad from the narrow drawer, and pressed Play on the answering machine.

As usual, the Judge had exaggerated for effect. Only three of the messages were from him, although each had escalated in tone. Two more were junk. Red simply asked me to call him, on his cell, whenever I woke up. Nothing urgent, he said, and the sound of his voice, soft and no longer angry, did a lot to ease the knot of tension in my chest. He just wanted to know how I was doing, he said, and to tell me they hadn't given up on the Crowder case.

My mind shifted immediately to the dead child, and it took a supreme act of will to push her image out of my consciousness. "'Sufficient unto the day is the evil thereof,'" I said into the silent kitchen. "Matthew 6:34."

None of it was my problem anymore. I'd done what I could, taken all my mind and body could stand. It was up to someone else now.

The last message was another hang-up.

I wandered down into the great room and curled up on the end of the sofa. I should call Red back, I told myself, make things right between us again. My head swiveled toward the open French doors. The wind had picked up, rattling the leaves of the palmettos and sending fallen pine needles skittering across the deck. Out over the water, flickers of lightning zigzagged across the horizon.

I had just heaved myself off the cushions, determined to leave all decisions until tomorrow and drag myself back to bed, when the unmistakable squeak of the screen sliding in its channel made me spin back toward the doors. A man stood there, his dark hair and mottled skin illuminated in a sudden flash of lightning, before he stepped tentatively into the room.

THIRTY-EIGHT

MAYBE IT WAS THE WAY he held out his hands, palms up, as if in supplication, that choked off the scream rising in my throat.

"Please," he said, "don't be afraid, Bay. I don't mean you any harm."

"What do you want? Get the hell out of my house!"

He didn't make any move to close the gap between us. "I just want to talk. To explain."

I risked a darting glance over my shoulder, judging the distance between me and the panic button on the alarm pad next to the front door. I had no idea how quick he might be, but the long trailing hem of my old bathrobe would slow me down. I took a tentative step backward, and he sensed my intention.

"Wait! I'm not going to hurt you. Just give me five minutes. Please! I'll stay right here. You can call the sheriff when I've finished. I won't run. I promise." A booming clap of thunder nearly drowned out the next word, although there was no mistaking the anguish in his voice. "Please!"

In the dim light drifting down from the kitchen, I could see pain etched across Harry Crowder's face. Not from any physical hurt, I thought, but from a place deep inside, some gut-wrenching misery that was tearing him apart. I felt some of the tension ease from my shoulders, but I stayed balanced on the balls of my bare feet, ready for flight or fight, whichever way it went.

"You're here about Deshawn," I said, and he nodded.

"And that poor dead baby." I spat the words at him and felt some small satisfaction when he flinched.

"Deshawn had nothing to do with that. It was I. I killed my grandchild."

It was the last thing I expected to hear. My knees trembled as if they might give way.

"May I sit down?" the professor asked, and I stared at him for a moment before pointing to the wing chair closest to the fireplace.

Like me, Harry seemed to be having a difficult time holding himself upright. His clothes were damp and wrinkled, as if he'd slept in them, and his usually neat dark hair stood out in tufts. He nodded and collapsed into the chair.

A few fat drops of rain splattered against the deck, and a long, rumbling growl of thunder rolled across the dunes. I moved around the opposite side of the coffee table and slid the French doors closed. I perched on the end of the sofa and flipped on a lamp. Harry squinted in the sudden glare, his head propped up on one hand as if his neck was too weak to bear the burden.

"Why?" I said into the sound of rain pounding against the doors. "How could you do such a monstrous thing? You're an educated man, a pillar—"

"I did it for my son. For Deshawn. You have no children, Bay. How can you possibly understand?"

"You're right. I'll never understand murder no matter how much you try to justify it."

"The child was ill," Harry said, his voice stronger now that he'd gotten the worst admission out of the way. "Belle sensed it right from the start."

"She delivered the baby?"

"Yes. Deshawn lied to us, his mother and me. He said the Marsh girl was having an abortion. We didn't know she was Catholic until it was too late. Aunt Belle kept their secret right up until the last."

"Elizabeth stayed out at the compound?" I asked, and Harry nodded.

"They thought we'd come around once the child was born." His laugh held nothing but derision. "They actually believed I'd let my son throw his life away on some…some oversexed teenager and her bastard."

I had no idea whether Elizabeth Marsh deserved that label or not, but the baby certainly didn't. "They could have married," I said sharply, "if legitimacy is that damned important to you."

"Don't be ridiculous! Deshawn is not getting married at eighteen. My son has a brilliant career ahead of him, and I won't have his life ruined before it even begins."

The small amount of sympathy I'd felt for Harry Crowder's predicament had evaporated in the cool air of my living room.

"So you killed your own granddaughter so your son could get into a good college?"

His smug expression wilted. "No! Please! That's not why I did it. It was Belle. She said the child had a defect, something wrong with its heart. She'd seen it in a vision. She said it would never be right, never grow up properly. It would be a kindness, she said. I did it out of love."

I really wanted to believe him. I wished I could.

"It doesn't really matter why, does it? In the eyes of the law, you committed murder. It will be up to a jury to judge your motives."

"You can speak to them," he said, and suddenly I understood the real reason he'd forced his way into my house. "You're respected, and Sergeant Tanner—"

"I'm not going to plead your case, Professor. They have lawyers for that. Find yourself a good one."

I rose and moved tentatively toward the kitchen, not turning my back completely on the wing chair where the confessed child-killer sat slumped, his elbows resting on his knees. Then a thought struck, and I moved back in front of the sofa.

"What about Deputy Graves? Did you run him down last night?"

I watched his face, and the surprise registered there seemed completely genuine.

"What are you talking about?"

"Malik Graves. He and Sergeant Tanner and I were at the compound last night. Someone came tearing up the road and struck the deputy. With Deshawn's van."

"That's impossible! I—"

"You what? Why is it impossible?"

"Because Deshawn couldn't—I was—"

I registered the exact moment he made the decision, and the panic fled from his eerie golden eyes.

"Yes. I did it. I mean, it was an accident, but I was driving the van."

"What were you doing out there?"

He took a moment to formulate an answer. "I was visiting my aunt." The man should have written fiction. I could almost see the wheels churning as he put together his story. "We had a disagreement, and I was angry. I wasn't paying attention."

"And Belle will corroborate your story?" I knew he was lying, but if she backed him up...

"Absolutely." The slim line of mustache above his lip quivered slightly, but he didn't look away.

"I see. What time was this?"

We stared across the room at each other while long rumbles of thunder rolled across the ocean.

"Whatever time it needs to be," he said softly.

"I won't let you do this, Harry."

"You have no choice. Let it go, Bay. Someone will be punished. For all of it. Isn't that what the law requires?"

"No. It requires that the *guilty* one be punished. And that's not you. At least not entirely."

"But you're wrong. I'm guilty of so much that I regret. And I won't let my son pay for my sins."

WE WAITED FOR RED and Lisa Pedrovsky in silence over steaming mugs of tea at the round glass table in the kitchen alcove. Neither one of us spoke after I'd made the call. Dr. Henry Crowder seemed to have made peace with his decision, and his eyes roamed over my kitchen and great room without really seeing any of it.

All of my arguments had bounced off the wall of his calm resolution to take responsibility for at least one of his son's crimes. I was absolutely certain he hadn't been driving the van that struck Malik Graves and then sped away. He'd all but admitted as much. And without a witness willing to come forward, there was no one to contradict his story about smothering the baby. He could have done it. I believed he was capable of almost anything to protect Deshawn's future. But how would we ever know for certain?

I listened to the storm move away out over the water and wondered about this bond between parent and child. Ben Wyler had died, in part, trying to protect his daughter from possible disaster. Harry Crowder was willing to admit to infanticide to keep his son from ruining his life.

On the other hand, Belle had tried to do the right thing, even though it meant great harm to those she obviously loved. She had played me almost from the moment my name hit the papers. Somehow she understood I wouldn't be able to resist picking at the skeins of the mystery of the dead child until I'd completely unraveled it. With guile and a great deal of insight into what drove and motivated me, she'd inexorably pointed me toward the truth. Her campaign had been cleverly orchestrated, with dropped hints and oblique clues, using circumstances to lead me exactly where she wanted me to go: straight into the heart of her community and her family.

I needed to hear it from the soft-spoken woman who had warned me that my friends were in trouble and had so accurately read the sorrow and longing in my own heart. I needed her to look me in the eye and tell me why.

Harry jumped when the sweep of headlights played across the ceiling, then settled back in the chair.

"You can still change your mind," I said, but he shook his head.

"Don't interfere, Bay, I beg of you. I was wrong to try and use you to help me mitigate what I've done. Believe me, it's better this way."

"I won't lie for you, Harry. If I can prove you weren't driving that van, I'm not going to cover it up."

"Why not? My life is already destroyed. My family will be humiliated, shunned. Think about what you could do for my son by simply walking away. Think about salvaging one life out of the ruins of all this." His gold-rimmed eyes bored into mine. "Try to imagine how you'd feel if he were your child."

I had no answer for that. A second set of headlights pierced the darkness, and a few moments later the doorbell rang.

A shiver ran through Harry's shoulders, but he held my gaze. With a last look at his determined face, I rose to open the door.

THIRTY-NINE

I RODE WITH RED in the front seat of his cruiser as we followed the patrol car carrying Dr. Henry Crowder off the island. The forty minutes or so it took to reach the Beaufort County Jail complex passed in near silence.

Once inside, my official statement about my conversation with Harry hadn't taken that long. Granted, it was all hearsay, but I'd related the crux of our exchange and signed my name. Whether or not it would ever be used, at least I'd done the right thing. Red wanted me to press charges for breaking and entering just to be certain they'd be able to hold him, but I couldn't bring myself to add to the man's troubles. It would be up to the county solicitor to decide which of the crimes, if any, Harry could be charged with. But if the professor stuck to his story about being responsible for the death of his granddaughter, I doubted anything I'd said would change the eventual outcome.

While I was there, I also gave a full statement about my actions and observations at the marina in Florida. Once it had been typed and attested to, the document would be forwarded to the local sheriff's office down there. All of us would have to go back and testify at some point about the deaths of both Kenny Briggs and Ben Wyler, but that was months or at least weeks down the road. I was surprised to realize that talking it all out had allowed some of the horror of those tragic events to recede.

At the same time I was being sworn, Red had been closeted in another room with his lieutenant, going over the same ground. I assumed they'd compare stories and make sure our accounts of that terrible night on the boat didn't differ on any of the important details. The nice thing about telling the truth is that you never have to worry about getting tripped up.

I said as much to my brother-in-law as we finally trudged out of the complex and climbed into the cruiser. Rain squalls out over the ocean continued to generate occasional flashes of lightning, but stars dotted the sky directly overhead.

"Aristotle said, 'The least initial deviation from the truth is multiplied later a thousandfold.' Harry should keep that in mind."

"Crowder's made his bed. It's out of our hands. And I'm too damned tired to discuss philosophy." Red's sigh echoed my own weariness. "It's been a long day. Let's get you home."

I leaned my head back against the seat, a dozen images flashing through my head: the cold, blue face of the dead child; the look of agony in Harry's eyes; the dim light glinting off Belle Crowder's brown fingers as they gripped my hand.

"Wait," I said, and Red turned to stare at me. "I need to do something first."

"THIS IS NUTS," he muttered as we headed out of Beaufort toward Sanctuary Hill. "*You're* nuts. It's almost damn two o'clock in the morning."

"Could we dispense with your assessment of my mental stability for a moment? How did your statement go? Do you think we gave them enough to get Kitty Longworth?"

"Who knows? The sheriff told me he heard from the guys down in Florida that she's sticking to her story about being kidnapped. Now she's saying it was all Briggs' idea, right from the jump, and she was an unwilling participant."

"That's not the story Sally told."

"I know, but there's no guarantee she'll testify. Kitty is her sister, after all."

I thought about Kitty's mad dash into the night with the gym bag full of cash. "But she left Sally behind when she ran. If we hadn't intercepted her, she would have been long gone without a backward glance. I think Sally will figure that out once she's had a chance to think things through."

"Don't count on it. I've seen families do some crazy things."

Like Belle and Harry Crowder, I thought. *And Deshawn.*

"So nobody's going to get nailed for Tracy Dumars?" I asked.

His head swiveled in my direction. "Briggs is seriously dead. You don't get much more nailed than that."

"I suppose. But don't you want to know why?"

Red flipped on the turn signal as we pulled onto the narrow paved road even though there wasn't another car in sight at that hour of the morning.

"My job isn't about why," he said.

"What does that mean?"

Red slowed as we approached the vicinity of the almost invisible dirt road. "Keep an eye out. It's right around here somewhere."

I leaned forward, squinting into the near total darkness. "There," I said a minute later, and Red swung the cruiser across the road and onto the verge. He left the engine running, the dash vents pouring blessedly cool air against my face.

"Juries generally like to have an understandable motive," he said, "but cops don't really care. Not so long as the evidence is solid. And this isn't going to trial. I mean, not Tracy's murder. They fished the gun out of the water. Caliber matches. It's registered to the dead kid's father."

"What about Ben?"

"Once they get ballistics on the bullet that killed him, that'll come back to Briggs, too. But like I said, there isn't going to be any day in court. I hope his daughters are okay with that."

"You killed the son of a bitch who shot their father. I'm sure they're more than okay with that."

He shrugged and dropped his hand onto the back of my neck. When I didn't pull away, his fingers stroked my skin in lazy circles, kneading gently. I rotated my head as the bunched muscles began to loosen.

"I'll give you about a year and a half to stop that," I said, and he chuckled. Then the import of his words about Tracy Dumars' death sank in. "Won't Kitty be tried as an accessory?

She'll at least do some time for the original scam on Tracy, right?"

"Doubtful. Like I told you before, Tracy supposedly gave up the money willingly. At least in the beginning. They might try to get her on fraud of some kind, but I don't think that'll fly. Best shot is accessory to murder, but with Briggs dead she'll probably skate on that, too."

"That's not fair, Red, and you know it."

"Fair doesn't enter into it. You keep confusing the law with justice. Not always the same thing."

I felt myself relaxing, my eyelids fluttering closed as exhaustion tried to drag me down into oblivion. I shook myself and sat up straighter. "Let's get going before I fall asleep right here."

His hand stroked my hair. "I know you must be wiped out. So am I. Can't we postpone—"

"No!" I lowered my voice. "I'm sorry, but I have to settle this in my own mind. I have to talk to Belle."

He sighed and pushed the door open. "Fine. If you're hell-bent on banging on that old witch's door in the middle of the night, let's get it over with. Maybe I can manage at least an hour's sleep before I have to go back on duty."

I swung the door open and stepped out into the heavy stillness. Red flicked on the flashlight. He took two steps onto the muddy road and stopped dead so that I stumbled into his back.

"What?"

"Quiet. Stand still."

I moved a step back and froze, the night breeze and the brusqueness of his voice raising goose bumps along my arms. "What is it?" I whispered.

"I smell smoke," he said, his head tilted up like a coonhound's sniffing for a scent.

A little gust from the edge of the storms still rumbling out over the ocean riffled the high branches and carried the not unpleasant odor of burning wood in our direction.

"A campfire?" I moved up alongside Red, our shoulders brushing.

"I don't think so," he said a moment before he took off running, the flashlight bobbing ahead of him, its loss plunging me into deep and boundless darkness.

"Wait!" I called, sprinting after the wavering light just as the first flames flickered into view among the trees.

FORTY

THE SNUG LITTLE COTTAGE with its antique plantation furniture
and hoarded treasures was fully engulfed by the time we stag-
gered our way past the compound and into the midst of the
small crowd. A few people turned as we approached, then
swung their gazes back to the crackling fire as if the sudden appearance of two white people—one of them in uniform—was
a usual occurrence in the middle of the night.

"Do you have hoses? Water?" Red gasped out. He was bent
over, hands on knees, trying to draw sufficient air into his lungs
after our sprint down the treacherous path through the heavy,
humid air now acrid with smoke.

"We can organize a bucket brigade." I spoke to a towering old
black man on my right who stood leaning on the handle of a
shovel. "We'll help. Where's the water supply? Do you have a
hydrant?" I stared up into his calm, impassive face. "We can still
save it."

His regal head lowered enough so that he could look me in
the eye. In a deep, sonorous voice that reminded me of the
Judge's, he said, "Please don't concern yourself."

Red was in heated conversation with a woman dressed in tra-
ditional African garb. The turban wound tightly around her
head glittered as the light of the flames caught its golden
threads. I could see him waving his arms as he spoke, but he
didn't seem to be having any better luck than I was.

"What's the matter with all of you? Are you just going to
stand here and let Belle's home burn to the ground?" Speaking
her name caused more than a few heads to swivel in my direction, but no one else spoke. Then another horrifying thought

streaked across my mind. "She's not in there, is she?" I scanned
the loose semicircle formed at the end of the quaint stone path.
"Belle!" I shouted. "Are you out here? Are you okay?"

"Please show some respect." The older man I'd first accosted
stepped in front of me.

"Respect? You're all going to stand around and let the
woman's house burn down? What in the hell is the matter with
you? Are you sure she's not inside? Did anyone—"

"Bay!" Red barked my name, and I was stunned into silence.
He took my arm and literally dragged me back out of the flickering light.

"What are you doing? We have to—"

"Be quiet, Bay. Please." He lowered his voice, and his arm
around my shoulders stilled some of the trembling. "There's
nothing we can do."

"But I don't understand! What if the whole woods goes
up?"

"It won't. They're prepared for things like this. The open
space around the cottage is there for a reason. Same with the
compound. It'll take the fire department close to twenty minutes
to get out here, and even then they won't be able to get much
equipment down that road. These people know what they're
doing."

I let myself sag a little against him. "But they're not doing
anything."

"Fire is different for them. It's a power, almost like magic.
The woman in the turban said if it's meant to be put out, it will
be. Otherwise, it isn't wise for humans to interfere."

I stepped away, out of the protective circle of Red's arm.
"Did it get hit by lightning? Is that what they mean?"

He shrugged. "I have no idea. All I know is that we're
basically trespassing here, so I think we'd be wise to stay out
of their business."

"But what about Belle? Was she in there? Is she all right?"

We whirled around as the roof collapsed into the gutted
interior with a *whoosh* that sent sparks flying up into the deep
black sky. A moment later, the tall, elegant man who had spoken

to me earlier stepped closer to the dying fire. Turning toward the assembled group, he raised his arms high above his head, and I gasped at the intricate whirls and images covering his naked chest. In the flickering light, he looked like an ancient African warrior.

"It is done," he said, and a low murmur rippled through the onlookers.

The man picked up the shovel he'd dropped. Others followed suit, and the thud of earth being tossed onto the smoldering embers echoed across the clearing. In a matter of minutes the men of the community had smothered the lingering tongues of flame until only a few smoking timbers and the charred bricks of the fireplace remained. One by one they began moving back toward the fence that encircled their compound. The women hummed, a low, moaning chant that made the hairs rise on the back of my neck. Even the few children, herded earlier into a small knot away from danger, fell into the solemn procession.

The leader paused in front of us, his black skin and the reds and yellows of his markings glistening with sweat. "We'd appreciate it if you kept what you've seen here to yourselves. We don't normally invite outsiders to our ceremonies."

"Is that what this was?" I asked, my mind suddenly crystal clear about what I'd just witnessed. "A rite? A cleansing perhaps?"

His smile revealed teeth so white they gleamed through the darkness. "Each takes away what he brings with him. We see what we wish to see."

With that enigmatic pronouncement, he turned and walked away, picking up the chant of the women as he swayed in time with the rhythmic beat. The sounds faded until Red and I stood alone in a silence so complete it felt like a presence.

WE TURNED WITHOUT SPEAKING and walked back toward the compound, following the path churned to mud by dozens of feet. The beam of the flashlight cut a welcoming hole in the otherwise impenetrable darkness. A few moments later we approached the gates, closed and barred now that the community was back inside. Something glittered, a brief flash as Red swept the light across the half-timbers lashed together with thick leather thongs, and I grabbed his arm.

"What's that?"

"Where?"

"Move the light back. Inside the gates. Over toward the left-hand row of houses."

He inched the beam left, and I saw the glimmer again, a white rectangle in a sea of blackness.

"There! See it?"

The shiny surface of the bumper sticker reflected the dim light back out into the night: IT'S OUR PLANET—KEEP IT GREEN.

"That's Deshawn's van!" I whispered.

Red stepped closer and stuck the flashlight directly into a gap between two of the timbers of the gate. The beat-up VW rested in front of one of the cottages, its left front fender crumpled, the headlamp shattered.

"Son of a bitch," Red said under his breath. He snapped his fingers. "Give me your pistol."

"What?"

"The Seecamp. Hand it over and move back out of the way."

I fumbled in my bag for the gun, suddenly remembering that his own weapon had been confiscated by the Florida sheriff's office. "What are you going to do?"

He jerked it out of my trembling fingers. "Go back to the road and call 911," he said between clenched teeth, "then wait there until someone comes. Go!"

"I'm not leaving you here alone!"

"Bay, get the hell out of here. Now!"

I turned and ran, sliding to a stop when I heard him pound on the gate with the butt of my pistol.

"This is the Beaufort County Sheriff's Office. Open up!"

I hung there in the darkness, my fear for Red overriding everything.

"Deshawn Crowder! This is Sergeant Red Tanner of the Beaufort County Sheriff's Office. Other deputies are on their way. Come out here now with your hands over your head! I know you don't want anyone to get hurt."

I could hear my heart pounding in my chest as a light clicked on inside the compound. It seemed as if time had been expanded, each second feeling like an hour.

Suddenly the towering black man with the intricate tattoos stepped up to the gate. Red lowered the gun a little but kept it aimed in the general direction of the compound.

"You have no authority here," the sonorous voice declared.

"You know that's not true, sir," Red replied in a calm, even voice. "You're harboring a fugitive wanted for a hit-and-run in which one of my deputies was seriously injured. Ask Deshawn to step out here, and we can all get on with our business."

"You have no authority here," the man repeated, but he turned as a hand appeared at his elbow.

"It's all right, Your Royal Highness. We're ready."

The older man spoke softly and rapidly, but in a few moments, he stepped away, his massive shoulders bowed.

The young man beside him, his skin almost golden in the glow, held his head proudly. His hand clutched that of a tiny girl, not much more than five feet tall. An aura seemed to shimmer from her mass of red hair. Red flicked the light in her direction, and the freckles across her cheeks stood out in sharp contrast against her creamy skin.

"Elizabeth Marsh?" Red asked.

The girl nodded and burst into tears.

I turned and sprinted toward the road.

DAWN HAD BEGUN to brush the tops of the trees when Red finally flopped down beside me in the sparse grass underneath the sprawling live oak that guarded the compound gates.

"What's going to happen to them?" I asked as my brother-in-law leaned his back against the massive trunk and slumped in weariness.

"Up to the solicitor," he said. "I'm glad I don't have to be the one to sort all this out."

"Did Deshawn admit to running down Malik?"

"Yes."

A tow truck would soon be trying to muscle its way through the trees to haul away Deshawn's crumpled VW van.

"How about the baby's death?"

"He and the girl both claim they had nothing to do with it. Belle and his father told them the child died of natural causes."

"You believe them?" I asked.

"I don't know. It could be the story Harry Crowder convinced them to stick to so he could take the blame. Both those kids are scared to death, although you have to give the boy credit for stepping up on the hit-and-run. He says he'd been arguing with Belle. Claims he and the Marsh girl wanted to go to the authorities and explain, but the old woman insisted they stay out of it. He says he sped away from her place and just wasn't paying attention. He never expected to encounter anyone walking along that track."

"But they've known since yesterday that the child was smothered. It was in the papers. They should have come forward anyway instead of hiding out here."

"I don't know, Bay. It's kind of hard to judge them when all the adults are encouraging them to lie. Tough call." He struggled to his feet and held out his hand. "Come on, let's go home."

"What about the fire?" I asked as we walked side-by-side down the deserted road.

The deputies who'd responded to my frantic call had escorted the two teenagers out just a few minutes ahead of us.

"What about it?"

Our shoulders brushed as the overhanging vegetation forced me to drop back.

"You know they burned her out," I said.

"The witch? You think she was in there?" He swiveled his head in my direction. "You're accusing them of murder?"

"No! And Belle wasn't…isn't a witch. No, they don't seem like violent people to me. I think they simply sent her away."

"Why?"

"I'm guessing they figured out she had a hand in the death of that baby. Maybe not directly, but she helped. And covered it up. They don't need that kind of grief coming down on their community, so they handled it in their own way."

Red kept up the pace, the beam of the flashlight swaying in time to his long-legged gait.

"Look," I said to his back, now barely visible in the blackness of the woods, "I've been thinking about this a lot. She played me. Us. When she found out I was the one who discovered the body, she gathered enough information about me to make some pretty good guesses about how I'd react. Then she set out to lead me right to the conclusion she wanted me to reach. I believe she wanted to tell the truth—about Harry and what he did—but she couldn't bring herself to betray her family."

"I think you're giving her too much credit."

"Why? She could even have left by her own choice. Before they set her house on fire. Maybe she had a premonition or something."

He swung around, and his voice told me his anger bubbled very close to the surface. "You seem awfully damned ready to accept all this voodoo stuff at face value, and I'm wondering why."

My fingers slipped of their own accord into the pocket of my slacks and fondled the two soft red pouches. Protection roots. Despite her manipulations, Belle Crowder had been concerned about my well-being. My thoughts drifted back to the first time she'd gripped the tender web between my thumb and forefinger. I'd felt only a fleeting stab of alarm, then a warm assurance had washed over me, as if everything she said made the most perfect sense. I suddenly realized her words had been playing in a continual loop in the back of my mind ever since...

"You've had a great sorrow.... It's good to remember, especially the love.... Let go, and find happiness. It's near. You just can't see it yet...."

"Bay? I said why have you been so willing to buy into this woman's act?"

His words came as if from far away. In my mind I still sat mesmerized in that cozy kitchen, with the encroaching trees dripping rain onto the slanted roof.... *"You'll know the truth. You'll hear it in the voice, and you'll know. Believe in your instincts. Act on them."*

"Because I don't have any reason not to," I said, and I could hear the wonder in my own voice.

"That's crap!" Red whirled away again and marched down the path. "You said yourself she played all of us. I don't understand why you're so damn calm about it. You could be dead wrong, you know. The arson squad could find her bones when they're done sorting through all that rubble back there. We may have just witnessed another murder."

I jogged to catch up. Suddenly it seemed like the most important thing in the world not to let him leave me behind. "You can have the arson guys investigate if you want, but I guarantee you they won't find any bones. Belle Crowder is gone. She's been banished, and her people have fixed it so she has nothing to come back to."

Red snorted. "And you're okay with that? You've been on my ass for the last ten days to find out who killed that baby. Now you're willing to let that old witch just walk away?"

I laid a hand on his arm, gripping hard, so he was forced to stop. "Listen to me," I said. "I'm not anywhere near all right with it, but there's not a damn thing either one of us can do about Belle Crowder. It's Deshawn and Elizabeth—and Harry—who are going to have to answer for the child's death."

His sigh mingled with the light breeze rippling through the underbrush lining the path. "I know it's not my job, but I can't get the image of that baby's face out of my mind. Someone needs to pay for that, Bay. Someone needs to pay."

I could hear the anger and the pain of it in his voice. I reached out and took his hand, the heat of his skin merging with mine. The rightness of it settled over me like a warm blanket.

"They'll pay, Red, you'll make sure of that. Because it's what you do. It's who you are. Rob was right about you. So was Belle. I just didn't want to see it until now."

In the dim light of the encroaching dawn, we stood facing each other in the deep, reverent silence of the hovering trees. I saw realization dawn on his sweet, familiar face, and I nodded. Red lifted my hand and brushed it gently across his cheek. "You continually amaze me, Bay Tanner. Have I told you that lately?"

"Not nearly often enough, Sergeant."

His stumbling words of love, spoken in the cocoon of the Camaro as we'd raced south to find Erik, hovered in the air between us. *"Trust yourself,"* Belle Crowder's voice whispered on the still night air. For a moment, the familiar panic rippled through my chest. I made one last effort to step back, but Red's strong fingers tightened around mine.

"Not this time," he said, his voice rough with emotion. "Not ever again."

I felt all the resistance of the past dissolve like the last wisps of smoke drifting up through the trees.

When our lips finally met, it felt like coming home.